VIOLET FENN

RED & DEAD

HARKER
HOUSE

First published by Harker House Publishing 2022

Copyright © 2022 by Violet Fenn

Violet Fenn asserts the moral right to be identified as the author of this work.

Cover design by GetCovers

First edition

ISBN: 978-1-7395926-3-9

This book was professionally typeset on Reedsy.
Find out more at reedsy.com

Contents

Oh Maggie, Maggie May, they have taken her away
And she'll never walk down Lime street anymore
For she robbed so many sailors and captains of the whalers
That dirty, robbin' no good Maggie May

Maggy May (trad.)

Harrington Street Hoolies

It's amazing how much you see around you in the split second after your brain realises you're about to die. As I flew through the air, I wondered whether I'd make a mess when I hit the ground. My cat, Grimm, was sitting on the steps of the fire escape, a vaguely curious expression on his face. A pair of magpies chattered in surprise from the roof of a nearby building and a pigeon did an emergency stop in mid-air, veering away sharply in order to avoid being taken down with me. I noticed that a window on the second floor of my block had a cracked pane. I was just wondering how long it would take for the landlords to get round to fixing it, when everything went black.

* * *

The day had been pleasant, as these things go. The sun was shining and business had been brisk in Flora's, the small, backstreet cafe I'd owned and run for the last two years. Harrington Street isn't really a through route to anywhere in particular—it sits a block back from the far more popular Mathew Street with its bars and music—and, unless you're local, you'd probably never know Flora's even existed. It had long been popular with students and local shop workers, but by the time I'd gone to look at it with my dad in tow, it had been boarded up for six months and its charm was definitely on the faded side. I'd never run a cafe before I opened Flora's, but I'd been a waitress at a coffee shop in the Bluecoat whilst I was at university. I'd figured it was probably a bit like that, just with more paperwork. And

I'd inherited some money from a great aunt I'd never even known—the best kind of inheritance, the sort that arrives out of the blue with no grief-laden weirdness attached to it. So it had seemed fated when a 'To Let' sign had appeared on the cafe—especially when I discovered the lease came complete with a flat on the top floor of the building. I'd given notice on my admin job in a small but very boring office, boxed up my meagre belongings from the room in the shared house in Edge Hill that I'd been desperate to get out of for the last three years and didn't look back.

These days, Flora's was the kind of cafe that sold *proper* coffee alongside pastries from a nearby bakery. The bakery owners gave me a good deal because I'd once briefly dated their daughter, before we jointly decided that having a shared love of 70s music wasn't enough to keep the flame of romance alight. I'd managed a week running the cafe on my own before dragging Izzy, my oldest—and most annoying—friend in to help. Izzy had moved up to Liverpool when I was in my second year of uni, declaring that she was 'bored beyond belief' by her job in a clothes shop back in Shropshire. Born to a Japanese mother who'd met her Welsh father whilst he was working in Osaka in the 1980s, Izzy had the vocabulary of a lairy sailor and the personal habits to match. Her sex life was a thing of wonder, peppered with hair-raising tales of ridiculous events and narrow escapes. She made up for it—in her mother's eyes, at least—by dressing permanently in delicate flowery dresses and dainty shoes and looking for all the world as though she'd just stepped out of the 1940s. Her shiny black hair was cut in the sharpest of bobs, and the faint Welsh accent she'd picked up from her father was still audible when she was either drunk or excited.

"Your boyfriend's back," she said as she came behind the counter and started fishing in the dishwasher for clean cups.

I looked up from polishing cutlery to see one of my favourite regulars coming through the front door. "Hey Sean," I said, as he dropped his satchel onto the table in the front window. He'd always chosen that table, ever since he started coming here a few months earlier. On the few occasions he found it occupied, he'd sit elsewhere with a faintly hangdog expression on his face until the usurpers left and he could reassert himself.

"Hey," he replied, glancing over with a smile. "Just the usual, thanks." I waited for Izzy to finish making the couple's drinks, then poured his large black Americano and took it over to where he was beginning his usual process of spreading out sheets of closely typed paper. I had no idea what Sean did for a living, but paperwork was clearly a large part of it. Izzy and I had decided early on that he was probably an academic of some description, but neither of us had ever had enough of a conversation with him to warrant asking. We only knew he was called Sean because Izzy had once overheard him ringing someone and announcing himself. He was definitely cute, though—around six feet tall with scruffy brown hair, dressed in faded black jeans and an untucked flannel shirt that flapped around, giving him the air of a distracted college professor.

"How's it going?" I asked.

He glanced at me with his amazing hazel-gold eyes, shuffling papers sheepishly under my scrutiny. I dropped my eyes, hoping I wasn't blushing like an idiot. "Oh, you know," he said, "no rest for the wicked." I grinned idiotically in response and retreated before I could say anything stupid.

"He definitely fancies you," said Izzy way too loudly, as she followed me behind the counter.

I scowled. "I can't date one of my regulars," I pointed out. "What if we broke up? That would be awkward."

Izzy looked unconvinced. "We can afford to lose one customer to your inept flirting, Lil," she said, waving vaguely at the packed cafe. "I think you could probably risk dating Sean."

"Chance would be a fine thing," I grumbled. "He's clearly some ridiculously professional businessman who just comes here for a bit of peace and quiet. Can you *imagine* how mortifying it would be if I tried flirting with him and he never came back again?"

"I think," she said carefully, "that you are just scared." She raised an eyebrow, daring me to argue. "And you are *definitely* out of practice when it comes to flirting. Here," she said, "let me finish emptying the dishwasher. You clean the tables and remember to smile. What?" she saw my expression. "It's a start. Shoo!"

And so the day had ended much the same as every other day, with me and Izzy bickering amiably. There was no denying that the mere thought of trying to chat up another human being made me cringe deep inside. After breaking up with Laura, I'd half-heartedly dated a couple of people I'd met through online swiping, because Izzy said I needed to 'get it out of my system'. I wasn't sure what I was supposed to be getting 'out', but I tried my best. The last attempt had involved an unexpected police raid—it's a long story—and I'd given up after that. Luckily, I'm not scared of my own company. And Izzy lived just a couple of minutes' walk away, in a tiny flat over a defunct record shop on the corner of Button Street. She'd been there years, despite constantly complaining about the odour of piss that regularly wafted up from the front steps, a side effect of the building being used as an emergency toilet stop for late night drunks.

"I'm off then," she said, picking up her bag and grabbing several pastries from a box behind the counter, where we kept leftovers that were going out of date. "You okay to lock up?"

"I'll manage." We had this exchange every day. I watched as Izzy let herself out and headed over to the doorway opposite the cafe, where a pale face emerged from underneath the heap of old blankets and sleeping bags. The face grinned as she handed the pastries over. I remembered I was out of cat food. Grimm, the enormous grey cat I'd adopted from a rescue centre not long after moving to Harrington Street, wouldn't be impressed if I arrived upstairs empty-handed. After pouring one last coffee into a paper cup, I headed out onto the street. Struggling to balance the coffee, I locked up and turned the small key that brought the metal security shutters down over the front windows. Settling against the wall, I waited for the ageing mechanics to clunk into life.

"That for me, Red?" asked a hopeful voice. Billy had always called me Red. He wasn't even the first to do so—it comes with the territory when you're cursed from birth with an untameable mane of carrot-coloured curly hair that flows erratically down past your shoulders.

"Who else?" I asked, heading over to the jumble sale on the pavement. A bony hand came out from the blankets and took the coffee. He gave it a

4

sniff and looked up.

"Did you remember the sugar this time?"

"Can't be having you rotting those lovely teeth of yours, Billy," I retorted, and got the gappy grin in response. "I'm sorry," I went on, "I forgot. I'll do better next time." Suddenly there was shouting further down the street. Turning to look, I saw a small group of men scuffling with security outside the hotel on the corner. Deciding discretion was probably the better part of valour, I took the decidedly un-scenic route down Dorans Lane to avoid any trouble and headed to the mini supermarket on Lord Street. I bought cat food, milk and a tub of reduced strawberries—with the vague idea of upping my intake of healthy fruit—before heading home the usual way, only to find the disturbance still going on outside the hotel. A small, blonde security guard was holding the shouting man back, her palm pushed firmly onto his chest. By the way he was gesturing over her shoulders, I guessed he was yelling at or about someone who was already inside the restaurant. Another man was standing in the road behind the pair and cars were having to slow down to navigate around him. He yelled incoherently as they did so, whilst a group of young lads—who didn't appear to be connected to anyone involved—shouted encouragement from the safety of the opposite pavement. I hurried past the shouting man and the patient security woman and headed for home.

It was still only 8pm when I got back to Flora's, but Harrington Street is narrow and gloomy at the best of times, let alone on a chilly night in early April. I made my way up the fire escape, looking forward to nothing more exciting than a leisurely bath and an evening of lounging in front of mindless television with Grimm. There's an internal staircase that goes from the cafe to the floors above, but I'd started using the fire escape as my outdoor space almost immediately after I'd moved in. The flats in-between the cafe and where I lived on the top floor had been rented out to various groups of students for the first year I was there. The last lot had done a moonlight flit, leaving the place empty apart from beer bottles, graffiti and open doors onto the shared stairwell. A commercial cleaning company had been in to clear out the worst of the mess, but no one had set foot in the place since. This was unusual in itself, given its prime location and the extortionate amounts landlords could charge for only barely habitable student accommodation. Once it was clear I wouldn't be getting new neighbours—and after establishing that the locks on the front doors of each flat had already been broken off for access—I'd begun using them to store books, spare crockery from Flora's and random bits of furniture that I'd found in charity shops but didn't have space for in my flat. I then changed the locks on the main door to the street and the supposed fire exit that led from my kitchen to the outside stairs, thus giving myself the run of the entire building without having to pay any more rent.

The fire escape had proved to be an unexpected joy. The emergency door on each level opened up to a metal platform on the rickety stairs and I'd gradually built up an extensive collection of plants outside my kitchen, the overflow of which was balanced on the lower steps. These days there was just enough space for one person to sit on the top step between the pots and watch the world go by whilst being spiked in the neck by an aspidistra that didn't seem to care that it was outside in all weathers and had now grown to the size of a small jungle palm.

I was halfway up to the flat before I realised Grimm was sitting near the top, perched delicately between a large mint and a waving fern. He was staring straight down at me with a nervous expression on his face, like a furry grey puffer fish that was about to go pop. As I got near enough to reach up and pet him, a faint clattering noise came from inside the building. I froze where I stood. There'd been an attempted robbery just after I moved in and I didn't fancy going through the experience again in a hurry. That time, a scruffy young man who'd been hanging around by the cafe counter as if waiting his turn had made an opportunistic lunge for the till drawer as I was handing change to the customer in front of him. The customer in question had turned out to be one of the very security guards I'd just seen outside the hotel, who had slapped the would-be thief across the face before marching him outside and—literally—kicking him down the road. But I didn't have a helpful customer with me this time. And I was already near the top of the fire escape, so it made sense to let myself into the flat quietly and call the police from there. I didn't have high hopes of a fast enough response to catch anyone in the act, but you never knew your luck. "Stay here, Grimm," I whispered. He sensibly did exactly that as I stepped over him. Fishing in my pocket for the keys, I put my shopping down carefully on the metal landing grill before quietly letting myself in. I didn't get more than two steps into the kitchen before a tall thin man dressed entirely in black appeared out of my living room doorway and stopped dead when he saw me, clearly as frozen with shock as I was. "What the *fu—*" I managed, before he came to his senses quicker than I did. He barrelled towards me and I only had a split second to register the fact that the would-be thief hadn't bothered to hide his distinctive face, before he sent me flying backwards off the top of the fire escape. As I fell, I saw Grimm sitting on the fire escape, quietly washing himself and observing the action. Then the ground came up to hit me.

On A Bed Of Basil

I'd only ever experienced complete darkness once before. I was a teenager, visiting my grandparents in their semi-detached bungalow in the modern overspill of an old village. An unexpected power cut had knocked everything out, including the street lights. I scrambled my way from the guest bedroom into their kitchen, only to find the back door open and the shadows of my grandparents standing on the tiny back garden patio. "Come and look, Lil," said Grandad. I wasn't sure what they could possibly be looking at in the dark, but I fumbled my way through the door to stand next to him. He was craning his neck backwards to look up. "See," he said, "not everything's visible until the lights go out." I stared upwards, wondering if he was finally losing the last of his marbles. Grandad had his 'moments', as Gran called them. He sometimes spoke to long-dead friends and relatives as if they were standing right next to him. But I loved him and was prepared to humour his oddness, so up I looked.

"Bloody hell," I said, as stars slowly appeared above my head. I heard Gran tut quietly.

Grandad laughed. "Told you," he said. "Didn't I?" As I stared upwards, more and more pinpricks of light appeared, as if my eyes were slowly taking in information and processing it into visible dots. I recognised the Plough constellation, but wasn't sure about the bright star low on the horizon. "Jupiter," said Grandad. "Only visible in spring and autumn. Look out for a red one as well—Mars pops up sometimes. And Venus too, when she can be bothered to lower herself to our standards." I was mesmerised by this secret space-world that I'd always known existed but never seen for myself. After that I always looked out for the planets that were huge beyond belief, but tiny from a human perspective. And I never stopped feeling quietly thrilled when Venus showed her face.

* * *

There were no stars in this night sky. It was nothing but jet black darkness surrounded by throbbing pain. I slowly became aware of my own body's existence again, as every inch of it began to make its indignation known. A reddish light crept gradually across my eyelids. I finally blinked them open to realise I was lying on my side in the pre-dawn shadows. When I tried moving, I was relieved to discover that everything seemed to work, even though it complained. I lifted my head and immediately banged it on something hard, which I realised with a shock was my car. I was lying on the ground in the carpark next to Flora's. Well, I *call* it a carpark—it's more like a patch of scrappy rubble and broken tarmac, through which the occasional dandelion and many, many nettles grow. There'd been an underground night-club here years ago, but the basement levels had been filled in and the surface-level building demolished long before I'd moved to Harrington Street. I'd cleared out enough space amongst the brambles for my ancient blue Beetle and left the rest to nature. I wasn't even sure that I had parking rights, but the lease that I'd taken on for the cafe had mentioned the empty space and *not* mentioned that I couldn't use it for whatever I pleased, so Basil the Beetle had sat nosed into the front of it ever since. It wasn't a particularly convenient parking spot, even without the weeds. The hydraulic barriers at the end of my street only lowered for a few hours each morning to allow deliveries through, so I had to plan ahead to even get the car out onto the main roads. Blinking slowly, I wriggled myself upright and sat back against Basil's front tyre. Looking up, I spotted Grimm watching me from the fire escape. *Holy shit, the burglar.* Panicking, I tried to get up, but the thumping in my head disagreed. Sinking back against the cool metal of the car, I could see that the kitchen door was still open and some of my pot plants had toppled over. Grimm was looking intrigued now,

9

rather than nervous, and was peering down as if wondering when I was going to get my shit together and finally put his food out. I risked turning my head to see if anyone else was around. Harrington Street was silent and empty, and I had no idea what time it was. I wasn't wearing a watch, because, like most people in the twenty-first century, I rely on my phone for everything. Right now, I had no idea where my phone even was. Light was definitely creeping up over the city and I could hear the occasional car in the distance, but no people. I wasn't far from the Liverpool One shopping complex, so I'd expect to hear sounds of life if it was anywhere near daylight hours. Deciding that sitting in a car park wasn't a good look for anyone, I forced myself slowly to my feet. Leaning on the car, I noticed a large dent in the front wing that hadn't been there before. A large, body-sized dent. Roughly the size of *my* body, in fact. Surely I couldn't have bounced off a *car* and not broken anything? I looked up at the open kitchen door, three stories above. The rail bowed out just where it would bend if someone had been thrown into and over it at speed. The dent in Basil's bonnet was exactly where a body would have landed, after being thrown over said railing. And I *definitely* hurt all over. There wasn't a bit of me that wasn't complaining about being upright—even my eyelids felt sore. But whatever had happened, I was alive, which was better than the alternative. Pushing myself up off the car, I felt something hard in my back pocket. It turned out to be my very broken phone. Well, that was just fucking brilliant. I'd actually kept this one alive for six months without damage, which was a personal record. Shoving its mangled remains back into my pocket, I slowly walked over to the fire escape, stretching my arms and legs tentatively as I did so. As I rolled my shoulders back, they made an unpleasant crunching noise. It sounded horrible but must have been needed, because suddenly I felt a lot better.

"You okay, Red?" Billy was standing in the middle of the street. He had his belongings piled onto his back like a pack-horse and was eyeing me warily. I wondered how long he'd been watching.

Leaning against the railing, I tried to sound as casual as possible. "Yeah, I just left something in the car." He didn't look convinced. Which wasn't surprising, given that Basil had been parked up for so long that ivy was creeping around his wheels.

"At five in the morning?"

I gave him a half wave and a tiny, painful shrug before heading slowly up the stairs to the flat, wondering gloomily what sort of mess I was going to find. My shopping was still outside the back door where I'd left it, my shoulder bag next to it. My wallet, keys and random collection of receipts and old tissues seemed to be intact, which was a pleasant surprise. I picked everything up and braced myself as I headed inside.

Nothing had been touched. It all looked exactly the same as it had the day before, even down to the dent left in the bed where Grimm and I had last slept curled up together. I went into each room in turn—not a massive task, as there's only four small rooms in the entire place—and didn't find so much as a footprint or handily dropped business card. This sort of thing was much easier to figure out in the movies. The main door to the inner stairs had, unsurprisingly, had its lock broken off. I slid the bolt across from the inside and decided to worry about fixing it later. Right now, I needed to go back to bed. Calling Grimm in from the fire escape, I stared out over the rooftops and wondered idly at the bright beauty of the sunrise, which was beginning to show itself across the rooftops. There were so many different scents in the air—warm bread from the bakery up the road, petrol from the cars beginning to make their noisy way into town, and a faint smell of stagnant water from the docks. I'd never been up early enough to notice it all before. I stood there for a while, just taking it all in. Grimm padded his way over and inspected me carefully, before deciding that I hadn't lost the plot entirely and was a safe source of kitty kibble. When he'd been fed and I was sure that everything was as secure as it could be, I climbed under the covers, still fully clothed. I was vaguely aware of Grimm leaping delicately up to wedge himself into the small of my back, before I lost consciousness.

* * *

I woke to broad daylight coming through the open windows and the absolute knowledge that I was about to be sick. Scrabbling my way to the bathroom, I collapsed onto my hands and knees and loudly vomited what felt like everything I'd ever eaten across the cold tiled floor, thankful there was no one else in the building to hear my pathetic groans. Then I sat on the loo with my head resting on the cool porcelain of the sink, whilst the world apparently fell out of my arse. The last time I'd been this ill was after a dodgy kebab from a late-night food van after Izzy and I had got so pissed that we'd taken a very scenic route home from an all-day drinking session on Bold Street. I'd still been at uni back then, when such behaviour was marginally forgivable. But the memory of the wrenching sickness had never quite left me and I'd been careful to never get that drunk again.

When I was reasonably sure that I was empty, I pulled myself upright. Wedging myself against the sink in order to wash my face with cold water, I peered into the mirror nervously. I'd expected to find a black eye at the very least, but there was nothing at all to show that I had, apparently, fallen from a four-storey building and lived to tell the tale. It briefly occurred to me that the vomiting might be connected to the fall. Perhaps I had less visible, but more dangerous injuries. But now that my insides had purged themselves, I was actually feeling much better. I was definitely pale, but then I always had been. Dad said it was the strong Celtic blood in me. My hair was sticking out in all directions, as if I'd put my finger in an electrical socket. Again, pretty much my day to day look. I stared balefully at the masses of red waves exploding in all directions and wondered, not for the first time, just how one human person could have so much hair. It was a miracle I'd never been mistaken for a rogue banshee whilst walking along the docks. Suddenly, I spotted a movement behind me in the mirror. *Shit.* It hadn't occurred to me that my attacker might still be in the building. I froze, unsure of what to do. But surely, if they'd been inside the flat when I returned and I'd somehow missed them in my dazed state, they'd have legged it when I fell asleep? Perhaps they'd been so freaked out by my Linda Blair impression that they'd hung around to check I wasn't going to die on them. Thoughtful burglars. That was a new one. I stepped softly out into the definitely empty living room and peered carefully round into the bedroom. Grimm was snoring happily in the nest he'd made in my duvet, and the only other noise was the distant sounds of life filtering up from the street below.

Once I was confident that no one else was in the building, I decided to clean up, have a bath and go back to bed, in that order. I staggered to the kitchen and opened the window to let in some fresh air, before using two full rolls of toilet paper to clean up the worst of the vomit. Then I got the mop and J-cloths out of the narrow cleaning cupboard that was tucked into a recess behind the back door and bleached the bathroom to within an inch of its life. Turning the levers that forced the ageing taps into life, I waited for the water to heat up and then put the plug in. Once there was enough steam to cloud the tiny frosted window, I stripped off my filthy clothes and dumped them on the tiled floor before stepping into the tub. I took bathing seriously; it was one of my main hobbies. The only storage in the bathroom when I moved in was a terrible mirrored cabinet from the 1970s that was bolted to the wall, had mould stains on the inside and filled with condensation every time I ran the hot water, so I'd installed a tall, narrow chest of drawers that I'd found in a junk shop. It was wedged into a narrow corner within reach of the bath and held endless bath oils and foams, alongside the stacks of the different hair treatments I kept buying, in the hope of one day taming my lion's mane. None had worked so far, but I always smelled delicious. I pulled out my favourite skin scrub, but was recoiling from the awful smell before I'd even unscrewed the lid. The damp must have got in and ruined it. What was usually a delicate, magnolia scent was overwhelming and sickly; cloying in its heaviness. The bowl of assorted Lush bars on the second shelf also lay reeking in their ageing glory, but I was going to have to use something. I picked out the plainest-looking one and gave myself a quick scrub over before throwing it as far across the floor as I could manage, then lay back in the water to rinse my hair. The bright morning sunlight coming in through the window was making my head hurt even through the frosted glass, and I decided I definitely needed more sleep. Adding 'find the source of the weird bathroom smells' to my mental list of things to do, I got out of the bath, wrapped myself in a towel and padded back to the bedroom. Giving Grimm an affectionate shove across the bed, I folded the towel and lay the dry side onto my pillow so I didn't have to think about my hair, and crawled back under the duvet. Luckily for me it was a Monday, the one day that Flora's stayed closed. I knew Izzy had relatives visiting and wouldn't be expecting to see me, so I had nothing to do other than sleep things off. I wriggled further down, put a hand on Grimm's fur for comfort, and slept like the dead.

Good Morning, Starshine

A loud hammering on the kitchen door woke me up. Only one person ever came upstairs, so I didn't waste time making myself presentable before answering. "Fucking hell, you look like shit," announced Izzy as I opened the door. I glared at her and pulled the towel tight around me in order to avoid flashing people on the street below. Izzy was perching on the second step down, one foot wedged against the rusty rail in order to avoid kicking a collection of unidentifiable greenery into the carpark below. "And you need to fix this," she nodded at the deformed top rail, "before someone falls off and breaks their neck." She pulled an oversized brown knitted cardigan around herself against the chill wafting up from the Mersey. I could taste sea salt on the air, along with stale doughnuts and a faint tang of sewers. Nice. "Anyway," she continued, "the dishwasher's broken. Again."

"Ugh," I replied helpfully, before relenting. "Okay, I'll come look at it." The sun was already up and it was a nice day, despite the chill in the air. "What time is it?"

Izzy tilted her head at me. "Just gone nine," she said. "It's not like you to have a lie in. Are you feeling okay?"

"Nine in the morning?" I asked, confused.

"Nooooo," she replied, "in the evening. Decided to start late-night opening on Tuesdays, innit. Of course in the morning." Fucking hell, I must have slept through an entire day and night. It had definitely done me good, though. I felt a million times better than I had the day before.

"Christ," I said, "I must have been more tired than I realised. Give me

15

ten minutes to get dressed, and I'll be down." I was probably going to have to fork out for a new dishwasher. The current one threw a hissy fit on a regular basis and I'd developed a knack for hitting it in just the right place to make it behave itself. I'd put off buying a replacement because anything electrical was a bit hit and miss once installed at Flora's. We'd once inherited a fridge from Izzy's parents when they'd refurbished their kitchen. Having worked perfectly for many years, it became temperamental the second it was installed in the staff kitchen (in reality, a single tiny room behind the counter that contained not much more than a sink, a small table and a toilet cubicle) and took to randomly switching itself off at inopportune moments. Eventually, I gave in and bought a replacement from Argos. This one had been okay so far, but had recently taken to making unpleasant buzzing noises if we filled it too much. The dishwasher was a similar story. Passed on to me by my parents when they'd decided they didn't actually need one for two people who were fastidious enough to do the washing up the second they used anything, it had worked perfectly—until it arrived at Flora's. We eventually decided that there must be an issue with the wiring down one side of the building, because the coffee machine and cash register on the other side of the room never had so much as a sniff of a problem. But it was in the terms of my lease that I couldn't change the plumbing without permission from my landlords. I didn't want to involve them, because that might involve them actually calling in at the café, which risked them realising I'd co-opted the middle floors and the fire escape. So we lived with the shonky connections and were on first name terms with most of the local repair shops.

"Oh, and there's a letter for you," Izzy said, fishing in her pocket. "It was on the mat when I let myself in. Apparently it is both private *and* urgent," the red stamps on the hand-delivered envelope agreed with this assessment, "so I thought I'd better bring it up." I opened it under her watchful gaze and pulled out a single sheet of white paper. The logo and address at the top of the letter was that of my aforementioned landlords, a property firm based in the Liver Building. I'd never met anyone from the company nor visited their offices, despite it only being ten minutes' walk away. Flora's had been listed on a commercial rentals website—I'd viewed it with an estate agent and done all the admin online before moving in. Reading down the brief letter, my stomach lurched and I leaned heavily against the doorframe. "Is everything okay, Lil?" asked Izzy. She made no move to leave, personal boundaries being something that, in her opinion, only applied to other people. I silently handed the letter over for her to read. "We're being evicted?" she squawked in horror. "They can't do that! What on earth will we do? And," she looked back at the letter to check, "they're only giving us a week's notice? That's fucking insane! We're not standing for it," she said firmly, handing the letter back to me.

I read it again. Silverton Properties were requisitioning the building for 'essential maintenance work' and they were very sorry, but would ensure I was duly compensated. The need for maintenance work didn't overly surprise me. Apart from the issues with the electricity supply, the roof had leaked for at least six months, and I sometimes heard scratching noises from the tiny storage cellar that sounded suspiciously like rats wearing hobnailed boots. Silverton Properties were offering me the equivalent of six months' rent in return for vacating the premises, a sum impressive enough to make me wonder exactly why it was so urgent. Maybe it was connected with the ongoing works on the next block. Years after the original Cavern club had been so sacrilegiously demolished, a belated attempt at salvaging its remains was made by the new owners of the plot. Which was when they discovered the Cavern had been built over an *actual* cavern. Or rather, what remained of one after the club's initial demolition had sent several tonnes of rubble cascading down into it. The surveyors who were brought in to investigate discovered that several streets in the area had been laid down over the remains of what was presumed to be old mine-workings. Victorian builders had been eager to take advantage of burgeoning industry and didn't always check how stable their footings were before adding towering new buildings on top of the precarious foundations. The cavern under the Cavern was the remnants of one of these mines. Local rumour had it that natural wells also existed at an even lower depth. Several nearby businesses had nervously brought in their own surveyors, just in case they, too, turned out to be perched precariously above an unexpected void into the underworld. A small section of Mathew Street was roped off even now. An unmapped tunnel had been discovered underneath the cellar of one of the endless bars that lined the busy street and an endless procession of contractors were being brought in to figure out just how much rubble and concrete would be needed to fill the void. But however justifiable my landlords' reasons for needing the building back, I wasn't going down without a fight. I'd been living and working in this building for two years with dodgy wiring and plumbing and no one had seen fit to check up on the state of the place, so Silvertons could fuck off if they thought I was just going to pack up and leave the minute they took an interest. "I'll have to go talk to them," I said. Stretching again, I gave an involuntary *ouch* as another joint made a creaking noise before apparently popping itself back into place.

Izzy looked concerned. "What have you done to yourself?" she asked. "Did you go out and have a skinful without me?"

I laughed hollowly. Izzy was much more sociable than me and we both knew it. She sometimes went out on the town with the women from her book club (she'd asked me to join several times, but I enjoy reading too much to accept being told what I *should* read, let alone then being expected to have a coherent opinion on it), or for an occasional coffee with a group of earnest students she'd somehow befriended at pilates class. My idea of a mad night out was sitting drinking coffee on the fire escape, watching Grimm chasing rats at the back of the car park. Glamour, thy name is Lilith. "I fell over on the stairs the other night," I said. Well, it wasn't a *complete* lie. "Gave myself a fright. Nothing major."

"Any bruises?" I pulled each of my legs up in turn, to see how much damage I'd done. Nothing.

"That's weird," I said. "I came a real cropper."

Izzy stood staring at me, her hands on her hips. "You really do look rough," she offered finally. "What exactly happened?"

"Honestly, I just tripped on the stairs and fell onto the carpark. Couple of steps up," I said hurriedly, seeing her expression. "I thought I'd have more to show for it than this, though."

"Turn round and drop the towel a bit," said Izzy. I did so obediently, like a toddler being told what to do by their mum. "Nothing," she said. "Do you have a headache?" She looked concerned.

"Nope." I definitely didn't have a headache, and I really was feeling much better. In fact, now that I'd vomited up whatever nasties had clearly been lurking in my system, I felt healthier than I had in a very long time. I suppressed a sudden urge to bounce energetically on the balls of my feet.

"Your eyes look weird." Izzy said, leaning forward and peering closely into my face. "Kind of...shiny." She stepped back again and gave me a suspicious look. "You're not taking meds again without telling me, are you?" Her concerns had some merit. I'd been prescribed a new type of antidepressant in my late teens and had such a reaction to it that I hadn't left the house for a week. I stayed hidden in my bedroom as my brain scrolled endlessly through fully conscious technicolour nightmares. Mum and Dad had assumed it was just the medication settling into my system and ignored it for a few days, but after a week of me being monosyllabic and confused, they'd asked the family doctor to visit. He'd taken one look and announced I was on the verge of psychosis and needed to be off the meds as soon as possible. It took a month to wean myself off them and sometimes I wasn't sure the effects had ever really gone away. I occasionally had dreams so surreal that my imagination couldn't quite shake them off. What if the surreal stuff was reality and the things we saw each day were just our imaginations? I spent way too much time thinking about it. And that *did* make my head hurt.

"No," I replied, walking over to the little mirror that hung next to the kitchen shelves. "I'm just tired." Peering into the glass, I could see what Izzy meant. My irises had a silver edge to them that definitely hadn't been there the day before. Could I have a brain injury after all? It seemed unlikely—if I'd landed on my head that hard, it would have killed me, not given me fancy eyeballs. I hunted around for something to tie up my hair and settled on a silk scarf that was hanging on the back of the kitchen door. I'd had it for years, after picking it up in a charity shop one windy day when I needed something to keep my hair out of my face, having walked blindly into traffic once too often. The fabric was a beautiful bottle green with gold threads. Holding it up to the light, I gazed at its glittery lines for a long second before using it to tie my hair up into a messy bun that focussed more on the 'messy' than the 'bun'. As I tied a jaunty knot on top of my head, there was a movement in the corner of my eye. Spinning round so fast that it was a miracle I didn't give myself whiplash, I faced the living room. It looked exactly as it always did—a large sofa against the wall that divided it from my bedroom, with a pair of ancient creaking armchairs on the opposite side. The small, nondescript coffee table sat in the middle of the room with books spilling all over it, as usual. Grimm sat perched on the windowsill, idly washing himself whilst peering out in the hope a pigeon might land on the window ledge. He couldn't get anywhere near the pigeons because of the thick glass, but that didn't stop him trying. I turned back round to find Izzy staring curiously at me. "What?" I asked.

"Nothing," she said. "You just seem a bit odd. Odder than usual," she clarified.

"Cheers."

Izzy looked unrepentant, standing with her arms crossed and eyes narrowed as she inspected me. "I assume you're going to get dressed before coming downstairs?" I looked down at myself, still wearing only the towel. My bare knees were determinedly un-grazed, as were my hands. I went back to the mirror and turned left and right in an attempt to find evidence of my dramatic fall, but there was nothing.

"It's weird," I said, in the understatement of the century. "How can I fall off a staircase without leaving a single mark?"

"Maybe you're bionic?" snorted Izzy. "Or perhaps you hit your head when you fell." Her tone turned serious again. "Maybe you should go up to A&E, just to be sure?"

I remembered how I'd repainted the bathroom with vomit before sleeping for a good twenty-four hours, and wondered if maybe Izzy was right. But I really didn't fancy schlepping all the way up to the emergency department. "I'll nip into the pharmacy on Castle Street and use that health check service," I said. "They can look at my vitals, at least. Can you manage without the dishwasher until I get back?"

Izzy snorted. "I manage without most forms of modern technology in that cafe," she pointed out. "I'm sure I can remember how to turn a tap on and wash some cups. Yes, yes," she was heading back out of the door onto the fire escape, "I'll be fine, it just needs one of your specialist arse-kickings. Go get yourself examined." With that, she disappeared back down the stairs, sandals slapping gently against the metal. I shut the kitchen door and checked the entire flat yet again, just to make sure there was no one sneaking around. When I was certain I was alone, I went into my bedroom and pulled on leggings, a short black skirt and an oversized grey sweater from out of my wardrobe, trying to ignore the smell of mothballs. I'd put some in the wardrobe a year or so earlier, after my sweaters went through a phase of turning into woolly lace. Rescuing my battered trainers from underneath the bed, I wedged them onto my bare feet and wondered again how on earth I'd avoided any major injuries during my enforced outdoor gymnastics display. All the aches and pains had gone now, and the strange silver tint to my eyes was the only sign that things weren't quite normal. I took a deep breath and tasted sea air on the breeze, which made a pleasant change from Harrington Street's usual aroma of takeaways and piss. Checking in the mirror that my hair was bearable for public viewing, I peered at my eyes again. Izzy was right—they looked weird. The silver ring around each iris was even brighter than before and their usual hazel-green colour seemed somehow faded. I knew I hadn't imagined my flight through the air—the bent rails of the staircase were proof enough of that—but how I'd survived without breaking something major was a mystery. On the plus side, I'd fallen from three storeys up and survived. That was a *good* thing, right? I petted Grimm, who was sitting on the bed observing me gravely with his beady yellow eyes, and headed out.

Big Mistake, Creep. Huge.

"I'm so sorry," the young pharmacist flustered. He was struggling to get his equipment to work, the blood pressure monitor having resolutely refused to give a result. He held the button down and forced it to keep pumping until I thought the cuff might pop, but it gave no result whatsoever. Whilst we waited for someone in the shop to hunt out a replacement machine from the storeroom, he decided to try a pulse oximeter instead. "Even if I can't take your blood pressure," he said with forced jollity, "I can at least reassure you that your blood is still pumping." After clipping the device to my finger, he spent some time peering into my eyes with a small pen torch. "Hmmm," he said thoughtfully, moving the torch from one eye to the other, "hmmm."

"Hmmm?" I squinted at him, from my position approximately four inches from his face. "Does 'hmmm' mean anything?" I'd told the woman at the pharmacy counter that my sister had been recently diagnosed with high blood pressure, so thought it prudent to get my own condition checked out. It hadn't even been queried—she'd just nodded and called the pharmacist without ever saying a word. I thought again about the strangeness of Sunday night's break-in. If the intruders had been intent on theft, they'd have made off with their loot at the time, but I was pretty sure that nothing was missing from the flat. Perhaps it was just a case of mistaken identity. Maybe someone had forgotten to send out change-of-address cards to their dealers.

"Hmmm," the pharmacist said again, stepping backwards and regarding me thoughtfully. He had glossy, dark brown hair cut into a polite quiff on top of his head, which faded out to a neat short back and sides. Brown eyes were framed by eyelashes of a length that most women would kill for and topped by a pair of neatly shaped eyebrows. I strongly suspected they'd been tamed with the help of the fragrant ladies of the Benefit brow bar in the John Lewis store down the road. After a long, silent minute, he shrugged. "I cannot get a reading," he said politely. "No reading at all. This is not normal. But of course if you really had no readings at all you would be dead and obviously you are not dead because you are sitting here in front of me right now."

"Oh well," I said, getting to my feet, "I just wanted to make sure I was alive." I grinned to show that I was in on the joke and he smiled back, clearly relieved I wasn't going to complain about his inability to conduct basic health checks.

"Well, you are either perfectly fine, madam," he said, opening the door out into the shop and standing aside to let me pass, "or maybe you are the walking dead. Ha!" With that, he closed the cubicle door on me firmly. I could hear him mumbling at his machines as I stepped back out into the street.

* * *

I got back to Flora's in time to help Izzy with the last of the lunchtime rush. We only had five tables inside, but it was warm enough that she'd put three of what we optimistically called the 'summer tables' out on the pavement as well. They were all occupied when I arrived, so I did a quick circuit and collected a towering pile of empty plates and cups. Heading inside, I dumped the lot into the big Belfast sink next to the coffee machine. Izzy had her head deep in the dishwasher and shot up at the noise, banging her head as she did so. "Christ," she hissed, "are you practising to become a ninja?" She straightened up, glaring at the machine as she did so. "It's still capable of working," she said. "I think it just doesn't want to."

I turned the taps on and rolled up my sleeves as the water filled up in the sink. "Been busy then," I said, nodding at the packed tables. "We should probably have a think about getting in some extra help."

"You appear to have forgotten about the eviction notice," said Izzy, keeping her voice low. "Do you think you'll be able to find new premises?"

"We're going nowhere," I replied, surprising myself with just how much I meant it. "Silvertons can fuck right off with their maintenance issues. If they want the place back that badly, they can come turf me out in person."

"Ooh, fighting talk," said Izzy. "I like it. With you in two ticks," this to two women standing at the counter, "just listening to my boss finally developing a backbone." She turned towards me as she dried her hands, narrowing her beady eyes. "Yes," she agreed, "we fight. And we really should get more help in. It would give you time to have a life outside Flora's. Won't that be fun?" With a grin, she turned back to her customers, leaving me to sulk quietly to myself whilst I washed up the crockery. I was quite happy with it being just me and Izzy in Flora's, but it would definitely be easier with an extra pair of hands. And what did she mean by 'growing a backbone'? Cheeky little scrote.

I washed and dried everything in record time, then decided to have a go at the work surfaces. Rooting around in the cupboard under the sink, I found a plastic tub of industrial cleaning paste. As I pulled it out, my hand knocked against something metallic. Peering into the gloom, I spotted a set of small keys hanging from a hook at the back of the cupboard. I didn't recognise them, so threw them into the cutlery drawer before setting to work scrubbing the worktops. When Izzy came back behind the counter, she leaned over and swiped the cloth out of my hands, holding it away from me in the manner of a dog owner who'd found their pet playing with something suspicious. "Who are you and what have you done with Lilith?" she demanded.

"Whaaaat?" I replied defensively. "Is it such a surprise that I'm cleaning up in my own cafe?"

"No, but you rarely wipe the work surfaces hard enough to take the top layer off." She pointed to where I'd been cleaning around the recessed electricity sockets on the back wall. The polished surface of the tiles had worn down to raw ceramic, all the way round each socket. "Are you sure you haven't taken something you shouldn't have?" I glared at her, but she blithely carried on, as she always did. It was one of the things I loved most about her. "Remember those steroids that acted like speed?" Of course I remembered. I'd been given tablets for a minor case of contact dermatitis after my skin had reacted to a new detergent we'd been using in the cafe. An unexpected side effect of the medication had been my inability to stand still, along with a constant urge to clean things. It was a shame I'd only had five days' worth, because I'd just been considering hiring ladders in order to clean the upstairs windows when the tablets wore off and I lost enthusiasm. One of the first floor windows was still cleaner on one side than the other from where I'd hung out over the street and had polished a good bit of the glass before Izzy had spotted me and started yelling.

I intensified my glare, which Izzy continued to ignore. "No," I said firmly, "I am not on drugs. Chance would be a fine thing."

Izzy snorted. "As if you'd ever cut loose enough to try illicit substances," she said, putting the polish and cloths safely back into the cupboard and latching the doors. "Not really your style, is it?"

I wasn't sure if I should be offended. Obviously, I didn't *want* to look like a drug user, but was I really that boring? "Maybe I'll start," I said archly.

Izzy wasn't falling for it. "You'll go back to bed, is what you'll do," she retorted. "I don't know what happened to you the other night, but you're not right at all. It'll be quiet now. I'm fine on my own. Now shoo!"

I did try to sleep, but gave up after twenty minutes of just staring blankly at the ceiling whilst Grimm rearranged himself endlessly on my stomach. He eventually settled into a position that enabled him to gaze directly into my face with his big, owl-like eyes. "Enough," I said, sitting up suddenly and sending him sprawling to the floor. He huffed slightly, then hopped back onto the bed, curled up in the dent I'd left in the mattress and immediately went to sleep. Clearly, there was going to be no afternoon nap for me. I decided to use my unexpected burst of energy to clean the flat.

By the time I noticed it was getting dark, every cupboard had been emptied, cleaned, organised and refilled. I found an old Dymo label printer at the back of a drawer, bought to label my university work a decade earlier. It still had tape in it, so I carefully labelled the contents of each cupboard. I'd got as far as my underwear drawer when I realised maybe I was taking it too far. Did I really need to remind myself which items of clothing were my own knickers? But I still couldn't shake off the feeling of edginess, so I decided to go for a walk down to docks in the hope of getting rid of some excess energy.

* * *

There was hardly a soul to be seen under the yellow lights of the Albert Dock, but that wasn't unusual at this time of year. In the height of tourist season there'd be people wandering around at all hours, but the Easter holidays had been and gone and it was too cold for outdoor drinking to have started in earnest. A sharp breeze blew in off the river as I walked down Mann Island and past the Museum of Liverpool onto the promenade. Taking up a slow jog as I wound my way across the Canning Dock gate and back to the river path behind Albert Dock, I was surprised at just how easy I found it. I hadn't travelled anywhere at faster than a brisk walk for months, but being on my feet in Flora's all day clearly had health benefits. Maybe I should take up running. I'd tried a few of those 'sloth to superstar' type online fitness courses over the years and really enjoyed them, despite never having made it past week three in any of my attempts to become Merseyside's answer to Paula Radcliffe. There was something about making a conscious decision to just go out and run for no reason that appealed to me. If I'd had a target in mind—a 5k race, say, of the sort that Izzy occasionally did with her pilates mates—I'd have hated it from the start, because that would mean there was potential for failure. But if I was just doing it for myself and had no one judging whether or not I was doing it *well*, then I could see the appeal. I'd always struggled to clear my mind. I had vivid memories of endless, boring afternoons at school when I was still young enough that the teacher expected the class to lie down for a brief nap in the middle of the afternoon. My classmates would wriggle around giggling for five minutes before dozing off in a sea of snoring and occasional farts, whilst I lay staring wide-eyed at the ceiling, wondering what good it was supposed to be doing me. My teacher had once spoken to my parents about it. I remembered them smiling at each other before telling Mrs Offsham that my brain was always too busy to sleep, but it didn't seem to be harming me, so what was the point of worrying? Mrs Offsham clearly thought that there was indeed a point to worrying, because she was having to deal with a five-year-old who'd rather stare blankly at her for twenty minutes at a time instead of curling up and sucking her thumb like a good little toddler. But she'd eventually learned to deal with it the same way I had—by switching off mentally and not acknowledging the person who's staring at you. Thinking about my poor beleaguered infant teacher made me laugh out loud. Accelerating into a proper run, I headed down past the arena and on towards the new-build housing at Kings Parade. Looping round the statue of John Hulley, I headed back the way I'd come. I idly wondered how fast I was capable of running if I got fit enough to really push myself. I once read a theory that suggested the human brain worked at only five per cent of its capacity most of the time and even so-called geniuses used maybe a fifth of their actual abilities. *What a waste*, I remembered thinking, although I had no idea how the verifiable geniuses (genii?) were supposed to make the most of the brain cells they weren't bothering to use. Maybe running was the same? I pushed my heels harder against the neat new paving slabs, and was rewarded with a burst of speed that felt as natural as breathing. It was as if I'd turned into the Flash, that speed-freak character in the DC multiverse who wakes up from a coma with the ability to outrun pretty much anyone on the planet. I hadn't been in a coma, though. Unless—perhaps the knock to my head *had* done something, after all? I wondered just how fast I might be able to run and picked up the pace without consciously sending the instructions down to my legs. Not only was I racing down the seafront at a speed that would have terrified anyone close enough to feel the draught from my pounding feet, I was doing it so easily that I could take time to figure out my best routes and avoid obstacles. Parkouring off the top of a bollard in order to avoid tripping over a pile of emptied fast food cartons that had been left on the floor, I raced on—only to race back and put the trash in the nearest waste bin in a fit of community do-gooding. I slowed as I reached George

Parade, trying my best to ignore the distinct tang of rotten fish and stagnant water. Rolling my head from side to side, I marvelled at how much better I was feeling. It was as if all my joints had realigned themselves and were now powered up and raring to go. It was certainly an improvement on being a vomiting mess. The steps in front of the canal link were empty, so I sat on the floor at the end nearest to the Beatles statue and leaned back against the stone. Closing my eyes, I wondered idly who it was who first decided the order in which the band's names should be listed. Someone who wasn't keen on Ringo, presumably. A tapping noise started up nearby. It was just loud enough to be annoying, and irregular enough to make me want to throttle whoever was doing it. I cracked open one eye and peered around, but couldn't see anything except a lone blackbird on the other side of the canal, pecking busily at a discarded chip wrapper. It took me a good few seconds to realise that the only potential source of the noise was the bird's beak tapping the ground. But I was at least thirty feet from it—too far to hear a tiny beak pecking at concrete. Shutting my eyes again, I decided that as soon as I felt more like my old self, I was going to kick people until I found out what exactly was going on.

"Hey, gorgeous." I turned sharply and saw a man jerkily settling himself down on the steps a few feet away. By the way he was struggling to balance, he'd had a lengthy session on the beer. "Whatcha doin' here on yer own?" He was struggling to string words together and the smell of cheap brandy and stale piss was coming off him in waves. Ignoring him, I clambered to my feet and slung my bag across my shoulders. "Hey!" a hand shot out as I walked past and grabbed my ankle. I kicked out automatically and the man howled, clutching his arm to his chest as he clambered heavily to his feet. He was bigger than I'd realised. His shambolic appearance had made him seem slight, but as he got to his feet, I saw he was well over six feet. He was definitely slender but wiry with it, and he loomed towards me with an expression of drunk aggression on his face. I might only be five foot six in my thickest socks and not normally renowned for my athletic prowess, but I'd been doing pretty well for physical strength recently. And it had been a difficult day. I took a chance and punched him straight in the face. "You bitch!" he screamed, lurching towards me as his collapsed nose spurted blood everywhere, "you ungrateful fucking *bitch*!" Oh, so he was one of *those*. The type who thought all women should be grateful for his aggressive attention and turned vicious when rejected.

My patience in the face of too much weird shit finally snapped. "What am I supposed to be grateful for?" I laughed, as he groaned to himself, "the attentions of a drunk loser?" I skipped backwards a couple of steps as he staggered towards me. His face was purple with alcohol and fury, a terrible combination against his floppy, strawberry-blond hair. "Wife kicked you out, did she?" I stepped sideways to avoid a clumsy swing. He was wearing a suit that had seen better days and shoes that had been expensive a very long time ago. "Sleeping in the office, are you?" Another swing. I was enjoying myself now. A passing couple who had stopped to see what was going on started walking slowly away, clearly deciding that I was more than capable of defending myself. I just hoped they were right.

"I'll teach you a lesson you won't forget," my would-be attacker hissed. "They all learn, eventually. And if you don't, then too bad." There was another scent mingling with the booze and sweat. Excitement, I realised. He was getting excited at the thought of scaring me. Well, we'd see about that. I stood my ground and dropped my bag so that he wouldn't be able to pull it around my neck.

"Come get it, big boy," I taunted, forcing myself not to duck out of the way as he grabbed me. His arms wrapped round me, far stronger than I was expecting, and he twisted me so I was backed into him. I could *definitely* feel his excitement now—it was pressing into my left thigh, very unpleasantly indeed. I reached around and under, grabbing the proof of his interest and squeezing hard. He dropped his arms and tried to double over, but I didn't loosen my grip. I could feel the tender flesh crushing underneath my fingers and grinned as he shrieked.

"Let go of me, bitch!" I squeezed harder in response. "You're fucking insane," he managed, hissing from between gritted teeth. Dragging him upwards by his most tender parts, I turned around so he was forced to meet my eye. I squeezed just a *tiny* bit harder and he squealed like a terrified piglet, tears running down his face. I leaned forward, holding my breath to avoid the acrid smell that was rising from him. If I didn't get rid of him soon, the street cleaners were going to turn up to hose him into the gutter, along with the rest of the city's rubbish. Unfortunately for me, he wasn't quite done. He swung an arm around hard enough to knock me off balance. I let go of him and only narrowly avoided falling over. As I scrabbled around, he caught hold of my arm and pulled me back against his chest again. His grubby hands pawed at me through my t-shirt and his breath was hot on my neck. "Come on," he growled into my ear, "let's have some *fun*." I threw my head back as hard as I could, and was rewarded with a crunching sound and an unearthly howl. Clearly, I'd finished the nose job. I swung around and hoisted him straight over my shoulders, cracking him back down onto the steps by the water. As I stood over his writhing body, a breeze blew in from the water, the fresh air swirling around him and making everything feel suddenly much better. I breathed deeply, clearing my lungs of the fetid smells of the docks and replacing it with the smell of life and power and strength and eternity and….*what*? Freezing with shock at the sudden rush of sensations, I stood motionless as my attacker flopped around at my feet like a dying fish. I breathed in again, very slowly. I could taste—no, I could *feel*—electricity and sex and rotting fish, all overlaid with a sense of power that was stronger than anything I'd felt in my entire life. The man at my feet made a sudden and horrible rattling noise, then fell silent. *Shit.* Gritting my teeth, I forced myself to lean over and check his neck for a pulse. Nothing.

Fuck, fuck, fuck. Just when I thought my day couldn't get any worse, I'd accidentally killed someone. It might not have been a very nice someone, but murder was murder. Manslaughter, possibly. To add to the general insanity of the situation, a creeping feeling of elation was buzzing through my veins, as if several gin and tonics had dropped into my system all at once and my brain had suddenly registered that it was party time. "Into the water with him." The voice came from close behind me and I stifled a scream. Spinning round, I saw a tall, dark-haired man observing events from a few feet away, with what looked distinctly like amusement in his eyes. He was in his early thirties at a guess, clean-shaven and with the look of a 1940s film

30

idol, an image that was reinforced by his dark blue woollen suit. He had eyes of palest sapphire, the light from the street lamps making them almost glow in the dusk. "I've knocked out the camera that covers this section," said my unexpected accomplice, leaning over to grab the man lying lifeless on the floor, "and there's no one else around. Let's get rid of the evidence before we're spotted." He picked the man up and dragged him over to the edge of the water, before looking up at me expectantly. Giving the corpse a careful push with my toe, it slid silently into the water and immediately sank out of sight. Staring into the black water for a minute, I wondered when I'd developed the morals of a particularly murderous alleycat. I looked up to question my partner in crime, but there was no one there. I stared around at the open space of the waterfront, which was thankfully empty of potential witnesses. Dusting myself down, I decided it was time to head home. My dishevelled reflection in the glass walls of the museum brought me up short. Stepping closer to the glass, I peered at the woman looking back at me. I was as pale as ever, despite the evening's physical exertions and my hair rippled out behind me like an orange cloud in the warped glass. But my eyes—well, my eyes were *something*. Pale, glittering silver, there was only a hint of the green that had previously been there. I was beginning to suspect that something really weird had happened when I fell off the roof. A low groaning noise made me turn towards the Strand. There was a dark figure walking in my direction. I straightened up and started walking slowly towards the road, hoping that the man wouldn't take too much notice of me. I needn't have worried. As he got closer, I realised that not only was he absolutely paralytic, he was also clutching a bleeding wound on his head. Whatever had happened when I took a flying leap off a tall building, it hadn't fulfilled my teenage dreams of turning into a vampire. The smell of the blood was undeniably strong, but I wasn't overcome with a sudden urge to lick it off the man's head. I altered course so that I'd pass him closely and took a deep breath, just to check that I definitely wasn't going to grow fangs. He was too distracted to notice a strange woman all but stalking him. As I got close, the scent of cologne and hurt pride—since when did emotions have flavours?—wafted off him. I sucked it in, feeling slightly light-headed

31

as I did so. To my horror, the man collapsed onto the concrete in a heap and for a second, I panicked I was going to have to deal with my second corpse of the evening. But as I took a tentative step closer, he mumbled something under his breath before curling up on his side and beginning to snore like an overgrown baby. Deciding that—for his sake, if not mine—it was probably safer to leave him there, I set off once again for Harrington Street.

There's A Ghost In My House

Scuffing my way home, I sulked quietly to myself. All I'd ever wanted was a quiet life. Yet here I was murdering someone and disposing of their body, all before bedtime. I was also nervous about who exactly it was who'd helped me. He'd definitely done me a favour, but now a complete stranger knew I'd just accidentally killed somebody. Come to that, why didn't I feel more concerned about the fact that I had just killed someone? Okay, so he'd been an asshole. And I was pretty sure that someone else would have done the same as me eventually, anyway. But the most violent I'd ever been before today was swatting wasps, and even then, I felt guilty if I killed them. As I turned onto Harrington Street, I gave an unsuspecting rubbish bin a disconsolate kick and watched with detached interest as it ricocheted off the walls like a giant bowling ball. Funny how I hadn't realised just how strong I was until I started losing my temper. And it was unlike me to lose my temper at all. I could remember a conversation with my parents in my teens, during which Mum asked if I'd ever actually had an argument with anyone. Apart from minor playground spats at school, I couldn't think of any. I generally found it easier to just ignore things I didn't like and go my own way. Grandad used to wink at me, saying, 'still waters run deep, Lil,' but I didn't really know what he meant by it. Maybe it was time to unleash three decades of built-up fury.

"How you feelin', Red?" Billy's voice broke through my daydreams. I turned to see him watching me with a concerned expression on his face.

Forcing a smile I really didn't feel, I stopped in front of him. "I'm fine, Billy." He didn't look convinced. "Honestly. It's just been a strange day."

"How much can happen in one day?" he asked. Before I even realised what I was doing, I walked towards where he sat wrapped in his collection of blankets and old sleeping bags and slid down the wall next to him. From here, I realised, he had a direct view not only into Flora's, but also through the front windows of my flat. I rarely closed the curtains, because I'd assumed no one could see in. Trying not to think about Billy peering into my bedroom, I turned to look at him. He didn't look remotely perturbed by me sitting next to him. Nor did he seem to think his luck was in, thank fuck. Instead, he was just looking at me with an expression of friendly—if slightly wary—interest. He was staring straight into my eyes and tilting his head as if to get a better view.

"Billy," I said, slapping his bony thigh through the endless layers and making him raise his eyebrows, "I caught someone breaking in last night. And then I fell off the fire escape," he opened his mouth to speak, but I put a hand up to stop him, "after which I woke up without a single bruise, despite having apparently bounced off my own car." I gestured towards where Basil sat opposite us, his dented nose glinting in the light from the street lamps. "Most of my night was spent throwing up, I have a banging headache and my vital signs are apparently missing in action." I turned to look him in the eye and beamed. "And I just killed a man for attempting to grope my tits." Billy stayed silent, which was probably the safest option. "So I think we can safely say that my day has been pretty fucking weird."

"What happened to your eyes?" It took me a second to realise what he was talking about.

"Nothing," I said. "I'm fine. Allergies. Anyway," I pushed myself back up the wall until I was standing in front of him, "I think I need to go to bed."

* * *

It wasn't until I'd let myself into the flat and fed Grimm that I noticed the woman sitting in my living room. "What the *fuck*?" I dropped the carton from my hand and the rest of the fancy salmon in gravy with steamed baby vegetables hit the floor with a splat. The woman was in her mid-thirties, at a guess. Her shoulder-length hair was strawberry blonde with a centre parting, and she had a delicate pale face with big eyes and a wide mouth. She sat in the armchair nearest to the window, wearing a wide-necked cotton top over loose jeans with rolled cuffs. She had her feet tucked under herself and looked thoroughly comfortable. This would have been weird enough, but she was also hovering a good few inches above the seat. And she was grinning at me as if we were old friends. "Lili!" the absolute, honest-to-god, real life ghost-in-my-house cried, getting to her feet. She bobbed up and down slightly. "I'm so pleased to see you!" She moved towards me with her arms outstretched and, in return, I did a very good impression of a terrified cat attempting to climb up the cupboards. The woman stopped in her tracks, her hands flying to her mouth. "Oh my gosh, I am *so* sorry," she exclaimed, "I haven't even introduced myself!" Pushing myself back against the wall as hard as I could, I wondered whether I could make it out of the door and, if so, whether I'd survive another leap from the balcony. Even if I did, I doubted Basil would.

"What the *fuck* is going on?" I squeaked. The woman stared at me for a moment and then burst out laughing. Full throttle belly laughing, right there in front of me whilst I tried to keep as much distance between us as possible. "AND YOU CAN STOP LAUGHING!" The unexpectedly authoritative tenor of my voice gave even me a jolt, but it worked. The woman stopped in her tracks, the grin wiped from her face.

"Oh my word," she said, a tiny smile already creeping back into the corner of her mouth. "Death clearly suits you, Lilith O'Reilly."

"How do you know my name?" I asked, somehow missing the more important part of her sentence entirely.

"We're family," said the woman. "I paid for this." She waved her arms around at the building in general. She had finally settled with her bare feet about an inch below floor level, which was disconcerting. I just stared at her wordlessly as she grinned and once again stretched out her arms. "Got a hug for your Aunt Kitty?"

* * *

35

I was sitting on my sofa, wondering if I could risk a cup of tea. Kitty was back in the chair, but now she had Grimm purring happily on her lap. I was pretty sure this shouldn't have been possible, on account of Kitty not actually being solid. But my traitorous cat had simply hopped onto her transparent knees and curled up for a nap. I could see straight through Kitty's legs to the tatty velvet fabric of the chair. But that wasn't stopping Grimm, who eyeballed me in a way that looked suspiciously like a triumphant grin. Kitty idly stroked him. Sometimes she even did it on the surface of his fur, rather than swooping her hand *through* him in a way that made me feel faintly sick. I could murder a cup of tea, I decided. "Why don't you put the kettle on?" she said.

I looked at her sharply. "Are you a mind reader?" That would be all I needed right now—someone who could read every single *wtf* thought that was currently going through my head.

Kitty laughed. It was a big, jolly laugh that was at odds with her hippy flower child appearance. "Don't panic," she said, as if I hadn't already been panicked by the ghost of my long dead relative appearing out of nowhere. "I recognise that expression, is all. Ma used to have the same look on her face when she was parched."

"You're dead," I said. I was never known for my subtlety.

"And you're very observant," replied Kitty, mildly, "yet here we are. Isn't this nice?" She peered around the flat as if this was a perfectly normal catch-up between friends. "I always wondered what happened to everyone after I'd gone."

"Haven't you been watching us? Isn't that what ghosts do?"

My dead aunt snorted at me. "You think I don't have enough on my plate without staring at unwitting relatives who wouldn't know me from Adam? Besides," she continued, "none of you could see me. I've tried."

I stared at her. "When did you try?" I asked, trying not to look too worried.

"Oh, don't look at me like that," said Kitty. "I'm not interested in your sex life, Lili."

"Are ghosts supposed to talk to their relatives like this?" I asked. "As if we're just gossiping over a cuppa? As if you're *alive*?"

Kitty looked at me levelly. "Well, we're neither of us alive," she said, "are we? So I'd say things have evened up a bit."

"What on earth are you talking about?" I said, frowning. "I'm sitting here, aren't I? In my flat, having spent the day working in my coffee shop. Thank you for the money, by the way, I wouldn't have been able to do it without you. I've just been out for a run and fought off a would-be rapist. I am exhausted and now my dead aunt is talking bullshit at me."

Kitty raised an eyebrow. "When was the last time you went running?" she asked. "*Proper* running, Lilith."

I ignored her and tried a different tactic. "I defended myself from an attacker," I pointed out. "He wouldn't have been able to grab hold of me if I wasn't alive. And someone helped me—they certainly seemed to think I was real."

Kitty arched a thin eyebrow. She had definitely been a fan of the tweezers when she was alive. "So you murdered a complete stranger and an unknown man just...*helped* you without ringing the police? And you think *I'm* the weirdest thing to happen to you today?" Clearly, Kitty had inherited the 'annoyingly persistent' gene that was so prevalent on mum's side of the family. "Lili," she said, in a more kindly tone, "I haven't been visible to any living person for decades. Not one of you has spotted me, even when I've been standing there with my heart breaking for you and desperate to give you a hug. Not even a flicker. But here I am, sitting in your living room and having a conversation and petting your cat. I'm inclined to think that something's changed. Aren't you?"

I gave it some thought and decided that it had undeniably been a weird twenty-four hours. I remembered the feeling of freedom I'd had whilst running along the river path—how it had felt as natural as breathing, but hadn't even made me puff. Taking a deep breath, I immediately started coughing. "I wouldn't bother if I were you," offered Kitty helpfully. She was still sitting—approximately—on the chair and Grimm was still pestering her for affection, but I could see her more clearly now. It was as if she was slowly materialising right in front of my eyes. Her hair was catching the light from the streetlamp outside my window and the lamp on the side table lit her with a faint glow down her left side. She was still faintly transparent, but with definite edges to her features that weren't there before.

"Bother with what? Breathing?" I could feel hysteria rising and wondered if perhaps I'd knocked my head harder than I'd realised. Maybe I was actually dead, and this was all just an effect of my synapses firing off in one last, impressive, neuron-related fireworks display. The coughing had subsided, so I concentrated on regulating my breathing into a slow, careful rhythm as taught to me by a well-meaning therapist years earlier. It felt *weird*. I must have bitten my tongue, because I could taste things on the air—the bleach that I'd used to clean the bathroom earlier, mustiness coming from the corner where the interior door opened onto the internal staircase, a faint tang of fish from Grimm's bowl on the floor in the kitchen... Laid over it all was a strange buzzing sensation, as if I'd bitten aluminium foil down onto a metal tooth filling. I raised my head slowly and looked at my great-aunt, who'd been dead for decades but was now somehow sitting in my living room petting my cat. "What the fuck," I said slowly, "is going on?"

Kitty gave me a sympathetic smile. "Well," she said, "you're dead. Sorry about that. But you're still here carrying on as normal—well, sort of normal—and no one else seems to have noticed. It's a rare occurrence you are, Lilith O'Reilly." She looked down at Grimm and gave him an extra scratch behind his ear, before looking back at me with a strange, sad smile. "Some of us would give anything to be in your shoes right now."

"Who the *fuck* would want to be dead?" This time, I managed not to choke on my anger.

Kitty sighed. "Well, not *dead* exactly," she allowed, "more kind of *un*dead."

I stared at her as though she were deranged. "Being dead but still walking around is not normal, under any circumstances," I growled.

Kitty was unperturbed. "No," she said, "I meant the act of being dead is normal. Normal reactions, normal behaviour. You're not a vampire," my eyes widened, and she raised a hand to stop me interrupting, "because vampires are horrible, feral things and you wouldn't be carrying on as if nothing had happened. You're just...*dead*, Lili. But your mind and body have decided they're not quite done yet. It's refusing to accept the memo, so to speak. It does happen," another rueful smile, "just not very often."

"How often?" I demanded, at the same time wondering if 'dead but not dead' might explain some of my more awful exes.

"Rarely," Kitty replied. "Honestly, I don't know exactly. I've missed huge chunks of time, Lili. There are definitely others like you, but I've only ever met one of them. If that's any help." She shrugged.

"It's no help whatsoever," I scowled. "I can't be dead. I don't *want* to be dead. There's too much left to do!"

"Like what?"

"I don't know," I replied. "Make Flora's a success. Maybe find someone nice to spend time with. A boyfriend or something..." I trailed off.

Kitty smiled kindly. "I don't see how being dead should stop any of that," she said, patting Grimm's head. It would have been cute, had her hand not gone straight through him. "Oops." The cat just made a contented noise in return and actually rolled over onto his back, demanding belly scratches. Kitty obliged.

"He's never once let me do that," I said, watching the pair of them from a safe distance. It was an even bet as to whether I was more nervous about the ghost or the cat right now. Grimm had been known to suddenly leap up and attempt to remove the face of anyone who dared stroke his belly, even if he'd been the one demanding attention in the first place. His contrariness was what I loved most about him.

"Maybe you're uptight—cats can sense that kind of thing." She smiled down at the cat and continued her ghostly petting. "When's the last time you saw your parents?"

I wasn't expecting that one. "What?"

Kitty looked up at me. She was increasingly solid, but I wasn't sure whether it was real or whether my eyes were just getting used to the weirdness. I noticed how green her eyes were. "Just asking," she said lightly.

"How did you die?" I deflected.

Kitty stared straight at me. If I'd hoped to throw her off balance, it didn't work. "Through choice," she said. "Not suicide," she added quickly, seeing my stricken expression. "it was accidental. But I chose to take the risks that led to it."

"What sort of risks?"

Kitty grinned. "Oh, you know," she said, "the risks one takes when nothing exciting ever happens around you and then someone comes along who makes life interesting again."

"The man on the seafront," I said. "The one at the cafe, when Jane and Diane reported you missing."

Katherine 'Kitty' O'Reilly had disappeared before I was born. And I mean *literally* disappeared. She had been born somewhere in County Cork in 1929. The details were vague because the family had moved over to England in 1932 and lost most of their paperwork in the chaos of their journey to Liverpool. My great-grandparents Callum and Rose had been offered live-in positions with a family in Shropshire; Callum as a gardener and Rose as a housekeeper. Their daughters Ivy and Kitty were six and four years old respectively at the time of their immigration; they settled happily in the countryside and attended the village school alongside the children of the 'big house'. The Big House is still standing and still called that by the locals, despite having been converted into apartments years ago. The gardens that Callum looked after are now allotments and there's a lengthy waiting list to get one. Rose's kitchen domain had been cut up with partition walling and was now both the kitchen and the bathroom for the biggest apartment in the building, the only one with direct access to its own garden.

Kitty had gone missing in 1963, whilst on a trip to Southport. She was travelling with old friends from the nursing school she'd attended in Liverpool during the 1950s. Jane Thompson and Diane Newstead had both gone to work for the NHS at the Royal Infirmary, but Kitty had found a position as a private nurse soon after they qualified, so it had been a good while since they'd seen each other. Newspaper clippings from the time are formal and sorrowful, with just a faint hint of 'probably ran off with a man'; my mum keeps them tucked into the back of one of her endless family photo albums. Kitty's friends told the police afterwards that they'd left her sitting reading her book in a cafe whilst they went for a walk. As they'd crossed the promenade towards the beach, a thin young man with floppy hair had waved at Kitty from the other side of the road and she'd waved back as if she already knew him. Diane asked if she was okay with being left alone. Kitty had replied that she had what she described as 'some catching up to do', but would see them after their walk. When Jane and Diane returned to the cafe an hour later, Kitty was gone. The cafe owner was questioned, but remembered nothing other than seeing her sitting quietly reading alone at her table.

No one ever saw her again. My grandma Ivy rarely talked about her younger sister. Quiet and reserved, Ivy believed emotions were for other people. She made it clear that, whatever had happened to Kitty, it was probably her own fault. "She had *ideas*, that girl," Ivy had once said to me when I was a curious ten-year-old who'd been badgering about her lost sister for longer than she was comfortable with, "it's no surprise she went to the bad." At bedtime that night, I'd asked Mum what 'going to the bad' involved. She'd laughed. "Anyone who doesn't toe the line has gone to the bad in grandma's books," she said, tucking me in. "And it's grandma who decides where that line is." Ivy had died when I was in my teens, and her husband Ted followed her seven years later. They left the bungalow on a new-build estate that was utterly soulless and filled with neat ornaments that no one wanted. Mum had immediately sold the lot and used the money to pay off the mortgage on our small, detached family home on the edge of town. And she paid off my student debts as a graduation present as a reward for me getting a very unexpected First in History, which was nice. But as far as anyone knew, that was the end of any family money. So it had been quite the surprise when we later discovered that I was the sole heir to Kitty's estate. No one had known Kitty even *had* an estate, never mind the minor fact that I hadn't been born until twenty-seven years after her disappearance. Mum had received a letter from a firm of solicitors in Chester just after my twenty-ninth birthday. They'd apparently been looking for me since I turned twenty-one, in order to fulfil their client's request that all her worldly goods be passed down to the eldest daughter of her niece. We never could figure out why it had taken them so long to find me—Chester's literally just down the road from Liverpool, and I've been on the electoral roll all my adult life. And why just me? Kitty's will had been specific about the money going to 'the daughter of the daughter' rather than 'children of', despite there being no children at all when the will was originally written. But the small windfall had enabled me to take a five year lease on the cafe, and here we were.

"That was him," nodded Kitty. "I didn't die then, though. We went away for a while, just the two of us. Then I was going to come back, but something happened and, well," she smiled softly down at the cat, "that was that. Shame really," she grinned up at me again, "I didn't even get to see the Summer of Love." I raised an eyebrow. "I died in '65. But as I say, it was through my own choices." She looked at me directly then and for a second it was as though the entire universe hid behind those green eyes. "I thought I could be like you, you see."

I stared at her dumbly. "Like me?"

"Undead," she replied. "Young forever, but still able to carry on with life. Doesn't that sound just marvellous?"

"It sounds very unlikely," I grumbled. "I don't recall reading any urban fantasies that had a thirty-something cafe owner as the paranormal heroine."

"I don't think it was supposed to happen," she said. "That fall should have killed you. Somehow it just…didn't. So you're still here. And now the city's stirring."

"Hang on." I was determined not to get sidetracked. And also I wasn't sure I wanted to know about stirring cities just yet. "You still haven't told me how you died."

Kitty sighed. "Jonny was like you," she said. "Undead, immortal, whatever you want to call it. I was arrogant enough to insist that I could become like him if we tried hard enough, and he loved me enough to try." I couldn't help but notice that her fingers were clenching with tension. Luckily for Grimm, they were still passing straight through him, even though they now looked solid. "He failed. *We* failed. But by the time I realised what had happened, I was long dead, and he was convinced it was his fault. He stayed nearby for a long time," I swear I saw a tear glittering in her ghostly eye, "but eventually had to accept I wasn't coming back. I was right there next to him, but I couldn't make him see me." I stayed silent, watching my long-dead aunt talking about someone she'd loved and lost decades ago. "When that man attacked you," she said, "you breathed him in, didn't you?"

I grimaced as I remembered the acrid bitterness in the back of my throat. "I don't know what it was," I said, "but it was fucking vile."

"I'm sure it was," she smiled tolerantly, "but didn't you also feel, well, *alive*? Sorry," she didn't look remotely sorry, "but that's the only way I can describe it. Jonny always said that taking people's energy made him feel alive. And he'd been dead for a very long time, I can tell you that much. Anyway," she was twisting her fingers again, and I watched them fade in and out through Grimm's dark fur, "Jonny had heard a theory that if a revenant—that's what you call yourselves, by the way—did that to a human over a long enough period of time, then eventually the human would die in the usual sense, but their mind and body would keep going. He wasn't confident that it would work, mind. But it's addictive—for both partners. So he took little persuading to keep going. I got physically weaker, but insisted that we had to keep trying. Of course, the inevitable eventually happened, and I died. But that was all." She was hunching down now, reliving her long distant memories. "At first, I thought it had worked—I was there in the room and so was Jonny and *ohhh*, he looked so beautiful! It was as if I could see his very soul, so it was. I went to hug him and he walked straight through me." Grief was etched into her face now and I wondered whether to stop her, but she was already talking again. "I was trying to tell him, *Jonny, I'm here! I'm here with you forever!*' But I couldn't make him hear me. And then I realised that I—my body, I mean—was lying there on the couch, cold and grey as a winter's afternoon on the Mourne mountains."

"I'm sorry." It felt like a pointless thing to say, but I meant it.

Kitty looked up at me and smiled. "Aah, you're a good 'un, Lilith," she said. "If there ever was a member of this family I could bear to be landed with in the afterlife, it's you."

The sheer volume of information that I was having to take in was making me feel lightheaded. I decided to start working through the practicalities. "You're telling me I can suck people's—what?" I asked her. "Souls?"

"I think it's more a kind of breathing in and absorbing of the life force? I'm sorry," Kitty shrugged, "Jonny never really explained it very well. And obviously I never got to experience it for myself. I'm not really much use to you, I'm afraid."

"Then why are you here?" I asked, the afterlife clearly not having furnished me with tact.

"Charming!" she said.

"I meant it literally," I backtracked. "I have zero filters, and if you're going to haunt me, you'll just have to get used to it." There was a tiny smile on her face again, so I figured I was safe. "You said yourself I couldn't see you before," she nodded, "but clearly you thought it was worth giving it another go. And you must have been watching me to know I'd been killed—or not, whatever this is—because otherwise you wouldn't have turned up here tonight. So what gives, Aunt Katherine?"

Kitty scowled. "If you use that name on me ever again, I swear I will haunt you for the rest of eternity," she grumbled. "I'm Kitty through and through and that's that. Katherine? I ask you!."

"Okay," I said, "why are you here, Kitty? And more to the point, how? And why didn't I just die when I fell off the roof? I haven't been letting anyone suck my soul," *chance would be a fine thing*, I thought to myself, "so why didn't I just go 'splat' and be done with?"

She pulled a face. "God, you're a vile child," she said with a grin, "Splat, indeed!" She laughed, but then looked serious again. "I wasn't lying when I said I don't know much about it." Her gaze drifted to the window, and she peered out onto the street. "I think you'll have to find one of the others and ask for some explanations." I wondered if Billy was out there. If so, would he notice the ghostly apparition in my window? Would he assume I had a friend over, or was Kitty invisible to everyone else?

Belatedly, I registered what she'd just said. "One of the others?" I demanded, "You mean I'm supposed to go find the nearest, whatever you call them, *revenant*, and ask them if they're running the Introduction To The Afterlife course this month? Fucking hell, Kitty," she narrowed her eyes at that, but I didn't see why I should censor my language for the benefit of a ghost who could have been watching me pee for all I knew, "this is *insane*. All of it—me sitting here, you sitting there with your hands *in my cat's head*, the dead bloke down at the waterfront. Absolutely fucking insane."

"Life isn't always sane, Lili," my aunt replied. "If it was, then the awful things wouldn't happen. They don't *need* to happen, they're just a product of a mixed up world. There's no need for hunger and poverty and all the rest of that shit. And there's no need to look at me like that, missy. I can swear with the best of the navvies when I feel like it. The misery? It's mostly created by humans in order to hold power over other humans. And now," she eyed me beadily, "no one has power over you, do they?" I must have looked confused, because she ploughed on. "What hold can anyone have over you now? You don't need to eat, so your living expenses are pretty much zero. You don't even have to breathe." I gaped at that one, but she carried on. "And it's best not to, because if you taste too much humanity you'll get addicted, or become poisoned by it, or both. Other than that, there's not much that can hurt you, because your body will just regenerate itself." I must have made a face that matched how I was feeling, because she stopped and looked at me expectantly. "Yes?"

"Am I imagining things," I said slowly, "or did you just say I can *regenerate?*" Kitty nodded. "Do you have *any* idea how ridiculous that sounds?"

She grinned at me. "I do, yes," she said. "Yet it's true, all the same. Your body's frozen in its terminal state and will pull itself back to that state, whatever happens to it. There are limitations," she added quickly, "so don't be getting your head lopped off. There's no coming back from that one, even when you're immortal."

"Noted."

"Although I heard talk of someone pulling their own head back on once, and they were back to normal in no time. Down south, I think." She frowned. "But otherwise—yes, it sounds ridiculous, but yes, it's absolutely true. You forget, Lilith," she said kindly, "I've seen it happen with my own eyes. Jonny once cut his hand on a kitchen knife—he was peeling an apple for me, it wasn't as if he could eat himself or anything—and he slipped, sending the blade into his palm. I screeched good and proper, let me tell you! I was half expecting him to pass out from it. Then I noticed there wasn't any blood, can you believe it? He was grinning at me like I was the silliest, funniest thing he'd ever seen. I asked him to hold out his hand and there was just the tiniest line left on his hand where the knife had been. Even that faded away to nothing as I watched. He was untouchable." She smiled wistfully.

"Where did Jonny go after you died?" I asked quietly.

Kitty gave me a sad smile. "Aah well," she said, "that's what I don't know. After Jonny realised, I wasn't going to wake up and join him in the afterlife, he spent a day and a night in that room with me. Just crying, silently. And then on the second morning he upped and left, just like that. I was left behind with my own cold body and I thought I might just break the world into tiny pieces with my grief. And that," she finished sadly, "was that. I've clearly faded in and out over the years, because I remember some things from back when you were younger. Then there must have been a gap of many years, because suddenly I found myself in this flat. You were wandering around looking confused, and it took me a wee while to figure out who you even were."

"You were here from the first morning I woke up dead?" Kitty grinned. Well, that explained the shadows flittering around the place. "And you just live here now?"

She shrugged. "I paid the deposit, did I not?" She grinned. "Might as well hang out for a while and see how it's going."

That was what I'd been missing. I felt like slapping myself in the face for not having thought of it sooner. "Why did you leave me the money?" I demanded. "I wasn't even born when you died—my *mum* was still a baby!"

"Jonny told me to," she said, as if it was the most obvious thing in the world.

"Let me get this straight," I said. "Your dead boyfriend told you that your baby niece would eventually have a baby of her own and *that* baby might appreciate a foot up the rental ladder forty-odd years later?"

"That's about the sum of it," she agreed. "Jonny said there was something going to happen with Rose's great-granddaughter—'the daughter of the daughter of the daughter,' was how he described it. And I knew I wouldn't be having babies of my own, on account of how my boyfriend was dead. So I figured it had to be someone on Ivy's side. Jonny had money of his own and paid all the bills, saying that my money was better put aside for 'the third daughter'. And that's how you ended up in this place." Kitty spread her arms and indicated our distinctly shabby surroundings. "I mean, it could do with a lick of paint, but…" she trailed off.

"I love it here," I said firmly. "And the only reason I don't redecorate is because my landlords haven't got round to sorting out the damp problem."

"You're not planning to leave, then?"

I frowned. "Why would I be doing that?" I asked, genuinely confused. "I've put a lot of effort into Flora's and I really do like it here. Anyway," I said truthfully, "Izzy would never forgive me."

Kitty's eyes lit up. "Can I meet Izzy?" she asked. "Any friend of yours, and all that?"

I tried not to look too obviously horrified. "You're *dead*, Kitty!" She squinted at me as if she didn't understand what that meant. "A *ghost*. Can you imagine? 'Hi Iz, I'd like you to meet my aunt Kitty. She's been dead fifty years, but she doesn't let it stop her.'"

"Perfect," said Kitty blithely. "I'm sure we'll get on just grand." With that, she went back to stroking my disloyal cat. I spent the rest of the evening staring at the walls and wondering what the hell I'd got myself into.

The Pier Head Zombie

I must have zoned out, because the next thing I knew, it was daylight and the sounds of city life were beginning to drift up from the street. I came to with a jolt and looked around for Kitty and Grimm. The cat was still snoring in the armchair, but now he was firmly on the cushion. As far as I could tell, there didn't appear to be anyone, living or otherwise, between him and the worn velour. "Kitty?" I called tentatively. No response. "Fucksake Kitty," I said more loudly, "at least let me know you're here, instead of lurking like a—" 'ghost', I nearly said. But Kitty *was* a ghost. Wasn't she? There was no sign of anyone or anything except me and Grimm in the flat and not a flitting shadow to be seen, however much I craned my neck into all the corners. Maybe I'd just imagined it all? Breakfast would make things better, I decided. I couldn't remember the last time I'd eaten—that couldn't be helping my strange mental state. Peering into the fridge, I found some wilting cheese slices and an almost-empty tub of spreadable butter that was going mouldy in the corners. Behind that was the tub of strawberries I'd bought from Tesco on the night of the accident. Already going out of date when I'd bought them cheap, they were now an unappealing soup of red mush. And they *stank*. I vaguely remembered Kitty's comment about not having to breathe. Surely I must have imagined it all? There was no way on this logical, scientific planet that I had spent an evening chatting to my dead aunt about how I was dead (but not) and no longer had anything to fear from pretty much anything. I must have just been having really weird dreams as a side effect of banging my head. But, despite the cynical voice in my head telling me it was the most ridiculous idea ever, I decided to test

48

Ghost Kitty's theories.

I took a deep breath and almost immediately started choking so badly that I ended up bent double and retching. Okay, that wasn't going to work. When I was sure I could stand upright again, I held my breath and started counting. By the time I'd got to three hundred elephants, I was bored with counting—but I still hadn't taken a breath. I wasn't feeling faint, nor was my face turning red. I stared at myself in the bathroom mirror for a while. My appearance seemed completely normal—if we discounted the silver-green eyes—and I was able to turn this way and that, checking out my appearance without once feeling the need to gasp for breath. Time to attempt breakfast again. I walked back to the kitchen and emptied it of everything that looked like it was going out of date. The only things left were the sad-looking cheese slices and what was left of a loaf of cheap white sliced bread, after I'd dumped the mouldy end. The not-breathing thing felt natural now and I happily pottered around, making toast and melting the cheese onto it under the electric grill. I found the brown sauce—never ketchup, urgh—and sat at the kitchen table to eat. The cheese tasted strong—so strong that I huffed a breath without thinking. Once I'd stopped spluttering, I forced myself to chew the food, trying not to retch at the overwhelming sensations. The toast was scratchy and dry, like cotton wool. The cheese was stringy and tasted as though I'd actually used ancient, rancid Stilton, rather than bland slices of supermarket cheddar. I swallowed—and nothing happened. Okay, so the food moved itself from my mouth down into my gullet, but it stayed there. I should have been choking to death and desperately hunting for a passerby to perform the Heimlich manoeuvre, but was actually just sitting calmly at the table, wondering how to get the food back out without having to resort to going down to the cafe for a spare pair of pastry tongs. I tried coughing and the lump of chewed horribleness dislodged itself slightly. It was a start. Standing up and leaning over the table, I made myself retch as though I was Grimm, trying to hack up a fur ball. It was a slow process, but eventually I got the awful lump back up into my mouth and spat it into the kitchen bin. Brushing my teeth to get rid of the lingering taste, I decided to assume—for now—that Kitty was real and her advice was valid. Just for today, I would assume that I didn't need to eat. Or breathe. Okay, so that one was weird. But surely I'd need to drink? I knew humans could survive an incredibly long time without food, but water was another matter. Going back into the kitchen, I filled a glass from the tap and took an experimental sip. The water went down in much the same way as I assumed it always had, having not really given it much thought before now. Feeling brave now, I switched on the coffee machine that was my one concession to luxury and filled the cup with grounds. When I had a steaming cup of black coffee in my hands, I opened the kitchen door and stepped out onto the metal platform of the fire escape. Perching on the top step, I felt the chill morning air on my skin and risked a shallow breath. I could smell—no, *taste*—the vapour in the air, a mix of ozone and pollen, with something faintly oily in the background. A ship's horn blew. There was a tang of heavy cloying silt and the hint of petrol from an engine, probably one of the tourist ferries that to this day still blasted out *Ferry 'Cross The Mersey* on every loop they made of the river. A shuffling noise from below made me snap my head around to look down at the street, where Billy was setting up for the day. He must have seen the movement, because he peered up at me, one hand shielding his eyes from the morning sun. Catching my gaze for a second, he gave me a salute before settling down into his blanket nest. I was sitting there, transfixed by the sight of sunlight slipping across the smooth surface of a green sleeping bag Billy was pulling over himself, when Izzy suddenly appeared at the bottom of the fire escape. I shot to my feet and my coffee cup went flying down into the carpark, where it smashed into pieces across the rubble.

"A'right, nervy Nora," Izzy called, as she made her way up the stairs. She had a piece of paper in her hands that was flapping in the breeze. Even from this distance, I could see the Silverton logo at the top of it. The corner was torn, as if the paper had been stuck down somewhere and then ripped off. I sat back down and waited for her to get to me, not wanting to risk any more accidents. As she rounded the top bend in the stairs, Izzy waved the piece of paper in front of her, as if it was on fire. "*This*," she said, flapping it more, "was on the front door when I got here just now. They're not messing about."

I took the sheet from her and read the eviction notice from Silverton Properties. The notice period mentioned in the previous letter had now been reduced to three days—apparently, according to the letter, because of the 'potential for severe danger to life and property' should they not be allowed to take over the building. If we ignored it, 'further steps would be taken, with utmost urgency'. I somehow suspected that Silvertons wouldn't be above sending in the heavies, if we didn't comply with their 'request'. "Three days?" I squawked, "I wouldn't be able to pack up to move *anywhere* with only three days' notice!"

Izzy was close to tears. "I don't want to close, Lil," she said, wiping at her face. "I like working here and I like being with you and I don't want to have to find another fucking job, for fuck's sake! I might end up working in bloody St John's. Can you *imagine?*" She pulled a woeful face at the thought of potentially having to find a job in the depressing shopping centre up the road.

I'd been pissed off when the first letter had arrived, and also worried that I might really have to consider closing Flora's down. But so much had happened in the last few days that it hadn't even crossed my mind again, other than for a vague thought about maybe popping into the Silverton office at some point, to find out what was going on. Now, with the increased aggression and my oldest friend standing in front of me with her face creased with worry, I was absolutely furious. "How *dare* they?" I muttered, almost to myself. "How *fucking* dare they?" I stood up suddenly, almost knocking Izzy backwards down the steps.

"Fucking hell, Lil," she said, clinging to the railing, "calm your tits a bit, aye? I know it's a crisis, but I'd quite like not to break my bloody neck in the process." I went past her down the stairs without replying, not even stopping to shut the kitchen door. As I got to the street, Izzy yelled after me. "What are you *doing?*"

I paused for a moment and looked up to where she was pulling the door closed. She looked down at me with a concerned look on her face. "We're not moving," I said, loud enough for her to hear. Billy popped his head out from under his blankets and watched the proceedings with interest. "I'm going to see the bloody Silvertons."

* * *

I'd adored the Liver Building long before I came to live in the city. On my first visit to Liverpool with my parents when I was ten years old, I stood on the waterfront staring up at the brick frontage that seemed to go on forever and spotted the tiny bird perched at the very top. Dad had told me there were two birds, and that they were, in fact, absolutely huge. I'd walked round to the other side of the building and found the second bird, but nothing would convince me they were any bigger than a crow. These days I knew *all* about the building and its avian mascots. Over three hundred feet of reinforced concrete, it was opened in 1911 as a home for the Royal Liver Assurance Group. That had, in turn, grown out of the Liverpool Lyver Burial Company, a working men's co-operative that was founded in 1850 to provide for 'the decent interment of deceased members' in the face of the poverty that had been hobbling the city for centuries. It stands thirteen storeys high, has endless elevator shafts and those tiny crows on top are actually cormorants, each of them eighteen feet tall, with a twenty-four foot wingspan. This random collection of nerdy information made it all the more surprising that I'd never actually been inside the building. Like anything that you see all the time, the Liver Building had rapidly become just another part of the scenery of my life, alongside remembering to put in bakery orders and dodging drunken hen parties stalking down the middle of Bold Street on Friday nights. I headed in through the main front entrance and was confronted by a long reception desk manned by a woman with sharply cut hair and a vocal tone to match. "Can I help you?" she demanded archly.

I could feel irritation stirring already. "You can, actually," I replied politely. "Which floor is the Silverton office?"

Sharp Hair looked faintly pleased with herself. "Nobody is allowed access to the Silverton's floor," she informed me smugly. "That area is private."

"I'll assume they're at the top then," I said. "Thanks for your help." Before she could make a move, I walked briskly past her and headed for the staircase at the back of the vast room. If I took the lift, then security might beat me to the top, but I was feeling pretty restless and figured a run would do me good. Racing up the stairs three at a time, I wondered again at my sudden improvement in physical fitness. I zipped up the floors like Usain Bolt racing for the last train home. I could hear shouting behind me, but I was faster than the voices. Feeling very pleased with myself as I rocketed up the last flight, I was stopped in my tracks by a tall, dark-haired man who stood waiting for me at the top, with one hand held out in front of him. I wasn't prepared and slammed into his outstretched palm, his hand smacking hard against my sternum for all the world as if I'd run straight into a concrete wall. Bouncing back, I regained my balance and glared at him.

"Can I help you?" His voice was deep and well-spoken. It had a slight inflection that made him sound like a newsreader who'd been brought in by the BBC in the hope of making them sound more accessible, without having to resort to employing people from north of Watford. I looked up and registered a handsome, slightly round face. He had wavy, dark brown hair framing a straight nose, cupid-bow lips and twinkling blue-grey eyes. He also appeared to be trying his hardest not to laugh.

"I would like to speak to someone about this," I said, holding out the letter that Izzy had given me the previous day.

He took it from me and shook it out, reading slowly. "It's fine, John," he said over my shoulder. I turned and saw that a security guard from the ground floor had finally caught up with me. John was blowing hard and was red in the face, but he waved weakly before turning and slowly making his way back down the stairs. "I don't see a problem," said the man. "Your landlord is clearly taking responsibility for what might be an unsafe building and is doing the right thing. I'm afraid I can't help you."

"I didn't ask for your help," I retorted. "I want to speak to the organ grinder, not the bloody monkey."

Before he could reply, the double doors behind him opened and a tiny white woman dressed in a black trouser suit walked up behind him. "Can

53

I ask what this is all about?" She had a cut glass accent and the poise of a ballerina. She took the letter from the round-faced man and scanned it briefly. Turning to me, she looked me up and down slowly, before finally meeting my gaze with a polite smile. "Aah," she said. "Lilith O'Reilly, yes?" I glared back at her. Everything about her screamed money and privilege. Not as thin as most rich women, she clearly had a tailor who knew how to make the best of what she'd got. Her crisp white shirt was cut as perfectly as the suit draped over it and I was pretty sure that the immaculately plain black court shoes she wore would show red soles when she raised them to kick you. She stepped forward and held out her hand. When I didn't move, she dropped it back down to her side without looking in the slightest bit offended. "Maria Silverton," she said. "I'm your landlord. Or rather," she waved a hand back towards the doors that were now closed firmly behind her, "one of them. We're a family firm. And we wouldn't normally ask a tenant to leave at such short notice," she smiled sympathetically at my grimace, "but we really do need to have some major repairs done on your building. I'm sorry." With that, she handed me the letter and nodded to the man. Before I realised what was happening, he'd swept me into a small elevator that I hadn't noticed, disguised as it was in the wooden wall panelling. As I opened my mouth to complain, he gave me a tiny wave and pressed a button. The doors closed, and I felt myself heading downwards. The *bastards*. By the time the doors pinged open at the ground floor, I was utterly furious. Walking out into the reception, I couldn't resist turning to kick the elevator door as it closed again and was satisfied to see that I'd left a dent in the metal. Pretty impressive, given that I was only wearing sneakers. Stupid bloody Silvertons and their stupid cheap metalwork. Pasting a polite smile on my face, I sauntered out past the receptionist, who eyed me nervously. She didn't drop her gaze until she was sure I was back outside on the steps.

I seethed quietly to myself as I stalked down to the waterfront. How *dare* that woman treat me so patronisingly? Her accent had been so precise that she sounded like she'd walked out of a Jane Austen novel and she was clearly used to using it to slice her way through life with no thought for others. *Well, let's see how she manages when she realises her tenant is a terrifying denizen*

54

of the undead realms! I thought to myself, already knowing damn fine that there was no way I'd be telling anyone about my deceased status anytime soon. I'd be evicted on the grounds of insanity and carted off to the nearest secure psych ward. *Until they tried to take your pulse and decided you'd be better off in a research lab,* said a traitorous inner voice. Shit. How was I supposed to exist in the normal world when suddenly I was anything *but* normal? Two days ago, I'd been an average woman in an average job in a city that didn't much care what anyone was up to, so long as they kept themselves to themselves. And now here I was, staring out at the ferry crawling along the Wallasey seafront on the other side of the river and suddenly my eyesight was so good that I could pick out individual passengers standing along the rail above the lettering that announced it as the *Royal Iris.* "I prefer the brightly painted ferry, myself," said a polite voice next to me. I tried not to look too obviously shocked as I turned to face Maria Silverton. She held out her hand again, and this time I shook it briefly. Her grip was firm and cool—the handshake of a woman used to getting what she wanted.

We gazed at each other for a moment, before I remembered why I was there. "You'll have to excuse me," I said, stepping away from her to leave, "I need to go figure out how to stop you evicting me from my home."

To my astonishment, Maria Silverton laughed, not unkindly. "I think we got off on the wrong foot," she said. Understatement of the century. "Perhaps you'd like to come back in and talk to us all properly? We, erm..." she trailed off, before visibly pulling herself back on track, "we didn't realise. About your...situation."

"Please stop talking in riddles," I said sharply. "It's been a long week, and it's only Wednesday. I won't be moving out of Harrington Street. If there's maintenance to be done, it can be done with Flora's in situ. The building's been there for a hundred years or more—it's survived a couple of world wars and several dodgy nightclubs, so I'm pretty sure we can manage whilst you install some rat traps."

"Rat traps?" Maria Silverton looked thoroughly flummoxed.

"I'm used to them, to be honest," I ploughed on. "The rats, I mean. And anyway, I've got a cat." It belatedly occurred to me I'd never checked whether the lease allowed pets. "A very well-behaved one. But if you'd sort the electricity out on the ground floor, I'd appreciate it. Now, if you'll excuse me," I started walking backwards as Maria Silverton stood silently watching me with an amused expression on her face, "I have a cafe to run." *And then I'm going to the pub*, I thought, as I weaved my way across the traffic on the Strand and headed up Water Street. *Let's hope that the undead can still get pissed.*

* * *

It turned out that no, the undead could not get pissed. "Your round, Lil," said Izzy, pushing her empty glass towards me across the table. We were sitting at one of the booth tables in the Pilgrim. It had become our favourite drinking spot whilst I was at university and that had never changed, even though it was a bit of a schlep now that we were both living closer to the waterfront. The cheap drinks had a lot to do with it. We'd had three rounds already and Izzy was clearly feeling the effects. I'd stuck to cider—maybe my system would cope better with something based on fruit—and had been careful not to drink too quickly in case I had a repeat of the vomiting incident. So far, so good—I couldn't feel anything trying to find its way back out—but neither was I getting drunk. The afterlife was looking really fucking boring so far, I thought to myself, as I scooped the glasses up and wriggled my way out of the booth.

"Same again?" I asked Izzy. She nodded, already staring at her phone to check for messages. There was always a man—or three—hanging around Izzy, just hoping she'd throw them a crumb of affection. I occasionally told her off for keeping people hanging, a criticism that she always vehemently denied.

"They enjoy the chase," she'd say firmly. "Nothing's worth having if you don't have to fight for it a bit." That didn't stop her shagging the brains out of those she actually fancied, usually leaving them asleep the next morning and sneaking out to give me a rundown of what they'd been up to. On several occasions she'd had to stay at my flat for a couple of nights, whilst the latest lovelorn sap slowly realised he wasn't going to get to repeat the experience of his lifetime. Whilst I waiting for refills, I became aware of someone watching me from the other end of the bar. I turned and, to my horror, realised it was the man who'd helped me dispose of my accidental corpse. He looked extraordinarily pale in this light, with dark shadowed eyes. He caught me looking and raised a glass of red wine in a silent toast. I nodded politely then looked away, feigning concentration whilst paying for the drinks. I could feel his eyes on me all the way back to the table. *Shit.*

"What gives with fanboy there?" asked Izzy as I sat back down. "He's still staring, in case you're wondering," she continued.

I resisted the urge to turn round. "Never seen him before in my life," I lied. "Now tell me who you've got on the end of your string this time, so I can lecture you about consorting with unsuitable men."

She had barely opened her mouth to speak when the barman appeared beside our table, holding a bottle and two glasses. He looked faintly embarrassed. "The gentleman at the bar asked me to bring you this," he said, placing the bottle in the middle of the table and a glass in front of each of us.

Izzy picked up the bottle and peered at it. "It's a bit dusty," she commented.

"That's because it's been on the top shelf since we bought it a few years ago," said the barman. "It's the most expensive wine we have. And that's the only bottle. The landlord fancies himself as a connoisseur—god knows why, when most of our customers are happy with bulk buying Jägerbombs." He gave the table an ineffectual wipe with his cloth and stood back. "I'm surprised he didn't just drink it himself, to be honest. No one's even noticed it sitting there before."

Izzy took a photo of the bottle's fancy wax seal and handwritten label and was busy googling before the barman had even got back to his post. I turned to at least acknowledge the gesture, but the man was gone. Just when I thought things couldn't get any weirder, Izzy looked up at me with a strange expression on her face. "Lil," she said in a squeaky voice, "this stuff sells for upwards of five hundred quid a bottle. Are you sure you don't know him?" She was pouring even as she spoke. "Because he sure as hell seems to want to impress you." She peered round the bar. "Where is he?"

"No idea," I said truthfully. "Fuck it." I picked up a glass. "Let's drink to weirdness."

"Shiiiiit," mumbled Izzy as I helped her up the steps out of the pub and onto Pilgrim Street. "That was some seriously good wine." The wine had indeed carried the expensive fruitiness that makes sommeliers talk about tarmac and sunshine and orgasmic rapture, and Izzy was absolutely, biblically smashed. I, on the other hand, was not. I was coming to the depressing realisation that I would never be happily pissed ever again. How would I get through Saturday night television without several large gin and tonics to fortify me? I guessed there was nothing to stop me drinking them—it appeared to just be food that came straight back up—but I was never again going to feel that lovely warm fluffiness of having had that tiny bit too much to drink. Izzy floundered forwards and would have landed in the gutter had I not grabbed hold of her arm. "Jeeeezus, Lil, you don't have to hold that tight," she said, shaking herself free. "If I'm covered in bruises in the morning, I'm blaming you."

"Not the chair that you fell over on the way to the toilet?" I asked mildly.

Izzy scowled at me and then giggled. "Why aren't you drunk?" she demanded, grabbing the top of a nearby wall. "I am...*very* drunk, but you don't look drunk. S'not fair." She made a show of standing upright. "I think..." she said slowly, "I need to walk it off." We wobbled our way down Duke Street and the few people we saw were careful to keep out of our way. I hoped Izzy was drunk enough not to notice how sober I was in contrast, but I occasionally faked a stagger to be on the safe side. We got as far as Hanover Street before we had to stop for her to throw up into a large ornamental flower pot, after which she looked much better. "I want to sit by the river," she declared, wiping her mouth with the sleeve of her cashmere cardigan. Tiny, well-fitted and expensive looking, it was also a pale grey colour that would not handle vomit stains well. Izzy gave her arm a half-hearted wipe against her skirt, which only spread the stain further. "It will make us feel better." With that, she spun around, nearly lost her balance again, then set off at a determined wobble in the direction of the Albert Dock. I followed dutifully behind her, occasionally putting out an arm to guide her back on course. When we got to the waterfront, I propped Izzy against a bollard whilst I bought a bag of steaming hot french fries from the little wagon which sold fresh doughnuts during the day and expanded its menu with various alcohol-absorbing carbs late at night. She fell on them gleefully and staggered off like Bambi. Any remaining elegance she might have had was destroyed by the mayonnaise she immediately spilled down her chin. I caught hold of her arm and guided her off the cobbles towards the safely paved pathway. We somehow made it across the lock bridge before Izzy gave up. She slumped down against the Pier Head sign and happily wolfed chips whilst gazing vacantly up at me.

"Why aren't you drunk?" she asked suddenly.

"I'm just not as drunk as you," I replied. "I thought you wanted to sit by the water?"

She wriggled happily on the filthy concrete. "Near 'nuff." I gave in and sat next to her, shaking my head as she proffered the wobbly bag of grease. There was a sudden loud splash from the dock behind us, but when I turned to look, I could see only darkness. Maybe my undead hearing was improving and I could hear fish now? Not that the Canning Dock had ever been known for its fishing opportunities. I took a couple of tentative steps forward and peered over the edge. There was definitely something moving deep in the water, I just couldn't figure out what. It was probably time to leave.

"Fucksake Lil, I've only just got comfortable," grumbled Izzy as I hauled her to her feet. "Why the sudden panic?"

"No panic," I lied, "I'm just cold." *Dead cold*, chortled a traitorous voice in my head. I stamped on that thought.

"Alright darlin'?" The rough male voice spoke before I'd got Izzy fully upright. I spun around to see a shadowy figure that looked like something straight out of a horror movie. Whatever it was clambered out of the water and over the metal railings. He was tall and his head tilted sideways so that he wasn't quite looking straight at us. A sinking feeling gnawed at the pit of my stomach and I took a step back as he lurched forwards. Izzy gripped my arm, fear pouring off her in waves. "Aaw, don't be like that, honey." Another step and the light over the Pier Head sign showed his craggy, damaged face

59

and leering eyes. There was no doubt, now—it was the creep I'd killed on George Parade. Or rather, the creep I'd *thought* I'd killed. Obviously I needed lessons in neck-breaking, because I seemed to have messed this one up quite badly. "Here, little kitties," he mumbled, through the mess of his face. "Why don't you come play?" Izzy and I both took another automatic step backwards and I could hear water behind us—the tide was in and high behind the dock wall. Fucking marvellous.

"Why don't you take a hike into the river, you dirty old man," I retorted. "I've had enough of you now."

"Would you mind telling me what the absolute fuck is going on, Lili?" Izzy suddenly sounded very sober.

"We had a disagreement," I replied, " although I don't think he remembers it. Anyway," I watched as the horror show on legs lurched closer to us, " he came off worse."

Izzy made a choked snorting noise next to me. "I can see that," she said. "You realise I'm expecting an explanation as soon as we get out of this?"

"Yeah, that's what I'm afraid of." I was getting thoroughly sick of having my quiet life disturbed. Taking a quick step forward, I grabbed the man's head and pulled him down hard against my knee. Twisting with all my strength, I heard a loud enough crack to be satisfied that this time I really had finished him off. Stepping backwards, I wiped my hands on my jeans as he slumped to the floor. There was no one around, and I was pretty sure that no security cameras covered this area. On the downside, I now had a body to dispose of.

Izzy interrupted my thoughts with a loud cough. "Into the river, I reckon." She was already moving to grab him by the arms and looked up at me expectantly. "Well, come on then," she said, "let's get going." I obediently grabbed the man under his other arm. His head flopped over onto my shoulder and his tongue lolling repulsively, all fat and greyish-pink. I tried not to retch as we dragged him towards the chain-link fence that stopped people from falling into the Mersey. "Drop him in," said Izzy. "With any luck, the tide will take him back out again for long enough that the fish get to have a nibble. Whaaaat?" She looked indignantly at me. "You want him unidentifiable, don't you?"

"Of course I do," I nodded. "I'm just a bit confused as to why you're being so, well, *practical* about it all." We pulled the would-be lover boy to the edge, sliding him under the lowest chain. The river was still high, lapping at the concrete as if waiting eagerly for its unexpected meal.

"Hang on," Izzy said, and rifled through her tiny handbag before pulling out a small penknife. To my silent surprise, she stabbed him hard in the belly without even flinching. "Lets out the gases," she explained. "We don't want to risk him bobbing up until we can be sure there's no trace of us on him. He'll reappear eventually, of course," she said conversationally, "but it'll be too late then. Coroner will write it up as a drunken accident, I reckon. Will you stop looking at me like that?" I clearly didn't, because she sighed. "I watch a lot of those real life crime dramas, don't I? It's amazing what you can learn from television."

"Most people settle for figuring out how to make a decent Victoria sponge," I pointed out. Izzy just grinned in response and pushed the body hard with her foot, sending him over the edge with a disturbing *splosh*. He sank quickly, and I hoped that he'd stay off the bottom long enough to clear the shallow edges. I turned back to Izzy, who was leaning against the metal railing post, looking distinctly nauseous. It occurred to me that murdering a man and disposing of the corpse might have been the easiest part of the evening.

I was right. She gave herself a visible shake and then grinned at me. "So, since when have you been a cold-blooded murderer with super strength?" she asked. I was beginning to think I was the one that should be scared - who'd have ever guessed that my delicate little friend would turn out to be so unflappable?

Giving in, I sighed and just went for it. "Since I died," I said. "A couple of days ago. Nights ago," I corrected myself. "I'm dead. Apparently. And it doesn't really matter if you believe me or not. In fact, it would be helpful if you didn't."

Izzy almost skipped with glee, then stopped abruptly. "Hang on," she said, before leaning over the fence and vomiting noisily into the water. "That's better." She wiped her face on her sleeve, stopping briefly to look wonderingly at the stains already there. "What a strange night it's been," she said. Then she fainted.

How Do You Sleep?

Honestly, this entire week could go fuck itself. All I'd wanted from life was to be left in peace to run my little cafe and maybe at some point meet someone who would tell me how well I was doing before offering to rub my feet ahead of an evening of mind-bending sexual gymnastics. Maybe they'd even get up early in the morning and cook me breakfast. Instead, I was facing an eternity of no breakfasts at all and imminent interrogation from my best friend. Izzy was curled up in the chair opposite me, wrapped in a blanket and looking slightly more aware of her surroundings. She stared beadily at me over a cup of tea. There was no sign of Kitty, although Grimm was making purring noises from the bedroom that suggested he had company. "You're a zombie." Izzy's tone was matter-of-fact and as sober as it ever got. I guess it's hard to stay in the 'happy drunk' zone when you've had to dispose of a corpse and listen to your best friend tell you they're dead, but not to worry about it. She'd already insisted on taking my pulse and timing how long I could hold my breath. I failed the pulse test entirely and Izzy got bored after eight minutes of waiting for me to breathe. She'd sat staring at me ever since, expressions of confusion and wonder alternating across her face. I thought she was he was coping very well, all things considered.

"I'm not a bloody zombie," I grumbled. "How many times do I have to tell you? And I'm not a vampire, either. Look," I waved an arm at her, "no sparkle." She laughed at that. "I don't know *what* I am," I confessed.

Izzy stopped laughing and looked thoughtful. "Well," she said finally, "vampires wouldn't sparkle, anyway. That was a stupid idea." She tilted her head and peered at me some more. "And if you *were* a bloodsucker, you'd have probably nommed me by now."

"Probably," I agreed. "Or maybe you just taste sour."

Izzy stuck her tongue out at me. She had a smile on her face, but when she spoke, her voice was serious. "You really did just fall off the roof and wake up dead?" Izzy was, I don't know... 'morbidly fascinated' was the only way I could describe it. Despite it being a far better response than running away screaming before returning with a flaming torch and a horde of villagers, I was feeling almost indignant that she was taking my revelations so well. She could at least look nervous, for fuck's sake. "So what gives with the creature from the Scouse lagoon?" she continued. "Why did you decide to off him?"

"He bloody well attacked me!" I said indignantly. "Last night. There's a limit, you know? What was I supposed to do—politely let him crack on with a spot of serious sexual assault?" She had no answer for that. "Anyway, I didn't 'off' him alone. I had help. And you're the one who knew how to dispose of a corpse! I didn't even know how to do that and I'm the walking fucking dead."

"You're still you though, aren't you?" she said. I frowned at the tangent, but she carried on. "It doesn't really matter if you're suddenly Lili the Zombie," she ignored the look I gave her, "cos you're still the same person you were last week. Just *way* more interesting. Sorry," she pulled a mock sad face. "But it's true. Earlier today you were just 'Lili who I've known forever', and now you're some sort of, I don't know, kick-ass undead vigilante or something." She smiled brightly as I scowled. "Stop looking so bad tempered," she continued. "For all you knew, I could secretly have been a crack-shot zombie killer with a brain pick in my pocket and a grudge against the undead. Don't look at me like that!" I wasn't entirely convinced. "Not yet, anyway. *It's a joke.* Honestly," she muttered to herself, "no sense of humour, you brain-eaters."

"So you're not going to run away screaming?"

"Are you kidding?" she looked up at me. "And miss out on the most excitement I have had since forever? *Ha!*" She watched me sip my coffee and raised an eyebrow. "I'm assuming you can actually drink that?"

I huffed a bit. "I *appear* to be able to drink fluids, but only if I do it slowly.

Food, nope. No more cake, no more chocolate, no more bags of fresh baklava from that shop up on Granby Street. Being dead is pretty fucking disappointing so far."

"Ooh, who's a snarky zombie, then?" cackled Izzy.

"I haven't tried to eat your brains. Yet."

Izzy considered this for a second. "To be honest," she mused, "I've always wondered why everyone expects zombies to walk round growling 'braaaaaains' all the time. If they're mindless brain-eating monsters, how would they know the word for brains, anyway? Hmmm?" She tipped her cup at me to emphasise her point. "Anyway, you're definitely not a vampire," she said this with certainty, "because you're nowhere near elegant enough." I scowled, and she ignored me. "And who helped you?"

"What?" She was jumping topics like a pentathlete, and I was confused. Izzy squinted at me. She was definitely sober now.

"You said you had help. With ol' creature from the deep. Who helped you and why did neither of you go to the police?"

"I'm not sure the police would be inclined to help a dead woman who murdered someone in self defence," said Kitty from behind me.

I spun around to glare at her. "Please will you stop doing that?" I hissed at my dear departed aunt, who was sitting a couple of centimetres down into the bookcase, my beloved Terry Pratchett collection still visible through her knees. A squeaking noise made me turn back round in time to see Izzy almost falling backwards off her chair, the blanket clutched to her face in fear. I had just about had enough. "WILL YOU BOTH JUST SIT DOWN AND SHUT UP?" My voice wasn't *loud,* as such; it was more as though I'd developed an ability to echo my words out from the bottom of the deepest, creepiest cave that had ever existed in humanity's worst nightmares. They both sat down and shut up, but Izzy looked distinctly as though she might faint again. "And you can wipe that bloody smirk off your face," this to Kitty, who did not wipe the smirk off her face. "Izzy," I said to the quaking bundle of fabric on the opposite chair, "this is my aunt Kitty. She's a ghost," I added, just in case the fact that Kitty was sitting *through* the bookcase wasn't evidence enough, "but she's okay. Mostly," I narrowed my eyes at Kitty, who wrinkled her pert little nose in response. Izzy sank back down into the chair, but didn't let go of the blanket. I gazed around the room at my terrified friend and my giggling dead aunt and wondered what on earth I'd done to deserve all this. Fuck my *absolute* afterlife.

* * *

Izzy had slept on my sofa, saying she felt safer with me around whilst she attempted to get used to the idea that all the teenage paranormal storybooks had been telling the truth. I was touched by her faith in me. Kitty had faded from sight after making Izzy promise to talk to her properly in the morning—she apparently had faint memories of the building Izzy's parents had their shop in and wanted to see photos. Izzy politely requested that I 'fuck off to bed, or go perch on a chimney stack or something' not long after Kitty disappeared. I'd settled on the sofa on the assumption that she'd feel better knowing I was there, but it didn't take long for her to inform me sharply that it's apparently quite difficult to doze off with a zombie staring intently at you. I pointed out in a hurt tone that I couldn't help not being able to sleep, but eventually gave in and went to bed. Curling up with Grimm, I stared at him instead. He didn't seem to care, pushing himself against me for ear-scratches before wrapping himself up in a ball and falling into that level of sleep peculiar to cats—snoring loudly, but with one eye open a tiny slit, just in case they miss something interesting. The strangest of all the strange things that had happened over the past few days, I decided as I stared at the ceiling, was that I didn't actually feel any different in myself. Izzy was absolutely right—I was still Me. Although Previous Alive Me wouldn't have handled the sudden awareness of the existence of the living dead as well as Izzy had. So why was I taking it so well now? Maybe it was simply because I didn't have any other options. I was definitely dead, there was no question about that. Izzy had persuaded me to let her have another attempt at finding my pulse before she went to sleep, with no luck. As dawn was breaking, I realised I wasn't holding my breath—there was no longer any breath to hold. I wondered how long I could go without blinking. That turned out to be limited to about fifteen minutes, but only because my eyes began to itch as they dried out and gathered dust. Tiptoeing carefully past Izzy into the bathroom, I ran the cold water and held my head underneath it with my eyes open. Had I tried that when I was alive, it would have been horribly uncomfortable, but now it just felt as though I was giving my eyeballs a really good wash. I wandered back to bed without bothering to dry my face and the water dripped onto Grimm. He woke with a start and glared at me with his wide yellow eyes, before loping off the bed and out into the living room, presumably to find shelter under Izzy's mound of blankets. Bored now, I went to stand at my bedroom window and looked out at the grey dawn sky that was starting to break up the darkness. Despite the deep shadows, I could see everything clearly. Death clearly worked wonders for eyesight. I'd been shortsighted in one eye for as long as I could remember, but now both eyes worked so well that it took me a few minutes to remember which eye it had been. "What on earth are you doing, dead girl?" Izzy appeared in the bathroom doorway just as I was pulling a particularly ugly face in an attempt to inspect the inside of my mouth. Somehow I'd assumed that I'd have shiny white teeth with which to terrify my enemies, but they appeared exactly the same as before, complete with a couple of large fillings towards the back. *Whatever happened to undead perfection*, I griped to myself as I tried and failed to check the top of my head for any grey hairs. I already had a tiny white streak at one temple and that was still there, but I quite liked it. I'd be happy enough if everything just stayed as it was. "Also, you look ridiculous. I thought the undead were supposed to be visions of power and elegance?"

"I'm not a vampire," I said. "We discussed that already." I started brushing my teeth with great ceremony, figuring they were going to have to last me a long time. Izzy got bored and wandered off. Then I got dressed, in an old-but-clean flowery dress, leggings and boots, with an oversized heavy-knit cardigan over the top. Walking into the kitchen, I saw Izzy had made herself a large pot of coffee and was perched on my windowsill, all the better to smoke out of it. "You know I don't like you smoking inside the flat," I said.

"You're hardly going to develop lung cancer," she pointed out, but obligingly put out her bent roll-up in the pot of Indian mint that balanced on the outside sill. I scowled at her. "Whaaaat?" she demanded, squinting at me. "I put it out, didn't I? Anyway, I needed it in order to cope with the realisation that my best friend is a newly fledged member of the undead."

"I don't see that it changes anything," I said, clattering crockery around on the draining board and finding myself a clean mug. "Enough in that pot for me? I really am going to lose my shit if I can't have my coffee."

Izzy looked dubious. "Where does it go?" I looked blankly at her. "I'm assuming you don't pee," she said, "so where does the liquid go?"

I thought about it for a minute. "I guess I'm like a pot plant," I said and saw her expression. "No, hear me out." She crossed her legs, still on the windowsill, and politely sipped her coffee whilst staring at me beadily. "Cos I *can* drink, but only a bit. And if I drink more than I can absorb, it just pours back out. From the top end," I said in the face of her grimace, "I guess it just doesn't go down if I don't need it."

"We need to find the others," Izzy said. I looked at her blankly. "You can't be the only one," she pointed out, "because much as I love you and believe in your individuality, I very much doubt that you are the only person to have ever woken up dead. Statistically unlikely, and all that."

"Kitty's boyfriend was a revenant," I replied, remembering the conversation with my dead aunt. "We're called revenants," I continued, in response to Izzy's confused look, "and no, clearly I'm not the only one."

"Well, where is he?" Izzy demanded. "Tell her to bring him here! He can give you a crash course in the afterlife."

"I don't think she knows," I replied. "She died a long time ago, Iz. The boyfriend went away, and she seems to have just popped in and out over the years, unable to communicate with anyone."

"Well, that's just stupid," said Izzy. "How are you supposed to know what to do? What happened to the Undead Welcoming Committee? They always seem to turn up in the books." I shrugged. Her guess was as good as mine. Her face suddenly lit up. "The man from the Pilgrim! He helped you the other night, so clearly he must be like you. He wouldn't have helped you otherwise," she pointed out.

"I don't know who he is," I said truthfully, "and nor do I know where he keeps disappearing to. But," I was surprised that a cartoon lightbulb didn't actually ping on above my head as the thought hit me smack in the face, "the Silvertons know!" I leaned forward and grabbed her arm, before dropping it in the face of her pained expression. "Sorry," I grimaced, "I forget how strong I am. But the Silvertons! One of them came after me yesterday and said she 'hadn't realised my situation' or something like that—they must be part of it all."

"Oh great," muttered Izzy. "Now our landlords are fucking zombies?" She frowned. "No wonder they're shit at keeping up with the maintenance. Too busy hunting for brains to actually keep up with the admin."

"They don't look undead."

Izzy tilted her head and gazed at me. "Neither do you," she pointed out, "apart from the weird eye thing."

I couldn't deny it—looking in the mirror that morning, the silver tint of my irises was unmissable. They seemed to have settled now—the original green was still there, but glowing slightly from the effect of the silver-grey ring around them. "Okay, so the eye thing is strange," I allowed, "but honestly, I didn't even think to look. They might all have weird eyes for all I know. I was too busy kicking their elevators to notice. They were being annoying," this to Izzy's querying look, "and I walked out, then one of them came after me and said they'd like to chat. I was fed up with it all by that point, so I ignored her. And that's when we went up to the Pilgrim."

"Maybe you should go back?" Izzy said. "Ask them for the introductory course. Ooh!" her face lit up, "maybe they can teach you to fly!"

I stared at her. "Why the fuck would I be able to fly, just because I'm dead? Aerodynamics disagree." I flapped my arms around to illustrate my point.

Izzy tried not to look too disappointed. "Okay," she said, sliding down off the countertop and shaking her clothes out, "you probably can't fly. But you really do appear to be dead," she grimaced, "so it makes sense to go talk to people who know what to do."

"Maybe," I said. "But right now, we have a cafe to run."

* * *

"Your usual, sir," I announced brightly, putting the coffee down on Sean's table. Which was more difficult than it sounds because—as usual—he'd spread paperwork all over the place. "What are you so busy writing?" The question was out before I could stop myself.

Sean looked up at me, clearly startled. "What?" he said, scrabbling around to make room for the cup before looking back at me. "Oh, me?" He was genuinely flustered. I noticed for the first time that he had crinkles around his eyes that implied he smiled a lot. I'd never seen more than a faint twitch of his lips, usually when Izzy and I were bickering behind the counter. To be honest, Sean had rapidly become so much a part of the Flora's furniture that I kind of took him for granted. But now I was looking at him more clearly, he was definitely worth my interest. I realised I was staring and looked away with an embarrassed cough, just as he spoke. "I'm a writer," he said. "Crime stories—the sort of thing you see for sale at airport bookstores. Good for a bit of beach reading, so I'm told."

"Should I have heard of you?" I asked.

He looked sheepish. "Maybe," he said. "I guess I've never had reason to tell you my full name." He suddenly thrust out a hand and I took it without thinking. I remembered to rein in my strength and managed not to break his fingers. His palm was warm and his grip firm. "Been practicing squishing tins of beans with your bare hands?" he laughed, then gave me a little formal nod. "Sean Hannerty at your service, ma'am." The name rang a faint bell.

"Lilith O'Reilly," I replied, grinning back at him. Then we both realised that we were still holding hands and awkwardly dropped each other's grasp at the same time. "Well, I'd better be getting back to it," I said. "I don't want to keep you from your work." Sean was still smiling as I made my flustered way back behind the counter. Izzy was emptying the dishwasher, but by the arch of her sharply raised eyebrow, I assumed she'd seen the entire thing.

"Ever heard of Sean Hannerty?" I hissed. I took longer than necessary to put two cups into the machine, in order to give myself time to collect my thoughts.

70

"The crime writer?" Izzy asked. "Yeah, my dad's got all his books. Why?"

"Because that's him." I tipped my head towards where Sean sat, now tapping busily into his laptop. Izzy dropped the glass she was holding into the sink with a loud clatter. "Shit! Aah phew, it's not broken. See?" She held the glass up to me, with her back to the room. "*That's* Sean Hannerty? Our Sean?" I nodded. "Bloody hell," she declared, finally putting the glass into the machine and shutting the door firmly, before switching it on with a cascading bleep of buttons and an ominous grinding noise from the machine's depths. "He must be worth a fortune," she mused. "Why's he working from a place like this?"

I scowled at her. "Charming," I said. "It's not that bad in here!"

"You know what I mean," said Izzy. "We're a tiny little backstreet cafe with no view of anything except the occasional rough sleeper snoring under their blankets. Why choose Flora's?"

"I don't know," I replied irritably. "Maybe he likes the rougher side of life." Izzy gave me her patented 'oh give over, you overdramatic idiot' look and turned away to serve customers.

I spent the rest of the morning wondering just what I'd done to deserve to be surrounded by so many idiots. Izzy kept flapping around and getting in my way and it felt like every second customer wanted something we didn't sell. Was lactose-free cheesecake even a *thing*? As I refilled the bean-hopper on the coffee machine towards lunchtime, the errant dishwasher made a clunky noise and halted mid-cycle. Water immediately started seeping ominously out through the door seals. Clearly, even the fucking equipment was determined to wind me up. I kicked the door of the dishwasher and it bowed inwards, forcing hot water out across the floor as I cursed loudly. "Bloody hell, Lil," hissed Izzy, coming behind the counter and reaching for the mop propped against the back wall, "what happened to pretending everything was normal?"

I glared at her. "Existing in a world filled with stupidity will do that to you," I growled, ignoring a young couple who had been standing at the counter looking at the pastries, but who were now gawping openly at me.

"I think perhaps madam needs an early night," said Izzy mildly. She picked up the mop and began to clear up the sudsy water that was lapping at her dainty feet. I opened my mouth to ask what the fuck my nonexistent sleep schedule had to do with anything, but was interrupted before I could let rip.

"Here, let me help," said a voice behind me. Before I had a chance to refuse, Sean had pushed past and, kneeling on the sodden floor, reached around to the back of the dishwasher. He stretched and grunted a bit, then the water stopped and he slid back out and up onto his feet.

"You're wet," I pointed out. Izzy gave me a look that she'd been using on me since we were at primary school—the one that implied she'd *like* to think I wasn't actually as stupid as I sometimes sounded, but that current evidence was suggesting otherwise.

"Ignore Lili," she said to Sean, "she's having a bad day. What she *meant* to say was thank you. Wasn't it, Lil?" But I was distracted, staring out of the window to where a dark-haired man stood looking straight at me through the glass. It was the same man who'd helped me dispose of a corpse and then sent over the bottle of expensive wine in the Pilgrim. I caught his gaze and he grinned in return, before turning and setting off in the direction of Temple Court. "Lilith?" I shook myself and turned to see Izzy staring at me, with Sean behind her. They were both looking at me as though they were concerned I might have lost my mind. It was feeling like a distinct possibility. I took a deep breath and tasted cinnamon, tweed, darkness and…strawberry shampoo? I leaned forward and sniffed Sean's hair, ignoring both his baffled expression and Izzy's look of outright horror.

"Have you washed your hair today?" I asked.

Sean frowned, and Izzy gave me a warning look. "Yes, but I don't think—"

"Strawberry shampoo?" It was suddenly really important that I knew I wasn't imagining it. Things were weird enough already.

"The bottle just says 'fruity', I think?" Sean tilted his head and looked at me through squinted eyes. "Does it really smell that strong?" He rubbed at his head then sniffed his hand, before turning to Izzy. "Can you smell it?"

"I can't smell anything other than insanity and waiting customers," said Izzy, pushing past both of us. "I'm going to serve these people and then I'll bring you something over, Sean." She looked at me again. "Our treat. Isn't it, Lili?"

"Err, yes. I guess so," I agreed, distracted by the sudden realisation that I could smell *everything* in the room. Sean's choice of shampoo wasn't even the start of it. By my reckoning, Izzy had used a masculine-scented deodorant that morning, the man in the armchair by the side door had a dusting of baby talc under his clothes and the young couple—who by some miracle were still standing at the counter—had *definitely* had early morning sex before heading out for a post-coital coffee. I wrinkled my nose in distaste. I had no issues whatsoever with other people's healthy sex lives, but I didn't need it making itself known via my nostrils before I'd even had lunch. Not that I was ever going to eat lunch again. "I'm going out for a walk," I announced.

Izzy turned to look at me. "What the fuck?" she said. "We're just about to get busy. You can't leave now!"

But I was already picking up my bag from under the counter and heading towards the door. "Sean, can you help Izzy? You know where everything is." Sean looked like a bunny in very fast oncoming headlights, but I didn't give either of them a chance to argue further. "I just need some air. Won't be long. Help yourselves to cake!" I headed off to hunt down the stranger in the long coat.

Tempting Fate

I turned onto Whitechapel and paced down the centre of the road in order to avoid the wandering tourists and endless shoppers chatting in doorways. A group of screeching women came towards me, six abreast across the street. They all wore garish pink sashes with 'BRIDESMAID' written across them in a silver font. The only exception was the woman in the middle, whose fully glittered sash declared her to be 'BRIDEZILLA'. In deference to the earliness of the day, they were all dressed in jeans and trainers, but had no doubt booked a suite in the Premier Inn down on the waterfront in order to change into tiny dresses and tottering heels later in the day. They would then spend all night drinking Prosecco and staggering between the bars around Rope Walks, before the inevitable finale in which one of them was sick in the gutter whilst the others had a fight. Or cried in small huddles about things that seemed important at the time, but would be forgotten before they made it down to their all-you-can-eat buffet breakfasts the next morning. I kept walking and didn't bother to move out of their way. They didn't notice me until I almost ploughed into them; scattering them across the street like giant pieces of confetti. One of them yelled that I was a fucking bitch, but I didn't stop to argue. I took a sharp left onto Church Street, and the smell of perfume wafting out of Boots made my eyeballs hurt. I was distracted by the overwhelming aroma of coffee that was flooding out of the Costa tucked into the front window of Next. Since when had everything smelled so *strong*? I'd never read any paranormal stories that mentioned the undead needing antihistamines. I was pounding up the street like one of those weird-looking speed runners at athletic events. Just as I had that thought, I realised that a family standing together just inside the entrance to the Liverpool One shopping centre were watching me with interest, their small children nudging each other and giggling. The mother bent to tell them off, but I could see her face crinkling with laughter behind her niqab. I made a conscious effort to slow down, but even when I paced myself against a group of determined office workers just ahead of me, it felt as though I was walking at the speed of an arthritic snail. I'd lost track of the man in the coat, but kept walking to the end of the street before taking a right. My quickest route would have been straight up Bold Street, but it was always busy whatever the time of day or night and I didn't want to risk my oddness being spotted again. I turned up Wood Street instead. It was empty apart from a couple of cyclists heading towards me down the cobbles, and there was no one to notice me ducking into a boarded-up doorway. I leaned against the metal shutters and tried to focus on the sign that had been stuck to the wall on the opposite side of the street in the hope of settling my head a bit. The sign announced an application for planning permission in order to allow a lap dancing club to open until 4am at the weekend. The text was tiny, presumably in the hope no one would notice it and be inclined to oppose the licensing request. I shouldn't have been able to read it from this distance, but I could make out even the smallest lines of print at the bottom. I felt as though my heart was racing, but although I held my hand against my chest, I couldn't feel anything.

Just as I was deciding that I should probably give up and head back to Flora's to apologise to Izzy and Sean, I spotted the man again. He was standing at the very top of the street, leaning against a wall and looking straight down at me. As I stared back, frozen, he raised a hand in acknowledgement. To my surprise, he beckoned me towards him. It was one thing following someone, but quite another to go willingly like a lamb to the potential slaughter. On the other hand, I was pretty sure he knew more about my current situation than he was letting on. And if there was anything I needed right now, it was answers. I started walking up the street. The man turned and strolled away as I got closer to him. I followed at a discreet distance as he stopped to negotiate the busy road before heading up

Bold Place. I crossed the road behind him, skirted the stone steps and the clumps of office workers who always used the spot for their coffee breaks, and walked slowly around to the side gate of St Luke's Church.

* * *

St Luke's is known to pretty much everyone as the Bombed Out Church, because that's exactly what it is. Built in the early eighteen hundreds, St Luke's was a busy parish church for more than a century, before becoming one of the most famous casualties of World War II. It was struck by a German incendiary device during the blitz on Liverpool in 1941 and everything except the external stone framework was destroyed. These days it's looked after by a caretaking group that keeps it maintained and available for the community. I often saw yoga classes taking place within its roofless walls, or art exhibitions attached to the railings that surrounded the ruins. Everything about St Luke's is open to the elements and visible either from the front steps, or from the streets surrounding the church grounds. I followed my mystery man to the entrance on Bold Place. The gate was usually bolted, but the man simply opened it and stepped backwards to allow me through. "Good afternoon, Lilith." His accent was what I'd have to describe as generic northern, because I've always been shit at working out accents. Yorkshire at a guess, but mellowed via an expensive education. "You seem to be managing well, considering the negligently behaviour of some of our community." He was wearing a long, dark grey wool coat over dark jeans and the sort of creased and worn leather Chelsea boots that had probably cost a small fortune but which were on their second decade of wear in return.

"Who the fuck *are* you?" I asked, more sharply than I'd intended. He oozed confidence and quality from every pore and, despite him having done nothing but help me so far, I could feel my hackles rising instinctively. He chuckled at that—a low, rich noise that felt like warm butter and treacle as it washed over me. "And you can stop that *right* now," I glared at him. "I don't know what it is you're doing with your voice, but I can do without being hypnotised without my permission, thank you very much."

76

He looked amused and held out a hand. "Ivo Laithlind," he said. "And I am at your service, Miss O'Reilly. I think some people call you Red?" I scowled, but said nothing. He must have been talking to Billy, because no one else ever called me that. "It's about time someone rattled the Silvertons' perch," he went on, with a grin. "You might be just the ticket." I took his hand and shook it, surprised to feel callouses and hard skin rather than the never-worked-a-day-in-his-life softness I'd expected. "And I am," he continued, "a friend of the family. Even if they don't bother to keep in touch." He shrugged in a 'families huh, whatcha gonna do?' kind of way. "I hope you enjoyed the wine?"

"That was very kind," I admitted. "Thank you. I suspect it was utterly wasted on Izzy and I, but we enjoyed it." *Before we spent the rest of the evening disposing of a corpse*, I thought to myself. Was that really only the previous night? "Anyway," I said, stepping away from him slightly, "why are you stalking me?"

Ivo gestured towards a wooden bench at the back of the churchyard. "Let's sit down and attempt to look normal," he said. "We owe you some explanations."

"So, you're telling me that there are others like me all over the country?" Ivo had been trying to explain things for a good half hour now, but all he'd managed was to confuse me even further. I turned to look at him and saw that he was gazing off into the distance, as if we really were just two friends having a quick catchup in the afternoon sun.

He smiled faintly. "And in other countries," he said. "We don't have the monopoly on this sort of thing, however much those in charge would like to think we do."

I digested this for a minute or two. Ivo sat silent and unmoving, as if he had all the time in the world. Which he probably did. "What do you mean," I said finally, "by 'those in charge'?" I'd been thinking that at least now I'd be the boss of my own destiny, but now I was supposed to accept that there were still other people in power? Fucking marvellous.

Ivo turned and looked me in the eye. "Red," he said, "there has *always* been a fight for power, from the dawn of humanity. People living in caves would hit each other over the head with rocks purely to have control over the next valley along. They often didn't even need the land, but the important thing was to control it. Nothing much has changed."

"How long have you been here?" I asked, not sure I wanted to hear the answer.

"Oh, a very long time," said Ivo, smiling again. "Longer than most. But that in itself doesn't give me power. It's still a case of establishing and maintaining allegiances. And knowing when to make myself scarce for a while, too, of course. Politics is an immortal beast in its own right."

"Great," I snorted. "I'm dead, but I *still* have to decide who to vote for? Do the undead candidates come canvassing door to door?"

Ivo laughed. "You wouldn't want some of them appearing on your doorstep," he replied. "I can promise you that. But," he eyed me carefully, "I think plenty would vote for you, Lilith O'Reilly."

I stared at him, appalled. "I've been dead less than four days, and so far it's been the same as being alive, just with added complications," I said. "I'm having nothing to do with undead politics."

"We'll see about that," he said. "You might not have any choice in the matter." I didn't like the sound of that. "Word gets around," he said by way of explanation. "Have you spoken to the Silvertons yet?"

"I tried," I said truthfully, "and they were bloody rude. The woman seems okay, though."

"Maria?" he asked. I nodded. Ivo snorted slightly. "She's a strange one, is Maria," he said. "If she's being nice to you, then it's because she thinks you'll be useful. The city's been waiting for someone like you, Red. Maria knows that. She'll want you on her side."

"I'm not planning on being useful to anyone except myself, thank you very much," I retorted.

"Then you need to be careful around the Silvertons," Ivo said, quietly. "They're in the habit of keeping things they think might come in handy, whether or not those things actually want to be kept. And you'd certainly come in handy. For one thing," he went on, "the rats didn't manage to kill you. And rest assured," he said in a tone that was far from reassuring, "they'd have liked to have killed you."

"Rats?"

"The...*things* that were in your building the other night. The ones who knocked you off the fire escape.."

I frowned. "But that was a man," I said. "A human man."

Ivo looked sceptical. "They might have been," he said, "once upon a time. But we're long past the era of fairytales now, Red. They've got a taste for human souls and you'd have been a grand prize."

I shuddered. Something occurred to me. "Human souls?" I asked. "Is that what I was tasting when that...that *idiot* attacked me the other night?"

Ivo nodded. "That's why I needed to speak to you," he said. "To warn you." He looked directly at me, a serious expression on his face. "That can't happen again, Red. The soul-sucking I mean. You won't get attacked again, not when...our sort realise who you are. *What* you are. But you can't take an entire human soul, not ever again. It's cruel and addictive and few get out once they're sucked in."

I stared at him. "Are you telling me that the creep down at the Pier Head was, in effect, walking, talking Class A undead drugs?"

Ivo gave me a wry smile. "That's not a bad analogy," he said, turning his face to the sun and closing his eyes in the warmth. "It doesn't really matter what sort of person they were in life—they all have a life force that can be taken from them. You felt the power surging, didn't you?" He turned and looked straight at me.

I struggled not to shuffle away along the bench. "Yes," I said honestly, "I did. And it was the most amazing thing I'd ever felt in my life." I looked Ivo straight in the eyes. "It felt grubby and unearthly and as if I could rule the entire world."

He gave a humourless chuckle. "That's why you can't ever do it again," he said, "because you'll think you can handle it until the time comes when you can't. And by then, you're no better than the rats."

I didn't ask him to specify whether they were rodent or human rats—I suspected it didn't really matter. "How do I feed, then?"

Ivo laughed—properly this time. "You don't need to," he said with a grin.

I boggled my eyes at him. "What do you mean?" I demanded. "All unearthly creatures of the undead realms need to feed on *something*. It's basically the law!"

"What, because books and films have told you so?" Ivo asked, not unkindly. "Red, humans have always struggled to understand things outside of their direct experiences. And when they don't understand, they fill in the gaps to suit themselves." He sighed. "It doesn't seem to have occurred to them that once you're dead, there really isn't any need for sustenance."

"So what keeps me going?" I asked. "Do I have a limited shelf life? Will I just shrivel up into dust when my reserves run out?"

"Do I look shrivelled to you?" asked Ivo. I didn't bother answering that. "Yet I'm more than a thousand years old." I gaped at him and he smiled calmly back, a tinge of sadness visible in his eyes. "It's a very long time, by any standards," he said, "yet here I am."

"What year were you born?"

Ivo laughed. "Dates weren't marked as well back then," he said, "but it was some time in the ninth century. I know," he saw my expression, "I'm probably the oldest man you've ever spoken to."

"You can say that again. And I've been out in Shrewsbury on a Friday night."

Ivo grinned. "I came to England from the north countries," he said. "And I did well enough for myself that, when I died, I was gifted the biggest tomb anyone had seen for generations. It was laid alongside the Trent, in the middle counties. I had dozens of my men for company in the afterlife."

"I hope the men were dead when they were buried with you," I said.

"They were by the time the tomb was closed in."

I changed the subject quickly. "What have you been doing for all this time?"

Ivo sighed. "I was peaceful," he said, "for a while. I have no memories of this new life until I was saved from desecration, almost two centuries after my death."

"Desecration?"

Ivo nodded. "William the Bastard invaded England and decided I was too much of a threat, even dead in my tomb." A short laugh. "And I was, too. People resented the incomers, but they remembered me—maybe not fondly, but with more affection than they felt for the new rulers. The Bastard found my tomb and gave orders to destroy it. My first new memories were ones of shouting and sudden blazing sunlight and the laughter of those trampling on the corpses of my loyal men. Instinct is a powerful impulse, Red. I was up and fighting them off before I even knew what had happened. Luckily for me," Ivo's expression suggested he wasn't actually convinced of his luck, "one of the Bastard's personal guard realised who I was and helped me escape. And," he continued with a shrug, "I've been here ever since."

"Here?" I asked. "You've been in Liverpool for a thousand years?"

Ivo laughed. "Heavens, Miss O'Reilly," he replied, "you really do need to brush up on your history lessons." I vowed to never mention my history degree. In my defence, my studies had mostly focused on the Victorian era. "Liverpool didn't really exist until the thirteenth century. Even then, it was just a small village. It only exists as it does now because Chester silted up, and industry had to move to the next available port. Chester had always had…issues," he smiled thinly, "so I didn't miss it. I went north to Jorvik and have been based there ever since."

"Why are you here now, then?"

Ivo looked surprised. "Do you never visit your relatives?" I shrugged noncommittally. "The Silvertons," he continued, "are friends of mine. I try to catch up with them now and then. Eadric doesn't like to travel if he can help it, so here I am."

A tiny bell rang in the back of my mind. "Is that the E. Silverton who runs the company?" I'd seen it on the header of the letter from the company's office. Urgh, I'd forgotten about the eviction. Even being dead didn't seem to stop life from being stressful. Yet another problem that the fantasy books had failed to warn me about.

Ivo grinned. "Officially he does," he said with a delicate snort, "but Maria like to think she's the power behind that throne. There's Nik, as well. Nikolaos Silverton. He's not related, and that isn't his original name. Eadric took him in a long time ago, when he needed somewhere to hide out. He's been with them ever since. You'll like Nik, I think."

"Why did the burglar want me in particular?" Ivo looked confused at the sudden change of topic. "The man who broke into my apartment," I clarified. "You said I'd have been a prize for him." I tried not to feel sick and mostly failed. "Why?" To my utter astonishment, Ivo patted my knee and left his hand there. We both stared at it for a long moment, before he thought better of it and folded his hands back in his lap. "And," I said, remembering the start of the conversation, "how do I survive, if I can't eat?"

"Firstly," said Ivo, "you really don't need to feed. The energy-sucking thing is delightful but utterly addictive and if you allow yourself to keep doing it, you'll be down with the rats before you know it." I shuddered. "You can drink, as you know. And it helps to do so, because even the undead can't avoid the basic science of evaporation. No one wants dried up eyeballs." I pulled a face. "But that's it. Think about it, Red!" Ivo grinned widely, animated now. "You're dead—really, truly dead—but your body just hasn't got the memo. Everything is in stasis, stuck as it was at the moment you died. You can't tire, so you have more energy and power than any living human can ever achieve. Your human body is no longer frail and damageable. And it has no limits on what it can do, because you don't have to worry about injury. You could climb the radio tower, if you chose to," he nodded over to where the Radio City tower was just visible above the rooftops. "Or run up the side of the Chinatown gateway and sit sunbathing on the top. I wouldn't recommend doing either, though," he continued. "People might ask questions."

"You don't say,"

Ivo grinned. "But there's something else," he continued, "and I don't quite know what it is. You've got...*power*, Red. More power than I've seen in a new revenant in all the centuries I've been on this godforsaken earth. It's interesting."

"What sort of power?" Maybe the payoff for an eternity without cake would be the ability to leap tall buildings in a single bound.

"A kind of...calmness," Ivo replied.

Oh well. A girl can dream. "I'm not sure that calmness is listed on the entry requirements for superhero school, in all honesty," I said. "Do I have dominion over all living creatures, at least?"

Ivo laughed. "Who would want that?" he asked. "Would you really want everything and everyone bowing and scraping at you because of who you are? Would you not prefer them to *choose* to be your friends?." He gave me a sideways glance. "It's as if…" he looked thoughtful, as if he was choosing his words carefully, "…as if, well… You're just carrying on as if nothing had happened. That's the strange thing. It's as if death comes naturally to you."

"Well, death comes naturally to everyone," I pointed out. "Although some more naturally than others, I guess. Anyway," I asked, "what am I supposed to do? Start running round the city centre scaring students and starting urban legends?" Ivo laughed. He had a nice laugh—deep and throaty and genuine. I turned to look at him. He was leaning back on the bench with his face turned to the sky, as if warming himself.

"Are we lizards?" I blurted out.

Ivo opened his eyes and turned to look at me, an expression of complete bemusement on his face. "Lizards?"

"Not actual lizard people," I ploughed on before embarrassment could stop me. "Not like the monarchy." Ivo stifled a snort. "Cold blooded, I mean." I took his hand, and he looked startled. "I feel normal to you, right?" He nodded. "And you feel normal to me. Normal temperature, I mean." I realised I was still holding his hand and dropped it abruptly. "If I touched someone who was still alive, would I feel cold to them?"

Ivo smiled. "Like in the vampire movies, you mean?"

"No! Well," I thought about it, "yes. Like the movies. Would I scare a human by touching them with my cold, dead hands?"

"Did the pharmacist look scared when he was checking your blood pressure?" Ivo asked.

"No," I said, "but to be honest, I think he was distracted by my lack of blood pressure."

"You still have blood pressure," Ivo squinted at me, "it's just incredibly slow. After the change, everything in the body slows down until it's almost imperceptible." He shifted on the bench. "Probably best not to get medical checks very often, though. You don't want people asking awkward questions."

"What kind of awkward questions?"

"Oh, you know," he grinned, "why aren't you breathing, why don't you have a pulse, how come your sleep pattern is practically nonexistent." He tilted his head at me. "That sort of thing."

"I *can* breathe though," I pointed out. "It makes me choke, I'll give you that. But I can still inhale and sigh," I gave a huge sigh to prove my point and Ivo was kind enough not to laugh when it ended in a coughing fit, "so no one's going to notice."

"They'll notice when you suck their life force and they're wondering why they need a good lie down every time they see you," Ivo said, and there was a serious tone to his voice. "If they even remember who you are. If you take it too far, you risk wiping their memory entirely. Or killing them. Get out of the habit of breathing, Red," he continued. "And you *absolutely* have to promise me you'll never suck another human's entire life from them again. Ever."

I frowned. "That man absolutely deserved it," I said, "and you know it."

Ivo nodded, but didn't lose the stern expression. "He did," he replied, "but you saw for yourself what happened when it didn't entirely work."

"Were you there?" I asked. "Were you watching me and Izzy that night at the Pier Head?"

Ivo nodded. "From a distance," he replied. "I was walking along the Strand—genuinely, I'd been to visit the Silvertons and stayed late, I wasn't stalking you—and recognised you and your friend sitting by the water. I did watch from a distance for a while, because I didn't know you were friends then. It wasn't exactly clear what you might be doing with a human." He ignored my indignant glare. "And then, of course, the waterlogged Nosferatu appeared out of the Canning Dock. But," he continued, "you seemed to be dealing with him well enough between the pair of you, so I left you to it and went home."

"Where's home?" I didn't want to think about Ivo watching me pretending to be drunk, or Izzy stabbing a dead man in the belly.

"I take a suite at the Hope Street Hotel when I'm in town," he replied. "They keep rooms for me on the rooftop, so I'm away from everything."

"Why?"

Ivo looked confused. "Why shouldn't I have some peace and quiet?"

"No," I said, "why do you need to be away from everything?" I looked at him. "You said it as if you needed to be kept away from people, not that you chose to."

He raised an eyebrow. "Sharp thinking," he said, in an approving tone, "I like it. Well," he grinned, "you've tasted the power of one filthy and thoroughly unpleasant human, so you know how powerful it is. Right?" I nodded reluctant agreement. "So," he continued, "just imagine how much more seductive it is when it's one of the many delightful young humans who wander this city. The sort who appreciate a friendly guide helping them out."

I narrowed my eyes at him. "Are you telling me you take advantage of drunken women?"

Ivo looked affronted. "No!" he said indignantly, "I absolutely do not. The very thought! And who said it specifically had to be women? I am simply trying," he continued, "to show that I understand why it's so tempting. It is also," he looked me directly in the eye, "utterly addictive. Heroin addicts have nothing on revenants who haven't learned to stay away from human souls. It hooks you in. And you'll struggle to ever get out."

"How do *you* manage it?" I asked. "How do you not accidentally damage your delightful young humans?"

A laugh. "I've explained to you how very, *very* old I am, Red," he replied. "When you've been around as long as I have, you develop mental strengths that are beyond the younger members of our community. Some get side-tracked by temptation and, of those who do, few get back out. Anyway," he said firmly, "there's no need for it. Your body becomes what the Victorians used to call a 'closed system,'" he did the quote marks in the air with his fingers. "It doesn't require sustenance and doesn't need to excrete anything. Although back then, they generally applied it just to sex in order to put people off." He sniffed. " It was a weird era," he said, "the nineteenth century.

85

Society pinned down by invisible rules like so many butterflies held by collectors' pins. Yet they were all living life to the full underneath the surface. Sometimes you have to go looking for life, Red."

"What was your favourite era?" I asked. I was genuinely curious—it isn't often you get to ask questions of someone who's been around for a millennium. Ivo laughed, but decided to humour me. He leaned backwards with his arms folded and, gazing up at the sky, appeared to give my question some serious thought. "Well," he began slowly, "sometimes the periods of upheaval and danger are the most exciting," he glanced sideways at me, "even as they're equally awful for most. You have to remember," he continued, "that I started my human life as a warrior. It was in my nature to go looking for the excitement. And of course," another fleeting smile, "it became easier when I had less chance of being killed. Permanently, I mean."

I remembered what Kitty had said to me when we talked about revenants in my living room. "Is it true that we can't die of anything other than beheading? I've got a ghost living in my flat," I said by way of explanation, "and she knows a bit about it."

Ivo nodded. "I sometimes forget the other dimensions are all still here," he replied slowly. "Yes, your ghost is right. The only way to definitively kill a revenant is to cut off their head. Even then," he continued with a smile, "it's best to burn them. Or at least keep the two pieces very separate. With some creatures I've met over the centuries, I wouldn't have been entirely surprised to see their bodies go searching for the missing head and put it back on, as in some of these newfangled movies you all seem to like watching." I suspected Ivo wasn't actually as old-fashioned as he sounded. He was even, quite possibly, taking the piss.

"Alright, grandad," I retorted, "we know you're from the age of the dinosaurs. No doubt you counted Nero as a good friend."

"Nero was long dead by the time I was walking the earth," Ivo pointed out mildly, "and as far as I know, he's stayed dead. I know Constantine, though. He's one of us, although he keeps to himself most of the time. Nice enough chap."

"Constantine?" I gaped at him. "As in the emperor?"

"Yup," he grinned. "Founded the Byzantine Empire, and all that stuff. Quite the busy boy. You should know this, though," he continued, "being a history scholar."

I frowned. "It wasn't my era," I said. "I mostly stick to the Victorians and Edwardians. Anyway," a thought had struck me, "how do you know what I studied?"

"I've been stalking you," said Ivo blithely, but I didn't miss the glance he gave me to gauge my reaction. "Only online, of course. You don't use much social media, compared to most people your age. It has been," he continued, "a rather fruitless task."

"If I want to see people, I generally just go see them," I replied. "And you haven't answered my question. Why have you been stalking me?"

"Your arrival into our world has been…unexpected," he replied slowly. "There haven't been any new revenants for a long time. I was trying to find out if there was any particular reason why you should be the first in over a century."

I digested this for a long moment. "I'm the first in more than a hundred years?"

Ivo nodded. "In this country, at least. Actually," he said, "it's nearer one hundred and fifty years. Maria's the most recent, before you turned up. And one of the strongest, both in will and in physical power."

"Maria?" I asked. "Maria Silverton?"

Ivo nodded. "She was reborn into our world in the late eighteen-hundreds," he said. "Nik was a few decades before her. And Eadric and I, well," he gave a short, humourless laugh, "we've been around since the dawn of time. Or so it seems." He gave himself a visible shake, then turned to me with a friendly smile. It didn't quite reach his eyes. "We go back a long way," he said, "and there'll always be a bond. No matter who or what tries to come between us." His expression hardened slightly. "Of course, there are more. They're everywhere, and some are more visible than others. Some we live alongside with and others, well," he paused, "let's just say that immortality can get quite complicated."

"I bet," I replied drily. "All those relatives to visit and no end to the birthdays. What on earth do you do at Christmas?"

"We get together and pull crackers and drink mulled wine, like normal people," said Ivo. He saw my expression. "What?" he grinned. "I'm not kidding! Honestly, we visit each other and watch movies and argue about who really won the Battle of Malplaquet. Eadric often wins the debates because he has a sharper memory, but I've been around longer and seen more things. It's fairly even."

I tried not to look as shocked as I felt. "Why would it have been dangerous for the...*rats* to capture me?" I asked, remembering Ivo's earlier comments.

His mouth twisted. "They'd want your power for themselves," he said, "no matter how forcibly they needed to persuade you." I shuddered. "Although you might have been able to get away from them, even so," he remarked. "Your running's improved recently." He gave me a sideways look, amusement on his face.

I blushed. "You watched that, as well?" Fucking hell, couldn't a girl have *any* peace around this godforsaken undead city?

"Not much of it," he said. "I just caught the tail end. Before you were ambushed by the Pier Head zombie. But," he continued, before I could say anything, "it was still rather impressive. And your strengths will develop for a while, yet."

"Do I get to fly?"

He genuinely snorted then. "No," he said, "you don't get to fly. We leave that to the witches. Sorry about that."

I wasn't sure if he was taking the piss again, so erred on the safe side. "Well," I asked, "what *can* I do?"

Ivo sat up, an animated expression on his face. "You can run, obviously," I nodded, "and you can climb, as I said. Perhaps not brilliantly right now, but that's something that most of us can do and your abilities will develop. I once climbed to the top of the cathedral," he nodded his head in the vague direction of the Metropolitan, "without anyone noticing. There are some grand views from the top of that central tower, I can tell you that for nothing." I raised an eyebrow. "Well," he said, slightly sheepish now, "everyone needs a challenge occasionally. Oh, and," he remembered something else, "you can swim. Underwater, I mean. For an awful lot longer than a human ever could. Remember," he said in answer to my confused look, "you don't need to breathe."

"Do you breathe, Ivo?" The question was out of my mouth before I could stop myself.

Ivo looked taken aback for a second, but then his quietly confident demeanour reasserted itself. "Sometimes," he said, flatly. "Imagine, Lilith," his voice had an urgent tone to it, "imagine living—existing—for *centuries*, without so many of the physical joys that humans can indulge themselves with. No delightful meals to entice your palate, no getting drunk with friends and waking up next to someone inappropriate, but curling up into them anyway and seeing where the morning takes you. In fact," he continued, eyeing me carefully as he did so, "no having sex with humans at all, until you're confident you won't accidentally suck the life out of them. And even then," a dramatically raised eyebrow, "huge care is needed." It took me a minute to register what he'd just said and when I did, my face must have been one of stricken horror, because Ivo looked concerned. He rested a reassuring hand on my arm.

"I can't have sex again? That's not fair," I wailed, "I haven't had sex for ages, as it is! I was kind of hoping that immortality was going to make me irresistible to the opposite sex. Well," I corrected myself, "*any* sex, if I'm honest. I just want to be desirable again. Is that too much to ask? What happened to being dead but delicious?" Ivo looked blank. "Never mind," I said, "even by my standards, that's a niche joke. Look," my tone was getting higher by the minute, "I know I'm hardly the female Casanova of the north west," Ivo suppressed a snort, "but I can't go without sex *forever!*" I ended my sentence just as a pair of older women walked along Roscoe Street behind us. The pathway was only a few feet from where we sat and by the muffled squeak that came from the shorter of the two women, they'd clearly overheard me.

"Red," Ivo said, "calm down. I want to show you something."

"Well, that's a new one," I retorted, "not. And I'm not falling for it, so you can think again, you grubby old man."

Ivo rolled his eyes. "For heaven's sake, you ridiculous creature," he said, "all I want you to do is hold my hands."

"Why?"

"I promise you won't regret it," he said. "And we won't be moving from this bench and everyone will keep their clothes on. Satisfied?"

"What do I have to do?" I grumbled.

"I've already told you," said Ivo, "just hold my hands." He turned slightly towards me on the bench and indicated that I should do the same in return. He held both his hands out, and I took them. "Look at me," he instructed.

I did as I was asked and immediately burst into laughter. "I'm sorry," I said, "this is all a bit weirdly intimate."

"Look at me, Lilith," said Ivo again, and this time I did. For a moment, there was nothing except the feeling of his soft skin against mine. "Breathe," he whispered, and as I did so, Ivo breathed out. He nodded at me. "And out," he said. Nodding encouragement, he slowly inhaled and exhaled, whilst I did the opposite. We were creating a circular breath, I realised—out of one and into the other, over and over. A warmth was growing in the very core of me—a feeling of excitement and hunger and desire, the likes of which I'd never felt before in my life. I held his gaze like a mouse in the face of a predatory snake. But there was no fear—just a clawing, urgent need to leap onto Ivo Laithlind and ride him like a bony pony. The realisation was itself enough to shock me into pulling away and I sat staring at him for a moment, utterly dumbstruck. My brain got the memo before the rest of my body did, and I had to force myself not to wriggle on the spot as I wondered just how exciting Ivo might be in bed. Actually, I was pretty sure we wouldn't get as far as bed. He'd be far more likely to just drag me into the nearest alleyway and pin me hard up against the wall, before—"Anyway," Ivo said blithely, breaking into my increasingly filthy thoughts, "I'm sure you'll have sex again. At some point."

"What the holy *fuck* was that?" I demanded. I edged away from him slightly, just in case my subconscious had me leaping onto his face before I realised what I was doing.

"It was a brief window into the levels of sensuality one can achieve whilst still fully dressed," he said. "And it comes from years of practice."

"So," I said, purely to break the tension, "rats. Why is it good that I'm the walking dead, rather than the…*rat* finishing me off when he broke in the other night?"

"If they'd absorbed your abilities, then they'd have been a force to be reckoned with, even by those such as Eadric and Maria."

"Abilities?" I was thinking again that maybe I was actually unconscious in hospital and all this was just my damaged brain pulling stories together out of all the terrible paranormal romances I'd read over the years. Any minute now, I'd wake up in a hospital bed with my parents sitting by my side and a nurse making them a cup of tea.

"You're not imagining any of this," Ivo said, ruining my daydream. "It's real. And you're real. Real and dead and right in the middle of a crisis, the like of which Liverpool hasn't seen for a very long time."

"Is it worse than that time they finished below Everton in the league tables?" Ivo looked blank. "My dad's a massive football fan," I explained. "I've picked it up by osmosis. G'wan the Reds and all that."

He grinned. "You've got more important sides to pick right now, Red." His light tone belied the serious expression on his face. "The Silvertons are going to want you with them, and right now there isn't much to stop them. And maybe it isn't a bad idea for you to swear allegiance and get yourself some protection." He put up a hand as a opened my mouth to speak. "Listen to me, Lilith O'Reilly," his voice had dropped to barely more than a whisper. "You have more power than you could ever imagine—you just need to find it and accept it. But be careful of those who'd like to control that power. For what it's worth," he went on, "I will support you in whatever decisions you make." He grinned. "It's about time someone woke things up around here."

The Renshaw Street Knitting Club

After saying goodbye to Ivo, I walked round to the front of the church and stood looking down Bold Street, whilst I gathered my thoughts. I was fighting a sudden urge to go absolutely batshit and just start throwing things or screaming at the top of my voice. Maybe if I had a fully public breakdown, someone else would take over and sort my life out. My *after* life. I was pretty sure that if I tried explaining the events of the last twenty four hours to a psychiatrist they'd take me in for assessment pretty quickly, so that was an option. *Yeah, if you want to end up with your brain sliced up like salami and stored in a medical research facility*, muttered my subconscious. I idly kicked a metal railing to the side of me and it bent the bars out of shape. Leaning down, I grabbed the metal and pulled it straight with a creak. Walking down the steps in front of the church—carefully, in case I accidentally knocked several hundredweight of old stone onto an unwary tourist—I decided to walk home down Renshaw Street. There would be less human contact than on Bold Street—mostly because Bold Street's been pedestrianised, whilst Renshaw is still a busy traffic route—but I could still practice the whole 'not breathing' thing whilst dodging students bouncing out of the shops and cafes. I'd only got about a hundred yards down the road when I heard someone calling my name. Looking across the street, I saw a tall Black man leaning against the doorframe of Mapp's bookshop and vaguely recognised him as the owner. He waved and then beckoned me over. On the principle that things couldn't get much weirder—a principle that I generally lived to regret—I waited for a gap in the traffic and ran across the street. I was getting better at physically controlling myself now and managed to only frighten one driver, a middle-aged man in a five-year-old Land Cruiser, who was driving one-handed and spilled coffee down his crisp white shirt when I bounced lightly off his bonnet in order to avoid being turned into an undead pinball.

The shopkeeper was dressed in a long black skirt, heavy boots, and an incongruously fitted pinstripe shirt that hung heavy with straps and buckles. He had kohl-rimmed hazel eyes, and I was utterly unsurprised to see a silver edge to the irises. "Well," he said, in a drawling voice, his accent anywhere north of Watford, "if it isn't our lord and saviour, miss Lilith O'Reilly." He gave a mock bow and gestured at me to enter. "I won't bite," he said with a grin, "unless you ask nicely." I scowled and stalked past him into the shop. I'd been into Mapp's several times in the past, so was reasonably sure it was safe. Unless, of course, the books themselves had somehow become sentient since the last time I visited and were now being watched over by a librarian with arms longer than his legs and a bit too much ginger hair. It wouldn't be the strangest thing that had happened to me in the past week. The woman who usually worked the till was absent, but there were three people at the back of the room, all sitting on mismatched chairs and surrounded by stacks of toppling books. As my eyes adjusted to the gloom, I realised they were all knitting. "Ever tried the yarn arts?" asked the man from the doorway. I turned to look at him, and he grinned in return. When I didn't reply, he rolled his eyes and sighed. "Okay," he said, "I give in." He walked towards me and held out his hand. I stared dumbly at it for a moment, then shook. He had soft, dry skin and a startlingly firm grip. "Gaultier Mapp," he said. "And as previously declared, I am, indeed, your servant."

"Cut it out, Mapp," said a sharp female voice from the back of the shop.

The shopkeeper straightened up and sighed. "Why do you always ruin my fun, Missy?"

"Because you're always being a pillock," said the voice. "That's why." It belonged to an angular Mediterranean woman of around my height. She had deep brown eyes and dark, reddish-brown hair that cascaded in thick waves down her back and over her shoulders, as if it had a life of its own. She turned to look at me. "You're Lilith."

"I know," I replied. I looked at the little group sitting with balls of wool in their laps and, somewhere in the far reaches of my brain, a tiny bell rang. "You're all dead, aren't you?"

Missy's eyes flashed for the briefest of seconds, before her expression settled back into that of your generic friendly stranger. "It's not safe to say that out loud," she replied.

Mapp snorted. "It's always safe in here, Missy," he said, "you know that."

She narrowed her eyes at him. "We don't know this—" she gestured at me "—*person*," she replied. Neither of the other members of the Undead Knitting Club had so much as acknowledged my presence. The one nearest to me appeared to be a very short man, with thinning grey hair cropped close to his head and faded blue jeans that were wider than had been fashionable for at least a decade. He wore a fisherman's jumper that I'd bet good money had actually seen the inside of a fishing boat, and his brown boots had an ominous-looking tidemark all the way around the bottom of the battered suede. I risked a small breath and was almost overwhelmed by the pungent aroma of decaying prawns and engine oil. Behind that was the scent of patchouli, overlaid with what I thought might be peaches. And beyond that, nothing. No, I realised, not entirely nothing—there was a cold, sharp smell, as if snow had fallen overnight and the sun was taking a while to warm everything up. It held notes of hyacinth and jasmine, along with a sharp thread of what I recognised as fox shit. My parents had rescued a Jack Russell terrier from the local animal adoption centre when I was in my teens and he loved nothing more than to race around the fields behind the house, looking for a nice fresh fox turd to roll in. He'd come bouncing in through the kitchen door with a proud expression on his face and a cloud of invisible stench following close behind him, almost always doomed to be ambushed by my mum, who would dump him under the shower and hose him down vigorously until he could be allowed back on the sofas. The fox shit smell was coming from the third person, who was of indeterminable height and/or gender on account of how they were curled up on the chair with their arms wrapped round their knees and their head bowed. They had black, greasy hair that hung lankly down over the nape of their neck.

Interestingly, the ball-creature had clearly done more knitting than the other two—I recognised a baggy shape hanging from their clenched fingers as being the back of an adult-sized sweater.

Missy followed my gaze. "Don't mind Heggie," she said, "he always struggles with new people. Don't you Heggie?" There was no response from the folded-up man. "Have some *manners*, you repulsive creature," growled Missy. She leaned forward and shoved the balled-up man off his perch, and he hit the floorboards with a thump. It sounded painful, but he made no move to unfurl.

"There was no need for that," I said to Missy indignantly.

She laughed in my face. "Who are you to say what I should or shouldn't do?" she asked. "Who are you to say what *anyone* should or shouldn't do?"

"*Missy*," Mapp's voice had a warning tone to it, "don't start."

"Start?" Missy said, dumping her knitting into a tote bag that was hanging off the backrest of her chair, "I will never stop, and you know it."

Mapp shook his head. "You'll have to excuse Missy, I'm afraid," he said to me. "She forgets her manners these days." Missy came to stand in front of me with her hands on her hips. She looked warily at me. There was no silver tint to Missy's irises, but I was still pretty sure that she wasn't your average human.

"Artemisia," she said eventually, thrusting her hand out at me. "Known to those I accept as Missy." I took her hand to shake it and she gripped hard, in the manner of small men with a lot to prove. I raised an eyebrow and squeezed back. "Owww!" she squeaked, pulling back as if she'd been burned. "Okay," she said slowly, "I'll accept that you're one of us. Maybe."

"But how can you be sure?" I asked her in a sarcastic tone. My patience was wearing much too thin for this bullshit.

She rolled her eyes. "Because you've got a grip that could crack walnuts and your eyes are fucking weird." We gazed at each other for a moment; a bloody-minded stalemate. She broke first. "Anyway," she said, slinging her bag over her shoulder, "it's been…nice," I doubted that, "but I have to go. I'm sure Mapp can fill you in on the gossip. He always does." With that, she stalked past us and banged out of the door. I was pretty sure she'd have liked to have slammed it behind her, but it had a soft-close mechanism and stopped halfway, before clicking shut slowly.

"So this is the gang's base," Mapp said brightly, gesturing benevolently around the room. I looked around at the endless shelves of dusty books. There was a wrought-iron spiral staircase at the back of the store that I'd never noticed before. It led up to a balcony that ran around the entire room, just wide enough for one person at a time, and then carried on up through a hatch in the ceiling. I'd noticed the double height of the shop's main room the first time I walked into it several years earlier. It was hard not to, as the roof was an ancient, stained-glass skylight that had faded to muddy shades of blue and green over the decades. Right now it was home to several roosting pigeons who squatted on the glass, their feathery bellies flattened down and misshapen claws just visible. I'd always assumed that the upper levels were accessed via ladders, but the spiral steps suggested something more permanent.

"What's at the very top?" I asked.

Mapp looked confused, but then his face cleared. "Through the hatch?" I nodded. "All of your hopes and dreams, my darling," he said dramatically. There was a low snorting noise from the short man in the jumper, who was still knitting quietly in the background. "Don't you start, Owain," he snapped. "Someone has to give Lilith here a proper welcome. It's not like anyone else is going to do it, is it now?" Mapp turned back to me. "It leads to the roof," he said. "Covered in pigeon shit, and you have to be careful your feet don't go through the tiles or you'll end up back in here via the quick route." He shrugged. "Nice views, though."

"Where did you all come from?"

Mapp looked confused. "I'm from Dingle, love," he said. "These days, anyway."

"What about before these days?" I sat down on the chair that Missy had vacated. "And what about your friends?" Mapp swung himself around the end of the little wooden railing around the cash desk, leaned over to pick up Heggie's chair, and lifted it over the prone body on the floor. Turning it away from him, he sat down with a flourish in front of me, leaning on the chair back.

"Well," he said slowly, "isn't that just the million dollar question?" He eyed me beadily. "How do I know I can trust you with our secrets, Lilith O'Reilly?"

I scowled at him. "You already clearly know far more about me than I do about you."

"Fair," he shrugged.

"Were you waiting for me?" I asked. "When I was walking down the street just now?"

Mapp looked sheepish. "That might possibly be correct," he said. "I wouldn't want to divulge my sources. But yes, I knew you were around. Had *joined* us, as it were. News travels fast in the underworld, Lilith."

"Lili," I corrected. "Friends call me Lili. Or Red," I went on, "apparently."

Mapp grinned widely. "Then we are officially friends," he declared, picking up my hand and shaking it vigorously. "And I prefer Lili, if it's all the same to you. It has a touch more class."

"Why is Heggie still lying on the floor?"

"Aah," said Mapp, prodding Heggie with the toe of his boot. "Heggie's well named, you see. When he gets nervous, he curls up in a tight little ball. He'll come back to us, eventually."

"Heggie," I said slowly, "as in hedgehog?"

Mapp grinned happily at me. "By jove," he said, "I think she's got it! She's a smart one, and no mistake. Isn't she, Owain?"

Owain grunted in response and then threw his knitting down into his lap. "Fuck that Missy," he spat suddenly.

Mapp pulled a face. "Really, Owain," he said, "there's no need. What's happened to you all today? We usually have a lovely time at our little get togethers," this to me, "don't we, Owain?"

Owen snorted. "Things ain't right," he said, "and you know it."

Mapp sighed. "You're right, of course," he agreed, "things aren't right. But Lili's here to help now, aren't you, darling?" Owain looked at me for the first time since I'd entered the shop. He had bright green eyes with the same silver ring around them as me. He was younger than I'd assumed—now I could see him properly, I'd have estimated him to be in his mid-thirties at the most. Owain would have been attractive, if he'd had a bath within living memory and was wearing clean clothes. He was painfully thin, but it belied a wiry poise that was reinforced by his beaky nose and sharp features. To my surprise, I realised Owain hadn't been knitting at all—he was, in fact, holding a small square of the most delicate lacework I had ever seen. The threads were gossamer-thin and brilliant white. Owain clearly washed his hands, even if he forgot about the rest of his body.

"That's beautiful," I blurted out, and both men stared at me. "The lace." I nodded to the fabric in Owain's lap. "How did you learn to do that?"

To my astonishment, Owain blushed right up to the roots of his thinning hair. "S'just like mending nets, innit," he grunted, but looked quietly pleased.

"Can I look?" I held out a tentative hand and, after a moment's hesitation, he dropped the delicate threads into my palm. Carefully spreading it out across my hand, I realised there was an intricate pattern to the lace, wending its way out from the centre point. I saw the tails first, then realised it was mermaids, writhing out towards the edges as if trying to escape, but the central circle of tiny stitching tethered them down. I handed it back to Owain.

"Sirens, see," he said. "They'll trap any man stupid enough to answer their calls."

"Maybe," I said slowly, "if a man is stupid enough to jump into open water after something he knows doesn't really exist, he deserves all he gets?"

Owain appeared to consider this for a moment, then grinned. "Mebbe," he said, "mebbe not. We'll see, aye."

"Look," I said to Mapp, "I really need to go home. I've got things to do, cafes to run. You know the score."

Mapp's face gave the distinct impression that, in fact, he absolutely did not know the score. But he smiled anyway and stood up. "Of course," he said politely. "It's all a bit much right now, I'm sure."

"You can say that again," I muttered. Out of the corner of my eye I spotted Heggie unravelling slightly, a beady black eye watching my every move. "Is everyone in the underworld as mad as a box of frogs," I continued, "or have

I just been really lucky so far?"

Mapp winked at me. "You're definitely lucky," he said. "But for whom, I'm not yet sure."

I was getting sick of riddles. All I wanted was to go home, apologise to Izzy and get into bed with Grimm. If I just stayed in bed for a while, maybe the weirdness would go away. I made my excuses and promised that I would absolutely visit Mapp and his friends again in the next couple of days.

* * *

I finally got back to Flora's to find Izzy locking up, ready to leave. She turned and scowled as I approached. "Well," she snarled, "thanks for leaving me in the lurch like that. What the fuck happened to your plans to carry on as normal?"

"I'm sorry," I said with a sigh, leaning against the wall. "Maybe it was too much to expect to be able to just keep going."

"Oh no you don't," said Izzy. "You're not dropping me in it just because you've been promoted to queen of the fucking underworld. I'm still boringly human, in case you haven't noticed," she bolted the shutters closed with unnecessary force and slammed the padlock shut, "and we've still got a cafe to run."

"Do you think this is *easy* for me?" I tried to shut down the note of hysteria that was determined to creep into my voice. I was scared that if I started shouting, I might never stop. Taking a deep breath for no other reason than habit, I tasted Izzy's fear and anxiety through a mist of Issey Miyake perfume and coconut hair oil. "Look," I said more quietly, "I'm sorry, okay?" Izzy's furious expression relaxed a tiny bit, but her body language still clearly implied that she might well throw the cafe keys down the nearest drain hole if the mood took her. I ploughed on. "This is fucking *weird*, Iz," I said in the understatement of the century, "and I'm still trying to get used to it. I followed that man because I knew he had some answers. And I need answers right now."

"Well, don't make a habit of leaving customers to pick up the pieces, aye?"

She frowned at me, but then grinned, despite herself. "You wouldn't have got away with it with anyone except Sean, you know. He was just so pleased to be helping you out that he barely noticed how weird you were being. Who'd have thought it," she continued, "my friend and Sean Hannerty! The crime writer and the dead girl—a match made in heaven. Or hell." Izzy snorted. "You're going to have to figure out how to behave normally if we're going to keep this up, Lil," her voice was more serious now, "because right now you're at risk of blowing it entirely. Anyway," she picked her bag up from the floor and hoisted it over her shoulder as she prepared to leave, "there's a note tucked under your doormat—someone from the Silvertons' office called in earlier and asked for you."

"What did you tell them?"

"That you were feeling under the weather and had gone out for some fresh air," she replied, "which wasn't even a lie. Anyway, he must have been half expecting it, because he had a letter ready in his jacket pocket and asked me to pass it on to you. I thought it might be important, so left it upstairs for you to find."

"He?" I'd assumed the visitor would be Maria Silverton, but clearly not.

"Yeah," said Izzy, "nice looking bloke. In his thirties, maybe? Talks like he's got a stick up his arse." The man who stopped me on my first visit, then. Nikolaus, presumably. "Is there a problem? I thought they were happy to discuss things?"

I tried to look more confident than I felt. "No problem," I lied. "I just need to sort the new lease out with them. It's probably just about paperwork."

"I'm sure you'll get it sorted," said Izzy. "After all," she grinned, "what would you do with immortality if you didn't have me and Flora's to keep you busy? Laters!" With that, she turned and strode off towards Button Street, her bag swinging and whistling under her breath.

I watched until she'd disappeared round the corner, then headed upstairs. I opened the envelope as distraction whilst sitting on the loo, trying—and failing utterly—to have a pee. Staring down at my bare knees, I noticed a spiky patch of hair that I'd missed with the razor. If I shaved it off now, would it grow back? Would I ever have to go to the hairdresser's again?

I gave up and stood, pulling my clothes back together and automatically washing my hands, despite no form of bathroom activity having taken place. *I'm going to save a fortune on sanitary products*, I thought idly, drying my hands and picking up the letter. Walking into the front room, I settled into the same chair Kitty had been in the night before. She hadn't shown herself so far this evening, and Grimm was also missing in action. I suspected they were hanging out together somewhere, the absolute traitors. Sliding a fingernail underneath the edge of the envelope, I opened it and pulled out a single sheet of paper. It had the same header as the previous letter, but this message was handwritten in immaculate cursive.

It would be appreciated if you could find time to drop by for a chat as soon as you return. We have much to discuss. MS.

You could say that again. After making sure that there was food down for Grimm if he ever returned from adventuring with his ghostly sidekick, I set off for the Liver Building.

New Kid In Town

Even though it was getting late, there was still a slow but steady flow of office workers exiting through the side doors at the end of their working day. I headed for the revolving doors at the front and was careful to enter at a slightly more sedate pace than I'd managed previously. As I walked towards reception, I spotted Sharp-Faced-Bob still in prime place behind the heavy wooden desk. She tilted her head in recognition as I approached. "Aah Miss O'Reilly," she said, actually cracking a smile. "I was told you'd be coming to see us today." *Oh, were you now,* I thought. *Very fucking smug of Maria Silverton to assume I'd jump as soon as she asked.*

I *had* jumped, though. I sighed. "Well here, I am," I said, smiling brightly. "As expected. No, don't worry, I'll see myself up." I was past her and up the marble stairs again before she had a chance to reply, but saw her gesturing to the security guard to let me through. *Too late, suckers,* I thought, *Zombie Lil's ahead of you.* As soon as I was safely out of sight, I broke into a run. Even at speed, I was more in control of myself now, and better able to judge how hard I could slam my feet down without damaging the marble. Not very hard, I soon discovered. Misjudging the last flight, I had to jam my heels into the floor at the top and felt a crunch beneath my feet as the stone crumbled. I looked down and stepped carefully away from the damage. I was pretty sure it was fixable. Hopefully.

"Good evening, Lilith." The man that had stopped me the previous day was standing in the open double doors that led into the Silverton lair. He had a definite expression of amusement on his face. "Aiming for a full rebuild of the Three Graces, are we?"

I held his gaze. "What's a bit of property damage between friends?"

"Indeed," said a polite voice. Maria Silverton appeared from behind him and stepped towards me, a smile on her face. I stepped back slightly, not yet entirely prepared to roll over and play doggo. She was unperturbed. "Come talk to Eadric," she said. I followed her into a huge and ornate anteroom that contained several large tables made of heavy dark wood, each with matching chairs. A pale cream, deep-pile carpet covered the floor. It felt like walking across expensively bleached grass. Enormous portraits in gilded frames peered down at us from walls painted in what my mum always called 'National Trust Green'. Between them were tall, arched windows. The middle one held a stained glass rendition of a Liver bird in a naïve style, as if the artist had been given a basic description and left to do their best. I followed Maria across the room to where a panelled staircase led upwards. She headed up the steps without checking to see if I was following her, her heels clicking on the wooden treads. Stepping through another set of double doors at the top, we emerged into what was, to all intents and purposes, an enormous living room. Looking out of the huge, arched windows on the far wall, I could see over to a massive cruise ship moored at the Stena dock to north Birkenhead and beyond. It was a damn sight prettier from here than it was at ground level. A polite cough to my right made me turn my head. There was a man sitting in an overstuffed armchair positioned below another window, this one looking out over the docks. He was the most exaggeratedly good-looking person I'd ever seen in my life. Well over six feet tall, this walking cliche had chestnut hair waving down to his chin and the faintest hint of stubble at his jawline. His pale skin and chiselled features made him look like a Celtic version of an ancient god and his eyes had the same silver ring as mine, fading to hazel with distinct gold flecks.

"Nice to meet you," he said in a disarmingly unidentifiable English accent, just a trace of Welsh lilting over the top. In fact, he sounded as though he could have come from my home town—although I was pretty sure I'd have heard on the grapevine if someone this ridiculously handsome had moved into the area. My mum prided herself on not being a gossip, but she never objected to her friends doing it for her. I shook myself—*bad Lili, objectifying someone like that!*—and attempted to rearrange my slack-jawed expression into something approaching politeness. "I'm Eadric Silverton," the man said, not moving from the chair. "And you must be Lilith O'Reilly?" He made it a question, but I was in no doubt that he already knew everything about me.

"Err, yes," I said, leaning down slightly to shake his hand. His grasp was firm, but not in a try-hard, macho way. His hands were dry and cool. Well practiced at the art of business casualness, I thought. "I'd like some answers, if it's all the same to you." Eadric smiled. I'd have expected someone with his looks to be saturnine or cat-like—all sly and sharp—but his expression was open and friendly. Maria stepped past me to stand next to him, her hand on his arm clearly implying ownership. *Oh, so that's how it is*, I thought, hoping the disappointment wasn't showing on my face.

"Aah, happy families." The man from the stairs walked into the room behind me. There was a distinct edge to his voice. I really hoped that my newly minted supernatural powers would eventually include understanding the subtext in conversations, because it was something I'd always been shit at. He flopped into the matching chair opposite Eadric and picked up a battered paperback from the floor. Turning away from us, he flung his legs over the arm of the chair and started reading, as if he was suddenly bored with the entire situation.

Maria rolled her eyes. "You were excited enough at the idea of fresh blood, Nik," she remarked to the man's back. I hoped she hadn't meant that literally. "Don't you want to have a chat with Lilith?" In reply, the man ostentatiously turned the page of his book, incredibly slowly. Maria rolled her eyes, an expression of resigned amusement on her face. "Come sit at the table, Lili," she said, "and we'll try to answer any questions you might have."

* * *

"Why don't we need to eat?" I demanded. "How do we keep going? Where does the energy come from?" They'd been trying to explain the basics to me for an hour now, but still none of it made any sense. I hadn't mentioned my earlier 'introduction to the afterlife' with Ivo—partly because I was curious to see if they'd give different explanations, but also because I wasn't yet sure who could be trusted. Eadric shrugged. The man even made a twitch of his shoulders look like an elegant catwalk manoeuvre. Pleasant as he undoubtedly was, his natural poise was grating. I'd spent a lifetime coveting the daintiness of those who pranced their way through life like delicate show ponies whilst I lumbered around like a baby elephant. Immortality didn't seem to have improved my abilities, if the amount of stonework I'd accidentally damaged in the last few days was any proof. *The afterlife is actually quite disappointing so far,* is what I didn't say. Instead, I just sat and waited for an answer. I'd learned quickly that Eadric carefully considered everything before opening his mouth. Verbal filters were alien to me, as Izzy reminded me every time I said something I really shouldn't. It happened a *lot.*

"Who knows?" He finally said. "I've put a lot of money into research since my death, but never found a definitive answer. Of course, science has improved somewhat over the last couple of centuries. Perhaps one day we'll find out." Maria squeezed his hand supportively.

"So, are you really ancient?" I asked, waiting to see whether his answers matched up with Ivo's.

Maria laughed. "I told you she'd be fun," she said to Eadric.

He gave me a wry smile. "I'm a thousand years old, give or take," he said and I reminded myself to look shocked. "I know. It sounds beyond the realms of possibility, doesn't it? Yet here I am." He sat back in his chair and slid a hand across onto Maria's thigh. "And with such a young wife. I should probably be ashamed of myself."

Maria shook her head and laughed. "He's about a decade older than me in human years," she said, "but it's a lot more than that in real time. Eadric died sometime in the second half of the eleventh century—no one's sure exactly when. I was born in eighteen-fifty-one and passed into the afterlife nineteen years later." She saw my expression. "Teenagers didn't exist back then, Lilith," she said with a small smile. "I already had a three-year-old child when I passed. And no, I don't know what happened to her." Her face hardened. "It took me a long time to accept myself as the godforsaken demon I'd become, and by the time I'd come to terms with my fate, it was too late to trace my little Mab. It was for the best." She smiled again, but it was tighter this time. "Of course," she continued brightly, "records are so much better these days. We already know all about you, don't we, Eadric?"

He nodded and looked at me. "We'll make all the necessary arrangements, of course," he said. "I have contacts at the hospital. They can provide paperwork to prove you were so badly injured in your fall that it wouldn't be possible for your parents to identify your body. You can get packed up and be on your way before they've even arranged your funeral." He kept talking, and I wondered how he hadn't picked up on the waves of panic that were ripping through me. "We thought you might like Scotland? Just until everyone who remembers you has died. Then you can come back and start again. If that's what you'd like, of course."

I got up out of my seat so fast that the chair flew into the wall behind me. I ignored the sound of wood panels creaking and leaned over the table to where Eadric and Maria both sat gaping at me, astonished expressions on their faces. Nik turned slowly in his chair to watch the entertainment, a grin breaking out on his face. "I'm going nowhere," I said quietly, but I was vibrating with fury to such an extent that I could feel it spreading through the heavy wooden table. Eadric could clearly feel it as well. He moved back in his seat a fraction, but not enough to show he was unnerved. Maria just stared at me uncomprehendingly. "I have had a *really* difficult few days," you could say that again, "and you are *NOT HELPING!*" I glared across the table. Patronising asshats, the pair of them. I leaned forward even more and this time a faint look of genuine apprehension flashed across Eadric's face. Good. "You," I pointed at each of them in turn, "do not own me. I am staying put. And more to the point, I am staying in Harrington Street." Eadric made a move to speak, but I stopped him. "Zip it, old man," I snarled, and I swear I heard Nik snigger from across the room. "Dead or not, this is the twenty-first century. Not the seventeenth, or whenever it was that people became entitled to do what they pleased in life."

"Twentieth," came Nik's helpful voice. "Depending on your interpretation of freedom, of course." All three of us turned to glare at him at once.

I turned back to Eadric and Maria Silverton. "What work actually needs doing in my building?" I demanded. "Because I can't see anything wrong with it, apart from the usual damp and dodgy electrics. You're pretty shit landlords, if you want to know." Their expressions made it clear that they hadn't wanted to know, actually, but now that they did, they would deal with it professionally. "And I have been a bloody good tenant. So we will just carry on, if it's all the same to you."

"We need it back in order to keep people safe," said Eadric. He'd apparently decided that the only way of getting through this meeting without destroying the city's most famous building was to go along with me. "There's an exit through the building and the others have found it. That's how they'd got into your apartment on the night you fell off the roof. They were probably hoping to find someone to feed from, but ran away when you fell, in case the police turned up."

"An exit from where?" They both looked uncomfortable at that. I leaned towards Eadric in order to make my point. "Eadric," I said in a sharp tone, "*what exit?*"

Maria put a hand across the table in a conciliatory gesture. "Lilith," she said calmly, "we need to make the place safe. If they come through there, then everything's at risk. You, us, all this," she gestured at the building around us, "the entire city. They want it back. And we have to stop them."

"Who wants *what* back?" Now I really was confused. Exactly how many undead creepoids were wandering around Liverpool? No wonder Paradise Street was such a mess on a Saturday afternoon. Maybe half of the shoppers really were zombies.

"The others," said Maria. "Others with a capital 'O'." She made hand gestures to show me what she meant. "Everyone who's dead, but isn't the same as us." She tried again. "You might call them the fae? I think that's what storybooks describe them as these days, anyway. I read a really good one once, about a fairy queen and a steamroller. Anyway," she smiled. "Ghosts, vampires, assorted supernatural creatures. Some are more common than others, of course."

Of course. "So vampires do actually exist?" I asked. "We're not just the

107

modern, polite version?" Maybe they'd take me in—it might be more fun than sitting in a fancy lounge with Mr and Mrs Old-And-Boring. Eadric looked uneasy.

"They're not how you imagine," said Maria. "They're...feral, for want of a better expression. And there aren't many around these days, anyway. The majority were killed off by the others when they began to draw attention to themselves. Whatever the movies might imply," she went on, "it's difficult to feed from humans on a regular basis. People become suspicious, even in a city as tolerant as Liverpool. They had something of a heyday after the second war, because everything was a mess and they were just one more problem in a city full of problems. But then cameras and televisions started coming in and suddenly people could keep visual records. Vampires do show up in photographs, you know," she said. "And they look like the monsters they are."

"So what are we then, if not monsters?" Nik broke in from across the room. "What gives us the right to say we're better than the others?"

From the way Maria sighed without turning round, I guessed they'd had this argument many times already. "We don't kill people, Nik."

"Some of us do," he said. "Is that not equally unethical?"

"*We* don't hurt anyone," Maria retorted. "That's the main thing."

Nik snorted. "Really?" he asked archly. Maria frowned. "Why don't you tell Lili about your wild phase, Maria?"

"It was the sixties," replied Maria calmly. "Things were...different." Nik looked unconvinced. "You weren't even here, Nik," she said sharply. "You were off having one of your episodes on a Greek island somewhere."

It was Nik's turn to look slightly uncomfortable. "I was trying to find myself," he said, narrowing his eyes at her. "It was a big thing," he went on, "you should try it sometime."

"I don't need to chase cabin boys around on Mediterranean yachts in order to know what I am," said Maria, glaring back at him.

It was left to Eadric to break the tension. "Stop it," he said, "the pair of you. What sort of impression do you think you're giving to the newest member of our family?" He smiled at me kindly. "You need to move," he repeated.

"It's the only safe way."

"No."

"That's it, just no?" His voice was incredulous. "You woke up dead, accidentally killed an innocent man—"

"—There was nothing innocent about that bastard—"

"—okay, so you realised you were dead, but not. You killed someone—yes, by accident, I'll allow that—and dumped him in the canal. And now you're standing here telling me you're going to hang around to see what happens next?"

"Yup." I could see Nik grinning in my peripheral vision. I suspected he was quite pleased to have someone else around to dilute the Silverton's bickering. "You lot are clearly rich. I mean," I gestured around the room, "Croesus levels of rich. And you must have contacts in high places in order to be able to fake my death. Un-death. Whatever." Immortality had also clearly failed to gift me with the ability to stop rambling whenever I got carried away. "I just need you to let me stay in Harrington Street and I'll keep out of everyone's way." Eadric was gazing at me with an unnervingly steady calm over the top of his steepled fingers. He *wants* to unnerve you, I reminded myself, remembering Ivo's warning. *He wants you to do as you're told so that there aren't any awkward questions.* Well fuck that shit absolutely sideways. I addressed him directly. "And I'd like you to make my property safe."

"*Our* property, I think you'll find." He really did have the sorting of voice that under normal circumstances would have my knickers melting off. Clearly spoken and warm, with just a subtle hint of temptation. Absolutely not my type, mind. I didn't go for the flowing hair, Viking-lost-in-the-twenty-first-century look. Never had. But I liked to appreciate beauty when I saw it. Shame he had about as much personality as an IKEA sideboard.

"Which I have the lease on," I reminded him.

He was unperturbed. "We will be...*understanding* with regards to the current situation," he finally replied. "You will be permitted to remain on the premises, but will allow us access for safety improvements. A workman will be with you tomorrow morning."

"Oh, and no one sucks *anything* from Izzy, understood?"

Eadric looked confused. "Izzy who?"

"The tiny human with the big mouth," said Maria. "She works in the cafe. And once told me to fuck off when I was standing on the steps outside her apartment building."

Go Izzy, I thought. "She was probably trying to prevent you getting piss on your expensive shoes," I said. "She was being *helpful.*"

"What about your parents?" Eadric continued, clearly determined to get the conversation back on track. "Aren't they going to start wondering why you're not looking older? Giving them grandchildren?"

"You won't be able to have children, Lili," said Maria. Softly, as if she thought it would come as a shock.

I looked at the pair of them as if they really had lost their undead minds. "Well, that's a fucking relief," I replied. "No need for contraception, ever again." There really were benefits to dying, after all. "I don't *want* kids," I said. "Never have, never will. I am thirty two years old and have yet to feel a single twinge of maternal instinct. Honestly," I shrugged apologetically, "it wasn't ever going to happen, even if I *hadn't* swan-dived off a building. And my parents know that."

"But they're going to realise you're not getting older," Eadric insisted.

I sighed. "Have you *met* my parents?" He shook his head to indicate that no, he'd never had the pleasure. "Because if you had, you would know that they're both in their seventies." My parents had spent years trying for a baby with no luck, only for me to turn up unexpectedly, just when they'd accepted it would never happen. And then my brother, years later, when no one thought it would happen again. "They'll be dead before I've developed major wrinkles. And people don't go grey in my family, anyway. My nan had black hair until the day she died and she was ninety-five. Oh," a sudden thought, "what happens if I cut my hair?" I tugged at the enormous scruffy bun that was perched on top of my head, just waiting for a Liver Bird to hop down off the roof and make its nest.

"Don't cut your hair," Nik laughed, "not unless you want a pixie crop for all eternity."

"Actually, that's not entirely true," Maria said thoughtfully, "things do grow and repair, eventually. But it takes decades, not weeks." She ran a hand through her hair. The darkest of chestnut waves slipped through her fingers and she smiled thinly. "Mine was cut off when I was still alive," she said, "to prevent lice. I'd like to get my hands on the bitch who did that, I can tell you."

"Lice?"

"I was in the workhouse. Up on Brownlow Hill. Decided I couldn't take it anymore, so I stole the head warden's stash of gin and laudanum, took the lot and jumped into the Mersey. Eventually I had to accept that I clearly wasn't going to die, so I clambered back out covered in silt and stinking weed."

"My very own swamp monster," laughed Eadric, catching her hand and pulling her to him before turning to me. "You can imagine Nik's face when I brought this creature home with me." A dry snort from the corner suggested Nik had definitely not been impressed.

"You're missing out the bit about Maria killing two innocent men before you found her," Nik said. Maria looked pained at that.

Eadric sighed. "It wasn't her fault that she didn't know what she was," he said defensively, patting Maria's arm. "It's not as though we can know in advance who it will happen to. As Lilith here has discovered only too well. Anyway," he said, changing the subject with about as much subtlety as a battering ram, "let's get the basics sorted and worry about the details later. I'm not convinced that it's a good idea to stay put, Lilith, but we're long past the days when rebels would have been killed and dumped in the sewerage system. Sadly. So I guess we'll just have to trust you on this one. And you might yet prove to be useful."

"And if you're not, we can always kill you," said Nik, pushing himself up from the armchair and coming over to the table. "Beheading gets rid of ninety-nine per cent of all known germs." He grinned at me. "Don't worry," he said, "we don't do that anymore. Not often, anyway."

"Stop it," said Maria.

Nik gave her a curious look. "Why are you defending a stranger?" he asked. "I've never known you be this welcoming to…incomers." He glanced at me, then back to Maria. "Lili clearly has some…strengths," he said. "I'd have expected you to see her as a threat, not a friend."

"You're being a brat, Nik," said Eadric sharply. "Lilith's clearly got a mind of her own, and that's better than not having a mind at all. She'll be fine."

"A handbook for the recently deceased would be useful," I suggested, hoping to break the tension. All I got in return was a full house of blank looks. Perhaps they weren't movie fans. "You know," I ploughed on, "basic rules for not getting found out, how to live when dead, that sort of thing."

Maria laughed. "Oh, I think we'll get on just fine, Lilith O'Reilly. You can run the first undead cafe in Liverpool and no one will ever know. Which is a shame," she mused, "because it would definitely pull in the crowds."

Cellar Door

I t was early the next morning, and I was lying on my bed staring at the ceiling, trying to make pictures out of the cracks in the plaster. I'd cleaned and reorganised the living room overnight, and when I'd finished that, I went out for another run. Turns out Crosby's really pretty in the moonlight. My phone rang suddenly, Viagra Boys blasting out from somewhere underneath my duvet. I fished it out and saw that it was an unknown number. Hitting the accept button on the smashed screen, I put the phone to my ear, expecting to hear Izzy griping about having lost her phone again and how she'd had to borrow one from a passerby in order to call me. She only ever asked men, and they always obliged. To my surprise, it was a deep, male voice on the other end. "Lili, darling," said Gaultier Mapp, "could you cope with having visitors? Heggie would like to talk to you."

* * *

Mapp and Heggie were already waiting for me on the fire escape by the time I'd got dressed and opened the kitchen door. Mapp was giving a good impression of lounging in a louche manner, despite sitting on nothing more glamorous than rusty metal stairs. Today's outfit was a kimono in dark green silk, with gold accents at the collar and cuffs. It draped elegantly down to the floor. Heggie was hunched on the lowest step, wringing his hands, with his hair hanging limply over his face like curtains. His feet were clad in grubby Green Flash sneakers and tapped lightly but frantically on the gravel around the base of the stairs. He looked up as I approached and I was surprised to see a round, well-padded face that looked no more than twenty. He had the glowing appearance of the recently scrubbed and his little black button-eyes watched me with what looked like wary excitement. He elbowed Mapp sharply and the older man shot to his feet in an attempt to prove that he hadn't been taken by surprise. "Lili!" Mapp cried, climbing over Heggie and coming up to greet me with his arms outstretched. "How lovely to see you again so soon." I allowed myself to be hugged, patting Mapp's back in a feeble attempt at jollity whilst he enveloped me in silk and what smelled distinctly like Samsara. He stepped backwards and gestured to his friend. "You've met Heggie, of course," he said. The little man flinched as I moved to put a hand out to shake his and I decided against it. It would be easier to talk if he didn't curl up into a ball again.

"Come up," I said, turning to walk back up to the top floor at a carefully human speed, so as not to be noticed by the neighbours. Although I was pretty sure no one in the vicinity would ever bother gazing out of their windows onto the beauty and glamour that was a patch of urban wasteland, I didn't want to risk ending up on YouTube if anyone spotted me scaling the building like Wonder Woman. The two men shuffled up behind me, bickering mildly as they went. Apparently, Heggie needed to buck his ideas up and Mapp should stop bullying Heggie. I opened the door to the flat and went to put the kettle on. Some habits never die, even when their mortal vessels do. Mapp sashayed in through the door, ducking to avoid banging his head on the frame, and Heggie came in slowly behind him, little eyes wide. I put the kettle on out of habit and started getting mugs out of the cupboard.

Mapp suddenly stopped dead, and I looked to see what had surprised him. An enormous grin was spreading across his face as he stared past me. "Kitty!" he cried, striding into the living room. I followed him, just in time to see him swing my aunt off her feet and into a tight hug. She was shrieking with delight and hugging him back with her transparent arms.

"How are you doing that?"

They both stopped and turned to stare at me. "How are we hugging?"

114

Mapp asked, looking confused. "Well," he said, stepping towards me with his arms outstretched, "you come here and I'll repeat the exercise and we can practise where our arms go."

Kitty was laughing behind him. "No," I said, "I mean, how are you hugging Kitty? She's a ghost!" My aunt shrugged in the universal sign for 'cannot deny it' as I stared at the pair of them. "Grimm can sit on her lap and you can hug her, *but she's a ghost!*" There was a faint tinge of hysteria in my voice. Just when I thought I was doing so well at this afterlife malarkey.

"Have you tried?" asked Mapp.

I thought about that for a moment. "Well, no," I admitted, "but I just assumed I couldn't?"

Kitty smiled and stepped forward. "Give it a go," she said, encouragingly. "It would be nice to hug family, after all this time." Not quite believing it would work, I held out my arms to hug my aunt. There was still that faint prickling sensation. And I could definitely still see through her, straight down to the floor. But she felt as real and solid as anyone I'd ever met.

I stepped back, a look of wonder on my face. "You're real," I said, "really real." Kitty laughed. I remembered something. "How do you two," I gestured at Kitty and Mapp, "know each other?"

They both grinned. "Oh, we go way back," replied Mapp, casually. "Met at a party in the early sixties, became, erm...*acquainted*, shall we say?" He winked alarmingly at me, and Kitty thumped his arm. I saw her hand actually connect.

"Don't embarrass my poor niece, Mapp," she said, laughing.

I stared from one of them to the other. "Are you telling me," I said, "that you two were...were a *thing*?" I'd forgotten that Heggie was behind me, and jumped when he snorted with what was presumably laughter.

Kitty grinned at me. "Would that be such a terrible thing?" she asked. "Would you not prefer that your dear old aunt had some fun whilst she was alive?"

"Of course I don't mind," I stuttered, "not that it's my place to mind, anyway. It's just..." I trailed off, embarrassed.

Mapp clearly didn't have the same fragile sensibilities as I did. "What does it matter who's alive and who's dead," he asked, "so long as everyone's having fun?"

"But I thought Jonny was Kitty's one true love," I blurted out. "Beloveds for all eternity, and all that."

"Lili," Kitty said kindly, "Mapp and I knew each other *before* I met Jonny."

"She left me heartbroken and inconsolable," confirmed Mapp. "And then she went and got herself killed and disappeared entirely. Until now." He grinned at Kitty and draped an arm around her pale, shimmering shoulders.

"Can I say my thing now?" asked a gruff voice from behind me. I turned to see Heggie staring at us all, his round cheeks pinking up in the face of our attention. "Only I want to go see Joe."

"You hang out with the wrong type of people," said Mapp, mildly.

"You're the wrong type of people and it doesn't stop you," pointed out Heggie.

Mapp laughed. "Very true," he said. "I cannot deny it. Let's all sit down together, and we can chat."

Determined to bring some normality to the insanity that appeared to be my life now, I insisted on making everyone a cup of coffee first. This included Kitty, who stared woefully at it. "I'm sorry," I said sheepishly. "Sometimes I forget that you're dead."

"We're all dead, Lilith," said Mapp, not unkindly. I looked up at him. Now he was standing close to me and the light was better, I could see that the silver line around the edge of his irises was far less intense than any I'd seen before, including my own. Mapp caught me staring, and I thought for a second he was going to say something. He appeared to think better of it and turned to Heggie instead. The little man was holding his coffee cup gingerly, as if worried it might come to life and bite him. "Spill the beans then, Hegs," he said.

The little man looked pained. "You know I don't like nicknames," he said.

Mapp rolled his eyes. "As if Heggie's your actual name anyway," he replied.

Heggie scowled. "I like it. Anyway," he turned to me and fixed me with his beady eyes, "you need to help Joe."

"Who's Joe?" I asked, with justifiable trepidation.. Joe was probably an evil troll who lived under the Anglican, if my week so far had been anything to go by.

"He's a man," said Heggie flatly. "He lives under the city and your bosses don't like him."

I frowned. "My bosses?" I asked.

Heggie sighed. "The Silvers," he said. "Silvers, Silvers, all about the Silvers."

Mapp nudged him. "Back on track, Hegs," he said.

The little man pulled his arm away from Mapp, and looked back at me. "Joe's people are going missing," he said, "and I think it's the Silvers' doing." Oh great. Not only was I dead, now there was a murderous turf war going on and I was expected to get involved. Worst week ever.

"They don't seem the killing type to me," I said.

Heggie shook his head. "You don't know them," he said, "or their friends. They've been powerful a long time. They won't give it up without a fight." It was the longest sentence he'd managed in my hearing. He paused for a moment as if it had tired him. "Joe's people aren't acceptable round these parts," he continued. "They're being encouraged into causing trouble!" His voice went up a few notches. "They're not bad people," he said, "not really. They get into poor company somehow. Not even Joe knows how it happens."

"Can't you just asked them?" I was thoroughly confused now. Who was Joe, and who—or, more likely, *what*—were his people? And what was happening to them that Heggie thought I might be able to help with?

"They don't talk," said Mapp helpfully. "Not ever in my hearing, anyway. I used to think it was because the teeth got in the way, but nowadays I reckon they just can't. I'm not sure whether they even have tongues."

"What *are* they?" I asked.

Mapp grimaced. "Most would call them vampires," he said slowly, "but they're not of any design you'd recognise from books or films. In fact," he glanced at Heggie, who was making a careful attempt to sip his coffee whilst looking thoroughly confused by the concept, "I'm not sure the city wouldn't be better off without them."

Heggie shot upright and scowled at him. "You stop that!" he cried, his voice squeaking slightly as if he was struggling to find enough air to force the words out. "Who are you to judge what's acceptable, Gaultier Mapp?" It occurred to me it was the second time that day that I'd heard someone being asked that question. Clearly, the denizens of the undead realms spend an awful lot of time wondering which creatures were superior to others. I suspected that they *all* thought they were, which was probably why they argued about it so much.

"I'm tired," I lied, "and I don't know anything about this Joe or his pets." Heggie glared at me. "Look," I said to him, "I'll come talk to you again, okay?" He simmered down a tiny bit. "But it has been a very long few days and I need to go lie down with my cat and ignore my ghost aunty for a couple of hours," Kitty didn't even bother trying to look offended, "and just let this entire shitshow settle itself into some semblance of rationality." They all looked at me as if they thought I'd be waiting a long time for rationality to seep in. I suspected they were correct. "Okay?"

"We're tiring you," said Mapp, getting to his feet, "and you being a new friend, as well. Come on," he said to Heggie, who looked as though he might be building up the strength for another outburst, "we'll leave Lilith in peace."

"I will come and talk to you," I reassured Heggie, who looked unconvinced. "And I will have a think about who I trust."

"Promise?" he asked.

I patted his arm. "I promise."

* * *

"That doesn't look very secure," muttered Izzy. We'd not long closed Flora's and were in the staff kitchen. Izzy was eyeing the small padlock that appeared to be the only addition to the door that led from the staff room down to the cellar underneath the cafe. A pair of surly workman had turned up as we were opening Flora's that morning. They'd shown me a card with the Silverton crest on it, before disappearing down the cellar steps without saying a word. We'd then endured almost an hour of what had sounded very much like drilling and arc-welding, whilst gritting our teeth and pasting fake smiles on our faces for our luckily tolerant customers. So I'd been expecting something more dramatic than a cheap padlock that looked like it had been bought in the DIY section of Wilkos.

"Maybe they found an opening in the cellar itself and blocked it up," I said, eyeing the stack of old bottles that the workmen had left in the corner. They spilled out of an ancient cooler box that I assumed must have been down in the cellar. I'd been down there once, just before I signed the lease on Flora's and wanted to check what I was getting for my money. A brief peek at the damp and mouldy cellar had convinced both me and my dad that I could probably live without the storage space. And after I'd taken over the upstairs floors, I didn't need it anyway. The little padlock certainly didn't look as though it would need much forcing, but presumably the Silverton minions knew what they were doing. And it wasn't as though I didn't have enough issues of my own to be thinking about.

In fact, I'd forgotten about all about the cellar until Izzy had mentioned it. My mind had been mostly taken up with wondering about the difficulties of relationships that crossed temporal realms. Could an undead creature of the night dare to imagine dating a famous novelist? Izzy and I had downloaded one of Sean's books to her Kindle earlier in the day and had been taking turns to skim it for any salacious bits during quiet periods. Sean was quite the king of the sexy bedroom scene, we discovered. He was also good with violent—and carefully detailed—murder. "At least he'll know how to deal with you when you give in to blood lust," Izzy had said, ducking as I half-heartedly threw a box of tea bags at her.

I got up and went to the door, giving the padlock an experimental shake. Izzy was right—the lock itself was small and not very sturdy at all. It was more the kind of thing you put on travel bags in the full knowledge that they'll almost certainly still spill their contents across the airport luggage carousel. Hardly high level security against murderous paranormal creatures. Especially as this particular door had always been difficult to keep closed anyway. It rattled in the slightest breeze and was usually forced shut with one of those little rubber wedges from a DIY store. I rattled the door handle and it shook in its housing, but the door itself didn't budge an inch. Peering more closely at the frame, I realised that the door itself was somehow fixed in place. I gave it a tentative kick—I didn't want to risk putting my newly powerful foot straight through it—and it was like hitting high tensile steel. I kicked harder, but all I got in return was a sickly vibration travelling up my leg.

"Want to explain what the fuck you're doing?" asked Izzy, her eyebrows raised.

"The door's completely stuck," I said.

"Isn't that the point?"

"That's not what I mean." I got a stool from the corner of the room and dragged it to the door, so that I could clamber onto it and inspect the top of the frame. "It's *literally* stuck. Pass me the torch?" Izzy scraped her chair out from under the table. I could hear her rattling round in the junk drawer whilst I stared in wonder at the doorframe.

"You need to stop hoarding crap," she said as she passed the little torch up to me. "No one needs menu cards from more than three Chinese takeaways. You only ever use Wok'n'Go, anyway."

"They do the best fried tofu," I said, switching the torch on. I aimed the light between the door and its frame.

"That you can't eat anymore," Izzy pointed out. I nearly dropped the torch. No more fried tofu! No more sticky rice covered in that salty shredded stuff that was sold as seaweed, but everyone knew was really cabbage. I stared down at her and she laughed at my stricken face.

"What?" I asked. "How would you like it if you realised you'd never be able to eat your favourite food again? No more doughnuts from the van down on Albert Dock. You'd weep for a week."

"Is that why you didn't have any chips with me the other night?"

"Yeah," I said, "I didn't want to be sick and blow my cover." I went back to peering at the door edges. "Then the Creature from the Black Lagoon went and blew it for me, anyway. Holy fuck," I went on, "that's one way to make sure no one can get through a door."

"What are you talking about?" Izzy was sitting on the table, her legs swinging idly as she watched me.

"There's metal all the way round it," I said, climbing down off the stool.

120

"I think they've actually fused the door and the wall together. Why would they do that?"

"Err, to stop the deadly demons getting in?" offered Izzy. "I'll be asking them to do the same to the door to the stairs, I reckon. I can use the fire escape, same as you do—better to keep the inside secure."

"You don't understand," I said, putting the torch back into the drawer and taking a moment to glare at the menus that would never again tempt me on a boring Saturday night. "There's no way into the building from the basement." Izzy looked blank. "It's a concrete cellar," I explained. "You've been inside it, you know this! There's that safe bolted to the wall that we've never used, but the door's open and its empty. That's it." Izzy looked unconvinced, before asking the obvious question.

"So why have they bothered blocking the door?"

"More to the point," I said, "*how* have they blocked the door? And what might be trying to get in that would justify so much effort to keep them out?"

"How did the intruders get in?" Izzy asked. "On the night you—" she faltered slightly, "had your accident?"

"I don't know," I said, realising the truth of it only as the words came out of my mouth. "There's been so much going on that I haven't had time to think about it much."

"You said that the door to the fire escape was open when you came home," said Izzy, and I nodded. "But the door to the inner stairs was broken through as well. You put the bolt on it." And hadn't done anything else with it yet, I remembered with a jolt. Izzy turned to look at me. "You're already dead. If you still need protecting from whatever's on the other side of this door, then I wouldn't like to meet whoever—whatever—it is on a dark and stormy night, is all I can say."

"I'd rather know what it is the Silvertons are so desperate to keep out," I said, thinking about what Heggie had said earlier. "I don't think the intruders are automatically the bad guys. That's just the Silvertons' opinion. Even Ivo seems to think they're not entirely trustworthy," I went on, "and he's a friend of theirs."

"Well, it's a bit late now," said Izzy, "seeing as how it's sealed off."

"The hatch in the car park," I said, suddenly remembering. "There's a manhole out there that looks more like a cellar hatch. When I looked around the place, the agent said I had to be careful not to leave anything on top of the hatch because it was needed for emergencies, but I forgot about it almost straight away. It's probably hidden under the weeds."

"What's that got to do with the cellar?" asked Izzy.

"Liverpool's got hidden tunnels everywhere, right?" She looked blank. "Everyone knows those big ones up at Edge Hill that go on forever, but there's also tunnels down here. Or rather," I said, "there are old docks underneath some of the streets. From before the new ones were built. You know the glazed viewing window on the street outside John Lewis?" Izzy nodded. We'd once ricocheted off the metal railings that surrounded it after too many pints of cheap cider one night. We had to go sit on the steps up to Chevasse Park whilst we got our breath back. "Well, that must go *somewhere*," I pointed out. There was a tourist tour that went down into the old docks, but I'd never done it. "What if the docks come up this far?"

Izzy looked sceptical. "I don't think anyone would need a dock this far back from the water, Lil," she pointed out.

I huffed at her. "I know *that*," I said, "but what if there are tunnels connecting things? Who knows what could be down there?"

"I'd rather stick with not knowing, if it's all the same with you," shuddered Izzy.

I sighed. "Where's your sense of adventure?" I said, and headed outside.

Going Underground

"You're not actually going down there?" Izzy was watching me from the back door, a worried expression on her face. She pulled her cardigan tight around herself as she watched me ripping away the weeds that had grown over the manhole cover in the carpark. I pulled satisfying chunks of nettle root out of the metal grate that covered the hatch, wondering why I'd always been such a baby about nettle stings. Even pushing my hands through the mat of fresh shoots with the brightest, spikiest leaves hadn't registered anything above a faint tickle.

"How else am I going to find out what the hell's going on?" I'd cleared away enough greenery to see the hatch clearly now. It wasn't the standard manhole cover you usually see on pavements. This one looked more like a metal version of those drop-doors outside pubs; the ones draymen use to roll barrels straight down into the cellar. There was a heavy iron grille over the top, made up of two panels that were hinged at the sides and padlocked together in the middle. The padlock was new. In fact, the padlock was identical to the one that the workmen had installed on the basement door inside Flora's, which was suspicious. "They've already been out here," I said to Izzy.

"Who have?"

I showed her the padlock, and she frowned. "However welcoming they're being on the surface," she said thoughtfully, "the Silvertons clearly don't trust you. You're the newest member of the gang and they're not going to let you into all of their secrets. Which," she pointed out, "is actually quite sensible. You've landed yourself on them like an escaped lunatic, having already murdered one of the local populace. You should probably be relieved that no one's come after you with burning torches and pitchforks." She took a small nail file from her cardigan pocket and began idly tidying her nails whilst leaning against the doorframe.

I straightened up and stared at her. "Have you quite finished?" I asked, brushing the dirt off my hands onto my leggings.

Izzy grinned at me. "Maybe you're a threat to them," she said.

I laughed at that. "Me? How?"

"Well, they clearly weren't expecting you," she pointed out. "And they've had it all set up quite nicely for a long time, haven't they? But then you come crashing through the doors of their ivory tower and suddenly they've got a rogue agent on the loose." I considered this for a moment. The Silvertons certainly took care to protect their privacy. But then most people would, if they'd accrued that much wealth. Even more so, if you had good reason for not wanting anyone to look too closely into your personal affairs. I wondered briefly how they explained to the tax man that their company directors had been the same people for centuries. Perhaps they took it in turns to move away or 'retire', before returning to the fold a few years after their supposed deaths. Or maybe they just had so much money that no one asked too many questions.

"Oh well," I said, "it'll do them good to have their lives shaken up a bit. Pass me the carving knife?" I saw Izzy's expression. "I'm not going to do anything awful with it! Just need something to lever this padlock off."

"This would be better." To my astonishment, Izzy reached up above the inside of the kitchen doorframe and brought down a crowbar. "I'd actually forgotten it was there," she said sheepishly. "Dad left it at my flat ages ago, after that spate of muggings." Izzy's father had an 'interesting' approach to justice, which basically ran along the lines of 'touch me or mine or anything that belongs to us and you'll be lucky to leave with your kneecaps intact'. Which was funny, because he always presented himself as the meekest and mildest man you could ever hope to meet. "Anyway, I brought it here after that incident with the would-be till thief and then forgot about it." I arched an eyebrow at her, but said nothing as she handed over the heavy bar. "Hang on," she said and ducked back into the kitchen, reemerging seconds later with a mallet. "From when we couldn't get the hot tap to work." Wedging the narrow end of the crowbar into the gap between the grill panels, I swung the mallet and landing a heavy *thunk* on the bar. The panels bowed out and the padlock shattered, sending shards of razor-sharp metal across the carpark in all directions. "Fucking *hell!*" Izzy shrieked, as she shot backwards and only stopped herself from falling over by grabbing hold of the doorframe. Grimm's puffed-up tail was the only bit of him visible as he shot up the metal staircase and leaped through the little window next to the door to my flat that I always left open for his use only.

"Sorry," I said. "I haven't quite got used to my strength yet."

"You're telling me," huffed Izzy from the doorway. "Don't go squidging any little baby cheeks any time soon, aye? You'll be ripping their faces off right in front of their poor mamas."

"I said sorry, didn't I?" I snarked. "Now mind yourself whilst I get this hatch open." I lay the pieces of metal grill neatly on the ground next to the hatch, then pushed the crowbar down in between the hatch panels. For a minute, I didn't think I was going to be able to do it. The metal panels were far heavier than the grill had been, and I thought they might be fused in the same way that the workmen had 'fixed' the door inside Flora's. I put my foot against the crowbar and pushed it sideways. Nothing for a second, then a slow, low creak and I managed to get a hand underneath the crack that had opened up in the panels. Using my weight as balance, I wedged my foot into the gap and pushed the edge of the trap door cover with all my strength. For a second it resisted, but then something shifted underneath me. It was as though the door suddenly gave up trying to keep me out. It flew up and over with a crash, leaving a gaping hole down into pitch black darkness.

Taking my phone out of my waistband, I used its torch to peer down into the abyss. There was a rusty metal ladder fixed to a square access hatch, just under the ground level cover. The ladder only had five rungs and I could see the floor of a tunnel beneath it. I glanced at Izzy, who was peering out nervously from just inside the doorway.

"How do you know it's safe down there?" she asked.

"I don't," I admitted. "But as I'm already dead, I can't see that there's much more could happen to me." Izzy didn't look convinced. Grimm had made his way back down the fire escape and was supervising proceedings from above Izzy's head, in-between washing his intimate regions. Oh, to be a cat, without a care in the world. No worrying about who was dead and who was alive, just a vague expectation of your food bowl being refilled regularly. "Look," I said, "give me two hours. If I'm not back by then, you can call the Silvertons office and they'll have to come rescue their newest offspring. Imagine the satisfaction that would give them."

Izzy looked unconvinced. "How will you know how long you've been?"

It was a good question. I was pretty sure the mobile signal wasn't going to be reliable underground. "There's a watch in the kitchen drawer," I said. "The back kitchen. A black box in the drawer under the sink. And I'll have the little torch as well."

Izzy disappeared inside and was out within seconds, the box and torch in her hand. She passed them over. "Since when have you even owned a watch?" she asked.

"Never," I admitted. "This is Kitty's. Mum gave it to me ages ago. I tucked it away for safekeeping and somehow just forgot about it." I took my aunt's watch out of its box and draped it over my wrist, twisting my hand to fasten the strap underneath. Then I undid it again and looked at Izzy. "What's the time?" She looked confused. "It's mechanical," I explained. "It needs winding up and resetting."

She pulled her phone out of a baggy knitted pocket and looked at it. "Six o'clock." I adjusted the time on the watch's dial and then wound it up. Holding it up to my ear, I made sure it was ticking gently before refastening it onto my wrist.

"Okay," I said, "I'll be back here by seven. In fact, I might well be back within minutes if the tunnel doesn't go anywhere. And I won't take any side routes, so that I can't get lost. Okay? I'll just go straight along as far as I can and see what's there." I looked up at her. "Deal?"

Izzy didn't look at all happy, but she nodded. "Be careful, Lil," she said.

126

But I'd already dropped out of sight.

* * *

I found myself in a narrow, brick-lined tunnel that wasn't high enough for me to stand completely upright. Reaching out my hands to touch the side walls, I was surprised to discover they were dry and slightly warm to the touch. The light coming in from the open hatch was enough to show that one end of the tunnel ended in a brick wall, just a few feet behind me. The bricks seemed newer than the rest of the tunnel. Turning back around, just a few feet of tunnel was visible in the gloom before it disappeared into endless darkness. Taking a tentative few steps forward, I stopped to let my eyes grow accustomed to the lack of light. I had the torch, but figured it made sense to check out my newly superhuman eyeballs. I could see tiny cracks in the mortar between the old bricks in the wall next to me without squinting, and the hairs on the legs of a small, scurrying spider seemed almost luminous. But I didn't appear to have developed full night vision as part of my unearthly transformation, which was disappointing. I reluctantly switched on the little torch and shone it down the tunnel. The beam showed nothing but darkness, and a lot of it. I reminded myself of what I'd said to Izzy—I was dead already, so there wasn't much to fear anymore. I was pretty sure the tunnels must have been part of the official infrastructure of the city at some point, or they wouldn't still exist this close to normal human life. On the other hand, any landowner who was aware of their existence would have almost certainly turned them into super-expensive subterranean apartments by now, so perhaps not. *Oh well*, I thought, *here goes nothing.* I stepped out into the darkness.

The tunnel seemed to go on forever. I'd been walking for a good ten minutes, keeping to a slow human pace in the hope of avoiding any unpleasant surprises that might hide in the dark. The biggest surprise was that I was still walking in a straight line; the light from the hatch on Harrington Street was still visible in the far distance behind me. I hadn't thought to figure out the tunnel's angle before I set off, so had no idea where

I was heading. It must have been inland, because my feet were still dry. The walls and ceiling of the tunnel were still the same aged red brick, but the floor had changed to dry, sandy shale within the first hundred yards. The roof height had increased, so I was now walking upright. I spotted a metal ladder on the wall ahead of me, and just beyond that, what looked to be a bricked-up dead end. Perhaps I could climb up and out to see where I was on the surface. But as I neared the ladder, I realised that instead of the tunnel coming to an end, it was merely making a sharp turn of almost forty five degrees to the left. Deciding to check out where I was before I explored any further, I put a hand on the metal rung and moved to swing up onto it. As I did so, a faint noise came from around the bend in the tunnel. Climbing carefully back down to avoid alerting whoever was down here with me, I stepped forward and peered nervously around the corner.

The tunnel continued running in another straight line, this one even longer than the section from Harrington Street. In the distance was a faint light, glowing in a flickery way that made me think it probably wasn't battery-powered torches. Against all better judgement, I ran towards the light, using it as practice for treading delicately rather than like a baby elephant. I even bounced myself off the side walls a couple of times, just to see whether I could. On the second attempt, I actually went right over the top, landing lightly on the balls of my feet like a top class stuntwoman. I was disappointed no one was around to witness that one. Slowing down as the light grew bigger and brighter in front of me, I realised that the tunnel walls were gradually widening. Whatever was ahead of me was clearly the end goal. Creeping along now, I pressed up against the bricks so that I was less likely to be spotted. I could hear voices ahead of me—at least two, and one much harsher and more aggressive than the other. It sounded as though they were arguing, which was presumably why no one was on alert for intruders. Wedging myself against the wall in the shadows just before the spread of light, I realised it was coming from a large fire. Enormous logs were stacked up in the centre of what appeared to be a cavernous section of railway tunnel. It ran horizontally across the open end of the tunnel I'd just run down and when I looked up, I saw a ventilation shaft in the centre of the cathedral-like roof. Either I'd been going downhill all the way without realising it, or the tunnel from Harrington Street ran into one of the higher areas of the city, because this space was *huge*. Each end was closed off with vast brick walls. There was a tiny opening in the side to my left, but it was so high up the wall that you'd have needed a very long ladder to gain access. Two…*people*, for want of a better word, stood in the middle of the sandy floor. They were close enough to poke each other as they spoke, and were both doing just that, with quite some vigour. The one on the left was short and squat, with arms that looked too long compared to the rest of him. I was making assumptions as to their gender purely because they both looked masculine and were wearing baggy trousers with braces over dirty cream flannel shirts. The short one was gesturing over the shoulders of the other, clearly concerned about something out of my eye line. The second man was taller, thinner, and had a distinctively long face. His greasy black hair was combed back and he had rat-like teeth. I realised with a jolt that he was the intruder who'd knocked me off the fire escape and started this insanity. It was all I could do not to stumble with shock, but I made do with gripping the stone wall so hard that bits of brick crumbled to powder in my clenched fist. The third member of the group was the most recognisably human. A small squat man with pebble glasses, he hunched on a boulder next to the fire and watched proceedings with what appeared to be amusement on his squashed, crinkly face. Suddenly, he turned in my direction. "Come in, my dear," he said amiably. I didn't move an inch. "It's taken you a while to find us." The other two clearly didn't have hearing as acute as his, because they both stopped and looked in my direction with expressions of surprise on their ratty little faces. The little man raised a hand slightly, and the rats stepped backwards. "You're here now," he said. "You might as well come in and say hello. I give my word that no harm will befall you."

Curiosity got the better of me. I stepped into the open space, but stayed close to the wall. "Where exactly am I?" I asked. "And who on earth are you?" The little man laughed and the rat-boys copied him, their chuckles sounding more like low hisses in the echoing chamber. It wasn't remotely comforting.

The man stood up and held out a hand to greet me. Even upright, he only came up to my shoulder. "I'm Joe," he said. "And I am pleased to finally make your acquaintance, Lilith O'Reilly."

* * *

"We have a lot of catching up to do," said Joe amiably, settling himself on a large sandstone block that was placed up against the curved side wall of the cavern. There were similar blocks positioned along the walls at regular intervals and the rat-boys perched on one each, awkwardly poised so they could watch us. There didn't appear to be any access points other than the one I'd come in through and the tiny gap up near the ceiling on the end wall. I was just wondering how the three men—okay, one man and two creatures—had got in themselves, when Rat Boy #1, the idiot who'd knocked me off the roof, sprang up from his perch. He skipped across to the end wall before leaping upwards and scurrying up the bricks and out through the small gap.

Joe grinned at my expression as I watched the poor man's Spiderman make his exit. "I'll show you how to do it yourself, if you like," he said, with a chuckle. He sounded more like a genial old uncle than a scary creature of the underworld.

"I'll give it a miss, thanks," I said and made a point of checking my watch. "I can't stay long," I told Joe. "I've got people on the surface waiting for me." Better for them to think I had backup ready to loom down the tunnels and kick some ratty arse.

"You mean the nervous Welsh girl and the cat?" Joe grinned. "We know all about you, Lilith," he said, before relenting. "My apologies," he said. "I so rarely meet new people that I have an unfortunate tendency to enjoy myself a little too much. We'll do basic introductions today and the full tour another time. If that pleases you?" Rat Boy #2 was still sitting, watching us from his perch. He gave an unpleasant snigger. Joe looked at him. "No need to be sarcastic, Benjamin," he admonished, before looking back at me. "There's an awful lot to see," he explained with a sigh. "I'm afraid this place has quite got away with me over the years."

"Where does it go?" It looked like a fairly definitive dead end to me. "Are we under the city centre?"

Joe smiled. "We're a long way from the streets, Lili," he said. "You need to know your way around these tunnels very well, before you go wandering alone. You never know what you're going to come across. Even I don't know what I'm going to find down here, half the time." His voice trailed off, then he visibly shook himself and smiled at me. Penfold. That's what Joe looked like—the little mole sidekick from the children's cartoon, Danger Mouse. I smiled and it clearly pleased Joe. He puffed himself up slightly and gestured around the vast space. "This is my favourite," he said. I wondered just how many tunnels Joe had to choose from. "It's warm and comfortable," I disagreed with the latter part of that comment, but managed not to say anything, "and the bricks are perfectly even. A triumph."

"Is there a Best Tunnel In Show competition?" I know. I can't help myself sometimes.

"There should be," said Joe happily. "My apprentices would surely win every time."

"You have apprentices?" Joe nodded. "As in, bricklaying apprentices? Underground?"

Joe turned his little round face to me and it glowed with pride. "Oh I've had apprentices down here for a long time, Lili," he said. "A very long time indeed."

A light bulb pinged to life in my head. A very tardy light bulb. "You're Joseph Williamson," I said. The Mole Man of Edge Hill beamed back at me.

A Whole New World

Joseph Williamson began digging his tunnels some time around 1810, and simply never stopped. I say 'he', but it was mostly the work of the endless tradesmen and apprentices that he kept in employment, at a time when jobs were hard to come by. The maze of tunnels began with the construction of arched brick supports that were built to cover steep drops behind the houses that Williamson's men were building in Edge Hill, on the south-east side of the city. Joseph had realised that it would be far more efficient to cover the gaping chasms with what was, in essence, a tunnel roof. That way his men could just fill in over that, rather than attempting to stuff entire chasms with rubble. Seemingly unable to stop—or perhaps simply unable to face the prospect of laying off any of his workforce—the eccentric philanthropist just kept on digging, creating an unmapped maze of architectural oddness. I'd been on a tour of the tunnels a few years previously, on one of my rare attempts to get to know the history of the city. I might know my way between the museums and pubs like the back of my hand, but I was woefully ignorant of the background stories. Laura, my ex, had been born and bred in Anfield and considered my interest in Liverpool history to be equal parts cute and also hilarious. She once told me with mocking pride that she'd never even done the Beatles bus tour. *'That's just for the tourists, girl'.* I'd tested her by asking if she'd ever heard of Pete Best and she gave me a blank look. So I did the tourist trail alone, joining endless Americans on walks around cemeteries and music trails, all the time hoping that I didn't bump into anyone who knew me well enough to mock my enjoyment of the naffer things in life.

I'd never seen anything as brilliantly batshit-crazy as the Williamson Tunnels. Even after years of archaeological excavation—including digging out an inordinate amount of toilet waste, the Victorian working class not being ones to find unexpected holes in the ground without putting them to good use—no one seemed to know just how far the tunnels extended. Each new dig uncovered more arches, some so small as to clearly be either purely ornamental, or perhaps a practice piece from a young apprentice who was just starting out. Others were gargantuan, cathedral-like spaces over rough, unfinished ground. There were endless anecdotes about Williamson giving his employees seemingly pointless tasks—moving rubble in wheelbarrows from one place to another and back again, was a popular one—for no reason anyone has ever been able to explain. I'd loved the whole, ridiculously untamed insanity of it all and for weeks afterwards had found myself wondering what else might be down there. Never in my wildest dreams could I have imagined my next trip down the tunnels would be as a member of the literal underworld. I gaped at the Mole Man, who grinned back. "Impressive, isn't it?" he said, rather unnecessarily.

"How far have I walked?" I asked. "It's miles to Edge Hill from Flora's."

"Aah well," said Joe, "we had to extend in order to stay hidden, didn't we? We're not as far away as you might think. Of course," he continued, "some people do know we're down here. We wouldn't be able to manage otherwise. I had a word with the manager when the excavations started all those years back and he makes sure that the archaeologists are kept away from this end. Wouldn't do to let the nobs at City Hall know that we're here right underneath their well-fed backsides." Rat Boy snickered unpleasantly. "She's not going to tell anyone, Benjamin," Joe assured him. Rat Boy seemed unconvinced. He sidled closer, his head tilted to one side as he looked at me with beady, coal-black eyes.

I glared back. "It's his bloody fault that I'm down here in the first place," I said to Joe. "If he hadn't barged me off the bloody fire escape, I wouldn't even know you existed."

"Oh, you'd have found us eventually, Lilith," said Joe. "We always knew you'd find us." He gave me a quizzical look, as if he was considering something. "But maybe Benjamin's right. It's perhaps a little too risky to allow you back outside. We really can't be letting the surface people know we're here."

"And who would believe her?" The voice came from behind me. I whipped round to find Maria Silverton standing at the entrance to the Harrington Street tunnel. "She'd be locked up quick smart and then where would you be, Joseph Williamson?" Joe had the decency to look faintly embarrassed. Maria walked towards us and Rat Boy couldn't get away fast enough. He scuttled up the wall and out through the little hole in the roof. Maria smiled thinly. "I'm glad to see that someone realises their limits," she nodded at his retreating feet.

"Why do you have to interfere so, Maria?" Joe looked put out, but not remotely chastised. "We need some fresh blood down here and you know it."

She glared at him. "Not by force," she said. "You know what happens to people who try to force others into things they don't want to do. Anyway," she turned to look at a dark corner of the tunnel that I hadn't noticed before, "what about that odd girl that needed somewhere to stay? What happened to her?"

Joe pulled a face. "She's still here," he said. "Won't let anyone near her," he must have seen Maria's expression, because he went on, "just to give her some food!" His voice was indignant. "For all your low opinion of me, Maria Silverton, I treat everyone who comes down here as a welcome guest. And mostly they choose to stay, so it isn't usually an issue." He sighed. "But this girl is the strangest thing I've ever seen, and I've seen a lot in my days." Maria moved towards the corner and Joe put a hand up to stop her. "She might be quiet now," he said, "but there'll be hysterics the minute you get closer to her. You mark my words."

Maria gave a little shake of her head and turned to me. "Come with me, Lilith," she said. "You're new as well, she might just listen to you." I doubted that very much, but followed Maria across the stony floor to where an iron gate was set into a crevice in the sandstone wall. Behind the gate was a small cave that had presumably started out as yet another tunnel, but which petered out into raw bedrock a few feet in. A low hissing noise made me look down to where a grubby bundle of rags lay on the floor. The rags skittered backwards against the side wall, a pale face emerging from them and glaring at us with the palest blue eyes I had ever seen. Maria stepped towards the bars and the creature recoiled, twisting its face away. I realised it had nowhere to hide from our unwanted gaze, and felt a pang of empathy.

"Where does she sleep?" I asked Joe, who had joined us but stood a few paces back. The creature seemed to make him nervous.

"She's been in there since Seamus found her," Joe tipped his head back to indicate Rat Boy #1. "A couple of days or nights now, maybe? I don't generally live by human time anymore." That would explain the stench.

"You say 'she,'" I said to Joe. "What makes you think it's a girl?"

Joe shrugged. "She seems…fragile, in some way? No need to look at me like that," he said to Maria, who was frowning at him, "I know that some of you women are as tough as old boots. Tougher than me, I reckon." He grinned, and Maria twisted a half-smile in acknowledgement. "I don't know, Lilith," he said, turning back to me, "there's just something, well…*feminine* about her." I peered in at the creature curled up in a ball with her back to us. She reminded me a bit of Izzy, back when we were kids and she'd failed to get her own way at something.

"Does she have a name?"

Joe looked embarrassed. "No, we just call her the girl," he admitted. Maria rolled her eyes.

"Then I'm naming her now," I said, surprising myself. I stepped forward and crouched next to the bars so that I was on the same level as the pitiful creature in its stone cell. "Hi Daisy," I said. I had no idea where the name had come from. It just seemed to suit her. I was pretty sure I'd never met a human called Daisy in my life. And this creature definitely wasn't a delicate little flower, but it would do. To my surprise, Daisy turned her head slightly, one big blue eye gazing balefully at me from her little huddle. "Where did Seamus find her?" I asked Joe. He turned to the boy and beckoned him over. Seamus slunk his way across to us, clearly not wanting to be questioned.

Joe put a hand on Seamus's shoulder and spoke quietly but firmly. "Please can you answer Miss Lilith's questions, Seamus?" he said.

The boy thought about this for a moment, then took a deep breath. "Shewasbythecathedral," he said, all in one breath. "Inthepleasuregardens." His voice had an Irish lilt, which didn't surprise me, with a breathy and very young tone to it, which did.

Joe turned back to me. "Seamus was worried that a breather might find her, so he brought her here for everyone's safety."

"A breather?" I asked.

"Surface dwellers," he replied. "Those who still breathe."

I narrowed my eyes at him. "You're breathing," I pointed out. "And I've been dead for days now, but I can tell you now that my lungs are still working." The smell from Daisy's cell was strong enough to make my eyes water at such close quarters.

"But neither of us actually *needs* to breathe," Joe said in a reasonable tone. "It's just our habit." He turned back to Daisy. She was still on the floor, but watching us carefully now. "I think she likes you, Lilith," he said.

I looked at the strange, frail girl curled up in a heap, and wondered where on earth she could have come from. "You don't think she's a…breather, then?" I asked.

"No, she's one of us," said Maria. "But not like anything I've ever known."

I crouched down and put the back of my hand up against the bars noticing Joe's worried expression as I did so. "I'm super-fucking-human, Joe Williamson," he winced at my language, "and I'm only just getting used to it. So you'll have to excuse me taking some risks for anyone who might be in the same position as me." I'd noticed Daisy edging closer as I was speaking and did my best not to shriek when she suddenly leant forward and pressed her face against the bars. To my horror, she shot out a long, pale tongue and licked my hand. Gritting my teeth, I held still whilst she sniffed my hand up and down and then gave it another experimental lick. Her tongue felt rough, like when Grimm occasionally decided to include me in his cleaning routine. She made a sudden lurch forward, but I was too fast for her. "Oh no you don't," I said sternly. She shrank back, but only by a couple of feet. "No biting. Okay?" I was sure she understood the intent behind my words,

136

even if she didn't know the exact meaning. "No. Bite." I grinned at Daisy as I wagged a finger at her. She tilted her head before raising a hand to look at her own outstretched fingers. Her hands were long and thin, even more so than the Rat Boys. Her fingers were almost alien-like. I realised with a jolt that they were webbed, a thin membrane stretching between them almost up to the first joint. I wondered if her feet were the same, but she had them tucked up tightly, out of sight underneath her. "She's cold and hungry," I said to Joe.

He shrugged. "We've tried her on pretty much every food you could think of, both human and not." I tried not to think about what 'not' might entail. "She throws it back at us, every time. When we tried to give her a blanket, she ate it. And then vomited it back up." Joe sighed. "Made a right old mess, so it did."

"Well, something needs to be done," said Maria, "but not right now. Let's get you back home, Lilith." She put a hand on my shoulder. I got to my feet slowly, still watching Daisy, who gazed back at me with those clear blue eyes. "Maybe you can talk to Daisy another time," she said, "and see if you can get any sense out of her. You're the only one she hasn't tried to eat."

* * *

After saying our goodbyes to Joe, Maria and I headed back into the Harrington Street tunnel. Joe stood watching us until we finally turned the bend and I felt safe enough to speak. "Joe's always been down there, then?" I asked. "Since the beginning of the tunnels?"

"Since the end, more like," said Maria with a chuckle. "Although they'll never end, I don't think. Not whilst Joe's around."

"I thought he died a couple of centuries back?" I couldn't remember the details that the enthusiastic tour guide had been so full of, but was pretty sure Joseph Williamson had been an early Victorian.

"I think Joe became so connected to his project that he simply couldn't leave," said Maria. I could see the faint light from where the tunnel hatch opened into the carpark. As we got to the ladder I'd seen on my walk down, she stopped. "Well, this is me," she said, swinging herself up onto the first rung. "This city's more connected than people realise, Lilith," she said in response to my confused look, and put a hand up to push the hatch above her head. It popped open easily, and Maria grinned. "Hydraulics," she said. "It's the future." She pulled herself up lightly until she was sitting on the edge of the hatch entrance. Above her I could see a stone roof of what looked like a crypt, with blue sky just visible through crumbling gaps in the stone. Surely not St Luke's? Maria looked down at me and her expression turned serious. "You will be fine, Lilith," she said. "It's strange and unexpected and probably all seems very unnatural to you right now. But you'll soon come to understand that maybe we're the most natural of them all." With that, Maria Silverton bounced up into the crypt and the door closed above my head with a neat *thunk*. There was the slightest scrape of a bolt being pulled across, then silence. And darkness.

I ran the last stretch of the tunnel, towards the daylight that filtered in through the Harrington Street entrance. Alone in the silent darkness, I felt the true power of my undead body for the first time. It felt as though there was no limit to how fast or how far or how high I could go. Everyone's had a dream about flying, right? That feeling of freedom you get as your unconscious self coasts across the sky on unknown wings, looking down on a world of scurrying ants and mundane problems that weren't even problems at all, if you only flew high enough. I was so carried away with the excitement of my own strength that I nearly crashed straight into the dead end of the tunnel and had to dig my heels in, sending showers of grit and sand everywhere. Leaning my hands against the warm wall, I wondered again why it wasn't cold and damp, as you'd normally expect. Turning full circle to inspect the tunnel more closely, I realised that there was another hatch in the wall. This one was much smaller than the access points in the roof. Crouching down to peer more closely, I saw it was actually a small metal door, complete with a tiny keyhole. *Curiouser and curiouser*, I thought to myself. My investigations were suddenly interrupted by a loud voice from above my head.

"Are you going to come out of there, or do I have to come in and fetch you?" I stood up so quickly that my head spun briefly and I put out a hand to steady myself. I could feel a faint thrumming from behind the wall. But before I could ponder it any further, Izzy's head dropped through the hatch, making me shriek. "Fucking hell Lil," she said, "you're a denizen of the undead realms and you're down there squealing like a baby? Poor show, mate." 'Mate' was not a word I'd ever heard Izzy use before. I looked up at her and realised that she looked really worried, her face all scrunched up as if she might cry.

"Sorry," I said and pulled myself up onto the access ladder, "I clearly need more practice at this undead lark." I bounced off the top rung and landed neatly on the scruffy rubble of the carpark. To my surprise, it was still daylight. I checked my watch. "I've only been gone forty minutes?"

Izzy nodded. "I sat here and waited," she said. "I figured that if I heard unearthly noises coming from the tunnel, I might be able to help." She saw my expression and coloured. "Well, I could have called your landlords. Or something." She clambered to her feet and looked down into the hole. "Did you find anything?"

Oh, just an entire subterranean world complete with mole-men and rat-boys, I thought. "Put the kettle on and I'll tell you the tale of my adventures underground."

* * *

"So you're telling me the tunnels might go on further than anyone realises?" Izzy was sitting on my kitchen counter-top, her legs swinging idly and kicking the cupboard doors with a quietly thumping repetition that was going to send me insane if she carried on for much longer.

"Oh, I think some people must know—PLEASE WILL YOU STOP KICKING THE CUPBOARDS!! Thank you."

Izzy sat frozen for a second before rallying admirably. "There is no need to use that tone on me, Lilith O'Reilly," she said. "I have a couple of things to say, okay?" I raised an eyebrow, but waited silently for her to continue. Izzy ticked her list off her fingers as she spoke. "One," she said sternly, "no using the voice of doom on me. It makes my ribs rattle. And I'm not deaf, so there is absolutely no need for it." Grimm was curled up in my lap and hadn't bothered moving, not even when I'd done The Voice. Cats clearly weren't as sensitive to paranormal goings-on as people always assumed they were. Or Grimm really was just thick as mince. The odds were pretty much even, I reckoned. "And two," Izzy paused for dramatic effect, "Sean was in the cafe earlier, asking after you. I think you've got an admirer." She grinned at my obvious discomfort. "Oh come on, Lil," she said, "you might be dead, but you're not buried yet! Why not have some fun?"

I sipped my espresso thoughtfully. Whether alive or dead, I couldn't manage without coffee. "You don't get it, Iz," I said. "It isn't as simple as just cracking on and enjoying my afterlife. What if I accidentally kill him?"

Izzy frowned thoughtfully. "Have you tried sitting somewhere busy for a while and just practising looking natural whilst not breathing? Isn't that more or less how the others learn to do it—by being around other people as much as possible?" Her eyes lit up. "That drunk you met on your way home after your attempted murder session down at the waterfront," she said. "You said you'd breathed him in? But he just fell asleep, didn't he?" I nodded. "So maybe," she said slowly, "what you need is to just get used to, I don't know, hanging out round the humans. Maybe? Tiny little breath here and there, just to get used to handling it. If you can breathe even just a tiny bit, you'll look less like a zombie when Sean takes you out on a romantic date." She grinned.

"It's supposed to be addictive," I said, hesitantly. But I was already thinking that Ivo had only said that I shouldn't take a human's *entire* soul. And he'd all but admitted that he indulged himself occasionally. "They learn to be very careful."

"So it's like going out on the beer but only having three G&T's, rather than finishing the entire bottle and ending up in the gutter," Izzy said. She looked pleased with her analogy.

"I think so," I said hesitantly. "It hasn't really been explained very well. Mapp and the others are friendly, but vague. And I think I've come as a bit of a shock to the Silvertons."

Izzy looked stern. "That's as maybe," she said, "but they're the experts at this stuff. Surely they're under some kind of otherworldly obligation to look out for you? Give you some training?" She caught my eye and grinned. "Apprenticeship scheme? Earn as you learn! How to be a zombie and other creatures." A delicate snort. "Look, I don't know how this shit works either, on account of how I am still very much alive. Sorry about that." She shrugged. "Sucks to be you."

"For someone who looks so presentable, you are actually a horrible little goblin," I informed her. "Who knows," I went on, "maybe I don't live up to the Silverton's expectations for their zombie horde. Anyway," I said, remembering the more interesting part of the conversation, "what did Sean say to make you think he's interested?"

"Oh, the usual," Izzy said airily. She started swinging her legs again, but saw my expression and stopped. "He hoped you were feeling better. Had I seen you today, are you single, that sort of thing."

"He asked straight out if I was single?"

"Well, sort of," Izzy said, "he actually said, did I know if you were dating anyone and if not, did I think it was worth him asking you out."

I gaped at her. "He did not?!"

She nodded vigorously, a broad grin on her face. "Yup," she said, "dead or alive, you've clearly still got it. Even if what you've got is dead and mouldering."

Mathew Street Meanderings

"Don't be long, okay?" I was standing outside Izzy's apartment building, watching her fumbling in her bag for the door keys. She finally waggled them triumphantly at me.

"See," she said, "I hadn't lost them at all!" She opened the door, just as a lanky boy wearing dungarees and an orange and yellow striped jumper was about to push it from the inside. He almost fell over her and stumbled his way down the steps, before loping off with a wave and a vague, 'Cheers, love,' in her general direction. Izzy sighed. "Standards are slipping."

"Even further?"

She pulled a face at me. "It's cheap," she said as she stepped inside, "and it's central. Who'd keep an eye on you if I didn't live close by?"

"I seem to be having quite the unexpected adventure, even so."

Izzy grinned. "You'll be fine," she said. "I'll be back at yours in an hour or so—just wander round for a bit and get used to things. Try not to scare anyone." We'd agreed that Izzy would stay with me for another night or two, to help me figure things out a bit. If nothing else, she'd promised to practise walking around town with me until I'd managed to regulate my speed. Human steps seemed so slow and lumbering now that it felt comical attempting to slow myself down in order to not stand out in public. Even just the short walk from Flora's to Izzy's place had involved me accidentally terrifying a group of students who'd been huddled behind the giant metal pillar on the corner. I'd decided on the spur of the moment to see whether I could climb it. Despite its smooth sides, it was the easiest thing in the world to scramble upwards like an oversized monkey. I'd then performed a

142

particularly spectacular dismount, swinging round and down whilst holding on with a single hand. Which is how I very nearly landed feet-first in the face of the teenage girl who was trying to light a suspiciously herbal-scented roll-up on the opposite side. There was a lot of shrieking and even more apologising as I landed on the ground and tried to make sure she was okay, whilst her friends gathered round, shouting at me. Izzy had intervened, informing them she was really sorry, but I had 'issues' and she had been taking me out for some air. She promised she would absolutely learn from her mistakes and ensure she had back up next time. We'd skulked the rest of our journey in a sedate manner, with the girls' sympathetic sighs and mutterings still audible behind us.

*** ***

I watched Izzy go inside and shut the door, before turning and heading through Rainford Square to Mathew Street. We'd planned this carefully. The idea was to give me a brief period on my own in a busy street, in order to see if I was capable of being around humans without getting into trouble. I'd put on the sunglasses that Izzy insisted would help—*you'll feel more inconspicuous, and no one needs to see those creepy eyes*—and started walking slowly past the endless theme bars that fill both sides of the street. There was a large group of tourists standing outside the Cavern Club—the fake replacement, just down the street from the site of the destroyed original. I leaned against a wall near them and pretended to stare at my phone. A notification of a missed call from my parents' number gave me a jolt. We only ever spoke once or twice a week, if that. Both sides worked on the principle that if something exciting or terrible happened, the other would be sure to find out soon enough. But they were definitely overdue a call. *Cope with this first and worry about what to say to mum and dad later*, said the chicken-shit voice in my head. Sort the freakish superhuman shit out first, deal with the 'rents later. Easy.

Putting my phone back in my pocket, I leaned back against the wall and hoped it just looked as though I was enjoying the ambience. I tried to zone out from my surroundings and allowed myself to take a slow, very shallow breath. It would be nice if I could avoid any more accidental manslaughter. As my mind cleared, I began to pick out individual scents on the cool evening breeze. Cheap aftershave and dried sweat from the man nearest to me, who clearly needed to up his hygiene routine. A generically popular, mid-price perfume on the older woman next to him, alongside a hint of nerves. I had no idea how I was suddenly able to smell emotions. Maybe it was chemicals sweating out of anxious human pores? And anxiety was the strongest scent of all, which came as a bit of a surprise. If I'd had to guess the most prevalent emotion amongst an average range of humans out drinking on a Saturday night, I'd have probably gone for desire. I opened my eyes to look at the people around me. Most of them would pass as being reasonably confident to the general public, yet every single one carried a mixture of sweat and underlying fear. The man nearest to me lacked confidence around women, I thought, and hadn't bothered washing properly because he'd long learned to assume that he wouldn't have any luck. Now it was on the cards, he had no idea what to do about it. The older woman—actually only in her forties at the most, I realised—really liked him, but wasn't sure whether he'd realised. I'd read all the articles about how humans only used a fraction of their brains and filtered most stuff out in order to avoid being overwhelmed, and now I knew why. This was *exhausting*. The woman who appeared to be in overall charge of the group was tall and neatly put together, with dark hair that streaked grey at the temples. Probably a deputy school head, or office HR manager. She was telling the doorman that they wanted to reserve a table for the evening and he was trying to explain that they were welcome to find their own table and take their chances with holding onto it. Deputy Head was clearly used to more upmarket venues, and her polite tone was getting sharper by the second. I strongly suspected that the entire group would be asked to move on pretty soon. A powerful scent of honey and ginger blew gently over me, its undertones made up of fresh sweat and testosterone. *Actual* testosterone—it was that clear. It was coming from the doorman, who was standing with his back to me. I edged slightly closer and risked another breath. Suddenly, everything felt *brighter*. Neon lights, and lamps in the windows of rowdy bars, and the flashing quick lights of mobile phones as people ambled past. God, he tasted good. I took another breath before stepping back again. The doorman unexpectedly leaned back against the corner of the doorway and waved the entire group inside with no further argument. Another security guard came out and must have noticed something was up, because she put a hand on his shoulder. He visibly shook himself and insisted he was fine, before greeting more customers on slightly wobbly feet. Okay, so I really was a risk to humans. I looked at my watch. Izzy would be waiting for me back at Harrington Street by now. I waited for a large group of people to walk past and tucked myself in behind them. And...*breathe*...oh god, this was so much easier. I could still make out individual scents, but there were enough of them that they mingled. *Human cocktail*, I thought to myself and grinned. I took the deepest breath I could manage and peeled off from the group, heading back past Izzy's and home to Flora's with a spring in my step.

"Addictive, isn't it?" said Mapp, dropping in beside me as I turned onto Harrington Street. I hid my surprise and kept walking, as if we did this sort of thing all the time.

"I don't know what you mean," I lied. Mapp sighed and stopped walking. I carried on, but he put his hand out and caught me by the elbow. He was stronger than I'd expected, and I had to spin round on my feet in order to not lose my balance. I glared at him and he sighed deeply in return. He was wearing a long crimson robe over matching wide-leg trousers and would have resembled a prince straight out of Arabian Nights, had he not also been sporting a faded black t-shirt underneath the open robe. It had 'Damned But Not Forgotten' scrawled across the chest in neon pink lettering.

"I mean exactly what I said," he replied, his voice more serious than usual. "It's addictive, it ruins people, and it's...well," he laughed sadly, "it's as easy as breathing." The faint silver rings in his eyes seemed brighter in the shadows of Harrington Street. For a second, I wondered just how old Gaultier Mapp really was.

"No one's specifically told me I can't," I said defensively, my arms folded across my chest.

"And that's interesting in itself," replied Mapp, "isn't it?" A group of women came giggling around the corner and Mapp guided me gently to the ornate chairs tucked away in the bend of the street, so that they wouldn't have to walk close by us. One woman gave us a curious look as she tottered past, staggering slightly on too-high heels.

"How do you mean?" I asked.

Mapp turned to face me, an unreadable expression on his face. "You're less of a threat if you're controllable," he said, "and the easiest way to make that happen is to have you willingly give up your free will in favour of a higher power. Addiction does that to you."

"A higher power?" I asked, hoping fervently that I hadn't accidentally found myself in an undead religious cult.

"Not God, Lilith," Mapp said. He laughed humourlessly. "Gods are easy," he continued, "whichever one of them you pin your hopes on. Addiction is more powerful than any god. It coaxes you in with promises of blissful eternity and then it spits you out when it's used you up. Did you ever take drugs when you were alive?"

"No!" I was shocked by the question. Did I *look* the type? But even as I thought it, I remembered Kevin Jonson. We'd been at school together and everyone expected great things of him. Even Kevin expected great things of Kevin. He went to Oxford—practically unheard of amongst my school cohort—and disappeared, presumably off flying high on the wings of academia. Four years ago, Izzy heard via her dad that Kevin had died of an overdose. He hadn't crashed in the way that the soap operas always portrayed it, though. No dirty needles and grubby squats for Kevin. He had indeed flourished at university, got a First in Economics and taken a high-flying job in the City. Pressurised jobs often spawn unhealthy coping habits, and Kevin was a perfect, terrible example. It was discovered after he'd died that he'd developed an expensive cocaine habit during his first years in London. It hadn't concerned anyone at the time, mostly because he was earning enough to pay for it. But then the girl he'd expected to marry decided that she didn't fancy being shackled to someone who was going to spend all their spare cash on little bags of white powder. She walked out a month before the wedding and, in a fit of 'fuck you' to the world, Kevin treated himself to one last weekend of hedonism. After that, he decided, he'd cut out the drugs entirely. The plan, according to a colleague he'd confided in, was to do so well in life that everyone would envy him and the ex would regret the day she walked out. But rather than turning over a new leaf, Kevin came out of that weekend with a newly discovered love of heroin. He had a plan, though. He'd only do it at weekends, so he could earn the money he needed for it during the week. The plan lasted less than six months before he was found dead in his office of a heart attack. He might have exited life with his reputation intact, had there not been a small box in his desk drawer which turned out to contain several hundred pound's worth of crack cocaine.

"No," I said again, less defensively this time. "Plenty of my friends did." I remembered Izzy's thankfully brief love affair with speed. She got unhealthily skinny and spent most of her time being way too reckless in pretty much every aspect of her life, before realising that she was just trying to make life more interesting. That was when she move up to Liverpool. "But I saw enough bad endings that it put me off for life."

"And yet here you are," Mapp smiled gently, "helping yourself to other people's energy. Like a succubus of old, without so much as a by your leave."

"I'd have to be having sex with them to be a succubus," I retorted indignantly. And I certainly wasn't doing any of that. *More's the pity.*

"Same difference when you think about it," said Mapp. "You're taking something *intimate* from them, Lilith," he frowned. "And they don't get to consent."

Suddenly I felt a bit, well, grubby. Predatory, like all the creepy blokes in bars that I'd shouted at over the years for making assumptions about how far they were allowed into my personal space. "So you're telling me you all behave yourselves around humans?" I asked. "And never, ever take without asking?"

"I don't do it, no," he said. "Never. So I don't need to ask."

I noted the personal response. "The others do?" I asked, and Mapp nodded in the gloom. I thought a bit. "What happens if I choose to?" He turned and frowned slightly. "I might decide that I don't care about your rules, Mapp. I woke up dead and no one bothered to give me the guided tour of the afterlife, so what's to stop me making my own mind up?"

He smiled at me, but it didn't reach his eyes. "They'll kill you," he said simply, "the same as they've killed all the others who've broken the unwritten rules. We can't afford to be found out, Lilith. It doesn't matter how much we all like you," well at least I was popular, "if you go round attacking humans, then you will have to disappear very quickly. Before word spreads."

"To who?" Mapp looked confused, so I clarified. "To whom will word spread? And," the million dollar question, "who will make me disappear?"

"The Silvertons will arrange an…accident," he said quietly. "They're in charge of keeping the peace. The rulers of this kingdom, if you like." I didn't like, but kept my mouth shut for now. "They'd have no option but to do it before word spread to the other kingdoms."

"Kingdoms?" I asked, frowning. "You mean different countries?"

"That as well," said Mapp. "But this country has its own kingdoms. Human politics and geography don't count for much when your life spans endless centuries, Lilith."

"Lili," I reminded him. "Lilith makes me feel like I'm being told off at school."

A small smile lighting up his grave face. "Of course," he said. "Humans will always fight for their territory, Lili, whether they're dead or alive. In fact, it's perhaps more needful *after* death, because we're no longer bound by laws that the populace can witness. Some still covet power. And the simplest way to achieve it is to take control over bigger and bigger areas of whichever country you happen to be in." He gazed down the street, in the direction of the Liver Building. "The Silvertons control this area. Up as far as Lancaster and Morecambe, and down as far as mid-Wales."

"How far east and west?" Mapp looked confused. "You've given me the north and south limits of the Silvertons'…territory," I said, "but how wide is it?"

His face cleared. "Aah well," he said, "all of it, to the west."

"All of Wales?" I hadn't expected the evening to turn into a lesson in political geography. But then I hadn't expected to wake up dead on a normal Monday morning in April, either. I looked at Mapp in astonishment.

He smiled again. "Yes," he replied, "all of it across to the coast. Eadric Silverton has a long connection to the area. And he holds onto it very tightly indeed." I thought I saw a brief clenching of the muscles in Mapp's jaw, but said nothing. "The southern boundary runs from just below Aberystwyth, across the top of Herefordshire and along to what's now Birmingham. It curls up around the city, taking in the old Potteries. Then the whole of Manchester and back up and over to the west coast."

"That's a lot of country," I said, which was an understatement.

"Eadric's been around for a long time," replied Mapp simply. "But his is far from being the biggest territory. That honour goes to Alba, north of the human border." Scotland, then. Someone I'd never met three days ago was sitting here and telling me all about how the 'United' Kingdom was actually still a mishmash of ancient territories with no mind for legal borders and I was just feeling pleased with myself because I knew where Alba was. I wasn't kidding when I told people that my history degree was likely the most expensive piece of useless paper I would ever own. Okay, so I could talk for hours about the socio-cultural impact of the Industrial Revolution, but it wasn't helping me figure out the meaning of land borders I hadn't even known existed. "But if you want the biggest territory by immortal population," Mapp continued, pulling me back to the conversation, "that would, of course, be Middlesex."

I knew that one. "London?"

"And its environs," nodded Mapp, looking irritatingly surprised that I understood. "The northern boundary is from above Coventry and across to Lowestoft. The western line is drawn from the east of Birmingham down in a near-enough straight line to the coast between Bournemouth and Southampton. She controls the Isle of Wight, if that helps you picture it." It didn't, but something else had perked my ears up.

"You said 'she'?" I asked. "London is run by a woman?"

Mapp grinned. "Oh, it certainly is, Lili," he replied, "and I think you would like her very much. She was still young when she took power, and it came as a shock to many."

"Young in which way?"

Mapp looked approvingly at me. "I think you're beginning to pick this up, Lilith O'Reilly." He said, ignoring my scowl. I never did like being patronised. "Elizabeth hadn't long joined us when the coup happened—or rather, didn't. The old king had long given up caring enough to keep an eye on what was happening. He was taken by surprise when his most loyal advisor lopped his regal head off one night without so much as a by your leave. Although having one's head chopped off would take anyone by surprise, regardless of the circumstance. Do you not think?" He winked at me in a most disconcerting fashion. "Unfortunately for the usurper, Elizabeth had already grown fond of the king and took matters into her own hands. Or perhaps I should say, her bed. In the way of so many wild women before her, she invited the culprit to her chambers and dealt the fatal blow just as he reached that blissful state that so many chase."

I was pretty sure that Mapp was just being filthy now, but I wasn't about to ask questions and risk outing myself as naïve. "You are not seriously telling me," I said, diverting the conversation, "that London has—had—more than one Queen Elizabeth?"

"Aah, she'd slap you silly if you called her by her title," grinned Mapp. "It *is* indeed her title, but she's called Lizzie by anyone who values their head."

"And how long has...*Lizzie*," I struggled, "been Queen of all undead London?"

"Not much over a century and a half," Mapp replied. "But believe me, she's made the most of her time."

"Clearly," I said drily.

He laughed. "She's a good woman," he said. "But," his voice grew serious again, "Ivo keeps trying to draw her into a battle for territory and she doesn't want any of it. He'll go to Eadric next. And I suspect Maria will agree to his requests."

My head was spinning at the sheer amount of unexpected information Mapp had managed to shoehorn into that one sentence. "Ivo?" I frowned, "He's another of the—what, kings?" Mapp nodded. "What does he want?" I thought of how Ivo had been so kind, helping to cover my tracks when I accidentally killed my tracker and chatting to me in the sunshine outside St Luke's. *Or*, said a rational voice at the back of my mind, *he helped you commit murder and dispose of the corpse in order to have something to hold over you. And he wasn't exactly clear about the risks of addiction.* Perhaps Ivo didn't have my best interests at heart after all. "And," I carried on before Mapp could reply, "why would Maria be agreeing to requests when it's Eadric who's in charge?"

Mapp sighed. "Eadric's been on this earth a very long time, Lili," he said quietly, "and everyone gets tired, eventually. *Most* get tired," he corrected himself. "Ivo's been around a fraction longer, yet shows no intention of slowing down. But the two of them go back a long way. And there's a loyalty between them that Elizabeth doesn't share. There is a small territory," he continued, "that lies between Ivo and Elizabeth's lands. It has borders with all three—Ivo, Elizabeth and Eadric—and Ivo has long believed it rightly belongs to him. He doesn't like there being any form of no-man's-land, right up next to his, because it might be used as a hiding place for those who would rise against him. Historically, the area has London's protection, but Elizabeth doesn't care enough about Ivo's feelings to help him out. He's nursing a growing grievance and is here to persuade the Silvertons that it's time he took what's his. And I think," he eyed me speculatively, "he has his eye on you as a bargaining chip."

I didn't like the sound of that one tiny bit. "Why am I flavour of the month?" I asked. "There must have been endless new members of this exclusively weird club of yours over the years," I pointed out. "Why not one of them?"

Mapp raised an elegant eyebrow. "That's where you're wrong, Lili," he said. "You are a rarity indeed. Not only have you sprung into existence for no obvious reason, when you should by rights have died in that fall, you're also carrying a power that we can all sense. It's fascinating."

"Gee, thanks," I scowled. "I've always wanted to be an exhibit in an undead curiosity shop."

Mapp laughed at that. "That was rather tactless of me," he allowed, "but the principle stands. You have power, and there's no getting away with it. The Silvertons might deal with it by allowing you to develop a drug habit in the hope of making you distracted and pliable, but Ivo will be after the same." He gazed at me with sharp eyes that I felt boring down to my very soul. If I even had one anymore. "I think he'll be wanting to take you away with him," he continued, ignoring my wide-eyed reaction, "so it suits him for you to get into trouble. He'll step in to save you from yourself, so to speak. He'll be hoping that the Silvertons will allow you to go simply because it's their easiest option. I believe, however," a calculating look, "that Maria might have something to say about that. I suspect she harbours feelings for Ivo Laithlind. So I very much doubt she would be impressed by the idea of him taking off into the Yorkshire sunset with the strongest woman this country's seen in centuries." Somehow, I got the impression that when Mapp said 'this country', he didn't mean England. Mapp's country was older and deeper—on all levels—than any modern political creation.

"You said Elizabeth was the strongest woman," I pointed out.

"Yes," he agreed. "*Was.*" We sat in silence for a while, both lost in thought. Just as I was veering off into a fantasy about being Queen of the Underworld and wondering what the costumes might be like, Mapp broke the silence.

"I need to visit Eadric again," he said, "and I'd like you to come with me."

"Me?" I said, with genuine horror in my voice. Mapp nodded. "Do I have to?" I wailed, sounding for all the world like a small child who didn't want to go visit a particularly scary great-aunt. "And why do you have to talk to him? Has your overlord summoned you?"

He didn't miss my sarcasm. "Eadric would never dare summon me," Mapp replied. "I'm one of his oldest friends. And one of his few staunch allies."

Mapp tried to insist on walking me back to Flora's, but I pointed out that it was less than a hundred yards down the street and we could already see it from where we were standing. After wishing me what seemed to be a reluctant goodnight, he strolled off down Button Street. As soon as I was sure that he'd disappeared around the corner, I walked towards the man who was waiting for me at the junction between Harrington Street and the main road.

"Hey," said Sean with a smile, pushing himself up away from the wall. He had his hands in his pockets and shuffled on the spot, a sheepish look on his face. "Was it that obvious I was waiting for you?"

"It was the constant staring that gave you away."

"Bloody hell, you've got good eyesight," said Sean, gazing down the street to the distant dots of the chairs that Mapp and I had been sitting on.

"Notorious for it," I smiled. Sean grinned back at me, looking for all the world like an eager teenager. "Anyway," I said, deciding to put him out of his misery, "what can I do for you, Mister Hannerty?"

He blushed. "I was, errr, wondering…" He coughed and seemed genuinely lost for words.

"Do you fancy doing something together tomorrow?" I blurted it out, and we both stood in shocked silence for a long few seconds. "I mean," *oh shit oh shit what if Izzy had got it all wrong and he didn't actually fancy me and I'd just made an almighty fool of myself fucking hell well done Lil,* "that's if you'd like to?"

"I'd love that," said Sean, relief flooding his face. "I really would."

"I've got to open Flora's first thing, but I could be free by lunchtime."

"Daytime date?" grinned Sean. "Is that your usual safety net—date in the daytime, so you can make excuses and leave quickly if it all goes to pot?"

"If it's in the daytime, then I'm less likely to get overexcited and just leap on you," I replied, and immediately wondered what the hell had happened to the last of my verbal filters. "Not that I do that sort of thing. Obviously."

"Obviously," said Sean, with a grin. "I don't mind when we meet up, so long as we do." I blushed again. He looked like an overexcited kid. It was the cutest thing I'd seen in a very long time. "I'll come to Flora's at eleven in the morning—if you're busy, I'll just have a coffee and wait."

"That would be lovely," I said, and I meant it. There was another awkward moment whilst we stood staring at each other, neither knowing quite what to do.

"Anyway," Sean finally broke the silence, "I'll let you get your beauty sleep. Not that you need it." Another goofy smile. "Tomorrow, then." He gave me a brief nod and walked away. He didn't look back. I gazed after him for longer than I'd have admitted to anyone, but his gaze stayed fixed firmly ahead. Finally, I turned and headed back towards Flora's, allowing myself to bounce giddily up onto the wall and tightrope along the top. I took the stairs four at a time and bounced in through the door of my flat in the best mood I'd had since I'd died.

* * *

"Do you think he can feel that?" asked Izzy, nodding towards where Kitty was sitting in the armchair, with Grimm curled up in her lap. Izzy and I were at either end of the sofa, watching my ghostly aunt baby-talking at the cat whilst enthusiastically swooping her hands through him. *Who's a beeyootiful pussycat then?*—a hand drifted through his head—*ooh esss he is! Grimmy is!*—a thorough rub in the general direction of what I assumed she thought was his back, but was actually somewhere near his lower intestines. The feline in question gazed up at her with a look of adoration I hadn't seen on a living creature since my mum once spotted Robbie Williams wandering round Selfridges in Birmingham. *Mum and Dad.* Shit. I was already well overdue a trip back home. I'd put it off the previous month, for no better reason than I just didn't fancy it. Of course, I didn't tell them that. I just gave them the impression that Flora's was too busy for me to take time off. Which was actually true—we'd been too busy for me to leave Izzy to manage alone for ages now—but we didn't open every day of the week. And it was only an hour or so's drive back to my parents' place in Shropshire. I just didn't want to, was the truth of it. I love my parents—they're both funny and sweet and have better taste in music than most people their age. But I'd left Shrewsbury as soon as I could—and now avoided going back—because it meant I didn't have to think about my brother. It didn't matter that Cally been gone over twenty years, he was still everywhere around me when I went 'home'. Every street that we'd walked together. The playground halfway where he'd loved going on the slide, despite it being made of horrible shiny metal that burned your legs when the sun had been on it. The paths that all led down to the river where I'd lost him forever...

We'd been on an adventure that morning, Cally and I. *'S'an advencha, Lil,'* he'd said, with a big grin on his face. We were going to hunt for a particular squirrel in the woods at the bottom of the fields behind our house. The squirrel was called Fred (Cally's choice, for no apparent reason other than 'he looks like a Fred') and we'd been quite successful in our attempts to tame him the previous spring. Fred would come haring across the field to our garden when Cally called him, before hopping up to balance on the fence post whilst we fed him monkey nuts. Cally really loved that squirrel. He drew endless scrawly pictures of it on paper taken from mum's printer. Fred failed to turn up one day and, although our parents did their best to persuade us both that squirrels just moved on occasionally, I'd overheard them discussing the fact that they were pretty sure Fred had been killed by the teenagers who liked to sit in the woods with air rifles, taking pot shots at the local wildlife.

But maybe we could find another squirrel that looked enough like Fred to convince Cally. One squirrel's pretty much the same as the next, I told myself as we headed off across the field to the woods, hoping my brother might have forgotten about Fred's distinctive pale ears. There was a little brook on the far boundary between the field and the woods, a shallow but fast stream of water that dropped down into the river a few hundred yards further on. I jumped the stream and held out my hands for Cally to balance as he picked his way across the stones that we'd long ago placed in the stream to act as stepping stones. I shushed him as we stepped into the woods and we walked quietly, both of us watching carefully for movement in the trees.

It didn't take long. "Lili, Lili!" my brother squealed. "Look! It's Fred!" With the world-weariness that only comes from being a practical ten-year-old tasked with looking after a naïve younger sibling, I pretended to see the squirrel. But Fred really *was* there. He was peering down at us from his perch on a high branch, clearly hoping that we'd at least remembered to bring the monkey nuts. "Fred!" Cally called, holding a nut up in the air. I wrapped my arms round his waist and held him up closer to the branch. He was a solid little boy and my arms almost immediately began to complain. "On the tree!" demanded Cally. "I sit and wait !"

"Okay," I said, pushing upwards as hard as I could. Cally scrambled for a footing and pulled himself up onto the branch. "Don't move from there," I warned. We were right at the edge of the wood, and the trees marked the line where the ground dropped away sharply to the riverbank below. I knew from a safety talk we'd once had at school that what looked like solid ground at the edge of the water was actually river weed tangled around reeds. And it was just waiting to grab unsuspecting ankles and pull children down into the depths. Miss Thompson, our stern and intimidating headteacher, had actually wiped away a tear as she told us the story of how three siblings had all died together on this very stretch of the river just a few years earlier. The brother had got into trouble and each sister had followed in turn, hoping to save the others. An entire generation of one family, wiped out in minutes. That story had stuck with me and I kept a careful hand on one of Cally's ankles. He was trying to stretch across to where Fred sat at the end of the branch, eyeing us beadily.

"Come on, Fred," pleaded Cally, as the squirrel eyed him warily from the very end of the branch. He leaned forward, and the branch bowed down alarmingly. I gripped Cally's leg even tighter. "Let me reach, Lil," he said and kicked out with his foot. I lost my hold and Cally wriggled further down the branch.

"Don't you dare move, Cal," I said, panicking. The branch was old and gnarled and creaked as he reached even further out over the edge of the bank. Fred lost his nerve and bounced off onto an upper branch, leaving Cally crying out in frustration.

"Fred!" The squirrel was now sitting above him and, before I could do anything about it—not that there was much I could have done from my spot on the ground—Cally twisted around and reached up. The branch gave an ominous creak and broke away from the trunk, depositing Cally on the very edge of a steep section of the riverbank. As I stood watching in mute horror, Cally jumped up and tried shouting for Fred again—which was when he lost his footing and fell backwards into the water.

I can still see the look of silent horror on his face as my little brother toppled over, as if in slow motion. Cally had been having swimming lessons at our local pool, but hadn't got the hang of it yet. As I yelled at him to stay still and float, desperately scrabbling my way down the bank in the hope of finding a branch to hold out to him, he started flailing. The current moved him further away, into the middle of the river. The last I saw of my brother was a tiny white face being swept away from me, endlessly beyond my reach. To this day, I have no real memory of anything between that last glimpse of Cally and the police turning up hours later to take my statement. Dad had apparently seen me out of the living room window, crying and stumbling my way across the field, and had come out to meet me. I'd garbled that Cally was lost in the river and 'it was just a squirrel' and that was all anyone could get out of me for days. Mum had called the emergency services whilst dad and all our neighbours had gone down to the river themselves, hoping Cally had somehow been swept up onto the shingle section that formed a kind of beach half a mile further down. They found nothing, despite Brian from next door stripping to his underwear and getting in the water in the desperate hope that he might find Cally tangled in the weeds.

It had taken three days for Cally's body to be found, just three miles downstream. I'd asked to see him, insisting that he might wake up if he heard my voice. My parents were in no fit state to discuss it, so it was left to my grandmother to explain that Cally had been in the river a long time and none of us were going to be allowed to see him. And he was most definitely not coming back, not ever. She made me a rare cup of cocoa on the stove with full fat milk and never discussed Cally again in my hearing. According to a newspaper report from the time, which I found years later during a bout of morbid curiosity, he was identified by dental records. The coroner's report stated that there was damage 'consistent with a fall and drowning.' No one blamed me for Cally's death. I was only ten—I couldn't be expected to have stopped him going into the river. It wasn't my fault at all. But I knew, deep down, that it was because of me that my brother didn't come home that day. I knew that the reason my parents often shut their bedroom door so that I wouldn't hear their soft crying was because I hadn't been able to keep my little brother safe when I should have.

Nope, better to shut it all down and not think about it. It wasn't as if I could bring him back. I just wished I could visit my parents without feeling sick at the thought of heading back into town along the by-pass and seeing the familiar turnoff. I knew Mum and Dad would drive up to Liverpool if I asked them to. But I definitely didn't want them visiting right now, when I knew just what was lurking in plain sight all over the city. What if my parents got ambushed by a rogue Ratboy? Or worse, Heggie and his worried expression and acrid vulpine smell. That alone would be enough to put anyone off their tourist activities.

"He doesn't seem to mind," I said to Izzy, who was still mesmerised by Kitty and Grimm. "Maybe it helps with his digestion." No, I'd have to go visit Shropshire, or risk my parents turning up anyway. "Can you look after the cafe for a couple of days? I thought maybe Todd might come in to help out." Todd was a friend of Izzy's family. He was very young and eager and had been asking me for a job for at least twelve months.

Izzy turned to look at me. "You're not going off on another killing spree, are you?"

"Thanks for the vote of confidence," I scowled at her. "I was thinking of visiting my parents, is all."

Kitty looked up. "Can I come?" I stared blankly at my deceased aunt. "I could do with a trip," she went on, "and I haven't seen your mum for decades."

"Aren't you, well…stuck?" asked Izzy. "To Flora's, I mean?"

Kitty looked thoughtful. "I think it's Lili I'm tied to," she said slowly. " Not literally," she must have seen my expression, " and not all the time. I didn't come with you down the tunnels, did I? Nor did I wander round with you the other day when you followed that man who'd been standing outside." She must have been watching from the window when I chased after Ivo, I realised. How awful to not be able to control where you went, or with who. The least she deserved was a trip out. And it might be fun to have company—even if it was of the ghostly kind.

"You think you might be able to get in the car with me and just come for a drive?"

Kitty nodded. "Can we give it a go?" she said. She sounded excited.

I sighed. "You have to promise not to frighten my parents," I warned. "No popping up into view or moving the crockery in a spooky fashion, okay?"

Kitty grinned. "A proper girly road trip!"

"Yeah," said Izzy drily, "the zombie and the ghost, out on the wild roads of Shropshire. Can't wait to see that one in the cinema. What?" We'd both turned to look at her. "Just don't get caught speeding," she warned, "'cos I cannot even begin to imagine how *that* would work out."

"I'm still just me," I pointed out, "for now, at least. It'll be years before I don't look as old as I ought to on my driving license."

"Yeah, but what happens if you ever have to do a breath test?" Izzy asked. "Or give a urine sample?"

I hadn't thought of that. "Well, I'll just have to stick to the speed limits, won't I?" Both my best friend and my aunt looked sceptical. "Anyway," I sighed, "I've got a more pressing problem than undead speeding tickets." I pulled a face. "I'm going on a date."

Good Luck With Acting Normal, Kid

Of course, the minute Izzy discovered I'd agreed to go out with Sean, she'd called Todd immediately, on the basis that it could also be his trial run for more regular work in the future. We definitely needed the help—especially now that being a fully fledged member of Liverpool's unofficial Club Dead was taking up a lot of my time. Izzy was so depressingly excited about my love life finally having a glimmer of potential that I'd eventually gone to bed and stared at my ceiling in a huff, whilst she and Kitty sat in the living room and gossiped well into the early hours. So much for all those paranormal novels about the glamorous afterlife. So far I'd mostly found it either stressful or tedious, and often both at once.

It was now daylight again, and I was busily throwing clothes around my bedroom in a growing panic. I'd opened up Flora's first thing, but Izzy had taken over almost immediately and told me to go make myself presentable. Surely there must be *something* in here suitable for a casual date? I needed to look as though I'd tried, without looking as though I'd made too much effort. Whilst also looking hot AF. Not much to ask. I ignored the increasingly loud ringing of alarm bells in the back of my head as I continued my search for the perfect outfit. It would be fine. It was just a *date*, for heaven's sake. Sean might become a new friend, if nothing else. Possibly intimate friends. Who almost certainly tasted absolutely delicious. *Oh god I must not accidentally kill Sean.* Absolutely not.

Eventually, I decided on a jersey dress that I hadn't worn in ages. Knee-length with a tiny floral print, the neck was cut low enough to be date-worthy, but not so low that I'd look like I was cruising for trade. I put it on over leggings and shoved yet another oversized cardigan on top. I couldn't help wondering what Sean might look like under those 'middle-aged lecturer' clothes. Maybe I should just be honest with him. *So anyway Sean, I should probably tell you I'm dead as a doornail—but on the upside, I'm going to have perky tits for the rest of eternity.* Grimm's face was just visible in between layers of blankets where he'd made his daily nest on the bed. Kitty was nowhere to be seen. I threw myself down on the bed beside the cat and tickled him under the chin, ignoring his murderous expression as he batted me off with his paws. Having impermeable skin was a definite advantage for the owner of a bad tempered cat. "Oh pusscat," I said to his impassive face, "why is it so difficult?" Owlish orange eyes blinked slowly at me. "It's not like I asked to be made immortal, is it?" I clambered off the bed and stared into the mirror. I looked like death warmed up. Ha ha. Pulling open the top drawer of the dresser, I rooted round for mascara and lipstick—at least I wouldn't look quite like I'd just been dug up. It would have to do. I tied my hair up out of my face and pulled on my trainers, before heading back downstairs to the cafe.

"Ooh, look at you!" said Izzy as I came in through the door and stashed my bag next to the till.

I turned to face her. "Are you sure it isn't too much?" I asked. "I don't want to look too try-hard, you know?"

Izzy snorted. "Only you could consider putting on some mascara to be trying too hard, Lil," she said with a sigh. "You look lovely. Seriously. No, don't start fiddling with things," I put down the coffee filter I'd been about to dismantle, "you'll only get into a mess. Anyway," she said, as I heard the cafe door opening behind me, "your date's here. Hey Sean," she grinned. I felt as though I must be blushing right up to my hairline again. A quick glance at my reflection in the coffee machine confirmed it. Being physically frozen in time clearly didn't stop blood moving around the body. I guessed that at least explained how fictional vampires never seemed to have a problem getting it on in the bedroom.

"Shall we go?" Sean's voice broke into my meandering thoughts about undead genitalia.

A woman who looked to be in her eighties was sitting alone at the table nearest the counter, watching us with a broad smile on her face. "Lucky girl," she said to me and, to my surprise, gave me a wink. "Have fun for those of us too old to bother any more, aye?"

Izzy wasn't even attempting to hide her sniggers now. I grabbed my bag and turned to leave, but she caught hold of me as I walked past her. "Try not to kill him, babe." I shook my head in disbelief and followed Sean outside.

As we walked out onto Harrington Street, Sean turned and smiled at me. "Hey," I said, small talk having never been my forte.

"Hey you," Sean returned with an easy smile. "Where do you want to go?"

"Your choice," I grinned. "This was your idea, after all."

He thought for a second. "Then we'll head up to the Walker," he said. "It's been a long time since I've been round it properly. And an art gallery is a good choice for a first date, don't you think?" There was a definite twinkle in his eye.

"Absolutely normal," I agreed. "Let's go." It was still sunny, but dark clouds gathering on the horizon threatened a break in the weather. We walked companionably up towards St John's Gardens. The wind was whipping up, and I was glad I'd tied up my hair. Casual was once thing—peering out through a wild curtain was another. I risked a couple of glances sideways at Sean as we walked. He seemed comfortable enough with the situation. It surprised me, given his evident nerves the previous evening.

"Have you always lived locally?" I asked as we walked. His hands were deep in his pockets and he kept his gaze straight ahead as he spoke.

"I was born and brought up here," he said, "but had a few years away when I was married. She was nice enough," he glanced sideways at me and shrugged, "it just didn't work out." When I didn't say anything, he carried on. "I've been back in town nearly three years now."

"Any kids?"

"No, it just never happened." *Phew.* Not that I had anything against kids in theory; I'd just rather not have to deal with them on a personal level. I risked a small breath and could smell Calvin Klein aftershave over the top of the strawberry scent that seemed to follow him everywhere. He must really love that shampoo, I thought. There was also an air of something else. Regret? I turned away and sucked in some fresh air, hoping to clear my head. "How about you?" he asked, turning slightly and giving me a crooked grin. "Any kids or exes that I should know about?"

I snorted. "None of either," I replied. "I mean, I've got exes—I've had my fair share of relationships," *way to go, Lil, real classy*, "ummm, not that any were serious." I wasn't making it any better. "No kids though. I'm thirty-two and never had a single maternal urge, so I doubt it's going to happen now." As we reached William Brown Street, a large group of tourists came towards us, chatting and laughing as they discussed where to go next. Moving aside to let them through, I took a breath without thinking and was suddenly surrounded by a choking whirlwind of adrenalin, sweat, and excitement. Somehow, I managed to turn it into a faked sneezing fit. I really did need to get out of the breathing habit. I followed Sean silently in through the busy atrium of the gallery, past the little gift shop with its tote bags and mugs printed with famous works of art. Despite having visited the Walker endless times since I moved to Liverpool, I'd somehow never done it in company.

Sean led the way, an air of excitement on his face. "Let's start with the best," he declared. "I like the older stuff." We walked around the corner to where a visiting exhibition of Renaissance art had been hung. It was glorious. I'd always liked over the top oil paintings, and the Renaissance gave them in droves. Huge, looming depictions of ancient events took pride of place in the centre of each wall, with smaller frames dotted in-between. We wandered slowly between the pictures, although I was struggling to make myself look at the paintings rather than Sean. Suddenly, he tugged my hand and pulled me towards the corner of the large room. "Look! God, I can't believe this is here," he said as we neared the small rectangular picture that hung inauspiciously between two enormous gilded frames. "Oh," he bent to peer at the information plaque on the wall next to it. "it's a print. Well, it would be, I suppose." His voice was disappointed. Straightening up, he put an arm casually around my shoulders, pulling me to him so that we could gaze at the piece together. I struggled to concentrate on the picture he was so keen to show me, acutely aware of his closeness. The print was small and entirely black and white—some form of etching. "*Melancolia,*" announced Sean, as if I should know what he was talking about. "One of my favourite pictures of all time." I gazed at the little print. There was a lot in it, for such a small piece of art. A woman in a long dress sat hunched in the centre, glaring out at the viewer with an extremely grumpy look on her face and what appeared to be a jumble of random items dotted around her. Sean sighed happily. "Just look at it." I looked. "So many thoughts and ideas and questions, all in one small engraving. No wonder the artist was considered the best of his era. Durer," he said to my unspoken question. "German, late fifteenth, early sixteenth century, almost certainly a genius. *Melancolia* is a puzzle in itself—no one's ever really untangled the true meaning behind it."

"I didn't have you down as an art buff, somehow."

He turned to me. "I'm a crime writer, don't forget," he explained with a grin. "I love a good mystery." Dropping his arm from my shoulders, he took my hand again as if it was the most natural thing in the world. I stared down at our hands mutely. "Come on," he said, "I'll stand here all day if you let me." We wandered happily for another hour, Sean occasionally telling me what he knew about the various artists and paintings. When we eventually emerged from the gallery, the sun was out and the streets were getting busy. "Fancy an ice cream?" Sean grinned. I hesitated for a second. Ice cream practically counted as milk though, right?

"That would be lovely," I replied with a confidence I didn't quite feel. We wandered back down to Williamson Square and Sean joined the queue at the Italian deli on the corner. "I'm going to wait out here," I said hurriedly, "save taking up space." He nodded cheerfully and stepped inside. I watched as he chatted to the woman in the queue ahead of him, debating which flavours they preferred.

"The absolute classic," Sean said as he came towards me, holding out a huge vanilla ice cream with a chocolate flake sticking out of it. "Had to argue for the flake, though." He had a big grin on his face. "Apparently it's not the done thing anymore. Come on," he said, "take it before it drips all down my arm."

164

"I…err…thank you." I took the cone from him and pulled out the chocolate stick. Would I get away with eating a tiny bit? Well, here went nothing. I took a small bite and swallowed determinedly. My throat immediately complained, but so long as I didn't open my mouth for a minute or so, the chocolate would probably melt. If my new dietary restrictions meant melted food only, I was pretty sure I could live with that. I dropped the rest of the flake into a flower pot when Sean wasn't looking. A shrieking seagull immediately landed to claim its prize.

"Heathen," said Sean when he saw me eating my flake-free ice cream. "The chocolate's the best bit, you're supposed to leave it to the end." We fell into step along the railings heading back along the sea front.

"Surely, if it's the best bit, you might as well enjoy it first," I retorted, ice cream dripping down my chin.

"I do like a woman who doesn't care how she looks," Sean remarked. I pulled a face."It's a compliment," he assured me, taking my free hand again and swinging it as we walked. "So, how many admirers do you have lurking in the background, Lilith O'Reilly? Will I have to fight for your attention?"

I tried not to look too pleased. "No, no lurking competition," I said, trying not to think about Eadric Silverton, who was gorgeous but married and nearly a thousand years older than me. And Ivo Laithlind, of course, whose motives I'd yet to figure out. "None that I'm interested in, anyway."

"Good," said Sean. He stopped and leaned back against a low stone wall. We were at an angle to the rest of the street and completely out of view of anyone unless they walked right past us. "In that case, no one will mind me doing this," and, without warning, he leaned in to kiss me. I was nearly lost within seconds. Sean tasted like a cool stream on a hot day, the smell of rain on warm stone, fresh and delicious. His tongue ran lightly along the edge of my mouth and my lips parted, but I forced down the desire to breathe. The buttons on his shirt dug into my chest as he pulled me against him. I felt a coldness seeping through me, pulling itself towards his warmth like quicksilver. I pulled away whilst I still had control. Sean looked dazed, and I was concerned until he spoke. "That was…interesting," he said, gazing at me thoughtfully. Before I could think of a witty response, he continued.

"Evidently, I don't kiss attractive women nearly often enough." The sky was darkening and heavy splats of rain began hitting us. "Perhaps we should continue this some other time?" A crinkled grin. "Let me walk you home." We ran, giggling like children as the heavens opened. Rain was splattering the streets and sending people scuttling into shop doorways. I was becoming practiced at moving at an acceptable pace now and matched my stride to Sean's. We headed down Harrington Street, staying close to the walls for shelter, and I could see that the front window of Flora's was steamed up. We were clearly doing good business with people hiding from the rain.

I stopped at the fire escape and spoke before I'd really thought it through. "Would you like to come in for a coffee?" I asked Sean. "You could meet Grimm, my cat."

Sean tipped his head sideways and appeared to give this option a lot of thought for a man who was standing in the pouring rain. "Yes," he finally said. "That would be lovely." *I really can do this*, I thought exultantly, as we climbed the steps. I was so conscious of Sean's presence behind me, his warm breath on my neck and a hand lightly on my shoulder, that I almost fumbled the lock. Had I been less distracted, I might have noticed the blood on the doorstep.

A Siren Calls

The smell hit me before the noise did. Fury and fear and—fish? A wild yowling was coming from the living room and I saw Grimm poised in the far corner, four-square and spitting furiously at something out of my eyeline. There was a plastic tub open on the floor—the remains of a tin of mackerel that I'd put away in the fridge for him. That at least explained the smell. Edging forwards, I risked a peek round the doorframe to see what Grimm was so pissed off about. In the opposite corner, crouching on the sideboard and spitting back at the cat, was Daisy. The creature from the cell deep down in the tunnels was in my flat—in my goddamn fucking *living room*—and she looked no less strange for being out in the daylight. She was perching on the balls of her feet and balanced with one hand on the wooden top of the sideboard, something dark and viscous oozing from the other. For a second I thought it might be blood, but then realised it was the mackerel. No wonder Grimm was pissed off. Mackerel was his favourite, and he didn't give it up lightly for anyone. He'd drawn blood on my hands more than once in the past, when I hadn't served it up as fast as he'd have liked. Daisy flicked a brief, unconcerned glance at me before grinning in a most unsettling manner at the cat. I saw that her knuckles had been bleeding. Despite Daisy's taunts, Grimm didn't try to get any closer to her, even when she held the mackerel up to her face and a long, narrow tongue curled out to pull it back into her mouth. A row of tiny sharp teeth glinted as she drew her lips back and hissed quietly with pleasure. Grimm took a careful step backwards. Footsteps behind me reminded me I wasn't alone and, before I could stop him, Sean put his head through the door next to me. Daisy leapt backwards in fright, falling down the back of the sideboard and crashing around as she struggled to pull herself out. Grimm saw his opportunity and shot forward to claim the last piece of fish that was lying forlornly in the middle of the carpet, before streaking past us out of the kitchen door. I shoved Sean backwards out of the kitchen door and only just managed not to launch him over the bent railings. Thinking quickly, I caught hold of his shirt and reached up to kiss him deeply, breathing him in as much as I dared. I just had to hope my theory would work. He took a step backwards, looking confused. "Go home and forget this ever happened," I instructed him sternly and, to my relief, it appeared to work. He blinked twice as if clearing his head, then turned and began making his way slowly down the fire escape. I just had to hope that he remembered where he lived. *Fuck my* actual *afterlife*, I thought to myself, before bracing myself to face the mayhem.

"What on earth have you been up to, Daisy?" I tried to make my voice sound resigned and vaguely parental, rather than angry. She'd managed to get herself out from behind the cabinet and was perched back up on top of it. I'd have perhaps had more gravitas had I not trod in a squashed pile of stinking fish that was lurking in the middle of the carpet. I shook my foot free and stepped over to the grubby creature that was responsible for ruining my love life. Daisy gave a friendly smile and gestured towards the floor, as if suggesting there was plenty of fish left for me. Christ. Up close and in daylight, I could see just how unhuman she looked. She was still wearing the rags I'd first seen her in. On closer inspection, they turned out to be a workman's boilersuit, which appeared to have started its hand-me-down life at least a couple of centuries earlier. Despite having the standard number of arms and legs and a vaguely female physical shape, despite her painful boniness, there was something slightly off about the overall picture. As I'd suspected when I first saw her in the tunnels, Daisy's filthy feet had webbed toes the same as her fingers, the membrane stretched thin as her feet splayed to keep her balance. Her long straggly hair was lacking pigment, rather than actually being blonde. I wondered for a moment if she might have albinism, but her pale eyes were surrounded by long dark eyelashes and heavy brows. There was no sign of aggression at all now that we were alone; if anything, she seemed friendly. "You need a bath," I said, and she cocked her head to one side, looking at me curiously. "Don't move." I had no idea whether she really understood me, but she obediently stayed put whilst I went into the bathroom and turned on the taps. Returning to the living room, Daisy was a pathetic—and frankly creepy—sight in the gloom. Only her blue eyes hinted at any humanity. I was wary about touching her, but I couldn't let her carry on in this state. Was it possible to catch diseases when I was already dead? I'd just have to hope not. She was much more amenable now, readily allowing me to tug her gently off the sideboard and towards the bathroom. "Wait there," I told her, holding my hand up in front of her in the universally recognised sign for 'stop'. To my relief, she stood obediently while I went into the bedroom and found several large towels. "Stay," I ordered, and she stood mutely on the tiles as I checked the water temperature. The tiny room was full of steam. I pulled my hair up into a ponytail and fastened it with the black band I usually kept around my wrist. The strange, filthy creature stood obediently still whilst I arranged everything, staring at me with a vacant smile on her face. Other people had an annoying sibling, but I'd been landed with what appeared to be a feral vampire traipsing around after me. Not for the first time this week, I wondered what atrocities I must have committed in a previous life in order to deserve the endless shittery that was being meted out to me in this one. I straightened up and turned to face Daisy. "Off." I indicated her clothes. She just looked at me, blank incomprehension in her eyes. I tugged at the t-shirt, then mimed pulling it off over her head. Realisation dawned, and she undressed with enthusiasm, throwing the stinking clothes into a heap on the floor. I pointed at the bath tub and Daisy dutifully climbed in and then sat motionless in the water. Christ on a fucking bike, I was going to have to wash her. I found an old flannel on the storage shelf and made a mental note to burn it later, along with the remains of her clothes. She'd just have to wear something of mine. I scrubbed her all over as quickly as possible and tried not to look too repulsed by the smell, which was merrily causing havoc in my olfactory nerves despite my best attempts at not breathing.

Her knuckles had stopped bleeding, so I just made sure they were clean. Daisy was as happy as a kid in a sweetshop, splashing her hands lightly in the water. She seemed to be enjoying the attention. I reminded myself that she couldn't help what she was, any more than I could—I just wished she'd stay well away from me. And Grimm's fish supply. Looking down at Daisy swooshing water around the bath with her webbed fingers, a happy smile on her face, I had an idea. Leaning out through the bathroom door, I rang Izzy.

After pulling the plug out for the water to drain, I dragged Daisy up and out of the tub where she stood dripping on the tiles. Wrapping her in a towel, I pushed her in the direction of the sofa. "Sit," I instructed. She sat, still smiling. It was *seriously* creepy. And that was coming from me, Little Miss Undead. With a sigh, I went to the bedroom and rooted in the drawers for anything old but serviceable. Black underpants, socks, and jeans. A faded ABBA t-shirt, from what I liked to think of as my ironic phase. It would all be far too big for Daisy's tiny frame, but was better than nothing. I took the clothes into the living room and Daisy's eyes lit up. She pulled her new outfit on with a speed that suggested she knew what she was doing. I talked to her whilst she got dressed, more to break the silence than in any expectation of her understanding me. "There, that's better," I said. "You look pretty, Daisy." Her smile widened slightly. I had a suspicion that Daisy understood far more than she let on. "Let me comb your hair." I only had a big wide toothed comb—nothing else would get through my own tangles—but it would have to do. I rubbed at her head with a towel as if she was a child and began to comb it through. Her eyes closed slightly with pleasure. When I'd done all I could, I stepped back and surveyed my work. Then I went to my bedroom and came back with an old pair of sneakers that I tugged onto her cold feet. Daisy looked almost presentable. She'd have passed for a teenage girl, so long as no one looked too closely. Her smile revealed her teeth again, glinting in the light from the lamp on the side table. A light knock at the kitchen door made her jump, and I put a hand up to reassure her. "It's fine," I said, "it's just Izzy. Izzy's a friend." Daisy sat frozen as I went to the door, keeping one eye on my house guest as I did so.

"Okay, so now the fish bloke in the supermarket thinks I'm insane," Izzy announced loudly from the fire escape. "Weirder than usual, anyway." Out of the corner of my eye, I saw Daisy getting up to watch us through the doorway. Izzy's eyes widened and she took a step backwards. "Who the fuck is *that?*" she hissed. I pulled the door closed until I was wedged between it and the frame.

"I found her in the tunnels," I replied, "and now she's found me back. They told me she was undead, but I'm not sure." Izzy looked at me as though I was mad, but said nothing. She was good at dealing with weird shit, no one could fault her on that score. I took the bag of fish heads from her. "Thank you," I said, already closing the door. I didn't quite trust Daisy around humans just yet. "I'll fill you in properly later," I went on, "I promise."

Izzy rolled her eyes so hard it was a wonder they didn't roll out of her head and bounce down the steps. "I'm holding you to that, zombie girl," she said and headed back down the stairs.

I took the bag into the living room and held it out to Daisy, who looked confused. "Food," I said, holding the bag out and reminding myself not to breathe. Daisy stepped forward and peered at my offering, before snatching it from me. Leaping back onto the sideboard, she immediately shoved her entire face into the bag. I busied myself cleaning the carpet whilst she ate, but was pretty sure it was a lost cause. I'd have to get Dad to come over to help me rip it up, before the stench of mackerel soaked into the floorboards.

"She could do with learning some table manners, that one," said Aunt Kitty. I shot up from the floor so fast that I nearly cracked my head on the coffee table. Kitty was sitting in the armchair and staring at Daisy, who appeared utterly oblivious to her presence.

"And you need to learn to sit in chairs properly, rather than hovering above them," I replied tartly. "Couldn't you at least announce your arrival, rather than just popping up like that? It's fucking unnerving."

Kitty stuck her tongue out and descended a fraction so that she looked as though she was sitting down, although I couldn't help but notice that one of her legs went straight through the leg of the chair. "No need for that sort of language, Lilith," my aunt said primly. "If you can't say anything nice, don't say anything at all."

I sighed. "Aunt Kitty, I am dead and you are a ghost. Language is kind of irrelevant. And that," I gestured to Daisy, who was by now happily picking fish bones out of her many tiny teeth, "is a living, breathing problem. What am I going to do with her?"

"Why, you take her back to the river, of course," said Kitty, as if it was obvious. "She needs to get back in the water sooner rather than later, or she'll start drying out. I thought her type had died off," she tilted her head as if to consider Daisy further, "but evidently not. Why are you looking at me like that?"

"You know what she is?" I'd been flapping around with my unwelcome house guest for hours now and here was my aunt telling me she could have explained it all straight away. "Why didn't you tell me earlier?"

"I wasn't here earlier," said Kitty, as if it was obvious. "I don't watch you all the time, Lilith. That would be creepy."

"Like you floating around my living room lecturing me about weird river creatures isn't?"

"No need to be like that," Kitty said. "I was out having a chat with William. He's a nice boy."

I squinted at her. "Who's William?" I asked. "I'm sure you're being purposely obtuse now, you mad old bat."

Kitty shrugged. "I'm not always fully here," she said. *You can say that again,* I thought. "Sometimes I sort of wake up and I know there's been some time missing. Perhaps I go into standby like one of those newfangled televisions you have these days." I was pretty sure that Kitty's idea of 'newfangled' involved polished wooden cabinets and lots of valves, but said nothing. "And of course you know William! He's outside every day, for heaven's sake."

An invisible lightbulb pinged on above my head. "You mean Billy?" Kitty nodded. "He can see you?"

"Izzy can see me as well, don't forget," Kitty pointed out. "But that's because she's emotionally very close to you. William and I are the same creatures," she went on, "so are as visible to each other as living humans would be. But Daisy here is a river girl. They've no ability to see me, but

I've never been able to figure out why."

"What do you mean, Daisy's a river girl? You're not telling me she's a bloody *mermaid*?"

Kitty laughed. "Mersey mermaids?" She snorted. "I should think not—they'd get eaten alive out there. No," she went on, "your Daisy's from an older time. Asrai, they're called. Water fairies. The stories would have them as tiny, timid little things, but most are more like your Daisy, there. Tall and strong and exceedingly dangerous to those who get on the wrong side of them. Where did you find her?"

So I told Kitty about the tunnels and the mole-men and how Daisy must have escaped and made her own way to me. "I think that's how she hurt her hands." Kitty pulled a face when I told her about the sandstone cell. "I don't think they were trying to keep her prisoner," I said, unsure why I was feeling the need to defend Joe Williamson. "They just didn't seem to know what to do with her." Kitty looked unconvinced. "I honestly think they were worried she might be a vampire."

"Get on with you," Kitty laughed. "Joseph Williamson knows exactly what vampires are like. And they're nothing like Daisy."

"You knew about the vampires, then?"

"What do you think those apprentices of his are?" She raised an eyebrow at me. "It's a big city, Lilith. And it's been here a long time. Not as long as some of the other places, mind. Just be careful if you ever go to Chester, is all I'm saying."

"Forget Chester," I said. "What am I supposed to do right now? With Daisy?"

Kitty looked at me kindly, as if I was a particularly dim toddler. "Take her to the river," she said. "Wait until it's quiet and just walk her down there—she'll sort herself out. You'll not see the back of her, mind," she warned. "She'll be attached to you, now she thinks you've saved her."

"But she saved herself!"

"That's not how she'll see it." As Kitty spoke, Daisy looked up and smiled at me with a blank expression on her face. "You've sheltered and fed her, so she'll feel that she owes you. The Asrai don't forget easily. Whether it's for the good or the bad."

* * *

I spent a very tedious couple of hours talking at Daisy and getting absolutely no response. She would occasionally offer me a fish bone, which I politely declined. Kitty sat with us for a while but then got bored and slowly faded away, her face the last thing to disappear. It was like being related to the Cheshire Cat, but a *lot* creepier. As soon as the streets started emptying, I pulled on my sneakers and gestured to Daisy that we were going out. She followed me like a child, which was both sweet and also very unnerving. As we went out through the kitchen door, there was a growling noise above my head. Looking up, I saw Grimm perched on the guttering, glaring down at us with his teeth bared. Daisy followed my gaze, baring her teeth and hissing loudly enough to make Grimm scoot backwards. There was a raspy noise next to me and when I turned to look at Daisy, she appeared to be snickering. "No," I said firmly. She narrowed her eyes slightly. "You leave my cat alone, you hear?" By the look on Daisy's face, I half expected her to stamp her foot like a toddler, but she gave herself a visible shake and smiled her creepy smile. "Exactly," I said. "Behave yourself. Now come on, we need to get you back to the water." I had no idea whether she understood anything I was saying, but she seemed happy enough to walk with me. We walked towards the river side by side, crossing North John Street in silence. There was hardly anyone around. Which was lucky, because Daisy was clearly enjoying being out in company. She took to grinning widely at the few people we did pass, making her happy little hissing noises. After the second person had nearly fallen into the gutter in fright, I took her hand firmly and kept her moving. I'd thought I was walking at a reasonable human speed, but Daisy seemed to have difficulty keeping up with me. By the time we'd got to the Strand, she was clearly struggling. I put an arm around her and tried to egg her on, but her long legs were dragging to the point I thought she might just topple over. Oh well, there was no point in having maximum abilities if I didn't use them. Stopping halfway down James Street, I turned to face Daisy. "I'm going to pick you up, okay?" I said. She was literally drooping in front of my eyes and didn't put up any resistance. Hoisting her up by her waist, I slung her over my shoulder like a sack of potatoes. I briefly forgot about not breathing and nearly choked on the smell coming off her. It was as though someone had set fire to a pile of dried seaweed—acrid and sharp, a mix of chlorophyll and sweat. There was no one else in sight, so I risked a slow jog as we got closer to the water's edge. Daisy began wriggling, and I put her down near to the railings. To my horror, she immediately began to strip naked, the clothes I'd given her flying through the air. *"Daisy!"* I hissed, but she ignored me and continued to fight with the sneakers I'd wedged onto her feet. Finally she managed to kick them off and leapt the railings like an Olympic hurdler. Before I could stop her, she stepped forwards and dropped into the murky water. I leaned over the railings in horror and was just wondering whether I ought to call the coastguard, when Daisy's pale face broke the surface a few metres out into the river. When she saw she'd got my attention, she gave me a slow, broad grin before somehow flipping up into the air and then diving back down into the water like the slickest of arrows. I stood watching for a long time, but the water was calm and inky black. The only movement I could see was a few slight ripples travelling across from the patrol boat near the opposite bank, cruising steadily from Birkenhead towards New Brighton. As panic began to rise, I reminded myself that Daisy clearly wasn't scared of the water. And Kitty certainly seemed to think it was what she needed. She'd be fine. But thinking of Kitty reminded me of what she'd said earlier, about her conversation with 'William'. It was time Billy and I had a proper chat.

Billy, Don't Be A Hero

"I'm just off, Red." Billy tried to sound apologetic as I stalked up the street towards him, but he was definitely being shifty. His backpack was towering over him as usual, and he had a red disposable cup from Costa Coffee in one hand. Steam was rising out through the vent hole in the lid.

"Why didn't you tell me you were dead?" I demanded.

"Why does it matter?" Billy's tone was defensive.

We stood facing each other like some bizarre undead stand-off. I gave in first. "Because I don't know what's real and what isn't anymore!" I wailed. My voice cracked slightly, and I realised I wanted nothing more than to have a bloody good cry. Billy stared at me, shifting nervously from side to side as if trying to decide whether he should leg it whilst the going was good. "Everything was normal and boring and I actually kind of liked it. And now *nothing's* normal and I am *scared*, Billy." I trailed off and stared at my feet, scuffing my toes on the pavement.

"Want to sit down for a minute?" Billy gestured to the doorway.

"Please."

So we sat down side by side in the cold doorway—but it *wasn't* cold anymore, was it, because my undead body didn't care about temperatures anymore—and we talked. Or rather, Billy talked—of how he'd arrived in Liverpool from Ireland in the 1860s and had long forgotten if he had any name other than William ('surnames weren't important back then, Red'), or whether he'd left any family behind. He had vague memories of a younger sister with hollow eyes and of parents who hadn't wanted him to leave, but he'd known even then that it was the best chance he had of making something of his life. And it had worked out—at least, to begin with. He'd been taken on as a general labourer at the docks and was kept busy from early morning til late at night, every day of the week. "Although we knew how to have fun as well," he said with a little chuckle. I turned to look at him. He was staring up at the sky, a wistful look on his face. "There were always women," he said, "and sometimes men as well." He turned and saw my raised eyebrows. "Aah, don't tell me you're shocked, Red," he grinned. "What difference does it make, so long as everyone's happy?" He gestured up the empty street. "It was busy beyond your every imagining around here, back then. People living side by side and on top and below each other. It was pure terrible as well, of course, but I had some good times. Some really good times." He leaned his head back against the shuttered door and turned to look at me. "Being dead's not all bad, you know," he said. "It's safer in lots of ways. There isn't much to fear in the world if the worst's already happened."

"What did happen to you, Billy?"

He sighed and went back to staring at the sky. "Aah, I got in the way of the wrong woman, didn't I?" I sat in silence, waiting for him to continue. "I had friends all over back then, some of them dafter than others. Tom was one such. He'd go off with any woman who showed an interest and didn't seem to care much whether they were just after his pay. I used to say to him, wasn't it obvious they were only hanging around the gates of the sailor's home on pay days? But Tom—well, let's just say he didn't much care about the motivation, so long as he got the results. Anyway," Billy shifted himself upright, hugging his knees, "there was this girl used to hang around and take advantage a wee bit. Helped herself to Tom's wages one too many times and he finally lost patience. Decided to go looking for her and demand his money back. He had a wife and babies back home and he was supposed to be sending the money back to them. His Niamh was a patient woman, but I don't doubt that patience would have worn out sharp had she known why he was sending her short some months. Anyway," he went on, "I said I'd go with him to make a witness. I thought she might be a fighter, see." He gave me a sideways glance. "Not that either of us planned to threaten her, you understand—I was more worried she might be the threat. And I was right," he continued, his grip tightening on his knees. "She must've known she was likely to get a comeback from any of the men she was stringing along, because she was armed. Just a pocket knife, like, but Tom wasn't expecting it. I was, though. When you grow up poor where I did, you learn to defend yourself. Tom though, well, he was a bit soft in some ways. So when I saw her move to take something out of her skirts, I pushed him out of the way and went to grab her." He fell silent for a moment. " And she slit my throat." I automatically put a hand to my neck in silent horror. "Last thing I remember of my life was Tom standing there absolutely frozen, the girl yelling at him to run before she did the same to him."

"What happened next?" I asked softly.

"Aah," he smiled at me, "I can't remember much for a while. On account of being dead, I guess." A lop-sided grin. "I didn't realise that to start with, mind. She must have shoved me down one of the alleys to be eaten by the rats, because that's where I was when I came to again a while later. No idea how long it had been, mind. Course, I thought I must have just been knocked out. So I walked back to my lodgings to lick my wounds, so to speak. But somehow I couldn't open the door. And then I shouted, because I knew my mates would be in there somewhere, but no one came. So I sat outside that doorway until it finally opened. And it was Tom, so you can imagine my relief! But when I spoke to him, he ignored me. I tried again, shaking his collar until it felt as though I might rip his head off, but then I realised I wasn't actually touching him at all. He just sort of brushed at his neck and carried on his way. It took me a good while to accept I was dead, I can tell you that." He turned to look at me. "So I'm more sympathetic than I might appear. I promise you that."

"Where did you die?"

"Oh, hereabouts," he said, "but it all looks different now. I knew all the streets and alleys like the back of my cold dead hand, but of course the bombs did for a lot of them. Did for a lot of people, as well." He went quiet for a minute, but then brightened. "Of course, there was fun to be had then, as well. Doesn't matter how big a war is when you're already dead, does it? Some of the others took the opportunity to come out more, back then. All those stories of flying beasts with glowing eyes, that people put down to bombing raids and adrenalin?" He grinned. "They really were just flying beasts."

"What sort of creatures?"

"Oh, witches and the like," he said, as if it was the most normal thing in the world. "Spirits. You know. And the vampires were around, for a while. I've not seen one of those for a very long time, mind. I heard that some have learned the knack of at least appearing human. They certainly don't look like the movie versions, so they must have figured out some really good disguises."

"What *do* vampires look like?"

"They're not glamorous and they're definitely not romantic," he said with a wry laugh. "They're dark, Red. In all ways. Dark-minded, nasty little things. Like rats." Billy looked around him as if there was a real risk that a vampire might eavesdrop on what he was saying about them.

"I can't believe I never realised you were dead," I said.

Billy rolled his eyes and sighed. "I'm just a rough sleeper in an empty shop doorway," he said. "What good would it do anyone to know that I'm a ghost? This city's full of ghosts, some still living and breathing. Ignored by everyone and left to the charity of others, without ever thinking to check the charity is actually there. Cities are heartless places, Red." He put a bony hand on my knee and we both sat staring at it for a while before he thought better of it and slid his arms back under the blankets.

"What do you do with the coffee and cakes that we give you?"

Billy snorted. "Does it matter?" he asked. "Where's the generosity in giving something and then demanding to know what becomes of it?" We sat in silence for a moment, then he relented. "I take it to George, round the corner. He's got a patch on Rainford Square. Likes coffee, but gets aggressive when there's no sugar in it. Prefer pain au chocolat over almond croissants." He looked sideways at me and grinned. "Just for future reference."

"Noted."

"What about your family, Red?" Billy asked suddenly. "Any brothers or sisters? Parents who'll miss you?" I automatically took a deep breath and immediately wished I hadn't. I was closer to Billy than I'd ever been before, and his scent was overwhelming. Not in the way people might expect of someone who lived on the streets—there was no sweat or stale odour. Rather, Billy smelled strongly—to me, at least—of pain. It was a sharp, metallic catch on the back of my throat, and it held echoes of hardship and suffering, alongside a tang of sea salt and sewers.

"Just parents," I said flatly, when I'd recovered my senses. "But they won't miss me, because I'm not leaving. Regardless of what other people think I should be doing." I turned to look at him, almost daring him to tell me I was wrong and that I should run far away, where no one would suspect me of being a monster.

"Well, that's good then, isn't it?" he replied easily. "It'll be nice to have company with someone who knows, but doesn't judge me for it." A wry smile.

"Why would I judge you?" I asked, frowning slightly. "It's not as if I'm your average human anymore, is it?"

Billy sighed. "Aah," he said, "they all judge, Red. All of them. The toffs and the moles, and the weird little creepy fellas who hang out on Renshaw Street. It was a relief to meet your Kitty, I can tell you."

"Yeah, she's a barrel of unexpected laughs, that one," I replied.

He laughed. "She's family, Red," he said, "and I reckon you'll be grateful to have her, soon enough."

* * *

"What do you mean, he won't remember?" Izzy was setting up the bakery delivery onto the display counter, occasionally pausing to eye me beadily as I cleaned and laid out the tables. After my unexpected heart to heart with Billy a couple of nights earlier, I'd failed utterly in any of my attempts to practise 'zoning out' and had managed to get precisely zero rest since. I really wasn't in the mood for an inquisition. I wasn't remotely tired physically—such a thing clearly wasn't even possible anymore—but my head felt as though it might burst. Everything I thought I knew about the world had been wrong and I'd only found out by dying. But it wasn't as though I could get comfort from knowing there was some form of afterlife. This particular limbo only seemed to be available to a few people, and there was no guarantee who would get it. I gazed at Izzy fiddling with a tray of pastries and wondered how I would cope with watching her age, whilst I didn't. I was prepared to lose my parents, but in that disconnected way most people are. Mum and Dad were getting older and would undoubtedly die one day, but that day was hopefully far enough in the future to not have to think about it much. But my best friend? Even if she lived into her eighties or more, I'd still be thirty-two in human terms. We'd look a strange pair if we were still going to the Pilgrim together. The thought made me smile, and I straightened up to look at her properly. "What?" Izzy said, "Have I got something on my face?" She brushed at her nose with her hand.

"No," I said, "I was just thinking how I'll at least be able to push you around town in your wheelchair when you're old and grumpy."

She scowled. "I might have a gentleman friend who'll do the pushing for me, thank you very much," she said. "Anyway, you haven't answered my question—why won't Sean remember what happened yesterday? It's not often that your date invites you back for coffee, only to find a stinking mermaid in the living room, is it?" She leaned into the counter display and wriggled a tray of apricot croissants until they were straight. "I think we're going to need to increase our order," she said, finally deciding the presentation was acceptable. "We're getting busier by the day."

"Sean won't remember because I wiped his memory," I said. "At least, I hope I did. Or if I didn't do it well enough, maybe I can convince him that my weird emo cousin is staying with me."

Izzy looked unconvinced. "Lilith O'Reilly," she said in a stern voice, "I demand that you promise me right this second that you will never wipe my memory."

"I don't want to wipe *anyone's* memories," I snapped. "I had no option!"

181

"You promise me right now, young lady." We glared at each other for a long second.

"I promise."

Izzy walked out from behind the counter and came over to me, her hand outstretched with the pinky finger extended. "Not good enough," she said. "Pinky promise, dead girl." I crooked my little finger into hers.

"Pinky promise," I said solemnly.

Izzy gazed at me thoughtfully for a moment, then nodded and released my finger. "I'm glad we've got that sorted," she said, as she unlocked the front door and pressed the button to start rolling up the shutters. She glanced outside and a brief look of panic flashed across her face. "Oh hi, Sean," she squeaked, turning to roll her eyes madly at me, "how's tricks?" I froze on the spot as Sean walked in, still apparently wearing the same clothes he'd had on at the weekend. He looked tired and dishevelled, but, to my relief, he headed for his usual table and dropped his satchel onto it.

"Sorry," he smiled vaguely at me as he settled into the chair, "I've had a really weird few days. Thought I might feel better for cracking on with some work." He started tipping his notebook and pens out onto the table in front of him, and Izzy stepped forward to catch a pencil that was about to roll onto the floor.

"I'll bring you your coffee," she said, leaving him rearranging his things on the table as we both scuttled behind the counter. "I think you need to work on your technique," she hissed at me, as the coffee machine ground slowly into life.

I stared across at Sean, who had already given up on his paperwork and was staring aimlessly out of the window at the empty street. "No one's given me a bloody owner's manual," I muttered back. " I'm having to work this shit out as I go along." I was worried, though. Maybe I should ask Mapp for some lessons. Just as I thought it, the door clanked open and the man himself walked in. He'd clearly learned to read minds since the last time I saw him.

"Good morning, lovely ladies," Mapp said with a genuine smile and a mock bow. Today's outfit was black bondage trousers over platform boots, topped with a red and black striped jumper with so many snagged holes that Owain could have used it as a fishing net. He looked for all the world like a Black Dennis the Menace on his way to a fetish night. A silver chain dangled from his nose ring across to a hoop in his right ear, which was also adorned with an ornately pointed silver cuff that wouldn't have looked out of place on an elf. His left ear carried only a diamond stud, which would have been elegantly understated had it not measured at least half an inch across.

"Coffee?" Izzy waved a mug at him.

"Only if I can stand here and gossip with you delightful creatures as I drink it," said Mapp, his grin widening.

"Honestly, Mapp," I said, "you're an entire book of cliches all wrapped up in pointy boots." He waved graciously in the manner of a queen greeting the proles through her carriage window. "To what nefarious honour do we owe this visit?"

Mapp clutched his chest in mock horror. "Forsooth, madam, you injure my feelings!" He leaned across the counter. "You promised to come visit our overlords with me," he muttered. "I'm just checking you hadn't forgotten."

I scowled at him. "I thought he was your ally," I said. "Not your boss."

Mapp buffed his fingernails casually on his jumper. It would have had better effect had he not got his many rings caught in the loose threads. Both Izzy and I watched in silence as he extricated himself with a muffled curse, before straightening up to grin brightly at me. "Bit of both, innit?"

I sighed. "Okay," I said, "I'll come with you. If," Mapp raised an eyebrow, "you promise to continue my introduction into the afterlife. And," I nodded towards Sean, who was now stirring his coffee very slowly, "I need you to check that I haven't hurt him."

Mapp turned to look and then frowned. "I thought we discussed this?" he said. "I already told you why it's not a good idea to take from humans, Lili."

"I didn't do it for fun!" I hissed at him. "I did it in order to keep my secret. *Our* secret, for heaven's sake. He came back to the flat with me, only there was a bloody Asrai in my living room and the cat was really pissed off...anyway," I trailed off, "it was complicated. So I did what I thought was best at the time. And now I need you to check that I haven't done anything awful."

Mapp sighed and strode over to the window. "Alright mate?" he said. Sean looked up and seemed utterly unperturbed by the arrival of a character from the Matrix. Before he could gather enough of his wits together to actually speak, Mapp bent and whispered in his ear. Whatever he said had the required effect, because Sean immediately brightened up. Within seconds, he was staring at Mapp with genuine curiosity.

"Can I help you?" said Sean, and it was in his usual voice. Izzy and I glanced at each other, the relief etched on both our faces.

Mapp grinned and dropped a leaflet on the table. "Just spreading the word," he said. "We have a get-together once a week, at my shop up on Renshaw Street." Sean had a polite expression on his face, the sort people muster when the Jehovah's Witnesses turn up on the doorstep. "Just a friendly community thing, you know?" Mapp went on. "Supporting each other through these hard times, yeah?"

"Erm…thanks?" said Sean, shuffling his notebooks with the urgency of someone who really wants to look busy all of a sudden. "I'll check it out."

"Great," said Mapp. "Maybe we'll see you up there one of these days."

Sean opened his notebook and picked up a pen in order to give off an air of being interested, but way too busy. "Yeah, sure," he said, already bending his head to write. "See you there."

"What did you say to him?" I asked Mapp. He was sitting on the worktop in the back room of the cafe, swinging his legs as he sipped an espresso and watched Izzy and I work through the open doorway.

He shrugged. "I didn't say anything." He eyed me over the tiny cup.

"Stop bullshitting me, Gaultier Mapp," I snapped. "You're quick enough to tell me when I'm doing things wrong, but you don't want to help me do them *right*, either. You are not being bloody fair, and you know it." He thought for a moment and then drained the coffee before putting his cup down and sliding off the worktop in order to come over to where I was refilling the coffee bean hopper. The cafe was busier now, with all the tables occupied and Izzy serving at the counter, so at least we wouldn't be overheard. Mapp leaned against the wall and gazed down at me, silver chain swinging gently across his face.

"I breathed life back into him," he said gently.

"What the fuck?"

He smiled. "It's a knack," he said, "and few have it. Plenty would like it, mind. So I generally keep it well hidden."

I stared at him, wide-eyed. "Who else knows about this talent of yours?"

"Not many," he admitted, "but a few have realised over the years. Usually when I've been forced to save them from their own stupidity. Eadric would know all about that." A wry smile. So that's why he didn't feel beholden to Eadric Silverton—the boss man owed him one.

"What about Maria?"

Mapp snorted. "Maria will never know about my…talent," he said. "She'd have me monetised and hired out to the highest bidders before you could sing the first two lines of *Maggie Mae*. Anyway," he continued, straightening up, "come with me to see Eadric. It might help you understand things a little better."

"Do I have to?"

He grinned. "It'll be worth it," he said. "I promise."

Who's A Pretty Bird, Then?

"Why do you need to speak to the Silvertons, anyway?" I asked Mapp as we walked along Castle Street. The old buildings on this stretch had somehow survived the onslaught by German bombers during the Liverpool Blitz of the early 1940s, with only a few modern buildings visible as architectural cement in between looming Georgian beauties. "And why isn't the Town Hall in the centre of the road?" Now that I was really taking in everything around me, the slightly off-centre position of the grand building at the end of the street felt really irritating.

Mapp looked confused by the change in topic, but rallied quickly. "Because it didn't used to matter," he said, coming to a sudden halt and causing a large, middle-aged woman to nearly walk into the back of him. She growled something about 'fucking idiot tourists' as she went past and we watched her stalking off down to the street to where the Town Hall sat in its awkward position on the junction. Mapp waggled an elegant finger left and right at the road in front of the hall. "The street used to go all the way across," he said, "and buildings filled that gap you see in front of you now. The Town Hall wasn't planned with a junction in front of it, so it didn't matter where it was. And it's Eadric himself I'm looking to speak with," he continued, as we started walking again, "not the rest of them." Turning down Water Street, Bertie, the inland-facing Liver Bird, seemed to peer down at us as we got closer. "Nik never cares about what might be going on," Mapp went on, "and he's not really family, anyway. Eadric's wild-woman might think she's in charge, but she'll learn." Mapp smiled to himself. It wasn't a comforting smile.

"What do you mean, Nik doesn't care?" He'd seemed interested enough when I'd last met the family, even if it had been in a faintly aggressive manner. "I thought he was Eadric's brother?"

Mapp snorted. "Is that what they've told you?" He seemed to find this genuinely funny. "Aah well," he went on, "I guess he's as much a brother as any of us. Eadric took him in when he needed help, and that counts for a lot."

"What had happened to him?" I asked. "Nik, I mean."

Mapp sighed. "Aah now," he said, "Our Nikolaus's story is a complicated one. He was very famous when he was alive. That makes it incredibly difficult to stay anonymous when you're supposed to be dead."

"Would I have heard of him?" I asked. "When did he die?" We were on the Strand now, waiting for a gap in the traffic. A large black Mercedes slowed down to allow us to stop. Its male driver was clearly mesmerised by Mapp, who, for reasons known only to himself, was now wearing a long black pencil skirt over his platform boots. He'd topped it off with a purple silk tunic that was draped with several long and heavy silver necklaces, each holding a variation on the biblical cross. I could make out a standard plain cross, a Celtic one, and what appeared to be an oversized rosary. I wasn't sure whether Gaultier Mapp went for the pick'n'mix approach to religion, or had just spent too long browsing the goth shop in town. He gave the man in the car a beaming smile and headed across the road with the confidence of Moses parting the Red Sea. As I moved to follow him, another car came from the opposite direction, way too fast. Without thinking, I shot forwards and was on the opposite side before Mapp had even got halfway. The Mercedes crawled away very slowly, its driver peering around as if wondering what had just happened.

"This is why we usually ask people to move away for a while after changing," Mapp said mildly, as he caught up with me. "However quickly you pick things up, you're going to accidentally do things that draw attention to yourself."

"I'm not going anywhere," I said firmly. "Anyway, you were telling me about Nik's secret identity?"

"I was telling you no such thing," Mapp retorted. "Nikolaus's identity is his business and no one else's. And given that there's at least one plaque in his memory in dear old London town, no one can blame him for being cautious." We were walking down the side of the Liver Building now. I headed for the front doors, but Mapp stopped at the corner. "Down here," he said, gesturing to steps that lead down to a small door I'd never noticed before. It was painted a nondescript dark green, peeling in patches to expose the worn oak behind it. The stairs down to it were old and rusted, with matching pipework that emerged and retreated through the stonework like giant robotic woodworm. If I'd ever noticed it before, I'd have assumed was the access point for the building's mechanic plant. Which was exactly what it turned out to be. When we got to the bottom of the steps, Mapp rummaged through the heap of scrap metal hanging round his neck and produced a key on a chain. It was small, but looked to be made of iron and was almost certainly handmade. He leaned forward to use it without taking it off and unlocked the door. A low hum greeted us as we stepped forward into a brightly lit, white-painted plant room, packed with machinery and more pipework. Mapp led the way and I followed silently behind, the door closing behind me with a heavy click. It felt for all the world as if we were walking through the bowels of a gigantic living creature. There was a large metal box against the wall at the back of the room, which I realised to my surprise was an old-fashioned elevator. Mapp used the same key to open the control panel and pressed a button to open the lift doors. He stepped inside and gestured at me to follow him, before pressing the only button on the inside panel. Heavy, coiled metal cables rolled slowly above the metal box, creaking their way around the loop of the elevator system and jerking us suddenly upwards. I staggered slightly, and Mapp put a hand out to steady me.

"For someone who could climb buildings on the outside if they cared to try," he said, "you're surprisingly ungainly at times."

"Thanks a bunch," I muttered. "Anyway," I said more loudly, "where does this take us?"

Mapp grinned. "To the toppermost of the poppermost."

* * *

The lift moved smoothly but slowly after its jerky start, and we stood there for what felt like a very long time before it finally juddered to a halt. I was ready for it this time and struggled not to look smug when I stayed unmoving as we ground to a halt. The doors creaked open onto surroundings that were as far from the basement's industrial aesthetic as was possible to imagine. We stepped out onto deep-pile crimson carpets in what appeared to be a small anteroom. The walls were painted the same dark green as those I'd seen in the Silvertons' luxurious offices and were again hung with large paintings in ornate gilded frames. But it was a smaller picture in the middle that drew my interest. Fractionally taller than it was wide, it depicted a man with his back to the viewer, with a woman playing the harpsichord to his left and another woman apparently singing on his right. The checkerboard floor the trio stood on gave it a contemporary feel. Something about the entire image felt incredibly familiar.

Mapp saw my curious expression and stepped over to lightly touch the painting's frame. "Yes," he said, "you recognise it. Vermeer can be very distinctive."

"But isn't it—"

"Missing?" He turned to look at the painting himself, one hand stroking his upper lip thoughtfully. "Yes, I guess that's as good a description as any." He traced the figure slightly with his index finger. "It got into the wrong hands and Eadric found out, so he...arranged to take possession." Mapp turned to look at me again, a smile on his face. "Eadric isn't fond of people who don't appreciate the value of what they've got."

"Talking about me again, Mapp?" said a deep voice on our left. I turned to see Eadric Silverton standing framed in the doorway. Once again, I struggled not to make incoherent meeping noises at the mere sight of him. Who needed personality when you looked like that? He smiled at me in such a way that I felt a sudden urge to check whether an extra sun had just risen in the sky. *Fucking hell Lili*, I thought to myself, *are you really so starved of male company that you collapse in a puddle of lust when a remotely attractive one finally steps into view?* But it wasn't that simple. Mapp was handsome by any standards—his outre dress sense wouldn't have worked on anyone without his height or physique, but there was no denying he was aesthetically pleasing to the eye. Sean—lovely, helpful, *normal* Sean—was cute rather than handsome, with his floppy hair and air of distracted college professor. Eadric was something else entirely—something not quite human. He radiated strength and power. *Old* power. Eadric Silverton had been around for a very long time indeed. I was more than a little bit nervous, standing so close to him. "Welcome back, Lilith," he said, stepping forward to shake my hand politely. I stepped backwards as Eadric moved past me towards Mapp and, to my utter surprise, grasped him in a bear hug. The two men held onto each other like genuine friends, rather than slapping each other's backs like most posturing men would have done. "Mapp, you bastard," grinned Eadric, as they stepped away from each other, still gripping hands, "it's been too long."

"Well, if you ever came down from your ivory tower, we'd see each other more often," replied Mapp.

Eadric laughed. "Don't start that again," he said. "You know I like it just fine up here. Anyway," he stepped back, "everything carries on very well without me, so why get involved?"

"That's what I'm here to talk about," said Mapp. "Something's not right, Eadric," he glanced at me before continuing, "and I think it's connected to our Lili, here. Nothing she's doing," he said quickly, as Eadric turned to look at me, "but caused by her arrival. The city is stirring. What's bothering me is that I don't know why."

"Come through," said Eadric, pushing open the door out of the anteroom and leading the way up a short flight of stairs, "and tell us about it." The reference to 'us' made me nervous. I assumed that Maria and Nikolaus would be waiting for us, but there was no one else around. And we didn't appear to be in the offices. A cool breeze blew as we followed Eadric through the door at the top of the stairs, and I found myself stepping out onto the open stone roof. The tower in front of us was open on all sides, its vaulted roof held up by enormous pillars. I looked to my right and gasped as I realised

WHO'S A PRETTY BIRD, THEN?

we were standing on the clock tower of the Liver Building, underneath the bird itself. "There's more," Eadric said to me. He had a boyish grin on his face that made him look years younger. "Come and look." He walked over to where a small, spiral staircase was bracketed against one of the pillars, twisting up to a heavy-looking wooden trapdoor set into the tower's ceiling.

Mapp caught my arm and tugged gently. "Very few ever get invited up here," he said. He spoke quietly, but I saw from Eadric's smile that he'd heard it. "Come say hello to the true heart of the city." I followed the two men up the steps, staying far enough behind Mapp to avoid his tunic blowing into my face. When Eadric got to the top, he pushed at the trapdoor and it obligingly popped upwards before sliding across, as if on rails. As I clambered out after the others, Eadric turned to look at me. "Impressive, isn't it?" he said. I gazed around the stone room, this one smaller than the last but laid out in a similar fashion. Looking through the openings between the pillars, I turned slowly to take in the view. The entire city sat below me, like a three-dimensional map. I got my bearings by looking for the radio tower, then along to the modernist outline of the Metropolitan Cathedral. Paddy's Wigwam, my dad called it. Not far past the modernist spikes sat the Anglican, its solidly Gothic presence looming over everything in its eyeline.

"Come on," said Eadric, heading towards an even narrower spiral staircase fitted half into the wall, "we're not quite there yet."

"You go in the middle," said Mapp, with the ghost of a wink. "Let him impress you." I wasn't sure that anything was ever going to impress me more than this view, but I did as I was told. Eadric led the way and Mapp brought up the rear, whilst I stumbled my way in the middle, distracted by the views still visible through the wall openings. Another trapdoor was pressed open, but this time with a creak, as if it wasn't used very often.

As he pushed himself up off the ladder and out through the top, I heard Eadric speak. "Hello my darling," he said in a soft, crooning voice. "How are you doing?" He didn't wait for an answer, leaning back down to grasp my hand and pull me up after him. I clambered awkwardly up through the trapdoor and out into fresh air. We were on the domed roof of the clock tower. To be more precise, we were standing next to it. A tiny walkway less than three feet wide circled the base of the dome, and below that was—

"—*holy Mary mother of fucking god!*" I'd made the mistake of looking down. I leaned backwards against the dome with my arms stretched wide, attempting to give myself as much contact with the building as possible.

"Wash out that blasphemous mouth of yours, Lilith O'Reilly," said Mapp, grinning as he climbed out of the hatch and onto the roof. He stepped over to me, perching casually on the walkway as if he was standing in the middle of Lord Street, gossiping with friends. He held out a hand, and I gripped it. I'd have definitely been hyperventilating if I was alive, but was desperately fighting the urge, in case the inevitable coughing fit sent me flying off to land in a splatted heap on Canada Boulevard. "If you fell off here, you'd just land on the roof of the main building," Mapp said helpfully. I glared at him, but it did help a tiny bit. I risked another peek, turning round to scan the city laid out below me like an urban scale model.

"Where's Eadric gone?" There was no sign of him. I briefly wondered if there might be another way down, but was pretty sure I'd have noticed it whilst climbing the ladder. Surely he wouldn't have jumped, just to prove a point? Bloody show-off revenants.

"Up here," came a voice from above my head. I peered upwards, careful not to lose my grip on the metal dome. I could hear a faint humming noise. It sounded was electrical, rather than mechanical—the sort you sometimes hear from fluorescent lights. I was looking up at the copper-green undercarriage of the bird. Even though I knew in theory that it was big, I was unprepared for just *how* big it was at close quarters. Eadric sat perched between its claws, his hand stroking the bird's heavy-set leg. With its head held high and huge wings spread wide, I had the sudden feeling that the cables securing the bird to the roof were as much to stop it flying away as they were for safety reasons. The humming was getting louder and there was a glow in the air. Could it be static electricity? We were very high up and the birds presumably acted as lighting conductors for the building—was I going to get a shock if I touched it? Could an electric shock harm me, anyway? Maybe I'd just end up with hair that looked even more as though I'd put my finger in an electrical socket. I gingerly stood up away from the dome and craned my neck to take in the entire bird, holding tightly onto Mapp for support. The glow was definitely coming from the bird itself, as was the humming. Just as I was wondering whether we were all about to be electrocuted, there was the distinct noise of creaking metal. Right in front of my disbelieving eyes, t he bird tilted its head to look at me. Mapp grabbed hold of my arm before I could topple backwards in fright. Eadric just grinned. The bird jerkily tilted its head a fraction further, as if sizing me up. It then slowly straightened up and settled back to gazing out to sea. The glow dimmed slightly, but the humming was still faintly audible in the background. It faded in and out rhythmically, as if—I stared up at Eadric, wide-eyed with shock. He smiled down at me, a look of peace on his face. "Yes, Lilith," he said, "the stories are true." He grinned up at the giant metal bird standing above him. "They're alive."

A City Made Of Magic

I stared up at Eadric, still sitting above me on the feet of a giant sculpture that had just come to life before my very eyes. His hair was blowing slightly in the wind and his shirt had come untucked. He'd wriggled round to lean back against one of the bird's legs and his trousers had rucked up slightly to show what looked distinctly like purple silk socks, just visible above a pair of battered Chelsea boots. If we hadn't been a couple of hundred feet above the ground, he'd have passed for a well-groomed hipster, just hanging around looking louche and waiting to be noticed. As it was, I had questions. A *lot* of questions. "Let's go down to the office," Eadric said before I could open my mouth. He gave the bird a last pat on its foot. The humming had settled into a low background breathing noise and the glow had all but disappeared, but I could have sworn that it twitched slightly at his touch. "I'm sure you've got things you'd like to ask."

"No shit, Sherlock," I muttered. Eadric headed down first, leaving me and Mapp to follow him. "Did *you* know the birds were alive?" I demanded, as I followed Mapp down the narrow metal steps.

He gave a gentle snort. "Of course," he said, as he got to the bottom and waited for me. As I stepped down onto the stone floor, he went past me back up the stairs. "Just need to latch the roof," he said in a muffled voice, as he reached up to fit catches back across the wooden hatch.

"What for?" I glared at him as he came back down and stood beside me. Eadric was already heading down the next staircase. "In case a fucking giant metal *bird* decides to clamber downstairs? What's it going to do—pop in to say hi to the tourists?"

"Bella's too big to get through the hatch," Mapp said reasonably, as we followed Eadric back down into the main building. "Anyway, she likes it well enough up there." He looked back at me as we went down the stairs and saw my disbelieving look. "Plenty of drama to watch over, darling. Bertie's the one who gets bored. Nik sometimes sits and reads him children's stories. It calms him down." He gave me a wide grin, and I had to fight the urge to smack him in the mouth. Couldn't anyone else see how utterly fucking *insane* everything was? I'd fallen off a roof, woken up dead, was being haunted by my dead aunt and had just met a real life Liver Bird that was about twenty feet high, weighed many metric tonnes and had turned its head to look at me. And I hadn't even been dead a fortnight.

We were back in the small elevator lobby. There was a narrow door on the opposite wall that I'd been too distracted to notice when we first arrived. Spotting a famously stolen artwork hanging casually on someone's wall tends to do that to a girl. The door opened silently on well-oiled hinges and Eadric stepped out to meet us. "You're getting slow, Mapp," he said with a grin.

Mapp raised an eyebrow. "Some of us like to appreciate the world, Silverton," he retorted without malice. "It wouldn't hurt you to do the same, occasionally."

"Oh, I appreciate the world," said Eadric, in a tone so even that it was unnerving. "I appreciate just how appalling it is to those who don't quite fit in. Anyway," he said, turning to me, "let's not drag the conversation down when we have company. A gentleman never argues in front of a lady."

"I'm not sure that I've ever been described as a lady before," I said, without thinking.

Both men stared at me, but Mapp broke first. "Then you've not been spending time with the right men," he answered smoothly, bowing deeply. "It would be my honour if you would find a large puddle and let me lie across it in order that you may be on your dainty way without moistening your..." he eyed my battered Converse, "...*delicate* shoes, madam." I laughed, and he looked pleased. Stepping forward, he put an arm around me. "I know it's weird, Lili," he said, squeezing my shoulders, "but nothing's actually changed.

195

Apart from you joining us, of course." A brief look flashed between him and Eadric and I wondered what I wasn't being told. "The tunnels, the ghosts, the birds—they've all been here a very long time. You just didn't know about them."

"Come through," said Eadric, gesturing through the door. We followed him into another room that was only slightly larger than the last. This one contained two heavy black leather sofas and was decorated in an almost identical style to the elevator lobby. I was pretty sure that I spotted a small Picasso sketch hung in an unassuming frame next to a light switch, but said nothing. I sat down on the sofa, next to a tall narrow window that looked out to the north. It was glazed, thankfully. I'd had enough high altitude river breeze for one day. To my surprise, Eadric sat at the other end, leaving Mapp to take the sofa opposite us with a faint twitch of his eyebrows.

Eadric looked over at him. "I assume you were coming here to check that the birds were still here?"

Mapp blushed deeply enough that it was clearly visible, then rallied. "It's a sensible check to make," he replied, "as you know very well."

"The birds will always be safe whilst I'm around," replied Eadric evenly. "You know that."

There was definitely something weird going on. Weirder than it already was, anyway. I was getting mighty fed up with them talking in riddles across me. "Where would the birds go?" I demanded, making sure that my sharp look hit both of them equally. "They're tied down, for fuck's sake. And I'm pretty sure that people would notice if one of the Liver Birds literally *came to life* and flapped off across the city on enormous metal wings. "Eadric smiled softly and again I wondered at the sheer aesthetics of him. He was so attractive that I was pretty sure that I didn't actually fancy him. His was the kind of beauty that's best put on display in a museum, rather than being left out for people to play with. Even in the very unlikely event of Eadric Silverton making a pass at me, I suspected I'd be too intimidated to ever accept his advances. And that was if I hadn't been skinned alive by Maria Silverton first. She didn't strike me as the sort of woman who'd tolerate anyone lusting after her man, let alone a random coffee shop owner who hadn't got laid in a while.

"The metal is just their visible form," Eadric replied. "It's the spirit inside the metal that's important. Without the spirit of the birds, it's said that the entire city would crumble."

"I'm really trying not to be insensitive here," I said, "but I'm pretty sure an entire city wouldn't literally fall to pieces simply because one of its most famous sculptures lost the ability to move its head. Anyway," I went on, "Liverpool was here centuries before the birds even existed! You can't tell me it wasn't a viable city before this building went up."

"It's symbolic, Lili," said Mapp. "Same as most things, really. None of the living inhabitants of this fair city know that dear old Bella and Bertie are actually alive, as it were. But they'd soon know about it if Liverpool lost its spirit."

"But where did they *come* from?" I said, trying not to sound whiney. Everything was getting madder by the day and showing no sign of calming down any time soon.

"Who knows?" said Eadric, with an elegant shrug. " Perhaps the city's innate magic was attracted to them in the same way that natural electricity is. All we know is that, as the building was being topped out, there was an immense storm. Workman who had balanced confidently on the most precarious of rooftop perches throughout endless howling gales during the construction were forced to climb down, for fear of being blown onto the streets below. There are tales of huge bolts of lightning hitting the untethered birds. And some say the lightning came up from the ground, rather than down from the sky."

"Lighting *does* spark up from the ground," I pointed out snarkily. "It just looks as though it's heading downwards."

"Yes, I know," said Eadric, "but it's usually caused by a charge building up and connecting the ground to the electricity in the air. This particular 'lightning,'" he actually did the quote gestures in the air with his fingers, "came straight up out of the ground and hit the birds directly. One strike on either side of the building, hitting each sculpture at the exact same time. The workmen only had another couple of weeks up on the roof after the storm, but stories began to circulate about how they never felt quite comfortable up there again."

"I've seen the photos," I said, "and I can't see how *anyone* ever felt comfortable balancing at that height."

Mapp laughed. "The irony was that the men were almost certainly safer up there than they'd ever been," he said. "Just a few days after the storm, a young apprentice slipped on the damp stone at the top of the clock tower and almost toppled right over the edge. But—and at least one of his workmates swore on a bible to having witnessed this—a sudden gust of wind pushed him back to safety."

"Could happen," I said in a cynical tone.

Eadric's face twisted into a small smile. "What about the day before the work ended," he asked, "when an older workman, just nearing retirement, was fixing the last cables onto Bertie and one snapped? It whipped round and would have knocked his head clean off, but the bird snapped it in its beak, before dropping it carefully at the man's feet."

"Oh, come *on*," I said, "you can't expect me to believe that?" The expressions on both the men's faces implied that yes, they expected me to believe precisely that. "No one would have been able to keep that sort of thing a secret. It would have been all over town!"

"Who's going to believe the word of a labourer who says a metal sculpture has come to life in the middle of one of the busiest cities on the planet?" asked Mapp. "Both incidents were assumed to be the rambling gossip of the working class who'd probably had a bit too much to drink that day. Both stories were forgotten very quickly. Leaving Bella and Bertie to watch over the city in peace."

"So why were you concerned that one of them might have left?" I asked.

Mapp looked shifty. "Like I said," he replied, sounding slightly uncomfortable, "things aren't quite right just now. And it started when you arrived on the scene. There's no getting away from it."

"I haven't done anything wrong," I pointed out, "other than fall off a building and die at a most inconvenient moment. Which was also not my fault." I looked from Mapp to Eadric, daring either of them to say differently.

Eadric sighed. "Nik's been saying the same for days," he said. "Something's different, but I can't figure out what. Maria's sure that Joe's rat-boys are looking to make themselves more visible." He looked at Mapp. "I'm sure you're aware of just how...*difficult* that will make things for the rest of us."

Mapp nodded. "Yes," he agreed, "but there's little we can do about it. And yes, I know," he said in response to Eadric opening his mouth to speak, "Maria thinks the city should be cleaned up, and the rat-boys with it. But we will not condone such behaviour. And certainly not towards a minority that has already been forced out to the very edges of society."

"Who's we?" I asked, given up any pretence of being subtle.

Mapp looked at me as if surprised to see me still in the room. "Those of us who don't live in ivory towers," he replied with a smiling nod in Eadric's direction. A sigh and a shifting of weight next to me suggested that this was a conversation the two men had had many times before. "Which I guess includes you, Lilith O'Reilly." Eadric stiffened beside me.

"Oh, no you don't," I said firmly. "I'm not taking sides with anyone. At least," I eyed them both beadily, "not until I figure out what's best for me. Me and Izzy," I corrected myself. "And possibly Kitty, although I think she's probably safe enough."

"Who's Kitty?" Eadric looked confused.

"My dead aunt," I replied, "who apparently now lives with me, whether I like it or not. She's a ghost, not one of...*us*," I gestured around the room, "but she certainly knows about revenants."

"I'd be interested to find out where she got that knowledge." Eadric's voice was mild, but there was a steely tone underneath.

"Someone called Jonny," I said. I didn't feel any need to protect the man who'd killed my aunt, however accidental it might have been. " He isn't around anymore. At least," I said, "not that she's told me. Anyway, it was a long time ago."

"Interesting relatives aside, Lilith," said Eadric, "I agree that you must make your own decisions as to your future path. As we have already discussed, I do not believe it is safe for you to stay in Liverpool. But—as we have also already discussed—you clearly have a mind of your own. You are capable of deciding your own fate. However precarious that fate might be." Well, that was comforting. Not. "And Gaultier," he said, looking across to where Mapp was lounging across almost the entire length of the sofa, tunic draped artfully across his knees, "the…others…are risking us all with their increasingly unbalanced behaviour. I am well aware that your own friends have learned to fit in with city life, some of them better than others. But Joe's inability to control his, well, let's call them apprentices, is beginning to make me nervous."

"It's making Maria nervous, you mean," replied Mapp.

"What am I nervous about?" asked Maria Silverton, walking into the room. She stepped across the thick carpet in her spike heels and came to an elegant halt between the two sofas. She looked like an unusually short Vogue model. "Hello Lilith," she said with a smile, "to what do we owe the pleasure?"

"I've been introducing her to the birds," said Eadric. A look of shocked surprise flashed across Maria's face before she managed to disguise it with a carefully interested expression. Her weight shifted slightly on her spindly heels as she turned to look at Eadric.

"How novel," she said brightly, "and so many wait years for the privilege." *And I bet you were one of them*, I thought. Interesting.

"Mapp thinks you're uneasy about Joe and the rat-boys," said Eadric, smoothly changing the subject. "We were just discussing the current situation."

Maria gazed at me, as if wondering when I'd been admitted to the inner circle. I was wondering the same myself. She turned back to Eadric and smiled. "We're looking weak, my dear," she said, "and that won't do. We have an image to uphold."

"I'm sure your image is just peachy, Maria," said Mapp, not moving from his reclined position. "You always make sure of that. Eadric's a big boy now. He'll manage things whichever way he decides is best. Are you okay, Lilith?" I'd breathed in sharply at his comment and was now trying to hold back a choking splutter.

Maria looked at me with interest. "Still struggling with it all, Lilith?" she asked. "Didn't Ivo bother to explain to you how things work whilst he was being so…helpful, this last week?"

"Ivo gave me some basic advice," I replied. Ivo had clearly been gossiping with the fam. "But nothing more." I was fighting the urge to smack Maria in her politely snarky mouth. "I have pretty much zero idea how any of this works," not entirely a lie, "as you all well know."

"We have been very remiss in our behaviour, Lilith," said Eadric, neatly cutting Maria off as she opened her mouth to speak. "I can only apologise. If you have questions, you are always very welcome to come and speak to any of us. Nikolaus will be here tomorrow. You might find his stories entertaining."

Maria snorted, the noise at odds with her elegant appearance. "You would be better to come to either myself or Eadric with questions you might have," she said. *Over my very dead body,* I thought.Eadric leaned over to a small side table, picked up an envelope and passed it to me. It was cheap and plain, as if it had been taken from a pack of supermarket budget stationery, but weighed heavily in my hand.

"I would be most grateful," he said to me, "if you would deliver this for me the next time you're down in Shropshire. Instructions are inside, along with the letter itself." He smiled at me and I swear my stomach did a backflip.

Maria turned to us, a scowl across her beautiful face. "Since when have we trusted strangers with our communications?" she said, leaning towards me as if to take the envelope herself. Eadric shot out a hand and gripped her arm firmly as I tucked the envelope safely away in my pocket. She stared silently at him, her expression one of stricken horror.

"Well, this has been lovely," said Mapp, getting to his feet, "but I wouldn't want to outstay our welcome. Coming, Lil?"

"What the fuck was that all about?" I demanded, as Mapp and I descended back to street level. We'd left Eadric and Maria in the tower room, the stony silence almost painful. He stared straight ahead of him and didn't reply. When we finally stepped out into the machine room, I had to wait for Mapp to find the door key from amongst his necklaces before he let us both out into the cool evening air. "Does Maria rule equally with Eadric?" I slipped a hand into my pocket and felt the envelope sitting there, the paper cool against my fingers.

Mapp snorted as he carefully locked the door behind us and we headed up onto the waterfront. "She might like to think she does," he said, linking arms with me as we strolled towards the river's edge, "but she underestimates Eadric. Maria," Mapp said with a sigh, "has made the mistake of confusing a lack of aggression with a lack of commitment. And the one thing that Eadric is committed to is his land—all of it. He'll no more cede control to Ivo than fly to the moon. And even revenants can't quite manage space travel just yet." He grinned and let go of my arm, leaning back against the railings. "Look up," he said. I followed his gaze, the railings behind me pressing reassuringly into my back. Most of the lights in the Liver Building had been switched off, leaving only a few bright squares dotted amongst the stonework. Small spotlights picked out the architecture, and a brighter light was trained on the Liver bird at the top, all the better to watch over the city.

"What am I looking at?"

"Shhh," said Mapp softly, "concentrate, Lili. Watch Bella. Carefully." I looked, but for a long few moments saw nothing other than cold metal lit by an orange-gold light. Just as I was about to give up and tell Mapp to stop being silly, I saw it. A faint glow that definitely wasn't manmade, creeping slowly outwards from the bird. In shades of green and blue with flashes of pure electricity, it was as if a miniature aurora borealis was spreading outwards from the bird's wings. Mapp nudged me and nodded towards the back of the building. Following his gaze, I saw the inland bird doing the same. His glowing halo was growing more quickly than Bella's, spiralling upwards into the night sky. As we watched, the birds'—what? Auras?—flowed upwards and across to the centre of the building's roof, where they began to swirl around each other in a delicate dance. The spirals didn't touch at any point—they simply twisted around each other, first stretching up towards the sky and then contracting back down towards the roof. I stared in wonderment as the halos made one last stretching helix before shrinking down and pulling back around each bird's head. A second later, there was no illumination at all, other than the usual mains-powered ones.

I turned to Mapp, who was still gazing up at the roof with a smile on his face. "I've never seen that before," I whispered.

He turned to look at me, the smile still on his face. "You've never been dead before," he replied. "We see the things that others don't. And the birds see you."

There Are No Secrets In The Shire

I f I could still dream, I'm sure it would have involved magical glowing
birds that spun in the sky in an eternal dance. But sleep was a lost
dream in itself, so instead I spent the night alternately polishing the
furniture and wondering how on earth I was going to manage the visit to
my parents without them realising something was different. "You'll wear
the finish off those chairs," observed Kitty, as she supervised me from the
armchair, Grimm sprawled traitorously across her lap.

I glared at the pair of them. "What do you suggest?" I asked tartly. "It's
not as if I can take a sleeping pill and escape this batshit new reality for a
few hours, is it?" Kitty idly rubbed Grimm's ear. Her fingers appeared to
me to just be rubbing against themselves, but the cat seemed to like it.

"But neither can you spend all of eternity wearing the varnish off
furniture," she pointed out in an irritatingly reasonable tone of voice. I
pulled a face and stalked out to rearrange the kitchen cupboards. Again.
Once they were cleaned and restocked to my satisfaction, I took a two-hour
bath. Lying in the near dark, I gazed thoughtfully at my legs, just visible
through the pillows of bath foam. They almost seemed to glow in the crack
of light coming in through the bathroom door. The tiny patch of hair on
my knee was unchanged in its spikiness, so I poked around in the bathroom
cabinet for a razor and shaved it off. Despite half-draining the bath and
topping the water back up three times, my extremities stayed determinedly
unwrinkled. I spent some time wondering about undead physics. As unlikely
as it seemed, I could find some logic in the human body going into a form
of stasis. But surely my fingers and toes should still turn white and wrinkly

if I soaked them in hot water for long enough? Apparently not. I lay back and slid under the water, my hair floating out around me like some kind of inner-city Ophelia. I opened my eyes and watched the bubbles floating aimlessly around above me. Some were getting caught in the tentacle-like tendrils of my hair that crept out across the surface of the water. Peering down the bath, I could just about make out the ghostly shapes of my knees in the dim light. I would never change from my current state. No wrinkles, no turning slightly flabby as muscles lost their elasticity with age, no grey hair other than the small streak already visible at my temple. Becoming a revenant in my thirties did at least mean that, to most people, I was just another generic woman living in a city with a busy and transient population. It would be at least a couple of decades before anyone started wondering why the woman running the local cafe didn't seem to be ageing. And even then, it was highly unlikely that anyone's first thought might be 'oh, perhaps she's immortal'. Because this sort of thing just didn't happen, did it? But, clearly, it did. And now I was a part of it, whether I liked it or not. *Sink or swim, Lil*, I thought, letting myself drop to the very bottom of the bath and resting my head on the enamel. I had to lift my feet out of the water to give myself enough room and could see them through the water, poking up into the air like a pair of white flags. I'd never been a coward. *Then you'd better learn to swim*, advised my inner voice. I pushed myself up out of the tub with enough force to send water flying across the floor, and stalked off, dripping, in search of clean clothes.

* * *

By seven in the morning, I was dressed and ready to leave. I'd texted mum to say I'd be with them early and received a thumbs up in return. My parents had never really got the hang of mobile phones. Theirs was one of the few households I knew that still had a landline. Although I'd never been around at the right time in order to verify my theory, I strongly suspected that my dad probably still announced their phone number when he answered it. I was sitting on the fire escape, attempting to play a mindless word game on my phone, still with the broken screen that was illegible in several places. "Are you nervous, Lili?" Kitty was floating in the open kitchen doorway behind me. I turned to look at her and it took me a few seconds to realise what was different.

"You've changed your clothes!" She was wearing a loose-fitting shift dress in a pale blue flower print. Her feet were bare and her hair was tied back from her face in a low ponytail. It gave her the air of a hippy schoolteacher on her holidays.

Kitty shuffled bashfully on silent feet. "Do you like it?" she asked, doing a small twirl. I was sure I could see the hint of a blush on her pale cheeks. "I got so sick of those jeans! I was daydreaming about a beautiful dress I'd once owned and thinking how much I'd love to wear it again. The next thing I know, I look down and there it is, already on me! I think," she said, gazing down at her feet, "it must have been a hot day, the last time I wore this."

"You look beautiful," I told my aunt, and meant it.

She wrinkled her nose in appreciation. "Thank you," she said. "But you didn't answer my question."

I hunched down on the steps and contemplated the street below. Kitty came to stand behind me. This was another fresh development. "Think you'll be able to leave the flat?"

She shrugged. "I think I can go anywhere you need me to," she replied. "It's you I'm connected to, not the building. But," she gazed over the rooftops, "I clearly don't have to be near you at all times. Sometimes I find myself sitting in the flat with lovely Grimm on my lap and it takes me a while to realise you're not around."

"It's been a busy couple of weeks," I said drily.

"Silly girl," said Kitty, but it was affectionate. She leaned forward to ruffle my hair, and it was like a gentle breeze playing through my curls. "I don't need you to babysit me. Heaven knows, I survived the sixties, and I was alive and vulnerable then. This modern age holds no fears for me. Well," she said thoughtfully, "I survived *most* of the sixties, at least."

"Yes, I'm nervous," I said abruptly. "In answer to your question. Yes, I am nervous. Because I need to go visit my parents who I love very much and somehow I have to make everything seem entirely normal. Nothing is normal, Kitty. We both know that." She moved to sit down next to me. This was the closest she'd ever been to me for any length of time, and I looked at her curiously. She was definitely...*there*, but not quite. There was a shimmering inner light to her, as if she was an extremely well programmed hologram.

She glanced sideways and caught me staring. "It's a strange old situation we've found ourselves in, isn't it?" I nodded and smiled my agreement. Kitty turned her gaze back to the rooftops. She looked thoughtful for a few long minutes, then turned back to me. "Here goes nothing," she said, a tentatively hopeful look on her face. "Road trip?" She had a hand up in the air, palm facing me. It took me a few seconds to realise what she was doing.

"Road trip," I agreed, and high-fived the ghost.

"Are you sure you're supposed to be going this fast?" said Kitty nervously, from her perch a few centimetres above the passenger seat. We were doing just over fifty miles an hour. I hadn't driven Basil for a couple of months and didn't want to risk shocking his system into engine failure.

I glanced sideways at my aunt. "You can put your seatbelt on, if you're that worried," I said.

Kitty scowled. "It's a heartless wretch you are, Lilith O'Reilly." I drove in silence for a few minutes whilst navigating the junction off the Chester road down towards Wrexham. Once we were back on a main road, I risked another look across at my aunt.

"When's the last time you were in a car, Kitty?" I asked.

She gazed out at the countryside whizzing past her window and looked thoughtful. "A week or so before I died," she said. "I remember going out for the day with Jonny. He'd not long bought a little yellow sports car. I'm remembering more and more, you know," she glanced over at me, "not that it always makes sense."

"What sort of car was it?" That seemed like a safe topic of conversation.

"An MG Midget," said Kitty, an air of confidence in her voice. "With a black soft top roof. It was a sunny day, so Jonny put the roof down. We drove up to Crosby with our hair blowing in the wind. Or maybe my subconscious is just making that up to make me feel better." Her voice grew quieter. "I'm not sure what's real and what isn't any more, to tell you the truth."

"You and me both," I said, and we drove on in silence for a while, each lost in our own thoughts. I'd always found the drive down to Shrewsbury tedious. It involved long stretches of dual carriageway that made the car bounce until my teeth chattered because the council rarely found the money to fix the endless potholes. To make things even more irksome, I'd opened the outer portion of Eadric's letter before we left and found nothing except another envelope inside it. This one was constructed from heavy cream paper and bore an address in the town centre. And that meant dealing with the rush hour in Shrewsbury—which was not known for its sensible traffic systems—before heading back home.

As we passed the turn off for Whittington, Kitty broke the silence. "Oh, I remember this," she said, peering back at the junction. "I think I drove down there with Jonny once. Something to do with his family." I put my foot down to overtake an elderly man in a battered Ford Fiesta and felt Basil groaning under the strain. I slowed again as soon as we got past him and patted his steering wheel sympathetically. Meeting Bella The Living Liver Bird had made me wonder whether my habit of anthropomorphising inanimate objects didn't perhaps have some benefits after all. Basil might hold off the self-destruct button a little while longer if I was kinder to him. We trundled steadily on for another half an hour, before finally heading off the by-pass and onto the road to my parent's house. "I'm looking forward to seeing the family again," she said.

I almost did an emergency stop in my panic. "You're not allowed to drop us in it, Kitty!" I'd thought I'd got a hold of my nerves, but now they were spiralling back up in my throat. I felt sick. I just needed to get through today and I wouldn't have to face it again for at least a month. And maybe by then I'd have got more adept at acting like a normal, living human. It all felt like a bit of a reach right now.

"I'm not going to do anything," my aunt retorted, "other than be there as support for you. You'll be fine, Lil." I clearly didn't look reassured, because she carried on talking. "You don't see them often—they'll be so thrilled by you visiting that it won't occur to them that anything's out of the ordinary."

"I hope you're right," I said, crunching Basil to a halt in a spray of gravel, "because we're here."

Mum was out of the house and halfway to the car before I'd even opened the driver's door. She was wearing jeans and a loose t-shirt that was covered in paint stains. She must be decorating again. I'd never met a wall that my mother didn't want to repaint, even if it was for no better reason than she had ten minutes free and didn't know what to do with herself. Sitting still was not in my mum's codebook. It never had been—sometimes it was tiring just being in her vicinity. Dad stayed back in the doorway, leaning against the frame. His arms were folded, and he smiled crookedly at me. He looked older, somehow. I hadn't seen them for a couple of months, but it wasn't enough to explain the slightly faded expression on his face and the way he seemed to use the door for support. "There's something wrong with him," said a quiet voice in my ear, "but I think he'll be okay."

I turned to look at Kitty, who was standing next to me, faded in the bright sunshine. "You're not to distract me, you hear?" I said, trying to quell my worries about Dad. If Kitty said he was going to be okay, then I was pretty sure she was right. Pasting what I hoped was an enthusiastic grin on my face, I stepped forward to hug Mum, being careful to neither breathe nor accidentally squash her.

"Aah, you're strong these days!" Mum shrieked happily, hugging me to her. "Must be the sea air doing you good."

"Our Lilith's always been the strong one," said Dad, straightening up with a noticeable wince. "C'm here, girly." He enveloped me in a bear hug and I was relieved to find that he hadn't lost any weight. His comforting bulk was still there underneath his baggy jumper and loose trousers. No jeans for Dad—he'd got into chinos in the eighties and had never lost his loyalty. "Smart *and* comfortable," he'd say, tugging at the fabric to show me, whilst Mum rolled her eyes.

"I've made us some scones," Mum said happily.

A flash of panic ran through me. I hadn't even considered that they'd expect me to eat. "Aah mum," I replied, trying to sound casual, "I'm off the cakes at the minute. I should have said."

She eyed me suspiciously. "I hope you're not trying to diet," she said, "because you are lovely as you are and anyone who thinks differently needs a slap. Have you got a new man or something? Has Laura come to her senses finally?"

I laughed. "No," I said, "no new anyone." Mum tried not to look too disappointed. "And I wouldn't diet for anyone else's approval, anyway. It's just," I thought quickly, "it's looking like I might be lactose intolerant, so I'm cutting things out to see if it helps. Coffee will do me fine." She looked at me strangely, but clearly decided to let it go.

"More for me," said Dad, already heading back into the house. "Excellent stuff."

We were sitting in the conservatory at the back of the house, a relatively recent addition that Dad had built himself after he'd retired a few years earlier. Some of the land behind us had been sold to developers over the years. New-build houses now sat in place of the view across to the town centre that had been there when I was young, but the patch directly behind the house had been kept for grazing. I looked out at the two small, fat ponies who had lived there for the past few years. They never seemed to get ridden, despite clearly being very well looked after. As I watched, one of them took offence at something I couldn't see and leaped up into the air dramatically, before taking off at a gallop on his stumpy little legs. His companion took no notice whatsoever and carried on munching. "Did I tell you they've closed that river path now?" said Mum, coming in with a tray of coffee. I tried not to show any reaction, but a flash in my peripheral vision suggested that Kitty had moved closer to me.

I took care with my words. "You didn't, no," I said. "I'm glad."

Dad harrumphed from his chair in the corner. "Should've done it years ago," he grumbled.

Mum must have seen my expression, because she clattered the cups down loudly and made a performance of finding the sugar. "Anyway," she said brightly, settling onto the wicker couch next to me, "tell us all about life in the city. How's Izzy doing? Has she broken any hearts recently?"

We chatted about nothing in particular, until Dad decided he couldn't hide his exhaustion any longer and pushed himself up out of the chair. "I'll leave you girls to have a proper gossip," he said.

Mum and I rolled our eyes at him as per family tradition. "Go have a nap, Geoff," she said. "I'll give you a poke before Lili leaves."

"Aye, you'd better," he said, reaching out to ruffle my hair, "or I'll have your guts for garters."

Once she was sure he was out of earshot, Mum turned to me with a stern look on her face. "Now then, Lilith O'Reilly," she said in a quiet but firm voice, "are we going to talk about the fact that you are dead?" She raised her eyebrows sharply at me. "Or were you planning to try to hide it from your mother?" I sat frozen, genuinely lost for words, whilst Mum just gazed levelly at me.

Eventually, I managed to pull some semblance of my wits together. "What are you talking about?" Mum held my gaze in complete silence, just daring me to deny it. "How…how did you know?" I stumbled. "And if you really think I'm dead, why aren't you wailing and crying?"

Mum snorted. "Why would I bother crying when you're still sitting here in front of me, bright as a button?" she pointed out. "To be honest, love, you look better than you have in ages."

"Gee, thanks," I scowled. "But I still don't understand. How did you know?"

Mum smiled. "You've got the eyes," she said. "But if I'm being honest," the eyebrows again, "the main giveaway is that your Aunt bloody Katherine is sitting right beside you."

* * *

Kitty had let herself become visible again as soon as Mum had spoken and we stared at each other in a combination of horror and amazement for a good few seconds. It was my aunt who found her voice first. "Well now, Helen," she said. "Since when did you have the family talent?"

Mum made a dismissive noise in the back of her throat. "Since when did anyone know I didn't?" she said, leaning forward to pour herself another coffee. "Top up, Lil?" I nodded mutely. "Did she bother wearing her seatbelt?" This to me, with a nod of her head in Kitty's direction. "Her sister used to hate wearing seatbelts, said they were designed to throttle people in the event of a crash."

"There, erm…there didn't seem much point," I said, weakly. Kitty was gaping at my mum. Her mouth was opening and closing silently, like a guppy whose tank was being drained. "How…how long have you known about all this?" I asked.

Mum sat back with her coffee cradled in both hands and gave it some thought. "Ooh, as far back as I can remember, really," she said. " I wasn't convinced it was entirely true until you turned up today, mind. It was Katherine there who gave it away."

"Kitty," said my aunt, her voice faint.

Mum nodded. "You always did prefer being called Kitty. You told me off about it once, when I was a young girl. That's when I started to think things maybe weren't quite as they seemed."

Kitty frowned. "You were born, when?" she asked Mum, "Nineteen-sixty-one?"

"Nineteen-sixty," said Mum. "I'd have been just about three years old when you left." She waggled an eyebrow. "There was…talk."

Kitty rolled her eyes. "I'm sure there was," she replied tartly, "but I was free and single and entitled to a life of my own. As Lili can tell you, I wasn't like this," she gestured at her not-quite-solid form, "until a good couple of years after that." I could almost see the cogs whirring in my aunt's head before she spoke again. "How old were you when I told you to call me Kitty instead of Katherine?"

Mum smiled. "About eight," she said, with a smug look on her face. "You visited me occasionally when I was feeling sad. Or just in a bad mood about things. Mum used to ask who I was talking to. After the second time she slapped me for it, I stopped telling the truth. But I knew you were real."

Kitty looked ashen, an impressive feat for a ghost. "I…I don't remember," she said, slowly, "not properly, at least. I know I used to talk to you when Ivy wasn't around, but I'd assumed it was when I was still alive. Oh," she wailed, "I wish I knew what was what!" I patted her knee in what I'd thought would be a reassuring manner, only for my hand to go through her leg onto the sofa below. Interestingly, I couldn't see my hand clearly, despite it having gone right through Kitty's leg. I knew it was on the sofa because I could feel the cushions beneath my fingers, but it was as if I was looking through thick fog. I wondered if there would come a point when Kitty was teetering between translucence and solidity and if I'd be able to feel her as my hand went through. Then I decided it was a grim and morbid thought that would not be allowed to run through my mind ever again.

"Who else do you see, Mum?" I asked, and we both knew what I actually meant.

Mum gave me a tired smile. "I've never seen your brother," she said, "however hard I've tried. Maybe one day." That explained why she'd always refused to move away from the family house. She was probably worried Cally might reappear and not have any family to greet him. "In fact I don't see many people at all," she continued, "which always surprises me in a town as full of ghosts as this one is. There's a couple of your kind," she nodded at me, "in the town centre. They don't bother anyone though, so I've never really given it much thought."

"A couple?" I asked, wondering if the undead grapevine was efficient enough for the local revenants to already know that I was in town. Perhaps I should have asked Mapp or Eadric whether there was any etiquette I had to follow. I might be expected to go pay my respects to the local branch of Soul-Suckers Anonymous for all I knew, or risk being kicked into the Severn for disrespecting the family. I decided I'd ask whoever it was I was delivering the letter to.

"There's an old woman who always shops in the market hall on a Friday morning," said Mum, dragging me back to the conversation. "And a younger chap—mid-thirties, maybe? I actually first noticed him because of his amazing dress sense. Sharp suits and cravats, that sort of thing. Not what you'd expect to be worn by someone his age, these days. I don't think they know each other, though. I've never seen them together, at least."

"Do you know where they live?" I asked. Perhaps I could get hold of one of them and ask them to be my local guide. Not today, though. I only had time to visit my parents and run Eadric's errand, because I absolutely had to be up and ready to open Flora's the next morning. Izzy had said she would be fine if I took an extra day off, but I'd been slacking enough already and told her not to be daft. And if I could get chatting with Sean, we might be able to start again. A noise from inside the house made us all look up in panic.

"Your dad's getting up," she said. "Not a word to him about this, you hear me? He wouldn't cope with it, not the way I can."

"Does he know you can see…different things?" I asked.

Mum shook her head. "No," she replied, "and he wouldn't want to. Very practical, is your dad. He's well aware that I believe certain things about the world, but we don't discuss it. It's my secret and I'm happy to leave it that way."

"What's wrong with him?" asked Kitty, who was already fading out.

Mum sighed. "Just age, the doctors say," she looked unconvinced, "but I'm not sure. He's hardly ancient, but he sleeps an awful lot. I was worried it might be dementia, but he seems sharp enough when he's awake. Anyway," she said brightly, "look lively, Dad's back!" Kitty disappeared just as Dad came through the door into the conservatory, looking far brighter than he had earlier.

"Want another cuppa, girls?" he asked me and Mum.

I shook my head. "I'll be needing a wee all the way back to Liverpool," I lied.

Mum smiled. "I'll have one, Geoff," she said. "Kettle hasn't long boiled." She waited for the sound of him switching the kettle on before speaking again. "You mind yourself, Lilith O'Reilly." Her voice was firm but anxious. "You're not invulnerable, even if you are immortal. I'm not prepared to lose both of you, you hear me?" I could feel my throat choking up. Getting up out of my seat, I went over to where Mum sat, looking smaller than ever. Leaning over, I hugged her, and she gripped me back with unexpected ferocity. "At least you still feel human," she said as I pulled away. She sniffed and rooted around in her pocket for a tissue.

"That's cos I *am* human," I pointed out. "Nothing's really changed. It's just that *nothing* changes."

"How's the love life?" said Dad, coming through the door with two mugs of tea and a bag of doughnuts under his arm. "Thought we'd have a treat," he said, putting the mugs down and ripping the bag open. "Lil?" he waved the bag at me. It smelled amazing.

Mum came to my rescue. "Aah Geoff," she said in a light voice, "the vile child stuffed her face at the services on the way down. She'll be sick if you force those into her as well."

Dad looked surprised. "I thought she was whatsit-intolerant?" he asked. "And what services? Who bothers to stop when it's only an hour or so down here?"

"Pulled off at Chirk for a wee," I said, "and McDonald's was open. Couldn't resist." I shrugged.

Dad rolled his eyes. "It's a bloody good job you've got your mother's metabolism," he said, cramming an entire doughnut into his mouth and then having to chew for ages whilst we waiting, "because otherwise you'd be the size of a house. God, those are good." He sat back and belched happily.

We chatted aimlessly for another hour. Dad filled me in on gossip about people I hadn't seen for years and wouldn't even recognise if I met them on the street. Mum corrected him as he went—'no Geoff, Sally ran off with that chap from Morrisons. It was Lou's husband who had an affair at Tesco'. I enjoyed the normality of it after the recent insanity in my life. But I was all too aware that I had to find Eadric's contact in town before I could head home. "Don't leave it so long next time," Mum said as we were saying our goodbyes on the doorstep. "It's always so lovely to see you." As she hugged me, she whispered in my ear. "You're going to have to invent a food allergy to stop your dad from trying to feed you."

I hugged her tightly. "Thanks Mum," I said, "you have no idea how much better I feel."

She stepped back to look at me properly, a smile on her face. "You'll be grand, Lilith," she said with certainty. "I just know it. See you again soon." This was aimed at Kitty, who I could feel was next to me. But of course, Dad didn't need to know that.

"Yes," he said, coming forward to hug me, "sooner rather than later next time, please." He felt reassuringly solid. Whatever might be wrong with him, he certainly wasn't fading away. I got into the car and reversed carefully off their drive, ignoring Dad's shouted instructions as I creaked Basil out onto the road. With a last round of waves and reassurances out of the window that I'd be back soon, I joined the traffic and headed into town.

Amazingly, I found a parking space just outside the address on the envelope. It was the only one on the entire street and had clearly been left because it was too small for most cars, but I managed to wedge Basil into it with only one unnerving clank of wheels against the kerb. I peered up at the town library in all its mock-Elizabethan splendour and briefly wondered if any of its famous inhabitants over the centuries had known there was a secret world hidden in plain sight. "I'm coming with you," said Kitty, breaking my train of thought. I turned to look at my aunt, who appeared to be actually sitting in the passenger seat. *She's definitely getting more real*, I thought to myself, and wondered if the pedestrians walking past us on the pavement could see her.

"I'm not sure that's a good idea," I said, remembering Eadric's none too enthusiastic curiosity about my resident ghost.

Kitty shook her head. "What if something happened to you? I might be stuck out here in this car forever!"

"Oh thanks," I said, "there was me assuming you were worried about me, but it's all about you, isn't it?"

Kitty grinned at me, unrepentant. "It's about both of us," she said. "After all," she raised an eyebrow questioningly, "what would Thelma be without Louise?"

Jack's Back

B lower's Repository looks ancient enough to have been built when Charles Darwin was still running down the corridors of the town library next door as a know-it-all pupil, back when it was still Shrewsbury School. All black and white Tudor beams and solid Jacobean stonework, the entire facade of Blower's is an outright lie. It was actually built in the early 1900s in a pastiche style, chosen to match its surroundings. Blower's had housed the reference section of the library for as long as I could remember, which is why I wasn't convinced by the address on the envelope. "You stay hidden," I hissed at Kitty as I walked the short distance down Castle Gates, my aunt nothing more than an occasional wisp in my peripheral vision. My plan was to go ask at the desk. With any luck, my intended recipient worked as a librarian, in the time-honoured tradition of spooky anti-hero stories. As it was, I hadn't even reached the door when Kitty shot past me into the stone archway next door, a blur of movement in the late afternoon sun. "It's here," she said. The faint outline of her hand waved towards a discreet brass plaque almost hidden in the stone behind the archway's gates. *JM* was engraved into the plate in copperplate script, next to a heavy oak door set into the stone wall. There was a brass doorbell below the plate, and Kitty waited expectantly for me to press it. "I'm not sure this is a good idea," I said, as I pressed the button. A bell rang once, somewhere deep inside the building. It sounded muffled, and as though it hadn't rung for a very long time.

"It can't be anything awful," said Kitty, "or the Silvertons wouldn't have asked you to visit."

"Don't be too sure about that," I said. "I'm pretty sure that a good two-thirds of the Silverton family would happily see me fall into the Mersey, rather than risk having to answer my questions." I pressed the bell again, in case it hadn't been heard the first time.

"Give me a bloody minute, would you?" came a voice from above our heads. I stepped back out onto the street and looked up. A small, leaded window had been opened on the floor above and the top half of a head poked out. All I could see was floppy dark hair. "I can't get the wiring to work," said the politely clipped male voice, "hang on. Aah," he continued, "that should do it. Come on up." The door clicked open with a modern-sounding thunk. I gave it a push, and it swung inwards on well-oiled hinges.

"Someone's good at DIY," I said to Kitty. "Come on, then." As I stepped through the door, I turned to look at her. She was clearly visible on the step behind me, but there was a look of pale apprehension on her face. "You wanted to come with me," I pointed out. "You're my wing-woman for this shit, don't forget." I tried not to look as impatient as I felt. It wasn't as though I *wanted* to be visiting random zombies, however cultivated this particular one might turn out to be. And I wasn't impressed at having been made Eadric's messenger girl. I had no idea what the letter was about, or who the recipient was. For all I knew, the whole thing could be a set up. There might be a welcoming party of machete-wielding revenant hunters up there. "I'm still trying to figure out who I can trust," I said to Kitty. She floated in the doorway behind me, poised a couple of inches above the step. I could see pedestrians walking up the hill into town through my aunt's torso, which was about as disconcerting as you could imagine. "But apart from Mapp, Eadric's the only one who's been remotely supportive. I don't think he'd put me in harm's way." Putting my hand behind my back so Kitty wouldn't see, I crossed my fingers. I was fairly sure that Eadric Silverton wouldn't have introduced me to the birds had he not trusted me. But perhaps I was giving him too much credit? Until I knew who this 'JM' was, I couldn't be sure it wasn't part of a plot to get rid of me. How could the Silvertons be sure I wouldn't tell people about them and their metallic rooftop avian collection? Not that I was going to voice my fears to my aunt, who was clearly as nervous as a ghost could ever be. "Come on," I said, with a confidence I didn't feel. "Let's go show whoever it is that nothing scares the O'Reilly girls." Kitty didn't look convinced, but she reluctantly eased herself through the doorway and floated next to me. We were standing in a tiny, dark stairwell, in which stone steps lead up to an open, arched doorway. I could see an ornate chandelier hanging in the room beyond, lit by what looked distinctly like low-wattage economy candle bulbs.

"Come on up," called the same voice as before. "I'm just trying to sort out this stupid wiring." I headed up the stairs before Kitty could think of a reason not to. She was all but invisible again, but the flickering in the corner of my vision confirmed that she was sticking with me. I stopped in the doorway and looked around me. We were standing at the entrance to what would normally be described as a studio apartment. It was one large room containing sleeping, eating and cooking areas, with a small bathroom visible through a doorway to my left. I say 'normally', because most studio apartments aren't decorated in a style more usually found in Versailles. There was a four-poster bed set against one wall. It was carved from what looked distinctly like oak and draped with an elaborately embroidered eiderdown in shades of red and gold. The two chairs that sat in front of the narrow leaded windows were heavy Chesterfields, their brown leather upholstery worn soft through use. The kitchen corner contained a full-size range cooker, with a Belfast sink underneath a small window. A wooden butcher's block on wheeled legs looked more authentic than any I'd seen for sale in kitchen showrooms. Dark oak floorboards ran across the floor throughout, laid with heavy woven rugs between the armchairs and next to the bed. The owner of the voice still hadn't shown his face. He had his back to us and was concentrating on a thick wire that protruded from what appeared to be a dumb waiter system that was tucked into the side wall of the building. "Oh *dash* it," he said finally, dropping the wire and turning towards me. Kitty whisked behind me, although what she thought anyone could do to a ghost was anyone's guess. "Sorry about that," he said. "It's been playing up for ages. What can I do for you?"

I wasn't sure who or what I'd been expecting, but it wasn't what was standing in front of me. He was in his mid-thirties at a guess, a slender white man with pink cheeks and dark hair that flopped over his face. I realised it must be the same man Mum had spotted in town. He was wearing dark grey corduroy trousers over brown brogues that were probably expensive some time in the distant past, topped with a long-sleeve cream t-shirt and a red plaid shirt. It only took a split second to register all this, but he was quicker than me. "Oh my word," he said with a breathy chuckle, "it's true, then. We've got new blood in the family." He grinned at me, his silver eyes twinkling.I was about to say something smart and probably inadvisable about not wanting my blood to be part of his family, when I realised Kitty was standing next to me. She was looking more solid than ever.

"Jonny?" she said in an incredulous voice. "Is it really you?" The man looked confused for a second, then a clear mix of s hock, regret and excitement all played across his face at the same time. I risked a breath, wondering if I'd be able to taste his true emotions, but there was nothing. I added 'ask Eadric if we're all unreadable to each other' to the rapidly expanding mental list of questions that in my head had been labelled 'Revenant 101'. There was a strange buzzing sensation in the air, as if static was building up on the surface of a balloon. It was coming from Kitty. She was glowing slightly around the edges and the man stood frozen to the spot, like a deer in headlights. I looked from him to my aunt and back again.

"Would anyone like to explain to me what's going on?" I demanded. The man gave me a brief glance, but Kitty didn't break her concentration at all. "Hello," I said, "is anyone listening to me?"

"Lili," Kitty finally said, her voice breaking slightly, "This is Jonny." I gawped at her and she saw it without turning her head. "Yes," she nodded, "the very same."

"What?" I asked stupidly. "But Jonny disappeared decades ago—you told me so yourself!" I'd have sworn Kitty was hyperventilating if it didn't seem such an unlikely reaction for a ghost. Jonny was still standing in the middle of the floor, apparently struck dumb with shock. "This is fucking *insane*," I muttered to myself in the understatement of the century. As if life—death—wasn't complicated enough already.

"*You deceitful, murderous, lying* bastard!" Kitty suddenly shrieked. As I turned to her in shock, she looked more real than she ever had before. Jonny's eyes widened in surprise and he only just ducked in time as Kitty picked up a large plaster bust of Shakespeare that was sitting on a bookcase and threw it at his head. It hit the wall and left a deep dent in the plaster, before dropping and smashing into pieces on the floor. I automatically grabbed Kitty, and it took me a few seconds to realise that I really was holding her. I could feel her shaking with rage and anguish, but she was already subsiding into my arms.

Jonny slowly picked himself up off the floor. "I never lied to you, Kitty," he said quietly. He was as white as a sheet and I could see his hands shaking. "I didn't want you to die."

"But you weren't honest with me," my aunt replied, more calmly now, "were you?" She took a deep breath and shook me off. Did ghosts actually breathe? Or was she feeling normal human emotions and just doing normal, human things in a way that I—still solid and functioning in the 'living' world—couldn't? I risked a breath myself and felt nothing. No, there *was* something. Kitty was giving off a faint air of quietly brewing fury that was building by the second. It tasted of firesmoke and seaweed and carried an overwhelming sense of betrayal.

"I didn't know for sure that it wouldn't work," Jonny said, his eyes pleading. "You were so desperate to believe, I couldn't bring myself to tell you just how unlikely it all was. And," he dropped his gaze, "I was an addict. I took from you and I knew it might kill you, but I kept doing it, even though I loved you more than I've ever loved anyone else." He looked up again, his eyes glittering. It hadn't occurred to me that revenants might still be able to cry. "I *loved* you, Kitty," he said. "More than anything. But I couldn't stop myself. You were eager and willing and I took complete advantage of that. There is nothing I can say that will change that." He held a hand out towards her and she looked at it for a long moment.

"You're right," she said finally. "There's nothing you can say." She was fading again now that her anger was retreating, and I could see the bookcase through her chest. A copy of Byron's *Childe Harold's Pilgrimage* sat propped against the shelf, right where her heart would be.

"Well," I said, "this is all very…unexpected." Jonny and Kitty both looked at me as if they'd only just remembered that I was in the room. "I think it's probably best if we leave," I said to the room in general. "You clearly both need time to think. I can bring Kitty back for a visit," I looked at my aunt, "if she wants me to." Kitty was shimmering in the air next to me, her face utterly expressionless.

"Did you have a reason for your visit?" asked Jonny. "Because I can't imagine that you'd have known to come here without instructions from elsewhere."

"Oh shit," I blurted, rooting in my pocket for Eadric's letter, "I'm sorry. I forgot." I passed the envelope over to Jonny. He picked up a letter-opener from a side table and slit the paper with practised ease. Unfolding a single sheet of cream paper, he scanned it briefly. When he dropped his hand, I saw the letter had been written in old-fashioned script, using a fountain pen. There was a single swooping letter at the bottom of the page.

"You'll be so kind as to tell Eadric that I am, as always, at his service," Jonny said politely. It wasn't a question.

"We'll be off, then," I said awkwardly, and looked round at Kitty. She wasn't there. I was well-enough accustomed to her by now to know when I was standing in front of empty space, rather than my invisible aunt. And this was a whole heap of empty space.

"She'll reappear," said Jonny. "She's just had a shock." He made a quiet, strangled noise that was halfway between a laugh and a sob. "We've both had a shock."

"Are you going to be okay?" I asked.

He looked at me and smiled. "Yes," he said, "I'll be okay. I've been waiting for Katherine for a long time, Lilith." His expression was indecipherable. "I'm sure I can wait some more. Come, I'll see you out."

* * *

As 'seeing me out' involved Jonny taking about six steps across the room to the door, I was down the stairs and back under the stone archway to the street in seconds. The door closed heavily behind me. "Kitty?" I said quietly, "are you there?" Nothing. What was I supposed to do now? I couldn't leave the ghost of my aunt wandering around Shrewsbury without company or supervision. I considered calling Mum and ask what she thought, but that risked Dad picking up and asking questions I couldn't answer. There was no option but to take Jonny's word for it. Hopefully, Kitty would stick with me, even though I couldn't see her. I unlocked Basil and dropped into the driver's seat, then sat for a while on the off-chance Kitty might materialise next to me. Nothing. When I spotted a traffic warden heading towards me along Castle Street, I gave up and pulled out into the afternoon traffic.

"That fucking *bastard!*" Kitty reappeared as I drove along the M53 through the glamorous environs of Ellesmere Port. I took a moment to wrench Basil back into our lane before responding.

"Do you think you might give some warning next time?" I asked through gritted teeth. I stared straight ahead and determinedly ignored the furious gestures coming from the driver of a Ford Transit who'd had to veer onto the hard shoulder in order to avoid being hit by over a tonne of ageing German metalwork. "And," I went on, slowing down in case of further disturbances, "is there really any point in losing your shit at Jonny after all these years?" I risked a quick glance sideways to where Kitty was frowning at me from the passenger seat. She'd resumed her usual visibility level—mostly there, but not entirely disguising the upholstery she was pretending to sit on. "I can't see that there was much he could have done at the time," I said, "and he was at least honest with his explanations."

"I should have *known* not to trust him," Kitty spat, "after what happened with his wives." Wives—plural, no less—were a new one on me.

"You didn't tell me he'd been married," I said, pulling out to overtake the same white van. Basil might have the acceleration of a snail with arthritis, but once he got going, he had a decent bit of poke in his engine.

"Twice," said Kitty. She'd folded her arms and was glaring out of the window at the grey skyline that was whizzing past. It started to rain, and I cursed Basil's crappy windscreen wipers. They'd needed replacing for at least eighteen months, but I'd been putting it off. Maybe I could get him properly reconditioned, now that I'd be saving money on food and heating. I'd realised within the first couple of days of my afterlife that I didn't feel the cold anymore, which was useful when you lived in a flat as draughty as mine. I wondered idly about death admin again. Nothing needed to change just yet, because no one actually knew I was dead. Or, at least, no one who'd be bothered by the legalities of a corpse wandering the streets of Liverpool as if nothing had happened. But the bank were surely going to wonder what was up if I hit my centenary and was still spending too much money in H&M of a weekend. I'd have to ask Eadric about it at some point.

"What happened to them?" I asked her.

Kitty sighed. "The first one died young," she said, "and I honestly think the stress of living with Jonny had something to do with it. This was a long time before I knew him," she glanced at me, "when he was still alive. He was a nightmare. Everyone knew the stories."

"What stories?"

"Oh," she said, "Jonny was infamous around Shropshire. Jack, he was called back then. Liked his drink and liked his horses. Didn't like anything else, very much. At least, that's what people said. Anyway," she went back to staring out of the window, "he had a daughter with the first wife, and then she died. Silly fool went and got himself a second wife, of course," she snorted to herself, "and this one was made of sterner stuff. Outlived him by a good few years, the clever girl." Kitty wriggled around—I wasn't sure whether a ghost would actually need to get themselves comfortable, or if it was just a habit—and lay her head back on the seat. "They buried her with him, regardless," she went on. "Which seems a bit bloody cruel, if you ask me."

"How can they have buried her with him," I asked, "if he's still up and walking around?"

Kitty shrugged. "Comes from a wealthy family, does Jonny," she said. "Those types don't spend much time caring, Lil. I doubt they even visited his tomb very often, let alone checked whether he was actually in it."

"But his second wife is?"

"Hopefully she's haunting the bloody life out of them," said my aunt, and grinned for the first time that afternoon. "Look," she went on, "I'm sorry for being so hysterical and dramatic today." I automatically moved my hand to pat her leg reassuringly and found myself stroking the passenger seat. Clearly, Kitty was back to her normal, incorporeal form. "I loved him very much, you know? And I didn't expect to ever see him again." Another sigh. "It takes a long time to get used to someone not being there. But eventually your mind settles to it and creates a new normality. So it's a wrenching shock when they reappear and that normality's ripped apart again. You know?" I nodded as we swung off the motorway and joined the A41 on our way to the Queensway tunnel. Cally popped up in my mind, running around the field behind our house and calling to me to join him.

"I think," I said honestly, " I'd at least want to give the new normality a try."

Kitty peered out of the windscreen at the dark clouds beginning to roll in the distance. "I think," she said, "there's a storm brewing."

We drove the rest of the way in silence. The barriers would be back up on Harrington Street, so Basil was going to have to brave the great outdoors until the next morning. I found a space on Hackins Hey and carefully locked him up. It was dusk, and Kitty was all but invisible in the gloom as she walked beside me for the few minutes it took us to get back to Flora's. I wondered if she could have just done the ghostly version of teleporting if she'd wanted to, but didn't like to ask. As I turned onto Castle Street with Kitty floating next to me, I couldn't hold it in any longer. "How am I going to find things out?" I asked her.

A flicker beside me suggested my aunt had turned to look at me. "Find out what?" she asked.

"Everything," I said, as we continued up the street. "Why I survived that fall, whether the Silvertons really are trustworthy. If Ivo Laithlind is a friend or an enemy. You know," I said, smiling despite myself, "the minor questions in life." We reached the turn for home and I stopped suddenly. Underneath the arched Harrington Street sign was what looked like a forensics tent. Several people in white paper suits stood around it, talking quietly amongst themselves. I thought of Billy and panicked for a second, then remembered that he was already dead. Pulling my phone out of my pocket, I saw several missed calls from Izzy. I muted my phone by accident so often that she rarely bothered to ring these days, so I must have missed something important. At least I knew she couldn't be inside the tent if she'd been trying to call me. As I stepped forward, a police officer came towards me.

"Closed off, love," she said, "you'll have to go round." I assumed Kitty had made herself invisible again.

"I live here," I said, nodding past the tent towards where Flora's sat, locked up and in darkness. "Can I ask what's happened?"

The officer gave me a kindly smile that didn't quite reach her eyes. "I'm sure you'll find out soon enough," she said. "In the meantime, I'm afraid I'll have to ask you to go the other way around." There didn't seem much point in arguing for the sake of it, so I did as I'd been told. The detour round Mathew Street and Rainford Square was a short one, but the streets were busy enough that I had to mooch along at a human pace. When I finally got back to Flora's, I found Izzy sitting at the top of the fire escape, waiting for me. Kitty was next to her, glittering faintly in the gloom, like a hologram whose power had been turned down. Taking the stairs four at a time, I bounced to a halt in front of Izzy. She raised an eyebrow at me. "Show-off," she muttered, getting to her feet. "You'd better let us in," she went on, "before anyone comes looking for you."

I was confused. "Why would anyone be looking for me?" I asked. Izzy looked tired and drawn. Something had clearly hit the fan with a thud whilst Kitty and I had been touring the borderlands, and I wasn't sure I really wanted to know what it was.

"There's been a murder," Izzy said flatly. "And I think you're the chief suspect."

Under Pressure

"What the *fuck*?" I spluttered. Kitty looked as shocked as a dead woman ever could.

"Can we just go inside?" asked Izzy. "It's been a long day and I'm not sure I feel safe out here in the dark." I hurriedly rooted around in my bag for the door keys and let us into the flat. To my relief, Grimm was asleep on the sofa, sprawled across the entire length of the seat cushions in that louche way only cats can manage. Izzy walked past me and scooted Grimm up so that she could flop down next to him.Kitty was more visible now that we were indoors. She floated across to the window and looked down at the street.

"I assume there's a body underneath that tent, then?" she asked.

Izzy nodded. "They found him in the middle of the day," she said, "when people were walking around and Flora's was really busy. Todd's great, by the way," she went on, glancing at me briefly, "we should probably keep him."

"Someone literally got killed on the street? In front of witnesses?" I asked. Harrington Street might have its creepy moments, but I'd always felt reasonably safe. There were certainly worse places to walk around alone in Liverpool.

"He was already dead when he was found," said Izzy. " A young American couple found him. They'd been into the cafe and were really nice. Paid their bill and left, and I thought no more of it. Then they came screaming back inside, a minute or so later. I thought there must have been an accident, it took a while to get any sense out of them. Turns out," she pulled Grimm up onto her lap and started stroking him like a comfort blanket, "the woman had literally tripped over a body. Just lying there on the street."

"And no one saw what happened?" I was incredulous, and also hugely suspicious. Harrington Street might not have been on the tourist trail, but it opened straight onto the main road. The spot covered by the forensics tent would have been clearly visible to passers-by at all times. I walked over to the window and stood next to Kitty. W e both peered out to watch what was happening below us. "Billy's still out there," I said. He was curled up in his sleeping bag nest and had the appearance of being asleep. "Has he been there all day?" I asked Izzy. "Surely he would have seen something as major as a body being dumped a few feet away?"

"He went off for an hour or so around lunchtime," she replied, "and came back just as the police were arriving."

I squinted suspiciously down at the street. As if reading my thoughts, Billy suddenly looked up. To my surprise, he waved at me. "I'm going down to speak to him," I said. "Maybe he'll know who it was, at least."

"I think you mean *what*," said Izzy wearily. I turned to stare at her and she looked up at me. "It was a man," she went on, "according to the Americans. But I went back out with them to see what had happened and honestly, Lil," she lay her head back on the sofa and closed her eyes, "I think it was actually one of your lot."

"What did it—he—look like?" I tried to squash down the panic that was rising in my throat. Since I'd been undead, I'd met several people I wouldn't miss if I never saw them again. But what if it was Heggie or Owain?

"Tall, thin bloke," said Izzy, "with straggly hair and thin fingers. Too many teeth for a standard human." One of Joe's ratboys. I tried not to let the relief show on my face.

"The man who pushed me off the fire escape," I said. "Could have been worse."

"The problem *is*, Lilith," Izzy said, "the police know something wasn't quite right. They were talking about him maybe having dental implants and weird fetishes. But if they take him for a post-mortem—which they will, on account of how people don't often just turn up dead in the street in broad

228

daylight—they're going to realise something's wrong. Aren't they?"

"I suspect Eadric will have contacts high up in the legal system," I said, "if not within the police force itself. Anyway," I went on, "it's not my problem. I wasn't here when it happened and they'd have no reason to be checking my medical information." I suddenly remembered what Izzy had said when I first got home. "What did you mean when you said I might be the prime suspect?" I asked her. Izzy looked pale, and I wondered if the events of the last week or so were finally catching up with her. Was it possible to get PTSD from realising that your best friend was a fully paid-up member of the walking dead? She cracked her eyes open enough to look at me.

"Eadric rang my mobile," she said, "just after it happened. So unless you've given him my number," I shook my head, "he's been snooping. I don't have my phone listed anywhere, as far as I know." I believed her—she'd changed the number a couple of years earlier after a dumped boyfriend didn't get the message, and rarely gave the new number out to anyone. "So he clearly has access to records." As she said it, my own mobile rang. I fished it out of my bag and stared at the unknown number through the cracked glass. I thought idly that I should probably get it fixed at some point, now it was becoming clear that I was going to be needing it a while longer. "Are you going to answer that," snapped Izzy, "or just stare at it all night?" I glared at her and poked the accept button more viciously than was strictly necessary.Before I could say a word, a voice at the other end spoke.

"Do not go anywhere," said Eadric sternly. "Nikolaus is coming to see you."

"No, he fucking isn't," I retorted. "I've just got in and there's been a murder and I have fucking well had enough for one day. Thank you very much."

There was silence for a moment. Then Eadric spoke again, more politely this time. "You might be in danger," he said. "People think you killed Benjamin." So I'd been right—it *was* one of the ratboys lying out there, being poked by the forensics officers who were still going in and out of the tent. They didn't seem in any hurry to move the body. No need to rush once you knew for definite that the corpse had stopped twitching.

Something important occurred to me. "If it's a ra—Benjamin," I said, "how

229

did he die?"

"I don't think it's a good idea to discuss things until I've reassured myself you had nothing to do with it, Lilith," said Eadric. There was something he wasn't telling me, I was sure of it.

"I was in Shropshire," I said sharply, "as you well know. I was running bloody errands for you, Eadric Silverton. And you haven't answered my question." I was sure I heard a sigh at the other end of the line, but ignored it. "How did the ratboy die? Because as far as I know, he was a vampire," Izzy jerked her head up at that, staring wide-eyed at me, "and assuming I haven't got my mythology majorly wrong, they don't die easily." There was a long silence, during which I was pretty sure Eadric considered whether it would be easier to simply drop me off the top of another tall building.

Finally, he spoke. "You're right, of course," he said evenly. *Strike one to me.* "Vampires are, by their very nature, difficult to...terminate." A brief pause. "Benjamin was drained of his soul."

I gaped at the phone. "I thought vampires didn't have souls?" I asked him. "Isn't that kind of the point?"

Eadric laughed. "You shouldn't believe all you read in books, Lilith O'Reilly. Look," he went on, "I have Joe waiting to speak to me and there will be a lot of explaining to do. He hasn't said anything yet, but I'm sure he's going to use Benjamin's death as a metaphorical stick to beat us with. In return for him keeping the...*boys*," he'd almost said 'rat,' but stopped himself, "out of sight as much as possible, we agree to make sure that they and all other residents of the netherworld are kept safe."

"Netherworld?" I snorted. "Is that what you call it?" Nether-fucking-weird, more like.

"However strange our... *world* might be," said Eadric levelly, "we look out for each other. Benjamin was killed by a revenant, Lilith." His voice dropped slightly. "We're the only ones strong enough to drain him until un-death becomes true death. Everyone knows Benjamin caused your own entry to our world—and many also know you've not been entirely happy about that fact. So you'll have to excuse them for drawing the obvious conclusions." I gaped at the phone. Two weeks ago I was nothing more than a bored cafe owner with not enough of a sex life. And now I was not only a reluctant member of a secret, undead society—I was also being accused of murder. I hadn't been this busy since that time I'd dated two boys at once whilst at uni and they'd both turned up for a surprise visit on the same day.

"I'm still not in the mood for an inquisition," I said stubbornly.

"Is your aunt with you?" said Eadric.

"Yes," I said, confused. I looked across at Kitty, who, by her expression, could clearly hear the conversation.

"She's your collateral," said Eadric. "You go anywhere outside that building and I will know about it, Lilith. Do you understand me?"

"I understand the not going outside bit," I said, "although I still think you're being a judgmental twat. But what's Kitty got to do with it?"

"You underestimate our abilities," Eadric said politely. "If you go anywhere further than the fire escape on your building, I will have her exorcised." Kitty and I gaped at each other in horror. "Do you understand me?" I was so angry, I had to fight the urge to race down to the Liver Building and have it out with Eadric Silverton in person. But my aunt—my poor, dead aunt, who'd only hours earlier had to cope with the reappearance of the love of her life—was clearly terrified. She had all but disappeared, only the tiniest shimmer of her outline visible against the glass panes of the window. As I watched, she disappeared completely.

"I understand," I said. "And I hope you understand that you are a bastard."

"You'll get used to it," laughed Eadric Silverton. "Eventually."

* * *

Izzy eventually fell asleep, still sitting upright on the sofa. I gently rearranged her so she was lying down, and covered her with a throw. There was no sign of Kitty. I was too tense to do nothing, so I went into the kitchen and rooted around in the junk drawer until I found the battered packet of emergency Marlboro Izzy had stashed there months earlier. Taking Eadric at his word, I decided that the fire escape was within my allowed boundaries. Grimm was already out there, perched on the top step and watching for mice in the car park below. Fishing a lighter out from the back of the cupboard where I stashed emergency candles, I went outside to join the cat. The metal stairs were set too far back for me to see the forensics tent, but quiet chatter wafting upwards told me that the site was still being guarded by police. "Fancy company for a bit?" To my surprise, Billy was standing at the bottom of the stairs, looking up at me. He had a blanket draped round his shoulders and the ever-present disposable coffee cup in his hand. I nodded silently, and he padded up the steps. When he got to the top, he sat down next to me and draped the blanket companionably around our shoulders. It smelled of cinnamon and patchouli oil, still with the background notes of suffering and sewers that I'd learned to recognise as Billy's signature scent. It didn't smell as awful as it ought to have done, weirdly. This new world I'd found myself in was an overwhelming mix of constant sensory input, filled to the brim with too much of everything. "Difficult being dead sometimes, innit?" Billy said. I glanced sideways. He was resting his chin on his hands as he stared blankly out onto the dark street.

"How do you manage it?" I asked, my gaze equally distant. "How do you cope with...*everything*, when there's so bloody much of it?"

There was a long silence, and for the first time in my life, I didn't feel the need to fill it with inane chatter. "Time," said Billy eventually. "A lot of it stops holding any meaning, after you've been around long enough. " I peeked sideways at him. He'd have been exactly the sort of man I'd have been attracted to, if we'd both still been alive. He was nice enough looking, but there was more to it than that. Something kind and safe lived behind Billy's pale blue eyes. He was the sort of man who put himself between his friend and danger with no thought for his own safety, and in return, he found himself abandoned on the streets of a city that had grown up and away from him.

"What keeps you here?" The words were out of my mouth before I'd had time to consider whether it might be too personal a question. "I'm sorry," I added hurriedly. "I didn't mean to pry."

"Aah it's okay, Red," he replied, twisting his mouth in the semblance of a smile, "it's a natural thing to ask." He shuffled himself around a bit on the step and I wondered how he could act and sound so *real*. He was sitting right there next to me as solid as you like, but I knew very well that he was no more alive than Kitty was. He didn't have a habit of disappearing as often as my aunt did, but then he hadn't just been threatened with exorcism. "Something keeps me here," he went on, "but I don't know what. I've chatted to Missy about it, but she can't work it out, either." Mapp's grumpy friend from the Renshaw Street Knitting Club. I'd forgotten about her. "Maybe something happened to me in life that I can't remember and it holds me here, for some reason." He turned to look at me. "Neither here nor there really, is it?" he said. "It's all I know, and sometimes that's better than the unknown."

"What do you think will happen?" I asked him, nodding my head in the general direction of the little white tent. "Will they check him out and realise his anatomy isn't quite human? Will they start carrying pitchforks and start hunting us down as the sun rises, do you think?"

Billy snorted. "Well now," he said, "that would be a bit pointless, wouldn't it? None of us turns into a sizzling pile of ash when the sun pops its face out. I think," he said, "we should all just carry on as if nothing's happened. And I suspect the police will do the same. They're overstretched and under-funded, and can well do without having to investigate a death than no one saw and no one will appear to care about. Plus, they'll no doubt have already had a phone call from the Silvertons. Probably offering to fund the station's Christmas party, in return for accidentally misplacing the corpse. Ol' Ratty will be wrapped up and sent off for a council funeral and that will be the end of it." He looked at me again, more carefully this time. "Or maybe it won't," he said, thoughtfully.

"Maybe what won't?" I demanded, lighting a cigarette and making a point of not inhaling. I didn't want to risk choking like an idiot just when Billy was finally spilling the supernatural beans. It was ironic that, now I could theoretically smoke myself sick without ever risking even a wisp of cancer, I couldn't actually even *breathe*, for fear of collapsing in a heap. Instead, I took a drag and immediately blew it back out of my mouth, amusing myself by making smoke rings and seeing how far I could push them away.

"Something's going on, Red," he said.

"You don't say," I replied, rolling my eyes to the heavens. "I'd kind of realised that already, to be honest with you." I didn't tell him how I'd sat with Mapp and Eadric whilst they discussed exactly the same thing. Puffing another smoke ring, I poked my finger through it before wafting it away with my hand.

"The birds are unhappy," Billy went on. "Something's disturbed them, and that's never a good sign."

"What?" I'd sent one particularly fine ring floating intact over the roof of Cavern Walks and was watching it slowly dissipate in the distance.

Billy sighed. "Have you always been this easily distracted?" he asked. "Only I could do with your full attention just now, Red."

I peered at him in the light from the kitchen window. Ghosts were strange things, I decided. Kitty was mostly transparent, with only occasional moments of visibility—pretty much how the story books and movies had always portrayed ghostly characters. Billy was something very different. He looked as real as any living human I'd ever met. I put a hand on his shoulder and gripped him briefly. His bones felt solid under my fingers and he looked at me as I gave him a quick squeeze. "You're real," I said, sounding stupid. "How can you be real but also a ghost? Are you sure you're really dead, Billy? Could you have had an accident at some point and just forgotten who you are?"

Billy looked as though he was trying to stop himself from laughing. "What on earth are you talking about, Red?" he asked. "Do you not think that if I was making my story up for entertainment purposes, I'd have perhaps made it a bit less depressing?" He snorted, despite himself. "If I was making it up," he went on, more seriously now, "there would have been dramatic tales of lost loves and witch's curses, with maybe a kingdom I needed to get back to, if only I could find a princess who wanted to kiss me." Another quiet snort. "You're real," he blurted. He turned to look straight at me. "You're real and running around Liverpool as if nothing's happened, Red. Yet we both know you're as dead as the proverbial doornail. Unless you're just a fantastic liar?" He eyed me beadily, one eyebrow raised in question.

"I'm not a liar," I said indignantly.

"And neither am I," said Billy, quietly. We sat in silence again for a while.

"What do you mean," I said eventually, "by 'the birds are unhappy'?" I glanced across at him. "What can have happened to upset a pair of copper statues?"

"You're being purposely obtuse, Red," said Billy, without malice. "You know as well as I do the birds are alive. Eadric Silverton introduced you to them. Which is notable in itself."

"Why is it notable?" Maria had clearly been pissed off by my visit to the top of the Liver Building, but I'd assumed that was regular romantic jealousy, caused by being made to feel left out. "Who cares whether or not I know the birds?"

"Red," said Billy, in that slow and deliberate manner parents use when they're explaining something to a mardy toddler, "this place had stayed unchanged for years. Decades. Centuries, even. The buildings and the people changed, but the city itself was always the same. Always calm and solid and *there*. But then," he tilted his head and contemplated me, "you arrived. And nothing's been quite the same since. I'm not the only one who's putting two and two together and making it add up to half a dozen right now, I can tell you that for nothing."

"Who else is wondering about my nefarious motives, then?" I kept my voice light, but could feel my chest tightening. What I really wanted right now was a week off. Just a few days of doing absolutely bloody nothing, in order to let my brain catch up with the madness of the last couple of weeks. I had a strong feeling that it just wasn't going to happen. *Sink or swim, Lil,* reminded the voice in my head. "I didn't *ask* to be pushed off a building, Billy," I said. I managed to keep my voice calm, but was struggling not to lose my temper. "And I *certainly* didn't ask to wake up immortal." *Especially now I know just how much political manoeuvring's involved,* I thought with a sigh. I tried again. "What's up with the birds?" I did okay with Daisy—maybe Eadric would let me back up onto the tower to have a chat with Bella. A bird-to-woman heart-to-heart, sort of thing.

"Their mother's gone missing."

Oh, now this was getting way too ridiculous. I glared at Billy in the dim light. "What the *fuck* are you talking about?" I demanded. "Even Eadric knows those birds are made of beaten metal and iron rods. Whether or not anyone believes the tale of the spooky lightning, it's a damn sight more believable than the idea of a, a—*mother bird* hanging around and keeping an eye on them. What did she do," I snorted, "hatch some metal eggs down in the docks and fly them up to the top of the Liver?" I made another inelegant honking noise and stared grumpily off in the opposite direction.

"Do you know the story about the third Liver Bird?" Billy asked, mildly.

I narrowed my eyes at him. "Isn't two enough for one city?" I said. "Where was the third one? Roosting on top of Radio City? I'm pretty sure I'd have noticed a third Liver Bird, Billy."

"If you're going to carry on like this," Billy said eventually, "I'm going to bed." He stood up and wrapped his blanket back around his shoulders. "Ask Eadric about the mother of the city," he said, turning away. "He knows." I wanted to say sorry and ask him to stay, but the words stuck begrudgingly in my throat. Everyone was talking in riddles and I was fucking sick of it.

"As if I'm going to ask Eadric Silverton for a history lesson," I muttered to myself. "As if."

On With The Dance

I decided to make a point of working in Flora's the next morning, but Izzy was ahead of me. She'd arranged for Todd to come in, *'in case you get distracted by the zombie underworld again, you know what it's like'* and the two of them seemed to be managing just fine. Kitty hadn't shown herself at all, but there had been enough flickers on the periphery of my vision to make me feel reasonably confident she was around. I kept myself busy by catching up with the accounts at the table in the back kitchen. *So even the undead have to file tax returns*, I grumbled to myself as I attempted to pull the paperwork into order. *How very fucking tedious.* The front door had been clanking open and closed all morning and I'd got used to it, so it came as a surprise when I heard Izzy saying, "She's back there, help yourself," to an unidentifiable visitor. I'd just hid my phone so that no one would realise I'd actually been playing word games for the last half hour, when Nikolaus Silverton walked in.

"Oh," I said, ungraciously, "it's you."

"Yes," he said with a friendly smile, "it does appear to be."

I scowled at him. "Come to tell me I'm being arrested by the spook police?" Without waiting to be invited, Nik sat himself down opposite me at the table.

"That looks...boring," he said, poking the pile of paper with a well-manicured fingernail.

"Yup," I replied, "I can't say it's my favourite way of spending a morning." We gazed at each other for a while. I glared and Nik just smiled amiably. He was more patient than me. "Out with it then," I snapped, "tell me what I'm supposed to have done."

"No one is assuming you've done anything, Lilith," said Nik politely. "But it does seem rather strange that all this trouble only started after you'd joined us."

"I haven't *joined* anyone," I pointed out sharply. "In fact, I've spent the last week or so being pulled in different directions by endless weirdness and everyone has a different story and no one seems to want to actually tell me the truth."

"Do you think Eadric lied to you?" Nik looked genuinely curious.

"No," I replied, "I don't think he lied to me. What I think," I went on, "is that no one is lying to me, but *everyone* is giving me only the information that suits them. Which isn't fair. And now," I glared at him, "someone has died and the first thing everyone thinks is *Ooh must be Lilith, blame the new girl!*" I said the last bit in a childish voice that I should have been embarrassed about, but I was rapidly reaching the end of my tether. I gazed at Nikolaus Silverton across the formica table. "For fuck's sake, Nik," I went on, "I *died*. I died, but somehow I'm still here. And if that wasn't confusing enough, now you're telling me that the inhabitants of fucking Netherweird," I ignored his scowl at that, "suspect my motives? I don't *have* any motives! So much for the afterlife being exciting and sexy and filled with adventures," I sighed. "So far, it's mostly just been a pain in the fucking ass."

Nik laughed at that. "It really isn't usually this dramatic when someone… joins us," he said. His expression turned thoughtful. "There really is something different this time. Unfortunately, we don't actually know what."

"When did you…*join*, Nik?" I asked him. "More to the point, *how* did you join? Because at the risk of appearing rude, you don't sound like a local."

Nik tilted his head thoughtfully at me. He seemed to spend some time considering his words before he spoke. "I was born in 1788," he said eventually, "and I died in 1824. I'm thirty six years old, but I've been that age for the best part of two hundred years."

He told me how he'd developed a reputation as a writer, and went travelling in order to find inspiration. "In reality, my private life was catching up with me." He then dedicated several years to "determined hedonism"

ON WITH THE DANCE

before getting sick. "I was a long way from home when I realised my time was almost certainly up." Things got hazy for a while, but then he woke up feeling better than ever. It was dark, and his relief at feeling well again lasted as long as it took him to realise he was in a coffin. "I got out of there quick-smart, as you can imagine," he said, a smile playing around the edge of his lips. "Gave the priest a good fright when he came to check the noise and the body was wandering around the chapel." The priest ran away, which was hardly surprising. "So whilst he was away panicking, I replaced my corpse with the body of a beggar I found in the street. No, don't look at me like that," he frowned, "the poor chap was already dead. And at least he got a decent send-off out of it. Then I travelled back to England as a passenger on the same ship that carried my coffin. I didn't attend my funeral," he went on. "It was tempting, but too risky. There's a plaque to my name in one of the biggest churches in the country," Mapp had been telling the truth, then, "and I've visited it a couple of times. It's fun to unnerve people occasionally." He smiled impishly. "Anyway, I'd brought enough money back with me that I was able to live comfortably in the countryside until people had forgotten. When I thought enough time had passed, I reappeared on the social circuit. Which is how I met Eadric." Nik had become a Silverton shortly afterwards. "You don't need to know my original name, it always complicates things." And now, almost two centuries later, he was explaining to me how I was either the saviour of the city or a harbinger of its destruction, but no one had yet decided which. "I'm not planning to destroy anything," I said, "let alone an entire city. Although I'd quite like to start with the stupid accounts." I glared at the sheets of numbers in front of me. "Right now," I said, "I have an awful lot of paperwork, but precious little money."

Nik grinned. "Aah, you'll make up for it," he said, "eventually. It's amazing how easily money accrues when you don't need to eat and won't get old enough to need to pay for care. She's cute," he said, on a tangent, nodding through the open doorway towards Izzy. "There's an interesting air about her. She'd make a wonderful addition to the family." It took me a second or two to realise he was serious.

"You want Izzy dead?" I hissed, careful not to let her hear our conversation.

"Absolutely not," said Nik. "I just think she's rather wasted on humanity." Great, I thought. I become superhuman and people *still* prefer my best friend over me. This was a touchy subject. On more than one occasion, I'd met someone I really liked, only to introduce them to Izzy and have to watch as their interest shifted from me to her. It wasn't as though she ever tried to steal people from me. If anything, she made a point of being rude and uninterested the minute she realised that any new beau's interest might be turning towards her. It was more that I just seemed to fade into the background when Izzy was around. Much as I loved my best friend, it had been nice to feel special for once.

I glared at Nik, who was still smiling benignly at me. "I think humanity still has plenty of use for Izzy," I muttered. I glanced through the door to where she was patiently translating the gesticulations of a couple who didn't appear to speak a single word of English. *And why should they,* I thought idly, *it's about time this country realised it isn't the centre of the bloody universe.* "Are there...netherworlds in all countries?" I asked Nik.

He looked confused. "How do you mean?"

"I mean it literally," I replied. "You call...this," I waved my hands around at the world in general, "the netherworld. Is it just in this country? Does every continent have one? Do I need an undead passport if I decide to go on holiday?"

"You died and were reborn into eternal life, yet your chief priority is whether you can go on holiday?" Nik looked as though he was struggling not to laugh.

"No," I said, "my priority is to figure out what the fuck is going on. But I reckon I'm going to deserve a holiday afterwards."

Nik grinned. "Lilith O'Reilly," he said, "if you can find out what's happening, then I shall pay for your holiday myself. Private flights, five star hotel, the lot."

"All inclusive?" I asked.

He looked bemused, but rallied. "Of course," he replied. "If that's what you want."

"Yes, I do want," I said. "I haven't had a holiday in years and I am bloody tired." I remembered something. "What's in the basement?"

Nik shrugged. "Nothing, now," he said. "But there's been activity down there recently—it's how your intruders got in on the night you died. There was a small entry hole behind the safe. So we had to make it secure. And in answer to your previous question," he went on, "yes—we exist all over the world. Some are more welcoming than others, and it's worth taking your time to figure out which is which, before you head off on your travels."

"Are they the same, though?" I asked him. "Revenants, ratboys, ghosts?"

Nik considered this for a moment. "Pretty much the same everywhere," he said eventually. "But appearances can be deceptive, Lilith. People aren't always who—or what—they say they are."

"Same old, same old." I stood up to stretch my legs out of sheer habit.

Nik got up at the same time. "I'll be off," he said. "I think I can safely reassure Eadric that you're not a threat."

"Am I still under house arrest?" I asked sarcastically.

Nik laughed. "No," he said, "you're safe to move around. I can't imagine you'd have stayed put for long, anyway." *But do you know about Eadric threatening Kitty?* I wondered, following Nik out through the cafe. Perhaps communications in the Silverton household weren't as open as I'd assumed. When we got to the front doorway, I saw that Billy's usual doorway was vacant. There was what looked like a carrier bag stuffed with other carrier bags wedged into the space, presumably to mark his spot.

"What do you know about Billy?" I asked Nik.

He looked blank for a second. "Oh him," he said, following my gaze. His voice was carefully neutral. Clearly there was something going on between the Silvertons and my resident homeless ghost. How on earth Billy could annoy anyone, I had no idea.

"Yes, him." I encouraged.

Nik sighed. "Maria doesn't like Billy," he said. "Says she can't see the point of him. She'd quite like to exorcise him, but Eadric says it's not her place to judge others." Fucking hell. The poor bloke was dead *and* homeless, surely they could cut him some slack?

"Maria sounds like an appalling snob," I retorted.

Nik suppressed a laugh. "Is your friend single?" he asked, peering back into the cafe.

"Leave Izzy alone." I glared at him. "She's a nice person who deserves someone more suitable. Someone who's alive."

"So we can only get it on with fellow monsters now?" Nik asked. He stepped out into the street, and I followed him. "What's that going to do for your love life?" Just then, I saw Sean approaching. He was wearing turned up jeans and a loose flannel shirt over a faded black t-shirt. He looked cute enough to eat.

We both stared long enough for him to notice. "Hi," he said as he got closer. He rubbed vaguely at his hair and pulled his shirt straight. "Lili, isn't it?"

"I, erm," I stuttered. To my astonishment, Sean held his hand out. After a moment's pause, I shook it.

"Sean Hannerty," he said, with a crooked smile. "Apologies—I should have introduced myself before now."

Nik snorted beside me. "Nice to meet you, Sean," he said, as Sean stepped past us into Flora's. "Good luck with that one, Lilith," he went on, in a quieter voice, "I'm off to attend to the affairs of the underworld." He strode off down the road with the air of someone who knew exactly what he was doing, and I envied that.

Then I had a rare and very overdue lightbulb moment. Scratch that previous thought. I knew *exactly* what I was going to do next.

Sometimes You Just Have To Do The Stupid Thing

Izzy seemed to be taking forever to close up Flora's for the night. Surely I hadn't always been this slow when I was human? I decided to mop the floors whilst I was waiting for her, in the hope of speeding things up. I had plans for the rest of the evening—and sitting around watching a human doing the cleaning wasn't one of them.

"Put that down!" Izzy cried, as I moved a table.

I stared at her in confusion. "I just want to mop underneath it," I explained.

Izzy looked at me as though I was a bit simple. "You are holding a *very* heavy table as if it was a drinks tray," she pointed out. I turned to look at my own hand, which was indeed balancing a table. "Put it down carefully!" I lowered the table sheepishly back into place. "You might be supernatural," she pointed out, "but the furniture isn't." I got sent to sit on a stool like a kid who'd been naughty in the classroom. "And you can stop that." I stopped tapping the toe of my shoe rhythmically against the dishwasher. "It's only just surviving your immortal promotion, as it is."

"What am I supposed to do, then?" I griped. Pulling a face at Izzy's back, I started polishing the water glasses on the top shelf. Thirty seconds later, all the glasses were sparkling, and I was back swinging my legs on the stool. "Sorry mum," I muttered. Izzy laughed. "Turns out there's a lot of hours in the day when you don't need to sleep," I griped. "I'm running out of things to clean."

"I can't see how never getting any rest can be good for you, immortal or not." Izzy tilted her head and peered at me. "You definitely look a bit hollow around the undead eyeballs, Lil. Maybe go into stasis tonight, eh? Just for an hour or two."

"I'm not a fucking alien," I grumbled, "and I don't go into stasis. I just...I don't know, actually. Switch off for a bit."

"Wish I could do that," she replied, checking she had her pilates kit in her enormous tote bag. "I just lie awake worrying about paying the bills. Or wondering whether my best friend is going to suddenly go on a brain-eating rampage." She looked at me. "I'll be back by ten," she said. "I've promised to go for a drink with a couple of the girls, but I'll be straight back here afterwards."

"Iz," I said patiently, "I'm dead. Even without you here to supervise, I can't come to much more harm, can I? " She didn't look convinced. "Honestly," I went on, "it's probably a good time for me to sit in on my own. Maybe Kitty will show her face if things are quiet enough."

"Don't do anything I wouldn't. Okay?"

I raised my eyebrows. "Well," I said, "that doesn't exactly restrict my activities."

She narrowed her eyes at me. "Death hasn't improved your manners, Lilith O'Reilly." She swung her bag over her shoulder and headed off. "Laters."

I locked up behind her and waited until I was absolutely sure she was gone. Then I raced up the fire escape to my flat.

"What are you plotting, missy?" Kitty's voice was right beside my ear as I walked through the kitchen. Turning fast enough to make the curtains sway in the draught, I glared at my aunt. "Just checking in," she said, floating across to the living room window. To my surprise, she waved down at someone. I assumed it was Billy. At least I *hoped* it was Billy, because the alternative was that Kitty was becoming visible to everybody. And that would cause a shitload of fuckery that I did not have the time to deal with right now.

"I'll be exorcising you myself, if you scare me like that again," I said.

Kitty feigned shock. "Ooh," she said, "how could you even say such a thing?"

"I wasn't exactly expecting you," I replied, "not after your reaction to Eadric's threat." I peered at my aunt, who seemed a little too bright-eyed for someone who'd been hiding in fear twenty-four hours earlier.

"Mapp came to visit me," she said. "Don't look at me like that, Lilith," I was gaping at her, my eyebrows all but disappearing into my hairline. "I'm entitled to have company. Anyway," she flopped down in the general direction of the chair and floated an inch or so above its surface, "he's quite the would-be protector. I don't think the Silvertons will threaten me again."

"If you single-handedly start the undead apocalypse," I said, "I will not be happy."

"Ha!" she said. "It might be the best thing for them all. Anyway," she gave me a beady look, "what *are* you up to?"

"Who says I'm up to anything?" I couldn't quite look her in her undead eye. Kitty squinted at me and I sighed. "Okay," I said, "I'm going back down the tunnels."

"To see Joe again?" she asked. "Why?"

"In the other direction," I explained.

Kitty looked blank. "There's another direction?"

"I don't know yet," I admitted. "There's certainly a door heading that way. It's small, and I have no idea where it leads. Could go straight into the sewers, for all I know. But if it was something to do with the council, we'd have seen workmen going down there at least occasionally. And workmen in the tunnel would mean everyone knowing about Joe Williamson and his band of merry vampires. The Echo would have been all over that shit by now. And they haven't, so I can only assume that it's all connected to Netherweird." Kitty rolled her eyes at me. "What am I supposed to call it?" I said defensively. "They call it the netherworld, and they're all fucking weird. Anyway," I went on, "I want to know what's down there. Someone—or something—is prepared to knock off the vampires in order to make me look bad, Kitty. And that makes me think they're not the sort of people who'll be happy to sit down to discuss it over a coffee."

Kitty raised an eyebrow. "How do you think your parents would feel if you didn't come back?" she asked. I shuffled uncomfortably. "They've lost one child, Lili—they won't cope if they lose another."

As if I didn't know. "Do you think I don't know all about how difficult it is?" I snapped. Kitty at least had the grace to look shamefaced. "I know what it was like to lose Cally, Kitty. I know because I was *there*." Kitty floated over to me and put her hand on my arm. She wasn't quite back to full strength yet, and I felt the contact as a patch of prickly pins and needles. I ploughed on. "I was ten years old, and I watched my baby brother die in front of me and I couldn't do a single fucking thing to stop it. So yes, I know how it feels to lose someone." I was gripping the key to the cafe shutters in my hand and felt a sudden crunch. I looked down and saw it was bent double. Fucking marvellous. I shook Kitty's hand off and bent to put the key on the floor. With a satisfying stamp, I got it more or less flat again.

"You might be undead," said Kitty quietly, "but you're not indestructible."

"How do you know?" I retorted. "I'm already dead, Kitty. It doesn't get much more terminal than that."

"I'm pretty sure that even the walking dead aren't invulnerable," she said levelly.

"Humph." I gave Grimm a pat before heading for the kitchen door. "I'll be careful, okay?"

Kitty gave a shrug. "It's your funeral."

"It'll be yours if I find a priest any time soon." I shot out of the door before she could reply.

* * *

Leaping down the stairs at full speed, I surfed the last turn on top of the metal railings, as if I was skateboarding. Bouncing off the end and landing lightly on my feet in the car park, I felt for the small set of keys that I'd tucked into my bra. It had occurred to me that whoever had hidden the keys underneath the staff room sink must have needed access to something close by, but without anyone else knowing about it. After checking that no one was watching, I stepped out into the carpark, opened the trapdoor, and peered into the darkness. Before I had time to talk myself out of it, I jumped down into the tunnel. Looking back up at the hatch, I belatedly realised that I had no way of closing the trapdoor after myself. I'd just have to hope that no one noticed the opening in the carpark. Or if they did, that it looked too dangerous and/or creepy for them to want to investigate. I peered down the tunnel toward the Edge Hill caverns. Nothing. No sound or light, not even from the very distant point where I estimated the access hatch to St Luke's must be. I turned to where I'd spotted the little door on my previous visit. Tucked right down in the corner, where the tunnel came to a scrappy end, was the small metal door. It was covered in grime and pale patches of algae, but the keyhole was clear. I fished the mystery keys out of my bra and knelt down to try them in the lock. The first one was too big, but the second fitted into the barrel and caught as soon as I turned it. The tiny door had a handle set into a recess on its surface. I gave it an experimental tug, and it opened smoothly, as if in regular use. I trod down feelings of unease and opened the hatch. Despite being set low in the wall, the door appeared to open onto another full-height tunnel. Sitting down on the rough floor of the Harrington Street side, I wriggled my way through.

The room I found myself in looked to be a disused cellar, its only contents a scattering of empty bottles. Some were made of green glass and were possibly Victoria, but most were generic Coke and Britvic. A few lonely flyers for club nights dotted the floor. Going by the drinks prices listed on them, they were probably from the 1980s. When I took a short, tentative breath, there was a distinct smell of damp that made me worry that moss might grow inside my deceased lungs if I inhaled too deeply. I walked across the room to an arched opening on the other side, the brickwork similar to that in Joe Williamson's tunnels. I wondered briefly if this was his doing, but it seemed doubtful that the Mole Man would have dared dig this far into town. Maybe someone else had been inspired by the Edge Hill workings. Risking another breath, I was surprised to discover that the bricks smelled sweet, almost like maple syrup. The archway lead to another tunnel, the floor of which dropped away steeply as soon as it left the cellar room. I decided that as I was already down here, it would be silly not to at least investigate where the tunnel went. It appeared to be a straight line, which meant it would go under Mathew Street. Perhaps it connected to the endless Victorian basements that were an architectural hang over from the old warehouses that used to dominate the area. Standing still for a moment, I was sure I could hear machinery somewhere in the distance. Then I noticed a flickering light coming from deep in the tunnel. Surely Joe's apprentices weren't here as well? Immortal or not, I didn't much fancy coming up against new and unknown ratboys. The light was faint enough to be almost imperceptible, but just as I was convincing myself I'd imagined it, I heard something cry out. Definitely some*thing*, rather than someone. It had an animalistic tone that made me worry it might be a dog or cat who'd got themselves trapped down here. Shit, shit, *shit*. Ratboys or no, I wasn't going to leave an animal stuck underground without at least attempting to rescue it. I leant back against the brick wall of the tunnel for a moment and thought things through. The air quality was better than I'd have expected from a brick tunnel underneath city streets. Not clean, exactly, but I didn't think there was any dust or other nasties in the air. I could taste damp brick underneath the sweetness, which was to be expected, and ozone from fresh running water, which absolutely was not. Even in the days before the docks, this area would have been at a safe distance from the banks of the Mersey, as well as from the Pool itself, when it used to run down to the river. I listened carefully, trying to figure out where the water might be. Nothing. Absolute silence filled the tunnel. It was oppressive and warm and—what? Not threatening, I was sure of that—I didn't have any sense of foreboding. The only way I could have described it was as an air of expectation. The tunnel was waiting for me to *do* something. I wasn't sure how I was suddenly aware of the feelings of a thoroughly non-sentient bit of man-made underground architecture, but I knew I wasn't imagining it. The tunnel *needed* me. I flattened myself back against the wall and lay my hands on the bricks either side, my palms outstretched. Letting myself sink against the sandstone, I tried to let it—whatever 'it' was—know that we were on the same side.

Then came the crying noise again. I realised it wasn't echoing through the tunnel at all—the sound was right inside my head. Something was in distress, and it was trying to communicate with me. Cursing my own do-gooding nature, I set off into the darkness.

And Then The Water Caught Fire

As I headed down the dark tunnel towards god knows what, I reflected that, if nothing else, life certainly wasn't boring anymore. But I did still *have* a life, despite being dead. Nothing that had happened since I swan-dived from four storeys up made any sense, but at least I was still around to attempt to figure it out. I was walking slowly now, slower even than human speed, wary of charging into potentially dangerous situations. There was still a definite feeling of the tunnel welcoming me. But why? I had a horrible feeling it had something to do with the unearthly crying noise. The noise inside my head was getting louder as I walked deeper into the darkness. It now sounded like that over the top pterodactyl screeching in the Jurassic Park movies, which definitely wasn't reassuring. But I knew I had to find out what it was. Somehow I'd landed up in this bizarre alternate universe in which mole men and ratboys lived under the streets and brick tunnels coaxed me into their bellies in order to—what? Eat me? Finding out that Liverpool itself was a sentient, carnivorous creature wouldn't be the strangest thing to have happened over the last couple of weeks. The flickering was becoming more visible in the darkness ahead of me. Flashes of gold, red, green and purple were growing in intensity, as though the air was shot through with threads of petrol. The temperature wasn't increasing, which was interesting. The tunnel was definitely still warmer than it should have been, but it wasn't getting any hotter. So not a fire, then. As I moved slowly forward, the sweet scent of fruit came back. Tropical, I thought—pineapple and mango, rather than apples and pears. And, strangely, bacon. I kept walking—and nearly stepped straight off the edge of the world.

* * *

The sheer drop had come with no warning. One minute I was heading slowly towards the light and the next, there was nothing beneath my leading foot. I somehow threw my weight backwards, ending up flat on the tunnel floor. Taking an automatic shocked breath, I tasted fish and smoke and fear and love and desperation, all emanating from the void in front of me. Rolling over onto my stomach and twisting round, I edged forward to where the ground fell away. About twenty feet below me in the gloom was a lake. Dark as pitch and showing barely a ripple on the surface, the water somehow seemed to invite me in. *Absolutely no fucking chance*, I thought, scrabbling a few inches backwards. Once I was reasonably sure I wasn't going to topple off the edge, I peered around the enormous open space. By my reckoning, I was right underneath Mathew Street. Threads of music caught on the edge of my hearing, like memories floating in the air. I reckoned the good money was on me having ended up in the cavern under the Cavern. Cheesy money would have been on the music being of the 'yeah yeah yeah' variety, but I was pretty sure it was actually jazz. The prehistoric wailing started up again and I realised that the sparking lights were coming from the edge of the lake. Rubble—some manmade, some apparently broken bedrock—sat in enormous heaps along the edge of the water. Somewhere behind the rocks was the source of the light. Looking down, I spotted narrow steps cut into the stone below me. So people *had* been down here at some point—but how recently? The recent subsidence issues in the area had been all over the papers. I was pretty sure that, had anyone known about the enormous, water-filled void space underneath one of the busiest streets in the city, I'd have heard about it. As I lay there pondering it all, the lights behind the fallen rocks began to glow more brightly. The noise in my head increased its volume to match. *Jesus fucking Christ*, I thought to myself, *I'm going to have to go down there.* There was nothing in me that fancied an underground swim, but neither could I ignore whatever was behind the rocks. The tunnel behind me seemed to urge me on, warm air pushing me gently towards the drop. "Okay," I said aloud, "you got me. What do you want me to do next?" In response, the flickering lights flared into what looked like a huge fire behind the rocks. The noise in my head intensified, until my teeth were gritting tight enough to give me an undead headache. "ENOUGH!" I yelled into the darkness. Silence. The lights dimmed slightly and the encouraging feeling from the tunnel changed to one of expectation. Wondering what the fuck I'd ever done to deserve an afterlife this complicated, I sat up and swung my legs carefully round over the edge. "I'm coming down," I said. "Don't attack me, okay?" A deep thrumming started up, and this time the sound was real. I thought it was coming from the lights, but couldn't be sure. There was only one way to find out. I wriggled over the edge of the tunnel floor and got my feet onto the first step, but then had to slide sideways in order to avoid toppling off into the dark water. Turns out that being immortal doesn't prevent you from absolutely shitting yourself in the face of danger. Once I was fully on the steps, I felt better. Standing up, I kept one hand on the rock face as I descended towards the water. The steps ended at the edge of the lake. The water was to my left, and the rocks loomed high above my head on the right. I gave one of the biggest boulders a tentative push and it stayed firm. I thought it was probably safe so long as I didn't accidentally dislodge things with my own strength, and began climbing carefully upwards. The light was seeping out from between the rocks as well as from behind it, and my suspicions that I was actually climbing a makeshift wall turned out to be correct. As I neared the top, the thrumming increased and the wailing started up again, but more quietly this time. "I'm coming," I murmured, "I'm coming." I was high enough now that I could almost touch the ceiling of the cavern with the tips of my fingers. There was a small gap in the rocks and I aimed for that, in the hope of at least being able to see whatever was trapped behind. This close to the source, the light was bright enough to be painful and, as I reached the gap, I had to shade my eyes in order to look through to the other side. There, writhing in excited fury, was an enormous, fiery bird.

It took me a few stupid seconds to realise what it was I was looking at.

This wasn't a metal sculpture, nor a living creature. This was more like a phoenix, made up of heatless, shifting flames. It was also, unarguably, a Liver Bird. It had the same proportions, just on a massive scale. And its cormorant-style beak was gripping tightly onto the piece of laver seaweed that might (or might not, depending on which histories you believed) have given it the name in the first place. "Bella?" No response. "Bertie," I tried, feeling even more stupid than you might imagine, "is that you?" Again, nothing. It was only a couple of days since Mapp had shown me the dancing birds at the waterfront, so I was pretty sure they were still perched up on their domes. Eadric would have probably blamed me for that as well, had they gone missing. Then it hit me. "You're their mother," I said to the glowing ghost bird. "Aren't you?" The flames roared for a brief second. The bird was clearly trapped, but I couldn't figure out how. It didn't appear to be solid, so in theory it ought to have been able to seep out through the gaps in the rock. "I'm going to help you," I told it. " Okay?" In response, the bird flared and tilted its head slightly. I looked into the glow of its eyes for the first time, and the tsunami of sensation that hit me almost sent me toppling off the rocks into the water. Fury and defiance and need and want and desperation all clawed at my mind. For a brief moment, staring into the bottomless glowing eyes of the firebird, I felt everything that the city had been through since its birth almost a thousand years earlier. The land itself was fighting for attention within the memories, all sucking marshland and deep slicing trenches, from times when its people tried to physically defend it from incomers. There was the smell of sea and mud and fish. And the pain and suffering of all those who'd arrived here hoping for new beginnings, only to find nothing except the agony of starvation. But threaded through the awfulness was strength and love and a determined independence. It tasted something like petrichor—the spirit of the city reasserting itself and folding its inhabitants safely next to the water beneath those wings of fire. *Christ*, I thought, *it's no wonder people either love or hate this place.*

I carefully avoided looking the bird in the eye whilst I decided what to do next. Clearly, it needed space to get past the rocks. But what then—could I get it out through the tunnel? I strongly suspected that the ground would cave in if I tried to move something so enormous and powerful through a narrow space underneath the city streets. I began moving rocks, figuring I could worry where the bird might go after I'd freed it from its stone cage. As I worked to make a gap, I wondered about the lake. The walls of the cavern were solid sandstone and had the same scrape marks I'd seen in Joe Williamson's tunnels. Man-made, then. I threw an experimental rock down into the water and it disappeared with an ominous sucking sound. I tried not to think too much about what might lurk under the blackness. The bird was calmer now, and I got the impression it was watching me. It had the manner of an abandoned dog that stops fighting back when it finally realises a perceived threat is actually potential rescue. "You could help me, you know," I said conversationally. I thought the bird actually gave this some consideration. It flared slightly, and the rocks shook as if they might suddenly collapse in on themselves. "No, no," I said hurriedly, "don't worry. I'll do it myself." The bird shimmered in the darkness.

Suddenly, I heard machinery above my head and remembered the industrial digging on Mathew Street. All I needed right now was a bloody JCB dropping through the ceiling. I worked faster, throwing rocks to the far side of the lake, where they built into a small cairn at the edge of the water. "I'm going to try to get you out through the tunnel," I told the bird, "but you're going to have to be careful. It would be nice if Flora's stayed in one piece."

"I rather think it's you who ought to be more careful about staying in one piece, Lilith," said a polite voice from behind me. I spun around. Maria Silverton was standing at the edge of the Harrington Street tunnel. Dressed incongruously in a dark blue trouser suit with spike heels, she was leaning back against the wall with her arms folded. Her casual pose made her look as though we'd just bumped into each other in a corridor at the Liver Building, rather than deep underground in the company of a wild mythical creature. She tilted her head and considered me. "Why did you have to turn up and spoil my fun, Lilith O'Reilly?"

"What the fuck's going on?" I spluttered. "What are you doing down here?"

Maria smiled. It wasn't remotely comforting. "I decided to make sure my prize was still safely tucked away," she said, "since your presence has been disrupting my plans. Wouldn't want it to escape before I could kill it off for good, now would I?" The bird screeched then, the noise very real indeed. Maria was jolted away from the wall, but recovered herself rapidly. "And of course, I find you down here sticking your idiot nose into things that are none of your business." She stood at the edge of the drop with her hands on her hips, glaring down at me. "If you hadn't appeared," she spat, "everything would be under control by now. This city has too much of a mind of its own, Lilith. We can't have that."

"What on earth are you talking about?" I asked. "What has the city itself got to do with anything? And," I glanced backwards to where the bird sat quietly now, seemingly waiting for something, "why the fuck is there a bird made of *fire* sitting in a cavern underneath the streets?" She smiled again, and it was fucking creepy. I noticed for the first time just how young Maria was, despite her grown up clothes and speech. An angry child, desperate to kick down other kids' sandcastles, just because they were better than hers. "This city," she said, "stole my baby." Her voice was quiet, but utterly venomous. "This city *owes* me, Lilith."

"It isn't the city's fault you lost your child," I said. "That was down to the actions of people. Awful people. What on earth could the city do now that might even remotely make up for you losing Mab?" Maria's eyes flickered at my use of her daughter's name, but she stayed silent. I felt the bird shifting behind me and wondered what my chances of survival might be if it decided to blow Maria sky high. Immortal or not, I was fairly sure that immolation would be terminal. "Come on," I baited her. "What can the city do to make *anything* better?"

Maria raised one arm and held the flat of her hand out towards me. *She's not a revenant,* I thought to myself in a moment of blinding clarity, *she's a witch.* A real life, honest to god, evil fucking witch. "The city can die," she said, and brought the rocks crashing down.

I didn't have time to do anything to save myself. The rocks tumbled me with them down into the water. Even then, I'd have probably got my shit together enough to swim back to the surface, if my too-recently-human instincts hadn't kicked in. I made the mistake of gasping for breath, and the cold, dark water was pulled deep into my lungs. I rolled around in the blackness in a panic, my lungs' autonomic attempts to cough the water back up foiled by the fact that I was still underneath it. My eyes opened on a roiling mass of bubbles and rocks, spinning round and taking me with them. Suddenly there was a loud booming noise, then a bright light snaked down into the water next to me. The firebird swooped through the water as if it was open air, flames whipping out behind it in defiance of all scientific logic. I fought down the urge to scream in panic and concentrated on getting myself the right way up. My lungs were complaining hugely at the unwanted watery intrusion and I desperately wanted to cough my undead guts up, but it was going to have to wait until I was back on dry land. The bird did a loop around me and I focused on it, wondering if it was solid enough for me to grab hold of. A shockwave went through the water and rocks started falling again. Maria was clearly determined to carry out her threat. The bird looped closer and, for a brief second, we hovered eye to eye in a terrifying underwater ballet. Then something grabbed my ankle, and I was pulled down into darkness.

* * *

However much I kicked and flailed, whatever had caught hold of my leg wasn't letting go in a hurry. It pulled me down to the bottom of the lake, where I bounced off rough stone and narrowly avoided cracking my head. Trying to wrench myself up far enough to see what was dragging me, I thought I saw a pale hand gripping my ankle. But just as my eyes were focusing through the black water, my captor took another sudden turn downwards again, dragging me with them. I was being knocked from all sides now and when I put out my hands, I felt the smooth rounded walls of what I strongly suspected was a drainage outlet. There was a noise behind my head and, when I tilted my head backwards slightly to look behind me, I saw a glowing light. The firebird was following us. I hoped to god that whoever had hold of my ankle knew exactly where they were taking me and were quick about it, because I didn't fancy our chances if a forty-foot phoenix decided to overtake us in such a narrow space. The tube changed direction and we lurched forwards instead of down. I smacked my face on the stone, hard enough to make me think I might have broken my nose. Even more worryingly, the increase in the light coming from behind me suggested the bird was catching up with us. *Oh well*, I thought, as I hurtled through the most claustrophobic water slide in history, *at least I tried*. I closed my eyes and waited for the world to fold in on me—and then I was pulled out into open water.

I knew the difference instantly, despite still being underwater and still being dragged along by my ankle. Not only was I no longer banging around in the pipe, I could feel slippery things bouncing against me that I thought were probably fish. My theory was confirmed when a large ray smacked straight into my face. It stayed there flapping for a second, before sliding off and away. The water was murky and, as I peered upwards, I saw the churning trail of a boat's propeller far above me. *We're in the river*, I realised, as the pressure dropped away from my leg. *We've gone through the drainage pipes and straight into the bloody Mersey.* I shrieked soundlessly in the darkness as someone caught hold of my hand. Flapping round in a panic to see what had got hold of me, I was greeted by a pale, delicate face. It was surrounded by blonde hair that was swirled into a halo by the water. Daisy grinned happily when she saw that I'd recognised her and started pulling me along again. Finally getting control of my faculties, I began to swim in earnest. Once she was satisfied I could keep up, Daisy let go of my hand and pulled ahead. Her webbed fingers and toes gave her an advantage, but I definitely won on physical strength. She changed direction and headed up towards the surface, with me close on her skinny heels. We breached the surface of the water at the same time, and the shock of the cold air made my lungs contract sharply. When I'd finally coughed up what felt like several gallons of water, I turned and floated on my back. It took me a few minutes to calm myself to the point I was reasonably sure I wasn't going to have a delayed panic attack, then I pushed myself upright again and trod water. For a second I thought I was alone, but then Daisy rose from the depths just in front of my face and I only just managed not to scream. She grinned at me, then pointed towards the shore. I turned my gaze to the city just as the firebird shot out of the water, midway between us and the waterfront. It climbed high above the city and started circling, orange-gold sparks flickering off it into the night sky. Just as I was wondering how it was that humans couldn't see such an impressive light show, I saw flickering above the Liver Building. Bella and Bertie slowly rose to greet the firebird. Daisy reached out a pale hand and I took it. We floated together in the darkness, watching the spirits of the three birds spinning round each other in a whirl of glittered lightning. It was so utterly mesmerising that it was a good few minutes before I remembered the reason I was night-swimming in the Mersey. *Maria.* I'd have liked to think she'd been dragged down with the rock fall. Or, even better, that the firebird had vaporised her as it escaped. But I was going to have to get to shore and find out for certain. "I have to go back," I said to Daisy. She turned to look at me. Letting go of my hand, she raised hers in a silent salute before flipping over and disappearing underneath the water. On my own, the Mersey seemed dark and intimidating. However protective Daisy was, I thought I'd feel much better when my feet were back on dry land. And I still had a murderous, vengeful witch to deal with. Kicking myself forward, I swam towards the lights of the Pier Head.

The Wild Hunt

Reaching the ferry terminal, I dragged myself out of the water and onto the mooring jetty. Bouncing up onto the roof of the passenger bridge, I ran along the top of it before jumping down onto George Parade. Luckily, it was late and there wasn't anyone around to witness me dripping my way across to the Liver Building. Unfortunately, the late hour also meant that the building was locked up for the evening. I didn't have time to get back to Flora's and hope Eadric would pick up the phone, so I went with the only option I had left—climbing the building. Choosing the Water Street side in the hope I'd be less visible to any passers-by, I briefly wondered how on earth one actually went about climbing the outside of one of the biggest buildings in the city. There was a flash of light above me and I looked up. Streams of golden light swirled high in the air. *The mother bird trusts you*, I said to myself. *Don't let her down now.* "Here goes nothing," I said, reaching my hands up onto the stonework.

Seconds later, I was climbing over the parapet of the roof balcony, amazed by my own abilities. Climbing up the sheer stone-faced concrete had felt as easy as, well, breathing. *Easier, these days*, I snorted to myself. The roof was in darkness, but dim lights were on inside. Deciding the current situation required speed rather than tact, I punched a small pane out of one of the windows and reached in to unlatch it. Clambering in, I caught my foot on the ledge and fell onto the thick carpet. I was just getting to my feet when a heavy hand landed on my shoulder. "Can I ask what you think you're doing," said Eadric Silverton, "or is that going to be a question I will live to regret?"

I whirled to face him, dislodging his hand. "Do you know where your wife is, Eadric?" His face darkened briefly, but then his expression smoothed out again.

"I'm not in the habit of keeping tabs on people, Lilith," he said politely, "and I would suggest you also refrain from doing so." As he spoke, Ivo and Nik appeared round the doorway, both looking confused when they saw me.

"Well, it's about fucking time you started," I spat at him, "because she just tried to kill me."

Eadric looked shocked, but recovered quickly. "That is a ridiculous accusation," he said, "and you will apologise this minute."

"Will I *fuck*," I said. "I was saving the mother bird, and Maria tried to stop me. She's up to something, Eadric. And if you don't know what it is, I would suggest that you find out as soon as possible. Because your darling wife is fucking unhinged."

"The mother bird?" Nik spoke from the doorway. "It's gone missing," he went on, "that's what's been disturbing Bertie and Bella. Where did you find it?"

"It's not missing any more," I said. "I freed it. Or rather," I admitted, "Maria tried to kill us both, and the bird escaped with me when Daisy came to the rescue."

"Daisy?" said Eadric, looking thoroughly bemused. "Who is Daisy? And why," he said, looking me up and down, "are you dripping water onto my carpets?"

"That's what I keep trying to *tell* you," I said. Christ, it was like trying to explain things to a slab of very handsome wood. "I went down under Mathew Street because I was trying to find out what the fuck has been going on, and what I *found*, Eadric, was an enormous fucking bird that was made out of *fire*." I was struggling to slow my rising hysteria. "Then Maria turned up. And then she tried to kill me. The roof fell down," I went on, my voice trailing off, "and I don't actually know whether she survived."

"How do I know you didn't push her?" said Eadric coldly. Shit, I hadn't thought of that.

I thought quickly. "Ask the birds," I said, holding his gaze. "They know the truth. Unless you don't trust them?"

He narrowed his eyes at me. "Where did you leave Maria?" he asked. He believed me, then.

"She tried to *kill* me," I corrected him, "somewhere underneath Mathew Street. There's a lagoon underneath the old Cavern, she trapped me in there."

Eadric turned and headed for the door. "You're not actually going out?" said Ivo, speaking for the first time. "Down onto the streets?"

Eadric stared at Ivo blankly, as if he didn't understand a word he'd said. "Why wouldn't I?" he asked.

"You haven't been outside this building in decades," Ivo replied. "Why now?"

Eadric looked at him as though he'd lost his mind. "Because," he said slowly, "my wife might be trapped underground. And," he went on, "if I find out that she really has been trying to bring this city down around me," he gave Ivo a look that made me quail, and it wasn't even aimed at me, "I will make her pay."

All this had occurred in a few brief minutes. I followed Eadric as he headed for the door. "I'm coming with you," I said.

He stopped dead and turned to look at me. "Why would you do that?"

"Because, well," I faltered, "she might attack you. If she's feeling threatened."

Eadric looked incredulous. "You think...*Maria* might be a threat to me?" he asked.

I stood my ground. "Yes," I replied. "She isn't who—*what*—you think she is, Eadric."

"I'm beginning to realise that," he said grimly. He set off for the stairs, with me in hot pursuit. We hadn't got more than a flight down before there was a clattering noise from below. As we turned a bend in the staircase, Gaultier Mapp came racing up towards us. Clearly having a day off from the goth lifestyle, he was dressed in a hot pink trouser suit, a matching feather poking jauntily out of his hair. The clattering was coming from the endless bangles stacked on his wrists. He looked up in shock as he saw the two of us bearing down on him.

"You've heard?" he said, turning to follow us as we continued downwards. "About Joe?"

Eadric skidded to a halt and turned on Mapp. "What the hell are you talking about?" he asked. "We're going after Maria. What's Joe got to do with it?"

Mapp gawped from me to Eadric and back again. "What's Maria got to do with anything?" he asked. "Unless…oh shit," he went on, "Heggie's gone to help Joe—there's been a disturbance in the tunnels and they think some of it might cave in. You don't think—?"

"*Nikolaus!*" Eadric's voice was almost as impressive as mine. Not quite, but enough to have Nik hanging over the very top bannister rail in seconds. Eadric looked up at him. "I'm going after my wife," he said, "and Mapp and Lili are going to help Joe and his boys." Me and Mapp boggled eyes at each other. "Can you and Ivo stay here, to make sure the building stays secure?"

Nik shook his head. "I'll stay here," he replied, "but Ivo's gone. Went down the fire escape at the back, said he was going to find out what the fuck was going on."

"Stay here," repeated Eadric, "but we'll be back."

"A'right Arnie," I said, because it is well established that I have zero tact. Eadric looked completely blankly at me for a second, then ignored my comment entirely.

"Go up to St Luke's," said Eadric to Mapp, "and use the access point there. That way, you're less likely to be seen. Make sure Joe and his…*creatures* are safe, then bring anyone who needs shelter back here. Understand?" Mapp nodded. "We'll worry about what to do with them after we know everyone's safe."

"You're not going down to the lagoon on your own?" I asked, trying to quash the rising panic I could feel in my chest. "How will we know if you're safe?"

"If I'm not," said Eadric flatly, "Bella will let you know soon enough. Now go."

* * *

We split up outside the rear of the building. Eadric disappeared over the Strand and up Brunswick Street so fast that I was pretty sure no one would realise they'd even seen him. "Come on," said Mapp, taking off across the road towards James Street. As I raced after him, I realised he was wearing spike-heeled silver ankle boots. They certainly didn't seem to slow him any, and I had to dig my feet into the ground to catch up. Luckily, it was an almost straight route up Lord Street and onto Church Street. As we raced up to where I knew we'd veer right onto Bold Street, I risked a sideways glance at Mapp. He was staring straight ahead, grim determination on his face. We were moving so fast that it felt like we'd dropped into one of those weird, slow-mo time slips you see in movies. "Joe will be okay," I reassured Mapp, amazing by my new ability to hold a conversation whilst running faster than a stolen Ferrari.

"Joe can do what the fuck he pleases," growled Mapp as we ran, "but if anything happens to Heggie, there will be a reckoning." I didn't know what to say to that, so stayed silent. Anyway, it was taking all my concentration to not hit anything as we turned onto Bold Street. We raced up the street so fast that we'd have been nothing more than brief blurs on even the most efficient of CCTV cameras. Late night drinkers wandering the streets probably just assumed the wind had got up. I'd lost track of the time, but there were still plenty of people around. I resorted to bouncing off parked cars a couple of times to avoid slowing down. We ran straight round to the back of the church, both leaping the fence like something out of an action movie. I skidded to a halt by the church wall. I'd only ever seen the access point from underneath and had no idea where it was on the surface. But Mapp was ahead of me. He'd already selected a key from his seemingly endless collection, and was trying it in the lock of the unassuming wooden door that was built into the stone wall. It hadn't ever occurred to me that there might be any other infrastructure to the church other than that visible from street level, which was bloody stupid of me. Every church had a crypt, didn't it? St Luke's turned out to be no different. Mapp pushed the door open and I followed him inside, waiting in the shadows of the ruins for the brief seconds it took him to lock the door behind us. We were inside a small stone room that was open to the sky, but had no other apparent exit. Mapp stepped silently past me and bent to lift what looked like a standard metal drain cover set into the floor. "Down we go," he said, gesturing me towards the pitch-black hole in the floor. I hesitated for a second, not wanting to admit that I was scared this might all be an elaborate trap. What if these apparent rulers of the netherworld really did suspect me of being the murderer? Mapp could be setting me up for eternal underground imprisonment. "Lili!" I looked at him. "Please?" The expression of anguish on his face was enough to send me jumping into the hole. I bounced off a solid floor, but somehow stayed upright. Mapp dropped down next to me and I saw we were indeed in the Harrington Street tunnel, at the point where Maria had exited after rescuing me from Joe and the ratboys. I turned toward Joe's tunnels just as shouting started in the distance. The shouting was followed by a low rumble. Mapp took off at warp speed, with me close on his pink satin tails. I could see light coming from round the bend, but this time it was bobbing, as if someone was carrying a lamp. There was a noise behind me and I jumped as a hand touched my shoulder as I ran. "She wasn't down there," said Eadric Silverton, keeping pace with me, "we'll have to find her later." I didn't have time to process the amount of insanity that was currently occurring around me, so just concentrated on keeping up with Mapp. As we rounded the bend like an undead version of the Three Musketeers, I saw Heggie coming towards us. He was half-carrying Joe Williamson, who was holding a lantern and clearly struggling to keep going. Evidently, not all immortals had the same stamina levels. Behind them loped Seamus, who kept looking behind him as if they were being chased by something.

"*Heggie!*" cried Mapp, "*keep going!*" Just as he said it, the roof fell in.

Mapp was running so fast that he smacked straight into the tumbling rocks as they fell. I skidded to a halt behind him. And I'd have stayed upright, had Eadric not thudded into me so hard that it sent both of us sprawling. In the movies, this would have been a comedy romance moment. I stared up at him lying on top of me and we locked eyes for a brief second. Then the panic reasserted itself—he shoved me into the wall as he pushed himself upright, and I'm pretty sure I kicked him in the bollocks as I sprang to my feet.

Only Mapp's lower torso and feet were visible under the rock fall, his silver boots sticking out incongruously into the air. Eadric and I started pulling boulders away, hurling them like bowling balls through the gap down towards Joe's tunnel. There was an enormous rock over Mapp's head, and for a second, I feared the worst. Eadric lifted it as I pulled at Mapp's shoulders. *"Mind my bloody suit!"* he suddenly yelled, and I flew backwards as he wrenched himself upright. He had Heggie clutched tight in his arms. The little man looked stunned but alive, which was more than I'd been expecting.

"You saved me," he said to Mapp in a quiet voice.

Mapp let out a broken, barking laugh. "Of course I did, you idiot," he said, putting Heggie down on his feet next to me. "What would I do without you?" Eadric and I eyeballed each other briefly, not wanting to intrude on the moment. Then Mapp shook himself. "Where the bloody hell has Joe gone?" he asked. We all scrabbled at the remaining rocks until the Mole Man was sitting on the floor of the tunnel, small piles of bedrock stacked up all around him. He appeared to be completely unscathed, which was more than could be said for Seamus. His broken body was just visible under the remaining rocks.

"He's gone," said Joe sadly. "I can feel it." He looked around at us, blinking rapidly despite the low light. "And my lovely tunnel," he said. "Gone. The witch is trying to destroy everything. *Your* witch," he suddenly spat at Eadric, who looked stunned. *"You* brought that witch into our lives, Eadric Silverton," Joe went on, "and it's you who needs to get rid of her."

"We can't do anything from down here," said Mapp, standing with his arm protectively around Heggie. "Let's get you both out, and we'll worry about the rest of it later."

"Back out into the church," said Eadric, coming to his senses. "It's safe there."

"Nowhere's safe with that bitch around," said Heggie, speaking clearly for the first time since I'd met him. "Nowhere."

"Come on," I said, pulling Joe to his feet, "let's get out. I'm sorry," I went on, "but needs must." He squeaked as I threw him over my shoulder. "I'm not going to hurt you," I said, already loping back along the tunnel to the St Luke's exit.

"I'm not scared," came the voice behind my head, "this is fun!" I rolled my eyes in the darkness and kept running. I could hear Mapp behind me, and by the muffled thumping assumed he was carrying Heggie. When we got to the metal ladder up to the church, Eadric went first, using only the bottom rung of the ladder to propel himself up through the hole. I climbed halfway up with Joe still on my back, then Eadric leaned back in to take him off me. Clambering up after them, I turned to do the same for Mapp, only to find him already pushing Heggie up and out through the hole ahead of him. He bounced out and slammed the metal cover down hard, before locking it and then slumping onto the floor. Heggie sat down next to him and put his head on Mapp's shoulder. Joe Williamson was looking around the tiny room in amazement, his eyes wide.

"Oh," he said, "oh!" He looked at me. "I haven't been outside the tunnels in such a long time," he said, craning his next to look up at the night sky. "I'd forgotten about the stars." I looked down at Mapp, who shrugged. Just then, a tinny rendition of *Another One Bites The Dust* by Queen broke the stillness of the night.

To my surprise, Eadric wriggled a small mobile phone out of his back pocket. "I do live in the modern age in some respects," he said tartly, seeing my expression. He pressed the accept button and put the phone to his ear. I could hear Izzy's panicked voice from several feet away. "She's safe," he said, in response to what I presumed was Izzy's concern about my absence. "What do you mean?" he went on, "who's there with you?" I stared at him as he listened to what seemed to be very fast talking coming from the other end. "Yes," he said grimly, "we know. We're coming now. Don't do *anything*, understand? Maria is…dangerous." I gaped at him as he put the phone away. "It seems," he said quietly, "that my darling wife has been harbouring rather more of a grudge than even I was aware of. We," he glanced at me, "need to stop her. You," he looked around at Joe, Heggie and Mapp, "will have to look after yourselves. I don't think she's after any of you," he looked at Mapp, "so I would suggest that you go back to the bookshop and stay there until we figure out what's going on." Mapp moved to get onto his feet, but Eadric put a hand out. "I mean it, Gaultier Mapp," he said. "I can't risk all of us. If anything happens to Lilith and I," he glanced at me in a way that was not remotely reassuring, "you will go to Nikolaus and take charge. Understand?" Mapp gave a silent nod before sinking back down onto the floor. Heggie patted his arm reassuringly. Joe was still staring happily at the sky, seemingly oblivious to the drama going on around him.

"What's going on?" I asked, in an example of possibly the stupidest question in history.

Eadric looked at me, and I felt his true power for the first time. Fury emanated from him in waves. "Maria is trying to kill your family," he said. "And we are going to stop her."

Some Days I Choose Violence

Leaving the three amigos in the church, Eadric and I dropped back into the tunnel. We made it to the Harrington Street end in seconds. Which would have been brilliant, had the exit to the carpark not collapsed in on itself. The tunnel now ended in a solid wall of rock. "She's trying to slow us down," said Eadric, as we once again began moving what felt like several metric tonnes of stone. Fresh air finally began to drift in. I was just thinking we must finally be near to clearing an exit, when I spotted something solid in front of us.

"My car!" Basil's rear end was hanging down into the tunnel, his front tyres somehow still clinging to the outside surface.

Eadric looked at me as though I were insane. "I will buy you another bloody car," he hissed, "if we survive."

"But I want *this* one," I wailed, suddenly feeling as though everything was a bit too much, actually, and maybe this was the tipping point at which I finally lost the plot and should probably be taken off for a nice rest cure somewhere on the south coast.

Eadric grabbed my shoulders and shook me until I felt my teeth literally rattle. "We don't have time to worry about your car, Lilith," he said. "My bloody *wife* is trying to take down the entire city. And she's planning to take your friends down with it as well. We need to hurry." *Izzy.* And Kitty, although I wasn't sure it was possible to kill a ghost. But it was the sudden thought of Grimm that made me move. Adorable, grumpy Grimm, who was the one true love of my life. I pushed at Basil's rear bumper and was rewarded by a loud creak as he lurched up and forwards, back onto solid ground. Suddenly, there was clear air between the tunnel and the outside world. Eadric pushed himself up and out, reaching down to pull me up after him. Looking upwards, I could see lights on in the flat. Shadows were moving around behind the windows and lights flickered outside in the air. Turning in the direction of the Liver Building, I saw the spinning firebirds still dancing in the air, splitting and recombining even as I watched. "The city's fighting back," said Eadric, as he headed for the fire escape.

To my relief, Grimm was sitting underneath the bottom steps, clearly hiding from the insanity going on around him.

"Good pusscat," I told him, as I leaped after Eadric onto the stairs, "you stay there." A faint yowl told me that Grimm knew exactly when to make himself scarce, and that time was clearly now. I sped up the fire escape after Eadric and only just stopped myself from going straight over the railings—again—as I got to the top.

"She'll know we're here," said Eadric quietly, "so once we move, we might as well do it properly. Okay?" I nodded, despite never having felt less okay in my entire life. Before I had a chance to rethink my position on the current matter, Eadric knocked my kitchen door off its hinges and strode into the flat. *You're paying for the repairs, old man*, I thought to myself as I followed him inside. There, in my living room, stood Maria Silverton.

Maria smiled widely as we stepped into the room. "Darling," she said to Eadric in a silky voice, "you've arrived. Would you like to help me tidy things up?" She nodded her head towards Izzy, who was pressed backwards into a corner. "I'd like her to bring the ghosts out to play," Maria went on, "but she refuses."

"I can't even *see* the bloody ghosts," lied Izzy, "let alone make them do anything. So you can fuck right off, you haggard old crone."

Maria's eyes flashed in anger, but she kept her voice calm. "You really shouldn't lie, Isobel," she said. "It never ends well."

"You'd know all about that, Maria," said Eadric quietly, "wouldn't you?" I slid along the wall next to him slightly, hoping to force Maria closer to him.

She whipped her head round to look at me. "Don't try anything stupid, Lilith," she said. "We wouldn't want anything to happen to your precious ghosts, now would we?"

"What ghosts?" I asked her. "there aren't any ghosts in here, Maria." She glared at me, but I was telling the truth. Out of the corner of my eye, I'd spotted Billy and Kitty out on Harrington Street, looking up at the window. They had their heads together, and I could only hope that they were coming up with a very cunning plan. "Why do you want them so badly, anyway?"

"Why do you care?" she asked me in return. "They're already dead. It's not as though they're any use to you."

"People don't always have to have their uses, Maria," said Eadric. I'd almost forgotten he was in the room. When I turned to look at him, I could see the sadness in his eyes. "I didn't rescue you all that time ago because I thought you might be useful."

She sneered at him. "And yet," she said, "I allowed you to rescue me precisely because I thought you could be very useful indeed." I gaped at her. Surely she wasn't going the full, cheesy 'let me explain my motives just before I kill you' route? "Ivo told me I would have to make sacrifices," okay, so she really was taking that route, "but that it would be worth it."

"What does Ivo have to do with anything?" Eadric asked, but I was pretty sure that I knew what was coming next.

"Everything," said Maria, with a shrug. "Ivo Laithlind is everything to me, and always has been. It's never been you, Eadric dear," she smiled pityingly at him. "It was always Ivo. I'd apologise, but, well—I don't actually care." She smiled coldly at him. "A century and a half of living with you," she nodded at him, "and your insular, reasonable approach. Eadric Silverton, always so reasonable and willing to live and let live. And then there's Ivo," she smiled again, this time with excitement in her eyes, "who's interested in nothing but what's best for himself. Which means power, of course. And power," she dropped her gaze briefly and looked almost coy, "is the ultimate turn-on. But here we are," her voice rose again, and she turned to glare at me, "being disturbed by this pathetic little *accident*. Yet you still didn't want to do anything about it," she scowled at her husband.

"I was doing plenty about it," Eadric said, and I turned to stare at him. "I was taking my time to find out whether Lilith might be useful to have around," he gave me an apologetic glance, "rather than going off at the deep end and just killing her without thinking things through first. But you don't like to be reasonable, do you, my *dear?*" He stepped closer to Maria, and she backed away. I saw my chance to move further along the wall. Maybe we could corner her near the window. Izzy saw her chance and shot out of the room. I heard her feet pattering down the fire escape and just hoped she didn't fall down the bloody great hole we'd left in the carpark. But rather than moving, Maria dropped her head and fell silent. Just as I thought I might risk approaching her, she began to mutter quietly. I took a breath. Maria suddenly tasted of cinnamon and seaweed and charred ash, with anguish and fury threading through it. Another one who'd been damaged by life. And she was intent on revenge, however long it might take her. Not like Billy, who was—there was a movement in the corner of my eye and I looked up. Billy was floating in the air on the other side of the living room window. Kitty was spinning around him and Izzy stood a long way below on the pavement, staring upward in horror. As I watched, Izzy turned and ran back to the steps. I couldn't figure out why she'd want to come back into the danger zone, but I had more pressing things on my mind. Maria was still talking to herself, but her words were becoming deeper and somehow less coherent, all at once. I managed to get round behind her, so that she was between me and Eadric, who was now staring at her as if hypnotised.

"*That bitch is trying to exorcise Billy,*" screamed Izzy as she flew in through the broken doorway. "*Fucking stop her!*" I looked out of the window behind me to see Billy floating on the other side of the glass like the worst example of horror movie possession. He was pale and glowing, his face drawn back tightly into a rictus scream of pure agony. As I watched, I could hear Maria chanting under her breath behind me. As she did so, Billy began to fade. I could see the roof of the Cavern Walks centre through his face now, as if he was literally draining away. Turning around, I saw Eadric standing on the other side of Maria, frozen in shock.

"Fucking *do* something!" I yelled at him, but he didn't move. Then I realised he *couldn't* move. He was blank-faced and unblinking, as if he'd been switched to standby. I ran past Izzy into the kitchen and began throwing things out of drawers. I knew what I was looking for, but hadn't used it for so long that I'd forgotten where I'd put it. Izzy was mumbling *oh god oh god* as I wrenched the doors off cupboards in my panic. Just as I found what I was looking for, there was an almighty crash in the living room and I turned to see Kitty—dear, sweet, timid Aunt Kitty—crashing through the window like something out of a Michael Bay movie. She was brighter and more solid than she had ever been. Her face twisted with absolute fury as she landed on Maria's back and sent her flying across the room with a howling crunch. As Maria hit the floor, whatever spell she'd held over Eadric broke. He looked around for a split second before realising what had happened. Launching himself forward, he pinned Maria down to the threadbare carpet. She didn't fight back—instead, she just lay there with her face pressed into the musty floor. She was still mumbling her incantation, and I could see Billy fading out through the smashed window. *"Get out of the way,"* I screamed at Eadric. He got out of the way just as I brought the meat cleaver down on Maria's neck. Sickening, it didn't go all the way through. I had to pull it back out with a horrible sucking noise in order to finally sever her head from her shoulders. I heard Izzy making faint squeaking noises behind me. Eadric scrabbled backwards as I stood over Maria's body, the cleaver still clutched in my hand. I watched in fascinated horror as more than a century of delayed ageing caught up with her in a few brief seconds. It was a blessing that Maria had been face down when I'd killed her, because I didn't have to see the decay wreaking its terrible havoc on her face. I stood and watched numbly as her skin dried and then desiccated, falling away to reveal blackened bones and unidentifiable lumps that I could only assume had once been internal organs. Even those began to crumble, the speed of decay accelerating until all that was left was small piles of ash amongst Maria's collapsed clothes. Her shoes lay on their side, lines of grey dust the only thing linking them to the rest of the awful mess on the carpet.

"Billy!" Izzy called. I looked out of the window to where Kitty was clutching Billy to her, their foreheads touching. Kitty was fading again now, but as she did so, Billy became more real again. *She's giving him her energy*, I thought to myself in astonishment. When they were both a similar level of translucence, they sank slowly downwards. I stepped over to the window and watched as they settled at pavement level, their heads still touching. "You can put that down now, Lil," said Izzy in a shaky voice. I looked over at my best friend, who was sliding down the wall onto the carpet. She sat huddled with her arms wrapped tightly around her knees, a safe distance from the mess that used to be Maria Silverton. She nodded at my hand and I looked down to where I was still holding the meat cleaver. Opening my fingers slightly, I let it drop to the floor with a thud. Eadric was still sitting in the middle of the room, his face white and expressionless.

"I'm sorry," I said, uselessly.

Eadric slowly looked up at me, as if finally realising what had happened. "We're all sorry," he said. "At different times, and for different reasons. The trick is to know when that sorrow is justified. For what it's worth," he went on, "I'm sad—but I'm not sorry. You did what you had to do, Lilith." He got to his feet and looked down at the remains of his wife. "I'm sure the city will appreciate your efforts." Something made me turn and look out of the window. Ivo stood in the middle of Harrington Street, just below the archway entrance. When he was sure I'd spotted him, he gave the briefest of salutes before turning away into the darkness. I turned back into the room with my mouth open to speak, just as Eadric picked up a tiny bit of dust from the floor and blew it into the air. It seemed to swirl with intention for a second, making a double twist in the air before disappearing with an audible pop. Sometimes, I decided, it's better to say nothing at all.

Hope Is The Thing With Feathers

"Y ou owe me a holiday," said Izzy, as she came behind the counter with a tray of dirty crockery. "I can't remember the last time I took a day off."

"That's because you can't bring yourself to keep away from the excitement," I said. "Don't deny it."

"That's as may be," she replied tartly, "but I could really do with a break from the bloody noise." There'd been heavy machinery running in the car park constantly for the last few days, ever since the tunnels had caved in and almost changed the course of all our lives. Eadric had pulled the right strings and paid the right people, and now the Echo was reporting on 'unexplained subsidence' in both the Mathew Street and Abercromby Square areas, both of which were being put down to pockets of underground gas. Now being dealt with, nothing to worry about, etc. Eadric and I had gone back down into the Harrington Street tunnel before the workmen were allowed in, to make sure the entrance to the lagoon was safely blocked off. We'd arranged things so it looked as though the tunnel ended just underneath the spot where Basil had taken his tumble. Basil himself was currently in the care of a specialist garage, who had assured me they could get him back into fully working order. This confidence was almost certainly eased by the fact that Eadric was paying the bill, and had told them to do whatever it took.

"It's the least I can do," he'd said, when we'd eventually gone outside to survey the damage. Maria had suffered the final indignity of being swept up with a dustpan and brush, her remains deposited into a small box that was currently inside a locked safe in Eadric's office. Her clothes had been taken out onto the car park along with the carpet, and burned. We'd discovered some decent oak floorboards underneath the carpet, so I was planning to polish them up. Maybe I'd buy some fancy rugs.

"Why don't we get Todd in for a couple of days," I said, "and you can bugger off to your parents or something?"

"I've got a date tomorrow," said Izzy, nodding towards where a particularly buff security guard was standing outside Flora's, watching over the repair work. "I reckon he'd appreciate me having a couple of days off, don't you?"

"He might appreciate it," I replied, "but whether he'll actually survive is another matter."

Izzy halfheartedly threw a tea towel at me. "What's the plan then, zombie girl?" She looked at me with curiosity. "Are you really going to carry on as if nothing's happened?"

I grinned at her. "We've got a prime position in town and a landlord who feels too guilty to charge any rent," I said. "It would be stupid not to take advantage of it."

"Is he really letting you keep the place?" she asked. "For nothing?"

"Yup," I said, "all ours. So I'm staying. Anyway," I said, as I turned to greet an elderly couple who had just come in, "Mapp wants to use it for his knitting group. Says the ambience is better here than in the bookshop. Maybe we can do more community-style things."

"Are he and Heggie," Izzy said as she bent to fill the dishwasher, "well. You know?"

"I have no idea," I said, reaching over her for clean cups. "And it's none of my business, anyway."

"God, you are a useless gossip," she griped. "What about your own love life?" I stared blankly at her. "Oh, come on, Lil," she said, "Eadric's single now! Well," she paused. "He's a widower, at least. Same difference."

"I don't fancy Eadric Silverton," I said, to her evident disbelief. "Also, I killed his wife four days ago. I'm kidding," this to a man who'd just stepped up to the counter, "just wishful thinking." He laughed, but shifted uncomfortably. "That kind of takes the shine off any potential romance, Iz."

"Huh," she snorted, "you're just overthinking things. What's a bit of murder between friends?"

* * *

"Is he out on the roof?" I asked Nik. He was sprawled across a large velvet Chesterfield chair, a paperback novel dangling from one hand. On closer inspection, it was faded old Mills and Boon romance. "You are so predictable, Nikolaus."

"The heroine has just swooned," he informed me, "and was caught by the terribly handsome Greek waiter. Some girls have all the luck." He grinned. "Yes," he went on, "his majesty is out on the roof. He's expecting you."

As I pulled myself up out of the hatch onto the tiny walkway around Bella's dome, I allowed myself to breathe the air blowing in off the Mersey. It still carried with it the scent of fish and mud and industry, but now there was a thread of something fresher running through it.

"It's hope," said Eadric. I looked up to where he was sitting at Bella's feet. He slid carefully down until he was next to me, leaning back against the dome. "Sit down for a minute?" he asked. Before I replied, he dropped lightly down so that his legs were dangling over the edge. I hesitated for a moment, then lowered myself down next to him. We sat in silence for a while, both lost in our own thoughts. "Thank you," Eadric said finally. I turned to look at him and he gave me a wry, beautiful smile. "The city's got its hope back," he went on, "and it's because of you."

"I had to murder your wife to do it, though," I pointed out.

"There is that," Eadric agreed.

"Why did she pick on Billy?" I asked. It had been bugging me that Maria had supposedly been after me, but ended up taking her fury out on someone else. I'd have asked Billy himself, but he'd disappeared shortly afterwards. Kitty assured me she'd spoken to him and he'd be back 'when he felt up to it'.

"I think it was Maria who killed him," Eadric said, his gaze fixed on the distant ripples in the Mersey. "Originally, I mean. Whether it happened before or after she became immortal, we'll likely never know. I suspect that

276

by the time I…*rescued* her," his voice cracked slightly, and I was careful not to look at him, "she'd been on this side of mortality for longer than I was led to believe."

"You think Maria was Tom's secret woman?" I couldn't keep the astonishment from my voice.

Eadric turned fractionally towards me and gave a small, sad smile. "It would explain her irrational hatred of Billy," he said, "don't you think? And also why she became so unhinged towards the very end, when you arrived in our world and turned everything upside down."

"What have I got to do with any of it?"

"You were the first real friend Billy had in a very long time," Eadric said, "and the first person he'd spoken to about what happened to him. I talked to him after the attack, just briefly. Billy's memories were coming back, Lilith. And I suspect," he went on, "there's plenty more lurking just under the surface. Maria couldn't risk him recognising her. Who knows what other secrets she'd kept from me for all this time?" He shifted slightly and for a second I panicked he was going to jump off the roof, before realising that he was actually getting something out of his pocket. "I can't deny that it's painful to know Maria never cared about me in the way I cared about her. But," he continued, "she was right in that I'd got complacent. And that's always dangerous. Ivo will be back, Lilith." I said nothing. "And I think he'll try to persuade you to join forces with him."

"Why would I want to support that lying, conniving bastard?"

"Because you're attracted to him," said Eadric. "Sometimes that's the most powerful impulse of all." I stayed silent. "Hold out your hand," he instructed. I frowned. "It's nothing awful," he said with a smile. "We've all had enough drama for several lifetimes." I held out my hand. "Now close your eyes." I sighed, but did as I was told. Something cold and metallic dropped into my palm, and then Eadric closed his hand around mine. I opened my eyes and he held my gaze, my hand still in his. He let go, and I slowly opened my hand. There, fastened onto a silver chain that felt heavier than it should have, was a small key. "That will allow you access up here," Eadric said, "whenever you want it." He glanced briefly upwards and then back at me. "I think Bella would appreciate your company sometimes. We—she likes you."

I gazed at him, wondering again at his sheer, overwhelming beauty. He was so close, near enough to touch… A metallic creaking noise brought me back to my senses. Looking up, I watched as several tonnes of metal bird leaned over to look me in the eye. Bella gave a slow wink, before creaking back upwards to stand guard over the city.

Our city.

THE END

Turn the page for a taste of what's to come in
THE HIGH GATE:
Netherweird Chronicles, Book Two

The High Gate

My phone rang just as I was balancing precariously on a ladder that had been wedged into place by a table that was slowly sliding across the floor. I was also being berated by my best friend Izzy for having no vision when it came to interior design. She had unilaterally decided that Flora's, the Harrington Street coffee shop that I owned and lived above, needed to be 'brighter and more welcoming', and I hadn't had the heart to stop her. "Red and pink absolutely works together, so you can wipe that look off your face," had been pretty much the sum total of our discussions, before she'd put a 'closed for refurbishment' sign in the window and spent two days dressed in a boiler suit, painting anything that stayed still for long enough. I actually really liked it, but kept a begrudging expression on my face because Izzy loves it when she thinks she's got one over on me. So now I was hanging gigantic Roy Lichtenstein prints on the headache-inducing walls, whilst Izzy shouted instructions. I'd have happily ignored the call, but my phone was playing *The Final Countdown* by Europe, which signified that it was either Eadric or Nikolaus. Both are capable of using modern technology but avoid it as much as possible on account of how one of them is two hundred years old and the other—well, let's just say that Eadric wrote some of the side notes in the original Doomsday Book and leave it at that. Dropping the box of picture nails to the floor, I did my best to ignore Izzy's indignant squeaking as I fished the phone out of my pocket. I nearly fell off the ladder as I hit 'accept' on the screen, and clambered down the freshly painted wall like a cockroach, hoping no one was walking past the windows to see it.

"If you don't come and do something with this repulsive pet of yours, I swear to the gods I will fillet and shred her and make a nice kedgeree."

I sighed. "Morning Nik," I said, heading behind the counter. Flora's was due to open in an hour and the bakery order hadn't yet been put into the display units. I started pulling warm pastries out of boxes and arranging them on the counter. The almond croissants smelled like heaven, and I cursed the fact that I couldn't eat human food. Izzy banged her way through to the staff room as I flipped the coffee machine on. At least espresso was still an option. "Daisy's a wild creature," I reminded Nik, "not a pet. I can't be responsible for her behaviour. You know that."

"Lilith," he said, "she climbed in through the bloody window and dumped a pike on Eadric's desk. It was still *flapping*." I could hear noises behind him that suggested the fishy incident was still ongoing.

"Was he sitting at the desk at the time?" Eadric Silverton wasn't known for either his humour or his tolerance for wayward river creatures. Daisy lived in the Mersey and was free to come and go as she pleased. Unfortunately for Nik and Eadric, her comings and goings were often via the top floor windows of their rooms in the Liver Building. And the fact that she climbed up the outside walls in order to gain access did complicate matters slightly. Luckily, she generally only appeared when it was quiet and she hadn't been spotted by the public so far—or if she had, they'd presumably marked her down as a stunt actor for one of the film crews that regularly popped up in town.

"Yes," replied Nik. "And he isn't happy about it." Yowling noises from behind him confirmed this.

"I'll come talk to her," I soothed, reaching for the jacket that was hanging on the back of the kitchen door. "She just likes company sometimes." There was a crashing noise at the other end, some muffled cursing, and then Nik came back on the line. He sounded tense.

"Fish pie," he said through obviously gritted teeth. "Get down here now, or I'm making fish pie."

It wasn't my fault I had a river creature as an accidental pet. I'd first met Daisy a few months earlier, when she was being held captive in a sandstone cave dug out underneath the city streets. No one actually wanted to keep her prisoner and she'd only been there a couple of days, but she stank to high heaven and had a spitting temper as well as several rows of the tiniest, sharpest teeth you could ever hope to never see in a human lifetime. So it was no wonder that Joe and the boys had locked her up whilst they decided what to do. And then I'd turned up and been nice to her and she'd attached herself to me like a lamb that's been bottle-fed and doesn't want to go back to the flock. I'd only been dead a couple of days at the time and didn't have a clue what the fuck was going on anyway, so I'd carried on being kind and got her back to her river and now we were all being stalked by an Asrai with momma issues. The regular piscine gifts might have been more welcome if more of us could actually eat. As it was, Izzy had installed a bigger freezer and bought a fish-themed cookbook. "I won't be long," I said to a grumpy-looking Iz, pulling on my jacket. I didn't feel the cold, but was becoming adept at fitting in with human behaviour. There was a distinctly autumnal nip in the air and people would be wearing an extra layer this morning, so I did too.

* * *

It took some coaxing, but I eventually got the Scouse Mermaid out of Eadric's office by tempting her with the tin of mackerel that I keep in his drinks cabinet for just this sort of emergency. After seeing her off into the water with a promise to visit again the next day, I headed back to Flora's. I'm pretty good at walking at a human pace now, even if I do say so myself. I've got the amount of times I scare random members of the public down to once or twice a week, max. And I haven't climbed a building without considering whether anyone's watching me for ooh, at least a couple of months. The sun was shining, passersby were smiling, and I had a spring in my step as I turned the corner onto Harrington Street. Sean, my very favourite customer, often came into Flora's early, spending hours at his favourite table writing notes for the insanely popular thriller novels that had made his fortune. We often chatted, and I was pretty sure he was going to ask me out again any day now. I say 'again', because Sean and I actually went on a date a few months ago. It ended with Daisy frightening the life out of him and me having to wipe his memory. Only I messed up the memory-wiping thing badly enough that my friend Mapp had to redo it—and when Mapp wipes memories, he wipes them *properly*. So Sean was oblivious to the fact we'd actually already had our first kiss, let alone just how arse-wrigglingly *hot* it had all been. But he was definitely showing interest, and I was determined not to miss out again. As I bounced happily down the street towards the cafe, I saw that someone was leaning against the fire escape that leads up to my flat. Tall, slender and with the palest skin I'd ever seen, they were dressed all in white from their fitted t-shirt and jeans, right down to their lace-up sneakers. Even their cropped, spiky hair was white as snow. I slowed slightly as I realised they were waiting for me and pasted on a confident smile that I didn't quite feel. I'd had one too many nasty surprises at the beginning of my so-called afterlife, and I'd been enjoying the relative normality of the last few months (if being undead and having a pet mermaid could ever be classed as normal). As I approached, the person pushed themselves upright and stepped forward to greet me. I could see now that it was a girl in perhaps her mid-twenties and, other than being painfully thin, she looked to be human. Probably a student from the art school, after a part-time job. I sighed with relief. Flora's seemed to attract outsiders and I was always happy to help people out where I could. After all, I knew only too well what it was like to be different. As I got closer, I opened my mouth to speak, ready to give her the standard 'leave your details and we'll get back to you' speech.

She beat me to it. "Lilith O'Reilly," she said in a soft, breathy voice. I thought I detected the faintest Irish accent, but couldn't be sure.

I stopped and looked at her warily. It hadn't been a question. She knew who I was—and I didn't think she was looking for work. "And you are?" I asked.

The girl tilted her head slightly and smiled. "My name is Mab," she said, and if my heart was still beating, it would have stopped there and then. Right at that moment, my phone started playing *The Final Countdown* again, and I didn't think it was a coincidence. Mab took a step forward, and I had to force myself not to back away. "You killed my mother."

"I can explain," I said. But *how* was I going to explain? There was no denying that I had indeed killed Mab's mother—and it had been horrible.

I'd chopped her head off with a meat cleaver in the living room of my flat, three storeys above where we were currently standing. It had been my only option at the time, but I was pretty sure Mab wasn't going to accept that as an excuse. Holding her gaze, I carefully slid the phone out of my pocket and pressed the speakerphone option. "It's not a good ti—"

"No, it absolutely isn't," interrupted Eadric Silverton. "The Queen wants to see you." I dropped my gaze from Mab and stared at the phone in shock. "You'll have to go to London."

"I'm a bit tied up at the minute," I replied, more calmly than I felt. "There's someone here you need to meet." I looked up at Mab as I spoke—but the street was empty.

COMING JULY 2023

Sign up to my mailing list to be the first to hear about upcoming releases and other interesting stuff - and get a FREE short story from Netherweird!
tinyurl.com/netherweirdstory

Author's Note

I've played fast and loose with both geography and architecture in this book, because it is a work of fiction and I enjoy carving imaginary worlds to suit my own motives. But almost everything is based on *some* kernel of truth—even if only on a mythological level. And the truth is almost always stranger (and much more interesting) than fiction.

There really was a massive, underground lagoon beneath the Cavern Club. Thought to have been dug in the 1850s, it was rediscovered to great excitement in 1982—and promptly filled back in with concrete.

Work to excavate Joseph Williamson's tunnels has been going on for many years and shows no sign of stopping. To this day, no one knows for sure why Williamson did it, or just how far across the city the tunnels actually reach.

Bella and Bertie have only been watching over Liverpool for just over a century, but it's a well-established legend that, should they ever leave, the city will fall. The third Liver Bird genuinely exists on a nearby building—let's hope she's supervising them carefully.

***

This book wouldn't exist in any coherent form if it wasn't for Toni Hibberd and Jayne Hadfield, who have the patience of an entire collective of saints. Thanks also go to Emily Davies, Katy Leckie and Donna Desborough.

Eternal gratitude to Winston Gomez and Joanne 'Tilly' Melia, for answering endless questions about people and places they'd mostly forgotten; the staff of the Liver Building and the RLB360; Tracy Whitwell, who Knows; Cressi Downing (thebookanalyst.co.uk), who was so politely constructive about the many early incarnations of this story that the only things I've kept are some of the names; Lucy Chamberlain; Li Zakovics for tea-making and ear-bending. Love you all.

Printed in Great Britain
by Amazon

19588172R00171